PAIN LOVES PASSION

MINA ALEXIA

Black Rose Writing | Texas

ISBN: 978-1-68513-173-9
PUBLISHED BY BLACK ROSE WRITING
www.blackrosewriting.com

Printed in the United States of America
Suggested Retail Price (SRP) $22.95

Pain Loves Passion is printed in Gentium Book

*As a planet-friendly publisher, Black Rose Writing does its best to eliminate unnecessary waste to reduce paper usage and energy costs, while never compromising the reading experience. As a result, the final word count vs. page count may not meet common expectations.

Dedicated to all the amazing souls
who made this book happen.

With love,

-M

Pain Loves Passion

PROLOGUE

I stood in the ashes of what we once were, with a bleeding heart in my hand.

I stood alone, as you walked away and never looked back... and I loved you all the while... through unfathomable agony.

An ocean of tears I cried for you; through summertime sadness, through autumn nostalgia, through cynical winter, through spring resurrection.

A decade of beautiful seasons that only passed to mock my deadness inside.

I. Could. Not. Feel.

And yet, I felt everything.

Are you haunted?

Do I keep you up at night?

Don't cry.

Don't shed a tear.

This love never lied.

This love never died.

It echoes in the halls of your soul,

It lingers in the caverns of your mind,

Like a shadow,

Like a ghost,

When I needed you most,

When I needed you...

CHAPTER ONE

VINCENT

It wasn't the way she talked or the way she carried herself in six-inch heels and skin-tight dresses that made me hate Lana so much; she was beautiful—stunning, in fact. I could never find a single flaw. Her European heritage was clear in her pale complexion and long blonde hair that she typically wore below her waist, tousled and windblown. Her aqua eyes were alluring... but they masked an agenda. Her sensuous lips were soft and sultry, yet poisonous. For a twenty-six-year-old, she had a body most women starved themselves to achieve. She was certainly attractive enough to make my father chase her for months before he finally put a rock on her finger. Upon first impression, one might even think she was absolutely "lovely," an intelligent woman who gracefully carried herself. So why did I hate her? Well, it was simple: Lana McKenzie was a bloody gold digger. She had masterfully crafted a persona that seemed to have fooled everyone but me.

My old man married this manipulative woman a year ago in March 2016 and moved her into the family mansion on the rich side of Atlanta, Georgia. My relationship with Lana was... well, what relationship? We had none. She was legally my stepmother, which was so absurd since I was five years older than her. I could have schooled her on a thing or two. *Christ*, I couldn't stand her. She was insufferable beyond comprehension. Every time I was around her, I wanted to give her a piece of my mind. Everything she did infuriated me. She had the charms of a proper witch—a *satanic* one, I should add. She presented herself as "sweet and caring," but I refused to fall for that façade. I knew right off the bat that Lana was only using my father to inherit a fraction of his fortune. Why else would she have married the man? No one could convince me she was genuinely "in love with him"—it was a load of bollocks, if you asked me. I can't believe my father married this woman just *four months* after Mum passed away. I'll never forgive him for this.

The rage I suppressed pounded louder than the bass in the distance as I walked along Rehoboth Beach, hypnotized by the soothing sound of the ocean; it overpowered the music that echoed from the house party behind me. I was vacationing in Delaware with my kids for the summer; they were staying with their aunt and uncle that night. The eleven-hour drive from Atlanta would have been too hard on my little ones, so we had taken a flight out to Dover and were staying with my wife's relatives for the week. The plan was to rent a vehicle in a few days and take a brief trip up to Ocean City to my family's summer home... Mum loved that property. I had so many amazing memories there.

It was in November 2015, two years ago, just shy of my twenty-ninth birthday, when my beloved mother Isobel closed her eyes one last time before she left us forever. She had lost her battle with breast cancer. She'd been sick for a while... I just didn't know. My parents had deliberately kept it from me until a month before her health took a turn for the worst. She died at forty-nine. So young, so missed. I loved her very much—still do. I was always closer to my mum than my father. There are reasons I resent him. Some things you can never take back once the damage is done.

I took a moment to pause by the shore and stared out at the sea, mesmerized by the waves rolling in at low tide. It was a tranquil night. I had strolled past some people near a bonfire earlier, but other than that, the beach strip was empty, just how I liked it. After Mum passed, I was used to the emptiness. I had shut down. Life never prepares you for loss. It just happens.

Surprise! Enjoy your trauma!

What a bloody joke. My wife Claire hadn't been able to help me through my grief because it depressed her. In hindsight, I should have started grief counseling. Instead, I buried myself in work to cope with the pain of losing Mum. I would've recovered like any normal person if my selfish father hadn't announced his spontaneous marriage to Lana in such a short time frame after Mum's passing. I felt betrayed, infuriated, and hurt. His "blossoming love life" had thrust me into a darker place that only prolonged my unbearable state of grief. How could he move on so quickly? I couldn't understand it until I realized my father had been vulnerable when Lana got her hooks into him.

She was a freelance editor and aspiring writer. Dad claimed to have met her on a flight during one of his business ventures. He had been flying out to Florida last year, and the woman sitting next to him was a "bombshell blonde." Allow me to sum up exactly how this fraudulent relationship began: they had drinks at the airport, which later led to a date, and once she'd discovered how wealthy he was, she was more than happy to sign up as his "sugar baby." My father looked great for his age at fifty-seven, but he'd grown a bit of a paunch and was losing hair. Mum used to always say that I looked just like my dad—a younger, more handsome, and taller version of him—I'm 6 ft. 3.

My parents had been married for over thirty years, and this was how my old man showed his respect? By marrying some slag who was young enough to be his *daughter*? I couldn't accept it. At first, I'd thought he was takin' the piss—but nope... the old bastard had introduced her to us for the first time *after* their sham of a ceremony in Vegas. He did all of this in secret. I didn't even know about Lana until *after* they tied the knot. I'm not sure if I'm angrier at my old man or just pity him for being taken advantage of by a money hungry woman. Sure, she's easy on the eyes, but she clearly weaponized her sexuality to lure and trap my father. I don't respect her. I can't stand being around Lana. I don't even like to utter her name out loud or in my head. There's nothing genuine about her. She's just a talented actress.

I remember the first time my father introduced us to his "blushing bride." He had invited me and Claire to dinner at the Sun Lounge, an upscale rooftop bar in Atlanta. What he forgot to mention was that he had a date with him that evening. As soon as I saw an attractive blonde sitting next to him, I instantly assumed she was an escort. The age gap between my father and Lana was painfully noticeable. She was dressed in a short, black lace dress that revealed too much cleavage. Perhaps it was wrong of me to have judged her like this, but she certainly looked like the type you'd find in a catalogue of an escort website. An anonymous source had confirmed my suspicions. Lana had a clandestine lifestyle as a sex worker. I would have dismissed the accusations... but there was evidence.

I was not prepared to hear, "Son, meet my *lovely wife* Lana." Her wedding ring was proof enough. It was an awkward encounter that not only enraged me, but I couldn't figure out why his new play-toy looked as if she'd seen a ghost when our eyes had locked... she was nearly in tears. I hadn't exactly given her the friendliest greeting. I couldn't hide my anger. Long story short, I had made a scene at the restaurant and embarrassed Claire when I told off my old man and hurled some insults at Lana before I stormed out. In retrospect, this wasn't exactly the best way to welcome someone into your family, but my outrage was justified. Lana McKenzie could never replace "Mrs. Luther"; that title belonged to my mother, even in death.

Regardless of our mutual animosity, we remained cordial for the sake of others around us. But whenever Lana and I were alone or in the presence of my father, we constantly clashed. I did my best to avoid all interaction with her. My strategy was simple: if Lana would walk in, I'd walk out; if Lana would speak, I'd talk over her and she'd zip it; if Lana would offer me drinks or food, I'd refuse and ignore her at parties. I didn't want to see her. I didn't want to hear that soft "sweetness" in her voice. I didn't even care to give her the courtesy of eye contact. She was beneath me and my family in every way. Breathing in her perfume always aggravated me—not because she doused herself in it, but because I didn't want my senses to awaken with pleasure.

"Vince!"

Suddenly, I was yanked away from my thoughts as I turned and saw Claire's cousin approaching in the distance. Jake Ross was a forty-year-old bachelor—no kids, never married, but attractive enough to have model material on his arm. Like myself, he was tall and athletic, except he had short blond hair and green eyes. He was the one who had invited me out to his friend's pool party that evening. I enjoyed spending time with Claire's extended family more than my in-laws.

"What are you doing out here by yourself?" said Jake, offering me a beer. He was clad in a pair of dark swim trunks, while mine were white.

"I just needed to clear my head, mate," I replied.

"You're really dreading seeing her again, huh?" He chuckled as we walked down the strip.

"What do you mean?"

"You know *exactly* who I'm talking about. You couldn't stop ranting about her all throughout our drive up here."

"I was venting."

"I'm curious to meet her."

"Trust me"—I sipped my beer—"you don't."

"She's definitely sexy. I looked at her socials—curiosity got the best of me. Lana's built quite the following."

"Well, that's probably the only thing she's got going for her: sex appeal."

"So, you're admitting she's sexy?"

Bloody hell.

"Give it a rest, Jake. I'm married."

"So what? That doesn't mean you're blind to attractive women."

"I'm not attracted to Lana. She pisses me off more than anything with her 'girl next door' facade. I don't buy it."

"All I'm sayin' is that she's smokin' hot! You can't blame your old man, Vince. You really can't."

"Yes, I can," I bitterly stated. "This is by far the worst thing he's ever done, and I know he'll regret it... only a matter of time. I know she's using him."

"Even if she is, maybe Max is cool with it—ever considered that?"

I clenched my jaw and swallowed my anger. Jake really didn't get it. No one did.

"Maybe this was his way of coping with bereavement."

"Oh, fuck off, mate... leave it out."

"You hate her that much?"

"She makes it easy to hate her guts."

"I remember when Claire shared some photos in our group chat a while ago... Lana's gorgeous! I haven't even met her in person, and I melted when I saw those eyes."

"She's *Satan* in disguise, I promise you."

He laughed at my rhyming rebuttal and gulped back his beer before he opened a text message on his phone.

"Gimme a sec, Vince—just need to respond..."

"Take your time, mate."

Jake mentioning Lana's photos triggered flashbacks in my head. I could never erase those X-rated images... tits out, arse in the air, hands tied behind her back... masked... collared, with a ball gag in her mouth—it was graphic... a masochistic display of sexual submission. Last year, I had received an anonymous email from one of Lana's past boy-toys claiming that she had been cheating on him throughout their relationship and prostituting herself to rich, older men. He had sent me a folder full of Lana's nude selfies... including some footage of her engaging in "self-pleasure," talking into the camera like a professional "cam girl." I still remember the way she moaned and giggled... the things she said:

You're gonna have to pay me more if you wanna see the goodies, Daddy Dom... I'm your holy goddess and your whore.

I hadn't even slept with this woman, but I knew what she looked like without her clothes on. I had *seen* things I could never unsee. It was a shocking revelation. Despite my raging hard on, I was absolutely appalled. When I had confronted my father about the email the following day, he had claimed to have received a similar email and assured me that Lana was never a sex worker, and that the compromising photos and videos were from her obsessive ex-boyfriend who had pulled her into his dark world of BDSM and abused her throughout their relationship. Dad insisted that the archived content in the email was all revenge porn, sent from Lana's angry psycho ex "André" who was out to sabotage their marriage—this was Lana's "explanation." I didn't buy it, though. She could have easily sold my old man a fabricated story to cover up her shame. He made me promise to delete the email and never mention it to Lana. He didn't want to re-traumatize her. I didn't follow through on his first request, but I kept my mouth shut and never confronted Lana about the alleged "revenge porn." I had my reasons for archiving the photos and videos—and it had nothing to do with me routinely clicking through the folder.

"Sorry about that," said Jake, pulling me back to the present. "It was work related." He took another sip of his beer and flashed a devilish grin. "Give me five minutes to cross-examine Lana, then I'll let you know if she's a 'gold-digger' or not. What do you say?"

Jake was a district attorney in Delaware County. My wife came from a family of successful lawyers.

"I don't need you to confirm the obvious." I paused again, glancing at the ocean as if it were calling out to me. Jake's cellphone vibrated when I was about to ask a question.

"Lana just tweeted."

"You're *following* her on Twitter?" I was genuinely shocked.

"And Insta... *Wow!*" He grinned. "Check this out... 'Kiss me by the sea / Unlock the deity / within you, within me / Divine synchronicity'... damn, I'm impressed!"

"I'm not." I rolled my eyes.

"She's not just a pretty face."

"Don't be fooled by Lana's online persona, mate."

I glanced at his phone and noticed that the witch had posted a pic beneath her little poem: a beach shot with the moon beaming down on the water. I was guilty of looking up her socials now and then. Last year, I had asked a couple of my mates to seduce Lana. My intention had been to test her character and see if she'd cheat on my father... perhaps even send a "racy" nude—but she never took the bait. In fact, she disabled her DMs altogether.

I kept my private life off the internet. Social media bred narcissism. Competitive attention seeking behavior was nauseating to me. I could understand why Lana used these platforms, but I didn't care about getting sucked into that superficial cyber-verse. Authenticity was truly a rare find.

"She's really something else," Jake broke the silence, sliding his phone into his pocket.

"She's bewitched you," I sighed.

"I *really* wanna meet her now."

"I think you've had too much to drink."

"I'm an excellent button pusher, Vincent."

"So am I."

"It's part of my job to ruffle feathers."

"I ruffle *hers* enough, I assure you. That's why Dad's always cross with me: nonstop arguments with Lana. I only agreed to this family holiday because of Claire and the kids."

"Well, try to make the best of it."

"That's the plan, Jake."

He finished his beer and looked over his shoulder.

"I'm gonna head back. You coming?"

"Soon."

"Don't be such a loner. The whole point of bringing you here was to get you to socialize."

"I know. I appreciate that."

"Claire mentioned you've been distant and still grieving when I spoke to her on the phone today."

I could feel my anger rising to the surface, building momentum like a powerful wave from a sea of fire.

"I'm fine, mate."

"You can't stay down in the dumps forever, buddy. If there's one thing we're all guaranteed in life, it's death. You're still in the land of the living... so, *live!*"

Please shut the fuck up and leave, I wanted to say.

He had no idea how difficult it was for me to lose my mother the way I did.

"Anyway," Jake continued, "let me know when that divorce happens. I'm interested."

I shot him a glare.

"Kidding!" He laughed.

Are you, though?

He turned and started back to the beach house as I fixed my attention on the waves in front of me.

Alone again in blissful solitude. I was in the wrong environment. I didn't want to be around intoxicated people. I wanted to find a sense of peace and solace in nature; that's what I really needed. My wife wasn't wrong about me feeling disconnected, but I was hoping this holiday would reconnect us and pull me out of the funk I was in.

Standing beneath the moonlight, a gentle tide rolled in and soaked my feet before it retracted with a soothing sigh... the song of the sea. There was something about the ocean that made me feel like I was home. I couldn't explain it, but I knew I wanted to retire near a beachfront property in the future.

Divine synchronicity...

Lana's poem popped into my head. I resisted the urge to glance at her Twitter profile, but eventually caved as I pulled out my phone. Her tweet was still up, attracting more "hearts" in real time as I read her poem and clicked on the midnight beach shot she had uploaded.

Is she still there? Is she with someone? I wondered, annoyed at myself for checking her profile again.

I suppose her ultimate weapon (apart from her being so fit) was her charm and magnetism. She knew how to attract people to herself. I refused to give her that satisfaction. I didn't want her femininity to infect me. She was a sickness, a *disease*, a flesh-eating virus. Too overdramatic? How about a sly, serpentine seductress? I find both metaphors very fitting. All I knew was that she had to go. I had to make my father realize his mistake before he'd keel over and die, leaving that bitch with complete access to his assets. No young woman in their right mind would marry a man that old and genuinely say they're "head over heels." I refused to believe it. Lana McKenzie was a con artist, and I'd sworn to reveal her true colors if it was the last thing I'd do.

CHAPTER TWO

VINCENT

It was a hot summer day in early July, and my kids and I were driving up to Ocean City, Maryland, from our week-long stay in Dover. It seemed logical to refuse my father's invitation to our summer estate, but my family loved Ocean City. Claire had insisted I pack up and take the kids; she would join us the following week because of her work schedule. The hour drive wasn't too bad, considering I had a six-and-two-year-old tagging along with me. I played classical music to bore Lilly and Milo to sleep... it worked. I wasn't in the mood to sing or distract them with games. My children were my world, but they were too young to understand what I was going through.

Twenty years ago, my father had purchased an expensive summer home on a beautiful 4-acre estate, close to the beach. It was my mother's favorite vacation property, and I had so many fond memories of her there. After Mum had passed, my father renovated much of the place, which pissed me off extremely. Lana had everything to do with it; I was convinced. It seemed as if he was trying to erase the memory of my mother in that home. Sadly, there was nothing I could've done to stop their plans to renovate.

My father, Maxwell Luther, was one of the wealthiest business tycoons in Atlanta. He had moved from Leeds, England, in his thirties with me and Mum, building his fortune in the automotive industry. I was only thirteen when we had immigrated to the United States and became citizens three years later. Technically, I was a "hybrid mutt," being half British, half Spaniard. Mum was raised in Madrid, Spain, born into wealth, just like my dad. My parents met when they were introduced by their fathers, who had been good friends and business partners. Merging both families through a marriage seemed more beneficial to my grandparents than Mum and Dad. When I was old enough, Mum eventually confessed that she hadn't been in love with my father when she agreed to marry him at eighteen. She had only agreed because of family pressure to make her parents happy. But the silver lining was that she eventually grew to love my father more than anyone in the world, which gave me some peace.

My childhood in Leeds was great, and my parents seemed happy. I still remember when Dad sat me down and told me we'd be moving to America. I didn't want to leave all my mates behind and start fresh in a foreign land. Sometimes I think the only reason my father had moved us was because he was secretly involved in organized crime, specifically with my mother's family in Spain.

My Uncle Joaquin and Uncle Dante had mysteriously died six months prior to us moving to the States in '97. I eventually asked my mother about it before I'd left for college, but she had insisted that my Spanish lineage was one to be proud of—free of any ties to a dangerous drug cartel. As the youngest living member of the Cortez family, Mum had inherited all her parents' assets when they passed away a few years after my uncles' tragic deaths. The Spanish authorities had ruled it as a murder-suicide. I had learned the truth through my own investigative digging online. My *abuelo* (grandfather) had been the one who had pulled the trigger. I had significant memories of him, which shocked me even more when I discovered the crushing truth of their deaths. Mum and Dad had lied and told me that my grandparents were killed in a car accident. As much as I resented my old man for making us move, I realized that he'd done it to keep Mum and me safe; to protect me from a world he didn't want me to know about or be involved in.

Adjusting to life in the United States wasn't a difficult transition. I was more popular at school than I was in the UK. Picking up American lingo had been a piece of cake, and my Spanish teacher loved me. But despite my efforts to hide my accent, some things you just can't get rid of. My British accent seemed to be a foundational part of my personality. It didn't bother me all that much, to be honest, seeing as it made me popular with the "birds" at my high school—though, I'd be lying if I said it was the *only* thing that gave me power and status in social settings. As shallow as it sounds, attractive people have more privileges in life. Don't hate me for saying it; it's a universal truth. I don't mince words in expressing my opinions, and I won't apologize for it.

I was twenty-four when I married my college sweetheart. Claire was a gorgeous redhead who had the entire package. We had been together for eleven years since we'd met at a party when we were both twenty. My wife was an accomplished lawyer, specializing in real estate law. She was everything I ever wanted: confident, successful, ambitious—I could sing her praises endlessly. It wasn't hard to fall in love with her. I always knew that I wanted her to be the mother of my children. We were married at my family's summer home in Venice, Italy, in 2010. The mansion accommodated our extensive guest list of two hundred people (most of which were my relatives and father's friends). It was a memorable wedding ceremony, and we later spent our honeymoon in Florence.

My wife got pregnant with Lilly within the first year of our marriage. I adored my little princess so much; she was my everything. I never thought I could embrace fatherhood with such joy, but my daughter was truly special and gifted. She took her first steps at nine months, and her ability to parrot back whatever I taught her was incredibly impressive. Mum had been teaching her Spanish before she passed away. I was fluent myself, but it hurt too much to step in as Lilly's teacher when I was drowning in grief. By the time she'd turned four, she was already reading children's books, writing, and learning how to play the piano. I had contributed to the creation of a child prodigy, and I couldn't have been prouder.

Claire took pride in Lilly's resemblance to me, as she had inherited my best features: light brown hair, olive skin, and bright blue eyes. Her little nose and lips were entirely her mother's, including her sassy attitude, which always made me laugh. She was the light of my life. Unfortunately, my spouse was diagnosed with postpartum depression after our daughter was born—that's why Lilly was so close to me; I practically raised her alone. Claire's depression lasted for a long time, even after she gave birth to our son, Milo. He'd been an unplanned pregnancy, but I loved him just as much as our daughter. I had high hopes he would be athletic, just like his dad. I would coach him to become a football star like Rooney and Beckham. Now, when I say "football," I don't mean the American kind—we Brits have it right. I never quite understood why Americans call their most popular national sport "football" when they're tossing the damn ball around with their hands throughout the game.

My mother had me at only nineteen. It was a home birth with midwives in a posh estate in North Leeds. She had suffered three miscarriages after me before deciding to throw in the towel and give up her dream of raising more children. Claire didn't want to have any more kids, so she got a hysterectomy last year. We'd already achieved our little nuclear family with Lilly and Milo, but Claire had stated that she did *not* want to change any more diapers. Personally, I would've loved at least one more child, but I wouldn't force my wife through another pregnancy. She was focused on establishing her law career and making senior partner at her firm; I didn't want to take that away from her.

But I digress... at thirty-one, I was more than happy with my life. I was lucky to have an amazing family with two beautiful children, and a wonderful home I had gained through my hard work ethic. I knew that I'd grown up with privileges that had opened many doors for me, but it bothered me to no end whenever my father offered his financial help. Even though I had a trust fund (including Mum's inheritance), I wanted to make my mark in this world, which was why I'd gone into commercial real estate. With my wife's legal counsel on land and building ownership, we made quite the team.

I was one of the most successful selling agents in Atlanta. It made me feel good as a man to know that Claire and I would never have to worry about finances, and neither would our children. This was one thing I was happy to have learned from my old man: being a good provider. He'd worked hard to build his company from the ground up, which I always admired, but I also wanted to pursue my passions and increase my wealth. Every man should make that his life mission before settling down.

Around 5:30 in the evening, I pulled up to the driveway of a three-story beach house that was built near the waterfront. Stricken with nostalgia, I paused when I stepped out of my white SUV. This place held so many fond memories. My mother loved it here. She had worked so hard on her garden through the years... but it was all destroyed now. After the renovation, my father expanded the house to approximately 6,500 square feet. It was the biggest lot in the neighborhood, comprising six bedrooms, four full baths, and two half baths. My mother, who used to be an interior designer, had meticulously picked all the furniture, wallpaper, and paint. After the renovation, Dad had replaced *everything* with modern luxury crap. It was a fancy house but didn't feel like a home.

We had several guest rooms, a study, a formal dining room, a living room, a great gathering room, and a finished recreation room in the basement. My father's architect had designed an open floor plan with skylights and vaulted ceilings, which demolished the historical character of the home. They installed hardwood floors all over the house—the only reasonable upgrade—but my biggest issue was that every trace of my mother's memory was gone, vanished, as if she had never existed. I could no longer feel her in the home with me. Visiting this place was now bittersweet.

As I unloaded the trunk, Dad's famous barbeque wafted from the backyard, which only made me painfully aware that I hadn't eaten lunch. I was starving—being on a Keto diet had its pros and cons. I was focused on bulking up a bit for the summer. If it made me vain to care about my physique, then I guess I was... combine that with my British wit, and it definitely resulted in the advantage I needed when closing deals with female clients, I'll put it that way.

My old man's red Corvette glistened near the bay garage. Dad loved this car. It was a vintage '67 and in great condition. He treated all his sports cars like his baby.

"Hey, stranger!"

I ignored her voice and continued unpacking, refusing to acknowledge her presence. Considering that we had no audience, there was no reason for me to be overly nice to her.

"Aunt Lanaaaaa!" Lilly rushed out of the car. "*I missed youuuuu!*"

I watched her from the corner of my eye as she ran into the arms of the "lovely" stepmom.

"I missed you more, angel!"

Bloody fucking great.

The woman was adorning my daughter with affection. It shouldn't have annoyed me, but it did. A lot. There was something about her that seemed so disingenuous. We hadn't even exchanged any words, and I was already fuming as I got Milo out of his car seat.

Claire got along with Lana just fine, but even *she* had doubts about her intentions. My children, on the other hand, adored the witch. Lilly was in the habit of calling the gold digger "Aunt Lana." What was I supposed to tell my little girl? Stop being nice to her? No. I wouldn't confuse her like that; she was just an innocent child who was full of love. I didn't want to poison her precious mind with the wicked ways of the world. It was still too early for rude awakenings. But Lana knew from *day one* that I wasn't her biggest fan.

"How was the drive?" Lana asked, holding Lilly's hand.

"Fine." I smiled curtly and walked past her. Idle chit chat was a waste of time.

"Your father's getting dinner ready. I hope you've worked up an appetite!"

Good God, why does she always sound so obnoxiously chipper? I thought, placing our luggage on the ground.

My strict fitness regimen meant that I always had an appetite, especially for some juicy sirloin steak.

"Vincent…"

The way she said my name ignited a passionate fury to blaze within me. Sensuality seemed to drip from her vocal cords every time she spoke. I couldn't tell if this was her natural cadence or part of her act.

I'm not your friend, Lana. We. Are. *Not.* Family.

"Do you need a hand?"

"No."

"You sure?"

Are you deaf?

"Let me help with—"

"*I said*, I've got it covered," I glared at her. "Thanks."

She stood for a moment while I returned to my task at hand, which only frustrated me further. A draft blew by, assaulting my senses with her perfume—whatever the fuck she had on. I didn't want to *smell* her. I didn't want to be around her.

"Can I take the kids inside to see their granddad?"

"Sure. Fine."

Short and sweet. Take them and go, Lana. Get gone. The less we interact, the better, I thought.

Once I got myself situated, I changed into a pair of white khaki shorts, and a white V-neck T-shirt and slides before I stepped onto the patio. I had tanned a bit, weeks prior, but I was looking forward to getting more sun. Standing on a newly renovated deck, I was reminded of everything that was missing in this professionally landscaped yard: Mum's flowers, her bird feeders, and her vegetable garden. It made my heart sink. The upgrades were beautiful, undoubtedly, but it still stung me. Dad had re-designed the pool and had added a solarium and jacuzzi. I had already fought with him about these upgrades—there was no point in complaining about it now.

"Vincent, my boy! Finally!" Dad hollered from the barbeque. He closed the lid and beamed at me. "I was wondering when you'd arrive—had me worried. Come, give us a hug!"

Clad in a pink Hawaiian shirt and blue swimming trunks, my old man always seemed to maintain an exuberant virility, despite his age. His receding hairline didn't affect his confidence in the least. I could tell he had lost some weight around his waist, but not too much—probably from all the *sex* he was getting from his gold-digging trophy wife. The reddish tint in his fair complexion meant that he'd spent too much time in the sun without sunblock, which only heightened the weathered lines of aging on his face. Despite my underlying resentment, I still loved him and was grateful for all his sacrifices, even though he had made a disastrous mistake by marrying that bitch. It was only a matter of time before Lana would ask for a divorce.

"Looking handsome as ever." Dad smiled proudly.

"I guess you can thank Mum. Her genes were superior."

"She would debate you on that, if she were here." He chuckled.

"Mum was always smitten with you, even after thirty years of marriage."

"Yes, well, your mother was a saint. God rest her soul."

My anger resurfaced again. It seemed as if my father were dismissively trying to close the subject, like he couldn't care to talk about her. How was he able to move on so quickly? Did he not care about my feelings? I watched him pick up Milo from his playpen before he showered him with kisses.

"I can't wait to take this little one on a fishing trip, Vincent! Remember those days, Son?" He placed Milo back in his pen and looked at me. "Where's the Missus?"

"Claire had a conflicting schedule, but she'll be here in a week."

"Splendid!"

My father's British accent was more prominent than mine. He was born in Collingham and raised in Knaresborough on the rich side of Yorkshire.

"How are you and Claire doing?"

"We're good," I replied, opening a Heineken as we walked back to the patio bar. It was more like an upscale outdoor kitchen. I took a few sips and watched my father flip some steaks on the grill.

"Gorgeous day, isn't it?" said Dad.

"Very."

"We'll take the family out on the yacht later."

I looked out at the ocean in the distance and felt a haunting sadness that caught me off guard. There were gentle waves in the water, with a boat harbor not too far from our dock. The lush greenery in our yard was so serene. In a few hours, cicadas would sing, and Lilly would go running around the garden, catching fireflies like she usually did in the evenings up here. She had a wild and spirited nature; she took after me.

"How's work?" Dad inquired.

"Work is... work. Sold a big property last week."

"You could retire early, you know that, Son?"

"I'm not ready to retire just yet. I'm making more money than Claire. She should quit her job so she can be with the kids more. I'm not happy with them being raised by a nanny—not exactly what I'd signed up for, but I guess that's my fault. We had never really discussed any details for child rearing."

"Uh oh." Dad frowned. "Trouble in paradise? I thought you said you two were doing well?"

"We are. It's just... she's not very maternal. I don't know... don't really want to get into it."

"Vincent, I don't want you spending your years slaving away like a workaholic. That's my way of saying 'don't become like your father.' I missed out on so much of your childhood because I was too busy with—"

"I know." I cut him off. "Look, there's no need to go down memory lane. I remember my childhood... sadly."

"Oh, come now... must we go there again?" He closed the grill lid and looked at me with an annoyed expression.

Evidently, I still had unresolved issues towards my father, but I just wasn't in the mood to hash things out and bury the hatchet. It wasn't the time, nor the place.

"*Da-da!*"

Milo caught my attention as I turned my head and watched him throw some building blocks in his playpen.

"Are you ever gonna teach that boy any other words other than the obvious?" Dad seemed unimpressed, per usual.

"He's not like Lilly," I said. "Stop comparing them."

"I'm worried he might have a learning disability. Was he screened for autism?"

"Jesus Christ, Father, he's not autistic! Even if he were, would you love him any less?"

"Of course not. I'm merely expressing my concerns—it's my right as his granddad." He opened the barbeque lid and took the steaks off the grill.

I tuned out Dad's voice for a moment and made funny faces at my son while he still had his eyes on me. Milo's laughter was adorable. He was a pudgy little fellow with big brown eyes, blond hair, and a dimpled smile. Claire would constantly say that he reminded her of this porcelain doll she used to have. He looked like Claire's twin when she was his age.

"... I know a really great pediatrician in your area, Vincent."

"Dad, give it a rest, please." I sighed and regarded him. "When my son is ready to talk, he will." I abandoned my barstool and walked over to his pen. Milo was perfect—no one could convince me otherwise.

"Daddy! Me and Lana made banana smoothies!"

I turned around to find my daughter grinning at me in her lavender dress. She held up a glass cup and insisted I take a sip.

"That looks delicious, Lilly."

I was about to reach for the drink when I noticed the *evil witch* walk out with a tray full of "poisoned beverages." She was wearing a short, white halter dress that reminded me of the one Marilyn Monroe had worn in her famous photo, except the hem of Lana's dress was much shorter. It was typical Lana McKenzie fashion—always showing off those tanned, slender legs. God forbid she covered up. I couldn't shake the image of her nudes out of my head.

She stopped in front of me and held out the tray. I avoided her eyes.

"Lilly poured a lot of love into these smoothies."

Can't say the same about you.

"Try it, Daddy!"

How could I say no when my little girl was looking at me with such expectation?

"All organic," Lana added.

I glowered at her and reluctantly grabbed a smoothie. Her pearly white smile never left her face, which only seemed to irritate me more.

"Well? Do you like it?"

I shrugged. "Tastes just like any other smoothie."

She rolled her eyes. "You're welcome, Vincent."

"I never said thank you."

"Would it kill you to say it?"

I had the perfect rebuttal prepared when Dad shouted, "Don't you two start again! Not around these little rascals!" He walked over to us and kissed Lana's cheek before he glared at me and said, "I'd like to be spared from your childish arguments, at least for a day. Make a truce for my sake, will you, Son?"

I would have much rather starved myself for a week than to make "nice" with Lana. She got on my nerves, and it was harder to hide it every time I was in her presence. I watched as she seated herself in a patio chair beneath an umbrella. Her peep-toe pumps looked painful to stand on, but she always made it seem so effortless to walk in heels. I fixated on her diamond anklet and noticed that her accessories were constantly changing; but the one thing that never left her body was a silver crucifix that she wore around her neck, clasped on a thin, silver chain. Her "faith" was just for appearances. There was nothing virtuous about this woman. I had long decided.

Holy goddess and whore...

Lana's seductive laughter echoed in my head as I did my best to purge the memory of that video footage. I had viewed it only once, but it permanently scarred my psyche.

Fuck my life, I thought.

Lilly sat on Lana's lap while I quietly spectated her affectionate display. Children were so naïve. Sometimes I missed the age of innocence, but I was grateful for my cynicism. It kept me grounded in reality; it shaped my existence, and I needed it. Lana had deceived everyone around her, but she couldn't trick me. I was hyperaware of the corruption that had rotted her soul. She didn't have one. It was all an act on her cosmic stage of life.

"Can you braid my hair like yours, Lana?"

"Of course, sweetheart."

Bloody hell.

The last thing I wanted was for my daughter to be "twinning" with a woman I despised. I didn't want my Lilly to grow up looking like a strumpet—not that she was old enough to have boys lining up, but I dreaded the day as her father.

"You're so pretty." Lilly smiled. "I wish my hair was like yours."

"Oh, honey, don't say that. Your hair is gorgeous! It's so soft and brown, like milk chocolate." Lana brushed her hair. "It makes your beautiful blue eyes stand out. I wish I had your hair color."

"Really?"

"Mhm."

"You can change it. My mommy dyes her hair cuz she gets grays sometimes."

This was true… all that stress from the job, combined with aging.

"I rarely dye my hair, sweetheart—too many chemicals in that stuff and it's not very healthy for you. Do you know what 'chemicals' are?"

"Yes. Daddy told me when we went to the science center last summer."

Christ, what is this? An anti-hair dye campaign?

Slightly annoyed, I made my way over and lifted my daughter out of Lana's lap.

"My turn, princess," I said. "Daddy's lonely."

She hugged my neck as I sat down on a lounger and held her in my arms.

"Why don't you impress Grandpa and tell him all the fifty states?"

Lilly named each one in quick succession while I sat there beaming like a proud father.

"Well done!" Dad applauded. "I think that deserves a reward, don't you think, darling?"

"I agree!" Lana smiled.

"Okay, how about… a pony?"

I sighed and said, "Dad, you spoil her enough."

"What's the point in acquiring wealth if you can't spend it on the ones you love?"

"She named the states—didn't write a prize-winning speech for world peace... hardly a reason to give her a *pony*."

"Well, the horse would obviously live at my ranch."

"You can't be serious."

"I want a pony, Daddy! Please, please, *please?*"

Here we go again...

Lilly jumped up and down and attacked my cheek with kisses. She was up to her usual tricks, melting me until I'd say yes.

Dad grabbed another beer from the cooler and smiled. "Can't I just buy her a car already? I'll park it in my garage until she gets her license."

"I doubt she'll want to drive something outdated."

"I'll get her a '55 Cadillac series 62—hardtop."

"She's just a child, Dad. She doesn't even know what vintage vehicles are, and I doubt she'll care when she's old enough to drive. Just take her out for ice-cream."

Lilly's eyes suddenly lit up with excitement as she clapped her hands. "*Yaaay!* Ice-cream tonight?"

"Yes." I ruffled her hair. "After you eat your dinner."

"You're the *bestest* daddy in the world!"

"*Bestest* isn't a word, Lilly," I corrected her. "You know that."

"But Tommy says it all the time!"

"*Tommy* isn't as bright as you. You don't need to dumb yourself down to make friends, my love." I was in the middle of lecturing my child when Lana rudely cut in.

"Vincent, just let her be a kid. You expect so much from her."

"No one asked for your unsolicited advice." I shot her a scornful stare.

"I'm sorry if I gave you that impression."

"You did. I don't need any commentary nor suggestions from you when it comes to my children, do you understand?"

She raised her hands in mock surrender. Dad didn't look too impressed with me.

"Lana's right, you know," he said. "Don't rush her childhood."

"I'm not rushing anything, Dad. I'm simply stating facts."

Lilly wore an eternal pout as I gently stroked her cheek and said, "Do you think Daddy's mean?"

She shook her head.

"Is Daddy too strict with you?"

I sensed some hesitation, but she slowly nodded.

"Oh, Lilly..." I kissed her head and squeezed her tight. "You know I love you, right?"

"Yes, Daddy."

"You know you're the light of my life?"

She slowly grinned.

"You're my little..."

"Sunshine!"

"That's right. I always want the best for you, my love." I kissed her forehead.

"Like in that poem by Buttling Eats?"

I laughed with Lilly. "William *Butler Yeats...* and, yes, sweetheart, just like in his poem."

"You've got her learning poetry already?" Dad smiled, impressed.

"She took an interest all on her own. I should share some of her poems; they're adorable. I read 'A Prayer for my Daughter' to her now and then, hence the reference."

"That's lovely, Son."

Lana crouched down to Lilly's level.

"You're such a special girl," she said. "Maybe you'll even be a famous poet one day." She winked at her and gently pinched her cheek before she turned around to help my father with the food.

I couldn't get Lana's cleavage out of my head. She had leaned forward so low that I could see... I didn't mean to look—it was just there in my face—and she was a tad on the busty side. Her soft, fleshy globes were popping out of her plunging neckline. I wondered if they were natural.

Probably fake, I concluded.

Lana caught me staring as she met my gaze.

Our eyes locked.

I wasn't sure why I couldn't look away, but I felt an energetic shift, filling my mind with a false sense of...

No.

It wasn't an attraction. Whatever it was, I chalked it up to her witchy ways. I would never be a victim of her beguiling beauty. She would never blind me, no matter how "sweet" and "kind" she attempted to appear. People like her were always agenda driven. I watched her set the table, remembering the times when my mother used to do the same.

"Dinner's ready!" Lana called out, pulling me out of my thoughts.

"Come on, love." I pecked my daughter's cheek and lifted her off my lap. "Let's eat."

∞

My father really knew how to barbeque. The steaks were delicious. I had been trying to balance my meat consumption, but it was easy to go overboard at summer barbeques, especially if Dad was behind the grill. We had frozen peach yogurt for dessert before I got up and put Milo to bed. When I returned to the patio, my daughter started complaining about ice cream.

"We can go tomorrow, sweetheart," I gently expressed. "You just ate dessert."

"But I wanna go *now!* Please, Daddy? You said Grandpa could take me this evening!"

"All that sugar isn't good for you, princess."

"But you *promised!*"

"I never promised."

"What's going on?" said Lana, stepping onto the deck. "Do I sense a pending tantrum?"

"Already in effect," I sighed.

Lilly stomped her feet in protest and scowled at me. "Daddy said I could have ice cream tonight, but he changed his mind." She moped, folding her arms in her chest.

It was all very animated and cute, I'll admit.

"*Awwww*," Lana sympathized. "Well, that's not very nice, is it?" She glared at me and sweetly said, "*Daddy* shouldn't make promises he can't keep."

Bloody hell, why encourage the child? I thought, scowling at the witch.

"Daddy wasn't expecting frozen yogurt for dessert. Maybe *Aunt Lana* should have reminded him about the ice cream plans. He's a busy man with a lot of responsibilities because he *works hard* for his money, unlike *other people* who don't do a damn thing."

"Aunt Lana isn't responsible for *Daddy Vincent's* poor memory. Not everyone is in the business of buying and flipping houses for a living. Other people have creative pursuits that are just as worthy of being recognized as *hard work*."

God, this woman really knew how to push my buttons. I looked at Lilly and noticed that she was on the verge of tears, which instantly made me feel like an ass. I crouched and held her hands.

"One scoop of ice cream, all right?"

"YAY!" She flung her arms around my neck and practically choked me. "Can Lana come with us?"

"No, I don't think she would—"

"I'd love to!"

Intolerable woman.

Her patronizing smile said enough. She was determined to make me suffer on purpose.

I cleared my throat and replied, "I'm sure my father would rather have your company instead."

"On the contrary!" He suddenly appeared from the sliding doors. "I spend plenty of *quality time* with her, if you know what I mean." Dad chuckled.

He was better off paying for escort services than marrying this woman; he could certainly afford it. I would have been able to handle that better than his decision to marry an ex-prostitute after four months of dating.

"Besides," he added, "someone's got to hang back and watch Milo. Why don't the three of you walk to the shop? It's only seven thirty. Lovely evening for a stroll."

"Let's go!" Lilly grabbed Lana's hand before she slipped her fingers into mine.

Bless her. I couldn't be mad at my daughter for placing me in an undesirable situation. It wasn't her fault that I couldn't get along with Lana. Sometimes in life, you have no choice but to lay your weapons and be the bigger person. This was one of those times.

CHAPTER THREE

VINCENT

The sun was setting on the horizon, dipping low in the champagne sky as its last few rays glimmered on the water. I loved summer sunsets, so tranquil and breathtaking, with splashes of color. Mum used to call them "cotton candy clouds." While she and Dad had grown up Catholic, I had rejected religion long ago in my teen years. At present, I was more agnostic with my beliefs. Was there truly an intelligent design to the magnificence of this earth? If yes, then surely God was an artist.

I strolled down a gravel path, with my daughter's hand in mine, ignoring the fact that Lana was also holding her hand, walking beside her. She had changed into some flip-flops, which took away from the extra height she had gained while wearing heels earlier—a sensible fashion decision, considering the tiny pebbles that crunched beneath our feet. My mind was clear as I gazed at the ocean, watching the waves sigh along the shore, hypnotizing me. I noticed some boats cruising by in the distance. The ocean air had a distinctive smell that reminded me of something... someone... a past life, perhaps—if such a thing existed.

Strange, isn't it? The idea of reincarnation. Esotericism and Eastern philosophy always fascinated me throughout my years at uni; I found it more profound than most Western ideologies. Now, when you "marry" the two together, a bastard love child is born: new age spirituality. Claire was obsessed with yoga, Sadhguru, and Deepak Chopra—all you had to do was scroll down her Twitter feed. I won't dwell on the horrors of British imperialism and colonization, but the idea of India being labeled as this "spiritual marketplace" for foreigners to "find themselves" is a prime example of Orientalist stereotypes. I had visited the historical land with my mum years ago, but my wife had never traveled there. She was in for a rude awakening. The West does a good job at projecting its own ideals on the East; that's Orientalism in a nutshell.

But to return to the topic at hand... whenever I was near the ocean, I felt like I was home. I felt this unbearable weight on my chest. I could not describe it... a sad sense of nostalgia that made me believe that a past life was possible. I couldn't prove the existence of the metaphysical, but if my 3D self also existed in a fifth dimension, I imagine he's got it all figured out in ways my human brain cannot even comprehend. The nostalgia I felt was like a short-lived awareness of a recollection... a flicker of something... an emotion? I could never connect the dots, whether I subscribed to Western or Eastern thought. I never had the answer.

"I love Ocean City." Lana broke the silence.

We had passed many houses without exchanging words. Lilly's humming had only distracted me further in thought. Normally, I would've ignored the step monster, but I figured engaging in civil discourse was the decent thing to do since my daughter was with us.

"It's just so beautiful here," Lana sighed.

"It is," I muttered. "I used to come here all the time when I was young."

"My mom never had a summer house. We never went on vacations—too poor."

And so conveniently rich now, I answered in my head as we strolled past an elderly couple.

"What's your favorite memory of this place?" she asked.

"Jet skiing with Dad. Mum would always have lunch prepared for us when we got back. She was a serious sandwich artist. I always thought she could run her own catering business."

"Your father doesn't really like discussing Isobel."

He's a bastard like that.

"Maybe he just doesn't want to upset you," I replied.

"I always encourage him to talk about her."

Right. And I'm desperately *in love with you.*

Her statement was just as insincere as my false declaration.

Lilly started singing along to a tune I couldn't quite figure out while she swung our hands back and forth. She had this random habit of making up songs out of the blue. Mum used to sing to her all the time in Spanish.

"My palms are sweaty!" Lilly exclaimed, releasing her grip.

She skipped ahead and twirled around while singing for her audience of two.

"Stay close, love!" I hollered.

We continued our walk down the path before I interrogated Lana.

"Why did you make my father renovate the house?"

"Really, Vincent?" She sounded offended. "I never made him do anything; it was his own endeavor. Max is stubborn as a bull. He's not easily influenced by others, much less me. I control nothing he does."

"The house was perfectly fine before. He bought our summer home for my mother."

"I never requested nor forced him to renovate, Vincent. He told me he wanted to spruce up the place and give it a new identity. I think he was having a hard time dealing with his grief. Maybe it was the memories that he couldn't handle. Last year, I had a discussion with him and had emphasized how upset you'd be with his plans to redesign the home. This place means a lot to you."

How did she know that? I had never sat down and had a one-on-one conversation with her about it, but there was no use in arguing.

I hated exposing Lilly to any form of confrontation; I'd had enough of it in my childhood, and I had long promised myself that if I ever became a father, I would shield my children from all of that. Having kids was an investment. No parent is perfect, but it's important to give a child the best shot in life at thriving. Lilly and Milo were my pride and joy; they'd always love me no matter what. That's what was special about the bond between a father and child: raise them with love and you'll get plenty back.

"Daddy, I wanna go fishing!" Lilly rushed toward me. "Can we go out on the boat tomorrow?"

"Sure, sweetheart."

"Promise?"

"I promise," I said with a smile.

"Vincent!"

A woman's voice caught my attention as I looked up and noticed Mr. and Mrs. Kent, our next-door neighbors, walking towards us. They were a happily childless couple—both retired physicians. Mrs. Kent had been good friends with my mother. She didn't seem to like Lana, which only made me respect her more. They had a charming white poodle that was walking with them—its name escaped me.

"Muffin!" Lilly let go of my hand and sprinted toward her canine companion.

I waved at our neighbors and monitored my daughter as we slowly approached them. We had a brief discussion before Mrs. Kent insisted we come over for dinner while we were still in the area. I told them I'd pass on the invitation to my father before I said goodbye and continued on our way to the ice cream shop.

"Do you know them well?" Lana asked.

"Obviously. You know, for a blonde, you sure fit the stereotype."

"I was just curious. My hair color has nothing to do with common sense."

"You mean your *lack* of it?"

"Don't be a prick, Vincent."

"This is me being nice." I glanced at her just in time to save her from face planting on the ground.

"*Crap!*" Lana drew a sharp breath and held onto me. Her cheeks were inflamed, I noticed as I helped her regain her balance.

She clutched my arm and steadied herself, shaking her left foot. "Sorry, I almost twisted my ankle there—stupid pebble."

"Clumsy, too."

"Be nice."

"I just saved you from falling on your arse in public. If I wanted to be a proper prick to you, I wouldn't have bothered. I don't exactly enjoy touching you, Lana."

She stopped in her tracks and looked at me in confusion. It made me uneasy.

"What?" I quirked a brow and thrust my hands in my pockets. "Expecting an apology?"

Lana seemed distraught, but I brushed off her weird reaction and kept walking ahead. Eventually, she caught up beside me.

"Thank you... for saving me."

"Um..."—I glanced at her—"sure."

It was hardly a heroic effort on my part. As awkward as it had been to come in close contact with her, something had happened when we touched. An image flashed before my eyes so rapidly that I could hardly make out what it was. I couldn't shake the feeling.

Lilly skipped ahead of us, dancing to some tunes that echoed from someone's yard. She loved music, which explained her talents.

"You're so lucky to have children," said Lana.

I truly was. I smiled and watched my daughter lose herself in her own imagination; something that seemed to die with aging. I didn't want her to grow up. I wanted her to be my little Lilly forever, as selfish as that was.

"I often wonder what kind of mother I'll be one day."

The world was full of people who did not deserve to be parents; Lana was one of them. It was a good thing my father had a vasectomy years ago. At least I didn't have to worry about hell spawn running around in his old age. Just the idea of that happening made me sick.

"I wish I had a brother or sister," Lana admitted. "Life would have been less lonely growing up." She ran her fingers through her hair and fanned herself before she pulled out a bottle of water from her white shoulder bag.

I watched several droplets trickle down the corner of her mouth, falling between her breasts. She released a contented sigh and wiped her lips.

"Lilly, are you thirsty?" Lana called out.

"No, thank you!"

"Vincent, do you—"

"I'm good. Thanks."

I advised my daughter to stay close before I looked at Lana and asked, "Why do you love my old man? Keep it G-rated, please. I don't need explicit details about your sex life."

"All my reasons are 'G-rated.'"

I felt her eyes on me as we walked side by side.

"He treats me with dignity and respect," Lana continued. "He's this rich, powerful man, yet he sees me as his equal."

How he saw her on the same level was beyond me, but I kept my mouth shut and listened.

"Max has such a big heart. He's just so different from the men I used to date—and that's a good thing."

Used to date? Or whore yourself out?

"Are you in love with him?"

She seemed to waver.

"Yes."

Bollocks. That was an obvious lie. But I avoided cross-examining her and changed the subject.

"Can I ask you something off topic, Lana?"

"Of course."

"How come you have published nothing yet? It's been well over a year now, and Dad said you've finished writing a novel. He always talks about it every chance he gets."

"I don't know. I guess I just... I'm a perfectionist. When I write, I feel so exposed. The idea of sharing my 'baby' with the world... it scares me to death."

"Why?" I genuinely wanted to know, which was unusual for me.

"Because I'm terrified that people will figure me out, like they'll know me... the *real* me."

I was right. She was a master class actress.

"Every artist wants to protect their art," she explained, "which is ironic because I'm my own worst critic." Lana sighed. "Look, I'm not saying that I'm being dishonest about who I am. I just meant that it's hard revealing the dark and personal stuff I keep locked away. It's easier to expose all of that in my characters; it's cathartic. A writer's vulnerabilities, weaknesses, twisted thoughts, and desires come out in their fictional world, intentionally or otherwise."

"And you're worried that... what? A psychopath will stalk you because he'll somehow identify you through a character in your book?"

"No... I'm worried the world will lift me up, only to crush me down. I've been through enough of that in life. I'm not exactly the luckiest person."

I scoffed at her. She became a millionaire overnight by marrying my father, and luck had everything to do with it—apart from her sex appeal.

"So," I said, "you're playing it safe?"

"I'm just trying to clean up my manuscript as best I can before I hand it over to an agent."

"Fair enough."

It must have been so convenient for her, marrying my father to further her career. He had connections in various industries.

"Do you read at all?" she asked.

"Not much, no."

Reading was a leisurely thing of the past; it had been such a long time since I had picked up a novel. I was too busy with work.

"What's your story about?" I inquired, sensing some hesitation.

"It's about a man and a woman living in Victorian England. They have incredibly intense chemistry... but their hate eclipses their passion for each other. It's a complex relationship that focuses on social class differences, gender roles, marriage, and a bunch of other topics within that cultural milieu."

I was half expecting her to describe some sleazy knock off version of *Fifty Shades...* Historical fiction I could respect, though I wasn't sure how accomplished of a writer she was. She never shared any passages or creative pieces with me.

"Why do they hate each other?" I asked.

"Because she didn't wait for him. She married another man, and he wound up settling for a loveless marriage once he finally gained all the wealth he'd dreamed of."

That seemed like a legitimate reason to resent a person... wasn't sure about *hate,* however.

"How come she didn't wait for him?"

"She met him after she married her husband."

"That's a ridiculous reason to hate somebody. But wait—I'm confused. You said she didn't wait for him... meaning... she knew him before getting married?"

"I don't want to give too much of the plot away, but she knew *of* him, not personally. He's her twin flame, and instead of waiting for their stars to align, she rushed into a marriage."

"No offense, Lana, but it just sounds like you're trying to sell some idealistic crap that is so far-fetched from reality." I had to laugh. "I guess that's why I'm no longer a romantic—true love isn't real. Fairy tale romances are just, well—fairytales."

"But my story isn't a fairytale, Vincent; it's a tragedy. I've told you this before. Maybe not in the traditional sense like Shakespeare's plays, but a tragedy."

"Let me guess, one of them dies? Suicide? Illness?"

"No."

"What is this new age rubbish I keep hearing about 'twin flames' and 'soulmates'? They aren't real. They simply don't exist." I wasn't sure why I was getting angry, but I could hear it in my voice. "You're either compatible with someone or you're not, Lana. It's that simple."

"You're disillusioned."

"I'm cynical."

"*Because* you're disillusioned."

"Does it matter what caused my cynicism? I'd much rather be a pessimistic realist than a gullible idiot."

She seemed to digest my words before she said, "I believe the worst pain in life is to find your twin flame and realize that you can never be together... all because of circumstance."

"It's a good thing you found yours, then."

My sarcasm was noticeable as Lana gave my arm a hard smack.

"Stop making a mockery out of everything I share with you!"

"Stop being so sensitive," I rebutted.

"You're unbearably sarcastic about everything in life, Vincent."

"I'm British, sweetheart."

"I can't tell if your sarcasm is a defense mechanism, or you actually enjoy being incredibly obnoxious?"

"It's high caliber humor—not for everyone, eh? Are you having trouble leveling up?"

"I have a Master's in English Literature, Vincent. I know the difference between Juvenalian and Horatian satire. I wish you'd adopt the latter than the former—you wouldn't sound like such an insensitive jackass half the time."

"And pass up on expressing my moral indignation and pessimism?" I laughed derisively. "What an insult to British tradition."

"You don't need to 'educate' me on the roots of your beloved customs."

"Are you trying to sound smart, Lana?"

"Your father goes all in with self-deprecating humor, but you're too arrogant to even jokingly tear yourself down, so you settle for the next best thing: undetectable sarcasm. 'What's wrong with a couple of laughs at the expense of someone else's pain?'"

"*Oh, please,* spare me your pathetic plea for sympathy. Appreciating cutthroat sarcasm does not make me sadistic."

"But apparently I'm a trigger."

"For what?" I snickered.

"Your cruelty."

What was wrong with this woman? Why was she deliberately provoking me?

"If you can't handle a friendly match of verbal jousting, then I suggest you avoid the endeavor entirely, Lana."

"You should have been a lawyer."

"I married one."

"How does Claire put up with you?"

"Just fine, actually—no complaints, especially not in the bedroom." I grinned.

"I didn't ask about your sex life."

"I was strictly stating a fact."

"One that I didn't need to know."

"Now that we're on the subject, how often do you fantasize about me, Lana?"

Why did I just say that?

"Stop grossing me out." She blushed.

"Don't worry, the feeling is mutual. If the survival of humanity depended solely on us, I'd happily let our species die off into oblivion."

She sighed, shaking her head. "You're so childish, Vincent."

"For not wanting to 'breed' with you?"

Lana gave no rebuttal as she increased her stride and caught up with Lilly. If I had struck a nerve, I was glad. She didn't have to like my honesty. The funny thing about the truth was that it hurt more than it made anyone feel good. I could only imagine how depressed and angry we'd all be if we could hear each other's thoughts.

ೞ

When we had finally made it to the ice cream shop, I'd bought my daughter a small cone with a scoop of chocolate ice cream, which she thoroughly enjoyed. I had also offered to buy Lana something, but she'd insisted she was still full from dinner. By the time we returned to the house, Lilly was less hyper, as she had spent most of her energy bouncing around on our stroll back.

"Daddy?" she said, walking up the steps of the front porch.

"Yes, sweetheart?" I released her hand to grab the key from my pocket.

"Can Lana be my new mommy?"

What?

The absurdity of her childish request baffled me as I met Lana's aqua eyes. She seemed equally confused and a little uneasy.

"Sweetheart, what are you talking about?" I crouched and cupped Lilly's angelic face. "You have a mummy already."

"But… she never hugs me. She… she never tells me, 'I love you,' even when I say it to her. Maria says that Mom loves me in her own way but… I don't think so, Daddy. Sometimes I think she hates me."

The tears in my daughter's eyes were like daggers in my heart. This is what I was afraid of: Lilly believing that her mother didn't love her and Milo. I had fought with Claire many times about her problem with saying, "I love you."

Maria was our nanny. I had hired her shortly after Claire gave birth to our daughter. The responsibilities of motherhood had overwhelmed her, so it seemed logical at the time to get some extra help with child rearing. My wife's refusal to verbally express her love had become an issue ever since she started taking classes with some new age "healer" who seemed more like a con-artist and cult leader (if you asked me), but she swore his sessions were helping her depression. According to *Guru Maharesh*, those three words were worthless; actions were more powerful.

So, whenever Lilly said, "I love you" to her, Claire typically responded with: "I'm grateful" or "I *appreciate* you." She had tried to "proselytize" me to her ridiculous indoctrination by explaining the importance of teaching our children that the L-word was meaningless unless you backed it up with action, but I couldn't get on board. To begin, I flat out disagreed with her, and second, I felt she had underlying issues going on—perhaps a childhood trauma that she refused to address, because ever since we had Lilly and Milo, Claire did a 180. She exhibited an avoidant attachment style with our children. As her husband, I did my best to be patient and supportive, but seeing my daughter like this... knowing she was sad and internalizing her pain infuriated me because my wife was creating unnecessary emotional scars.

"Lilly," I whispered. "Don't cry, sweetheart." I brushed her tears away and hugged her close to me. "*Shhh...* it's all right, darling. Mummy's still a little sick. Give her time. We must be patient with the people we love. I know for a fact that she loves you more than anyone in this world."

"More than you?"

"Yes." I smiled. "You're her favorite. She would sacrifice everything for you and Milo in a heartbeat. Don't you ever doubt that."

"Then why doesn't she tell me she loves me, Daddy? Why doesn't she hold me like you do, or like Lana does? She never tucks me in at night or reads me stories."

"Mummy has a very important job, Lilly. She helps many people, and that means making sacrifices. That's why we hired Maria to help and make sure that you and Milo are happy and taken care of. You're happy with her, aren't you?"

"Yes, but..."

I hated seeing Lilly in tears—hated it more than anything. Claire was to blame for this. I was tired of making excuses for my wife. It wasn't fair to our kids. I wanted her in therapy, but she had this tendency to quit after a few sessions. Sometimes I wondered if I had married a covert narcissist.

"Now," I muttered, "no more tears, my love."

Lana touched Lilly's shoulder and said, "Maybe I can help?"

"Mommy's mean and Daddy's lying, Lana!" She hid her face in Lana's skirt and started sobbing. "Mommy doesn't love me and Milo!"

"*Lilly*," I stressed, "that's not nice to say about your mum. It would hurt her feelings if she were here right now."

"*I don't care!*"

I rubbed my temples, feeling hopelessly helpless. It was upsetting to watch my child put on such a juvenile display in front of Lana. I didn't want my daughter airing out our dirty laundry. My marriage problems were mine and Claire's alone. Lana was the last person I'd confide in.

"I don't want Mommy to come!"

The front door suddenly opened as I heard my father's raspy voice behind me.

"Good Lord, Vincent... what's all the commotion?"

"Nothing," I replied, facing him. "Lilly's having a tantrum."

Lana held her close and tried to calm her down while I spoke to my father.

"I was worried," he said.

"We saw the Kents and got held up. Helen invited us to dinner next week."

"I have no interest in eating that woman's dreadful cooking. She talks a lot and had spread so much gossip about Lana in this neighborhood when she found out I'd remarried."

"She was probably just as shocked as I was, Dad. I mean... four months is hardly—"

"It was none of her goddamn business! Besides, she was more your mother's friend. I'm surprised her husband is still alive. I'd

have blown my brains out long ago, had I lived with that woman!"
He chuckled.

"Dad, Lilly can hear you."

"My apologies, Son. Why is she crying?" He called out to her. "Come here, princess..."

It broke my heart to see the way my daughter clung to Lana. Claire never had patience for her neediness, which begs the question why she wanted a child if she was so resistant to meeting their needs?

"She's fine, Dad," I said. "Lilly's just a little upset that her mum couldn't make it," I lied.

He took Lilly's hand and pried her away from Lana. "It's almost bedtime, darling. How about you come inside and read Papa a story? Would you like that?"

My daughter seemed to cheer up. She loved reading, especially to her granddad, since he praised her so much. Claire was always too busy to be a mother to her during bedtime routines. Her court cases always took precedence over everything else—our sex life included.

"I'll meet you two in the gathering room afterwards," said Dad. "Please don't get in a tiff."

"Don't worry, Max. Vincent's on his best behavior this evening."

Hardly.

When my father left, I was alone again with the sea witch, standing on the porch while the sky darkened.

"Is everything okay with you and Claire?"

"With all due respect, that's none of your business, Lana. Keep your nose out of it."

Direct and straight to the point. Mind you, I was irritable and moody, but I wasn't willing to divulge my marriage problems to a woman who was clueless about what it meant to be in a *real*, committed relationship. Contrary to what I'd said earlier, she should have had enough sense to conclude that things were *not* okay with me and my wife. Lilly certainly made that crystal clear. Claire's postpartum depression had emotionally crippled her. She never had a problem telling me she loved me in the past. Whatever was going on with her, it was affecting our daughter and I wasn't happy about that. Fortunately, Milo was still too young to understand, but he wouldn't stay that way forever.

"I'm sorry," Lana weakly uttered. "I didn't mean to pry."

"Why didn't you attempt to defend Claire, since you're such 'good friends' with her?" I said with contempt.

"What did you expect me to say? Lilly caught me off guard."

"Yeah, well, she didn't mean it."

"You think I don't know that?"

"There is no way my Lilly would ever want *you* for a mother if she knew who you really are." I was about to leave when Lana blocked my exit.

"Why do you have such a hard on for hating me?"

"Please," I chuckled. "You *wish* I'd have a *hard on* for you."

"Pervert!"

"You're the one who mentioned me having a bloody 'hard on,' not me."

It was a stare down.

No.

It was the calm before the storm.

I felt a subtle vibration in my body, as if I were standing close to a live wire. I feared that if I touched Lana, I'd get zapped.

"I'm not this awful person you're determined to believe I am," she calmly said, hugging her arms, as if to protect her energy from me. "If only you realized how deep your words can cut, Vincent."

"Which words? The part where I basically called you an unfit mother?"

There was a palpable pain in her eyes. I had hurt her. I must have. That pathetic mask of happiness that she wore every day was no longer there; somehow it had slipped. It left me confused. Lana's toxic positivity always triggered my mood swings, but in that moment, right there, I felt as if I was finally seeing through her persona. Something shifted inside of me; a plate tectonic movement of anger, resentment, and a certain sensation... but I couldn't identify it.

I wanted to respond, though she robbed me of the opportunity to defend myself when she calmly walked off and slipped back inside, leaving nothing but the fragrant smell of her perfume.

Roses.

Now I knew why I hated her scent so much: it was familiar. It reminded me of the ocean, which was strange because the smell of sea air was far from "rosy." I just saw... something... an unexplainable past life memory that plagued my mind in distorted flashes. Did I hate Lana in that lifetime, too? I shut my eyes and took a deep breath. This was going to be the longest three weeks ever.

CHAPTER FOUR

VINCENT

After reading *The Lorax* several times to my daughter, Lilly finally nodded off. Dad had tried to put her to sleep earlier, but she wanted me to read to her like I did most nights before bed; it was our little ritual, which I enjoyed. My mum used to read to me when I was a child. I guess I sort of picked that up from her: spending quality time with my children. Even though Claire and I were having problems, I didn't regret fatherhood. My kids were everything to me. Deadbeat dads didn't deserve to be parents. It saddened me to know that while I hugged and kissed my children every night before bed, orphans were starving on the streets somewhere; kids were being sold, neglected, and abused. This was the dark side of reality. Where was our benevolent God? Why would he allow such atrocities and injustices? Religious folk can be so quick to judge the atheist—but when you think about all the human suffering that continues to pile on through the epochs of time, it either tests your faith or makes you lose it entirely.

Lana told me something last year, and it sort of stuck with me since. She accused me of having "an impenetrable titanium heart"—and this was *not* a compliment; it's all about context and tone. We had been arguing, of course. Personally, I wasn't offended. I had a strong sense of self. I knew who I was, so her judgment of me did not crumble my self-worth. Many have accused me of being a pompous ass, but I preferred Lana's label of "titanium heart." The imagery was attractive to me—made me feel strong when I attributed my meaning to the metaphor. See? It's all about your *perception* and how you *respond* to external stimuli. I didn't need a bloody guru to tell me that.

Careful not to wake my daughter, I switched off her bedside lamp and quietly crept out of her pink bedroom before I checked on my son. Claire refused to breastfeed him. She couldn't do it with Lilly, either. There is nothing disgusting about breastfeeding. Those who shame young mothers in public need to get their heads screwed on properly. My assumption was that pornography was the culprit; it warps the mind. Nurturing an infant is a beautiful maternal display of love. Apparently, cleavage is fine and acceptable, yet breastfeeding in public is a serious social offense? People like that can piss off.

Yes, Lana... perhaps I have a titanium heart for those who don't deserve to breathe, I thought to myself.

I'd rather just ship 'em off to an island and blow it up. How's that for "world peace"? Extreme, I know, but we cannot achieve a utopia with the existence of oppressive ideologies. I don't think I possess the patience needed to teach misguided people about changing their harmful views. It seemed easier to just "kill them off"— hypothetically speaking, of course, I wouldn't actually do it. But that's sneaky politics for you... combine that with religion and you have a dangerous weapon for mass control. Isn't this how genocides happen? You only need to look at the Abrahamic faiths and their fanatics. It was a paradox, really. On one hand, each monotheistic religion promotes "peace and love" while simultaneously radicalizing nut jobs into carrying out acts of violence. I didn't need religion to guide my moral compass. Anyone can misinterpret spiritual teachings to justify their evils.

I tried not to dive in too deep with these thoughts as I headed downstairs, following the beautiful sound of sad piano melodies. At first, I thought my father had turned on the stereo, but I was pleasantly surprised to find the gold-digger sitting by a grand piano in the corner of our renovated gathering room. The walls were in earth tones, and the dimmed pot lights in the ceiling offered an ambient, calming effect. The focal point of the space, however, was the custom brown brick fireplace that had a massive viewing area, cast iron andirons and ceramic glass covers. It was the only thing that added a rustic feel to the room. A blown-up photograph of a forest hung above the mantle. This space was easily my favorite part of the house because of the large bay windows that offered a gorgeous view of the ocean. Sunrises, sunsets, and moonlight were breathtaking to witness from this room.

No one seemed to notice me as I leaned my weight against the doorframe and listened to Lana's impressive performance. She didn't have any sheet music in front of her, which made me think it was an original composition—nothing that I was familiar with. My mother had signed me up for lessons when I was eight years old. I played professionally all the way into my twenties. I was an accomplished pianist in her eyes.

Dad was sitting in an armchair with a drink in hand, entranced by the music. Stringed instruments were incredible; they seemed to move even the hardest hearts, *especially* ones made of titanium. I couldn't seem to look away as I watched Lana, admiring her feminine features. She had won the genetic lottery; I'll give her that much—didn't mean I had to like it. My eyes wandered from her face to her slender neck. I wasn't sure why I found clavicles to be so attractive on women; Lana's were so well defined. Everything about her was just... so... *feminine*. It occurred to me then that I had never seen her in sweats, or even a T-shirt. Lana McKenzie was a high maintenance woman, which conveniently fit her role as my father's little plaything. It seemed ridiculous to refer to her as my stepmother, because of our small age gap. Maybe that's why I had difficulty taking her seriously. Her presence lacked authority— couldn't say the same about my wife, however.

I respected Claire's work ethic, though I didn't agree with her views about stay-at-home mothers. I didn't see it as a loss of freedom and autonomy. Indeed, I was a firm proponent of feminism and female empowerment, but if toxic masculinity and the "MGTOW" movement were problematic, then so were neo-feminism and toxic femininity. To me, motherhood is a beautiful sacrifice; the most important, hardest job in the world. You only get one shot at raising kids the right way. You can't press rewind and delete little slip-ups here and there, much less the monumental parenting fails. I guess I was just disappointed that my wife didn't embrace motherhood the way I'd expected.

Harmonized melodies echoed around me as Lana stayed focused on the ivory keys. I didn't need such concentration when I played. My hands were dexterous, and I knew many classical compositions by heart. Still, she played well as I stood there, motionless, studying her as if she were my muse. I hadn't expected her to look up and catch me staring, but she did. It didn't seem to throw her off as I held her gaze for as long as I could before she finally looked away and finished her classical piece.

"Bravo!" My father applauded. "That was exquisite! Such raw talent!"

Lana's eyes were warm and disarming as she smiled and stood up.

"You play so splendidly, my dear." Dad continued to praise her. "It's been ages since Vincent filled this house with music."

"Maybe you should ask him." She pointed at me.

My father whipped his head around and chuckled. "What are you doing standing over there, all by your lonesome? Come, Vincent... have a drink with us."

"I didn't mean to intrude." I reluctantly stepped inside.

"Nonsense! Sit next to my beautiful wife and entertain your old man. It's been so long. A duet would be nice. How about it?"

"I'm sure Vincent would prefer to play a separate piece, Max," Lana answered.

"Afraid of a challenge, my boy?"

I knew what he was doing, but I humored him and moved next to Lana on the piano seat. I could tell she was nervous as she scooted over to give me more space.

"Are you familiar with any classical composers?" I asked her.

"I love classical music, but I've had no lessons—Mom couldn't afford it. I'm just... self-taught."

"Can you read sheet music?"

"Not that well."

"Know any songs?"

"Um..." She seemed to ponder for a moment. "'Apologize' by One Republic. Do you know it?"

"Yes."

"Do you know how to play the duet version?"

"No, but I can improvise along with you."

"On with the show!" My father grumbled impatiently.

"Okay, you ready?" I asked her.

Lana nodded.

"You lead, I'll follow."

She took a deep breath and positioned her fingers over the keys. Her hands were beautiful, trembling slightly.

"Close your eyes and take a deep breath," I advised, hoping it would help.

She exhaled slowly and composed herself before she played the first few chords in 4/4 time. I waited on beat and joined her, playing the lead melody in a higher octave.

Much to my surprise, we sounded decent. Lana never messed up her notes, despite how nervous she initially was. Her confidence appeared to have increased by the second. Our fingers accidentally brushed against each other now and then: a liquid movement my old piano teacher would have praised us for, had she been there.

When we finally reached the chorus, Lana's singing voice blew me away. Her vocal range was just unbelievable; it evoked an unexpected reaction within me; something I had never felt before.

Why was this woman focusing on a writing career when she could have easily been a fan favorite of *American Idol*? Her voice sent chills down my body. I didn't know whether to envy her or praise her hidden talent.

We were sitting so close to each other—too close for comfort. All throughout the song, I realized one thing: I was enjoying myself. Was I possessed? Had she finally bewitched me? Her voice seemed to have a spellbinding effect. Had I known she could sing like this, I never would have come on this stupid vacation. Why was this happening? Why did I feel...

I stole a quick glance and noticed a tear roll down her cheek. Was this song sentimental? Who broke her heart? Did she truly have a heart to break? Everything had faded around me... everything but Lana.

When we reached the final chorus, I had goosebumps all over my arms that didn't seem to disappear, even when she stopped singing. That magical voice still echoed in my head, as if to taunt me, knowing that I'd...

Bloody hell. I wished I'd never heard it.

My father's voice faded in as I looked up and noticed that he was on his feet, giving us a standing ovation.

"Flawless!... [*claps*] ... Beautiful! Master class performance! Such a gorgeous voice! Doesn't she sing beautifully, Vincent? She's blessed with a voice of an angel." He continued to praise her as he walked over to a bar cart and poured himself another glass of brandy.

"That truly made my night." Dad smiled. "With all the arguing between you two... who knew that you could make such beautiful music together?" He chuckled.

Lana met my gaze. I wasn't sure how to interpret her silent signal, or so it appeared. What was she trying to tell me? Perhaps it was just a respectful exchange of admiration from one musician to another. Her subtle smile seemed to show that.

"You play really well for someone who's only 'self-taught,'" I said.

"Is that sarcasm?" She scowled. "You don't believe me?"

"I was being genuine, Lana."

"Oh."

I could have sworn she blushed.

"Thank you."

Dad's phone suddenly vibrated as he stood up. "Back in a jiffy— need to take this." He left the room, leaving us alone together, *again.*

I felt uneasy and unsure of myself. I guess it was the awkward silence and the fact that we were still sitting together on that piano seat.

"Look, Vincent... I... I want you to know that despite our differences, I really care about you. I know you think I married your father for the wrong reasons, but I genuinely love him. I consider you all my family... the *only* family I have." Her eyes brimmed with tears.

I wasn't sure how to react. Seeing her in such a vulnerable state was unfamiliar territory for me. After all this time, why now? It had to be an act. She must have had an ulterior motive. What was her angle? I never bought into Lana's bullshit story about "loving" my father. What made her think I was going to change my mind now?

"I don't trust you," I finally confessed. "I don't think I ever will."

"Why can't you just try? We never seem to get along. I feel like every time I try to do something good, you only hate me more."

My blood pressure was rising. It took every bit of strength to resist erupting in anger.

"Let's avoid this conversation," I suggested, trying to calm down.

"Don't you want to resolve this with me?"

"No, I don't."

"There are tons of horrible people in the world, Vincent. I'm not one of them."

She was pushing me. I had warned her.

"How many times do I need to repeat myself? You took advantage of my father, Lana. He was vulnerable."

"That's not true, though!"

"It *is*!" I lost my temper. "You can't convince me otherwise."

"How can you still think that way about me? It's been over a year... have I not proved myself? I love your dad. I love this family."

"If you truly cared, you never would have agreed to marry my *idiot* father, who was *clearly* not in his right mind after my mother died!"

"Are you really gonna hold a grudge against me because of that?"

"I mean, for fuck's sake, Lana! Where the hell was your compassion? Your common fucking sense? You couldn't just let my family grieve, could you? You just *had* to get married four bloody months after she passed away!"

I had lost control of my emotions, but it felt good to remind her that my opinion of her had not changed. No one could change my mind about Lana.

"Vincent, please just—"

"You expect me to respect you, but I can't!" I raged. "You did a great job of destroying that by yourself. If you had any sense in your head, you would've turned down my father's proposal."

I wanted to tell her about that email, but I had promised Dad. I had to keep my mouth shut.

"As I said before, all you did was take advantage of a grieving old man who probably felt unbearably lonely and convinced himself that the best way to medicate and mend his broken heart was to take on a new wife. Well, you're a poor substitute, mark my words. You're nothing but a cheap version of 'Mrs. Luther.' You can never fill my mother's shoes. Do you hear me? *Never*."

Fresh tears spilled down her face as she looked at me, so clearly wounded.

Good.

I had no regrets.

Lana caught me off guard when she stood up and left the gathering room without breathing a word. It was foolish to have thought that she'd defend herself. I seemed to have had this amazing talent for making her run away from me. She rarely fought back. My wife, however, always had a hard time throwing in the towel and backing off from an argument. Both women had opposite personalities, yet somehow got along. It was beyond me.

... ashamed of yourself, mijo.

I wasn't sure if I had created this voice in my head, or if my mother's ghost was reaching out to me from the other side. Whatever it was, it didn't pull me out of my limbo state as a wave of emotions washed over me. While I drowned in feelings, my father's voice miraculously saved me from overwhelming despair.

"Where's Lana?" he asked, standing near the threshold.

"She's *your* wife. How the bloody hell should I know?" I replied disparagingly, brushing past him.

CHAPTER FIVE

LANA

The house was eerily quiet as I padded through the darkness and stepped into the kitchen in a silk, ivory camisole. It was too hot to cover up. The air conditioning had stopped working during the night, but that didn't seem to bother Max; he was fast asleep. He could have slept through anything. Humidity always kept me up. It also didn't help that Vincent's scathing words were looping in my mind like a broken record. He had such a charming accent and a deep, husky voice—it only heightened his attractiveness. But whenever he got mean, he turned ugly, and it hurt.

Desperate for air, I cracked open a window and looked out at the ocean. The moon was full and large in the sky, casting its silver reflection on the dark waters below. It mesmerized me. This place was an idyllic vacation spot for anyone with a family. I only wished she could have been alive to experience this with me... this life. It wasn't fair. I would have been the best mom ever. I hadn't been very far along for an ultrasound gender reveal, but I always sensed that the life that had been growing inside of me was a girl.

As tempting as it was to sink in self-pity, I opened the freezer and reached for a bucket of chocolate mint ice cream. It was time to eat my feelings; eat them all away until I couldn't feel the pain. I hadn't binged in a long time, but this evening had been rough on me. I found a big spoon and sat cross-legged on the floor with my back against the fridge, feeling like I was thirteen again. The waterworks had begun, and all I wanted was to numb myself.

Food wouldn't yell at me or abuse me. Food wouldn't beat me up. Food wouldn't tell me I was a "worthless, piece of shit who would amount to nothing in life." Food was my friend. Food gave me comfort when my mother was too strung out and high on a cocktail of opioids. Food made me feel safe when I didn't have a father to shield me with his love. Food had convinced me that the *only* way to be free from all my anguish was to fill myself with everything that made my brain feel good, only to make my belly swell with pain and regret. And so, I'd purge and purge, until I emptied myself of all those unpleasant feelings, as if to reverse my shameful self-indulgence. The evidence of my guilt in a fucking toilet bowl.

Pathetic.

Flush it. Flush it away. Pretend it never happened. It's out of your body, you got it out. Next time, you'll control yourself. Next time, you won't go overboard.

It took me years before I accepted I had an eating disorder. My battle with bulimia ended when I was nineteen, when I'd finally moved away from my toxic home environment. But the demon was still there... watching, whispering, waiting. When you grow up with trauma, it leaves you feeling empty, so you do whatever you can to fill that void because you desperately want to survive. This leads to addiction and substance abuse. I didn't want to lose my life. I just wanted the pain to stop.

My chest felt so heavy as I sobbed in silence, stuffing my mouth with gobs of green ice cream. Was this a relapse?

No.

I wouldn't puke it up. Just a few more bites and I'll stop, I told myself. Vincent would've shaken his head at me in disgust had he walked in on me like this.... so pitiful. I was certain he would have shared a few harsh words reserved just for me. He always knew how to make me feel so inferior and worthless. It was getting harder to pretend as if his words didn't affect me. The things he had said earlier had truly broken my heart. I never wanted him to hate me. I was worried something like this would happen when Max had suggested we tie the knot. Intuition is always right. It was tempting to pack up my things and leave my wedding ring on the kitchen counter, followed by a lengthy apology letter to Max. I wanted to hit the road and just drive with no destination—much like how I felt in life: perpetually lost. This feeling had been torturing me for months now... my need to just run away.

Sadness filled my empty well as I wept uncontrollably. I kept thinking about the life I had lost in my womb. He had no idea. He either remembered and just didn't care, or I was so insignificant that he'd managed to erase me. I guess that's what happens when you settle for a one-night stand with someone who saw you as nothing more than a conquest.

The more I ate, the more I cried. I was binging and unable to stop. Why was I doing this to myself? Why was I punishing myself for caring so much? Vincent was wrong. I deserved an apology, and yet, here I was... hurting myself with food at twenty-six.

I genuinely loved everyone in Maxwell's family, especially Lilly. She was like the daughter I always dreamed of having. I saw so much of her father in her. Vincent was often very blunt and cruel to me, but every time I caught him showing that little girl nothing but love, it made it difficult for me to believe that he was eternally evil. I had entered my husband's life during the most difficult time for Vincent. I thought I was lucky to not have to deal with any jealous stepdaughters. Little did I know that having a monster for a stepson (who was older than me) was just as bad, if not worse.

Unable to stop, I dug into the bucket and scooped up a generous serving of icy goodness, ignoring the brain freeze that followed when I scarfed it down. I couldn't stop crying. I felt so stupid for sobbing on the kitchen floor, breaking down like a hormonal pregnant woman. What was wrong with me?

Oh God. I panicked. *Someone's coming.*

Footsteps echoed down the hall, approaching the kitchen.

I froze.

Please, not him... not him...

The tall island had obstructed my view. I couldn't see who had entered until he came around and stood just a few feet away from me.

Fuck. My. Life.

"What are you doing eating on the floor like a dog?"

Vincent's glacial eyes pierced right through me as I dropped the spoon inside the frozen bucket and set it down. I felt hopelessly defeated. He was wearing a pair of black boxer briefs without a shirt on. It felt good to know that I wasn't the only one who had ventured out half naked; we could share the embarrassment. But knowing him, he would target me alone.

"Did your parents never teach you proper table manners, Lana?"

"If you're trying to make me feel any lower than I already do, you won't succeed. This is as low as it gets for me."

I tried to push back my tears, but failed. All I could do was hide my face in my hands and stifle the sobs.

"Lana..." he spoke in a hushed voice.

It did nothing to console me. I couldn't stop weeping and feeling sorry for myself. Vincent's muscular body slid down beside me, which only stressed me out more. I didn't want to be attracted to him, especially since he despised me. I felt his hand on my shoulder and didn't know what to make of it. My heart was pounding. Why was he trying to be nice? He slowly rubbed my back and did something I never thought he'd do, *ever*: he comforted me.

"Don't cry... Look, I'm sorry. I was being an ass."

"You don't have to say that." I sobbed, hugging my knees to my chest. "I know you find me repulsive. You made that perfectly clear earlier."

"I don't."

"You hate me. No matter what I do, you hate me."

"I don't hate you, Lana. Hating someone is like wishing them dead. I don't want you dead, I just…"

I finally looked at him and thought my heart had stopped beating. He was so unbelievably attractive. It was unfair.

"You were right about what you said this evening." I sniffled, wiping my tears. "I should have thought things through before marrying Max."

"It doesn't really matter. He would've gotten his way, regardless. He always does."

"Vincent, I didn't marry your father for money." I examined his expression, desperate to read his thoughts. "I know you don't understand Maxwell's relationship with me, few people do. But I feel like no one has the right to judge me, because money had nothing to do with my decision to marry him."

"Then what other reason? You're gorgeous. You could have any guy you wanted. My father's—well—*old*. Please help me understand."

"I was in an abusive relationship for a long time."

I didn't want to open up about how I was trained to tolerate sexual abuse, all under the guise of a "healthy BDSM lifestyle." André was *not* a "dom"—he was a *weak* son of a bitch who sadistically hurt me to empower himself. He broke my trust in every way.

"My ex used to beat me," I uttered, controlling the pain in my voice. "When I finally left him, I had nothing. I felt like I was robbed of my identity, completely stripped of who I was. I wasn't sure how I was going to survive, but somehow, I managed. Meeting your father… Max was the first man in my life to show me unconditional love.

"He wanted to do everything in his power to help me pursue my dreams and asked for nothing in return, only friendship. We started out as friends, but I fell in love with him. I fell in love with his soul. Not everyone is shallow and superficial, Vincent. Maybe that's how you judge me based on your own prejudice, but that's not who I am." Tears misted my vision again as I tried to force them back.

I wanted to tell Vincent everything I had been keeping to myself. But what difference would it have made? I had tried to get through to him before in subtle ways; there was simply no positive impact—no way to reach him inside.

He stared right through me with his arctic eyes, as if he were trying to find a lie in my truth.

"Let's get you off the floor," he said, standing up and holding out his hand.

"Thank you."

Was this the beginning of a newfound friendship?

Don't hold your breath.

Vincent smelled of body wash and aftershave. I had a hard time looking at him because my eyes kept wandering to his chiseled abs. Max was a sweetheart, but he was no longer blessed with an athletic body that came with youth. I still loved him, regardless.

"Did you wake up because of this heat, too?" I asked, hoisting myself up on the island countertop.

"Yeah... one of the hottest nights of the year." Vincent opened the fridge and grabbed a bottle of water.

He tipped it back against his lips, hypnotizing me with the bobbing motion of his Adam's apple. Afterwards, he reached for the tub of ice cream that I'd left on the floor and was about to put it back in the freezer when I said, "Pass it over."

Vincent set the bucket next to me while I opened a drawer and pulled out a spoon.

"You should try some. It'll cool you down."

"No, thanks."

"Come on, just one bite." I scooped a spoonful and raised it to his perfect lips. "It's the best mint chocolate I've ever had."

He seemed reluctant as he shot me a quizzical look.

"Don't glare at me like that," I sighed. "I didn't poison it."

"You sure about that, *stepmother*?"

It was my turn to raise an eyebrow this time. But much to my surprise, he gave in and took a bite.

I smiled when he did, watching as he nodded in satisfaction.

"Oh—here..." I giggled. "Let me..."

A drop of ice cream was melting near the corner of his mouth, so I reached out and wiped it with my thumb. I was about to lick it off when he grabbed my wrist. Time seemed to stand still as Vincent locked his heated gaze on me. I felt so powerless with his seduction. He possessed me in a way I couldn't understand. I couldn't look away, as he brought his face closer, parting my legs and moving between them. His fingertips made me shiver. My heart kept hammering in my chest as he slid his hands up the sides of my neck, cupping my face.

Is this actually happening? I asked myself, half panicked.

The man who had seen me as his mortal enemy was finally waving a white flag. I couldn't wrap my head around it. All I knew was that he was going to kiss me, and I was freaking out inside.

This is wrong, I repeated in my head. But I couldn't move. I didn't want to.

"Vincent, what—"

My breath quivered right before he shut me up and crushed his lips against mine.

Heat.

Passion.

Desire.

The spark had ignited an inferno that dangerously blazed around us in that dark kitchen. My heart slowly opened and blossomed while he kissed me with an urgent need; an endless hunger that consumed me. Alarms were going off in my head, but my body refused to listen. He had shattered me and put me back together... through a kiss. How weak I was. This was wrong. This was bordering on *adultery.* We were both married. I knew I had to stop this, but my arms found their way around his neck, pulling him closer between my legs as I kissed him back with equal fervor.

Needing.

Wanting.

Craving.

This wasn't enough. I wanted more... so much more. Vincent seemed to gain more confidence as he dominated the intensity of our kiss, as if to challenge the karmic energies of the universe, daring it to strike us down if this feeling was wrong. I was so stimulated I could hardly think straight. Everything about this man intimidated me. I felt like a mortal woman who had tragically fallen for the Greek God of war; he groaned as I ran my fingers through his thick mane. It was at this moment that I realized how much I had suppressed this desire, ever since I'd laid eyes on Vincent. As soon as he grabbed my hips, I broke our heated contact and pulled back.

"We have to... stop," I panted, resting my forehead against his.

His evident arousal throbbed against my inner thigh, driving me mad with lust. I had a primal need. I was starved of intimacy.

Think this through, I kept telling myself.

"Lana," Vincent breathed with me, holding the side of my face. The way he said my name sounded like a desperate plea, so different from his typical icy tone.

His kiss had been so passionate. We sat there for the longest time, catching our breaths, as if we had finished a vigorous workout.

"Vincent, we can't—"

"I can't think," he blurted out, meeting my eyes. "There's no bloody way I can rationalize anything around you, Lana, and it's making me crazy."

His lips drew closer as he kissed me again, this time with feral aggression. I tried to push him away, but he overpowered me.

"No... Vincent"—I mumbled between kisses—"*Stop.*"

"I can't... you don't want me to."

He glided his hand along my inner thigh, parting my lace panties. I should have been freaking out, but I was so deliriously aroused. All logic had disappeared. I *needed* to be penetrated. It was the only way to open that cosmic window: a shortcut for our souls to touch.

He slipped a finger inside of me and I instantly unraveled. A breathy moan escaped my lips as I tried to push his hand away, but it was no use. My body had surrendered to amplifying pleasure; pleasure that Vincent was giving me. Unable to stop myself, I reached into his boxers and pulled out his steel, hard shaft, stroking it while he drove his digits deeper into me.

This was by far the most erotic experience I'd had on a kitchen counter, sitting there with my legs wrapped around him, panting, vulnerably exposed. I refused to slow down as I stroked him faster, determined to make him feel as good as he made me feel. We both seemed to work towards a mutual goal... kissing, touching, biting, until...

"*Fuck!* Lana, I'm—"

I panicked when he moved my hand away. But the fear in my heart only heightened when he wrapped a powerful fist around his shaft and buried himself inside of me.

A violent thrust.

A pulsing explosion.

This was it. We had done the unthinkable.

I felt Vincent's breath on my neck as he groaned and filled me to the hilt. He silenced my pleasurable moans with an insatiable kiss as I returned his affection. I had broken my vows while in submission to this man. We were both adulterers now. An avalanche of guilt raced over me as I slowly realized the consequences of our impulsive actions. Now that the fog had cleared, we were no longer possessed by our animal instincts. What was Vincent going to do? Expose my infidelity? Slaughter me with insults? I wanted to cry. I had never expected this situation. Setting boundaries with men was hard for me.

After a minute of heavy breathing, Vincent finally calmed down and whispered, "This can't happen again."

"I know."

"Look at me," he demanded.

I met his heated gaze and drowned in him.

"*Bésame.*"

The way he spoke Spanish always made me weak in the knees. My desire for him only strengthened my decision to fulfill his request as I leaned into his lips.

"Wait." He stopped me. "Don't do it if this is nothing more than wild sex on the counter."

I stared at him and held his face. This was so much more than just "sex." It meant more to me than he could ever imagine.

"Lana."

My actions spoke louder than words as I pressed my mouth against his. Ecstasy. Euphoria. His kiss was addictive. I couldn't get enough.

When he pulled back for breath, he looked at me and said, "Ask me."

"Ask you what?" I pulled him in again, desperate for his heat.

"The same question... [*kiss*] ... ask me... [*kiss*] ...what you mean to me?"

"I can't," I confessed.

"Why not?"

"I'm afraid of the answer."

His penetrating eyes never left mine as he caressed my cheek and softly kissed me full on the mouth. I couldn't stop things from escalating. We had already crossed a line we never should have crossed.

When Vincent finally withdrew, I stared at his handsome features, tears filling my eyes.

"Hey." He frowned. "What's wrong?"

"Please tell me you remember... please tell me I'm not crazy."

Compassion seemed to pour from his gaze as he moved his lips to my ear and said, "Do you honestly believe I could ever have feelings for a whore like you?"

My eyes snapped open as I shot up in bed, drenched in sweat. Max was no longer beside me. Confused and slightly traumatized, I threw my legs over the mattress and made my way to the bathroom. Vincent's sinister confession still echoed in my mind as I turned on the tap and splashed some water on my face. I was shaking all over, physically affected by nocturnal imagery. I'd never had a dream like that before—so sexually graphic.

A beautiful nightmare.

Had my subconscious fueled this dream? It felt so real. Mom always said I'd have nightmares if I ate too much sugar before bed; she was right. I felt so nauseous. My belly had swelled from my shameful ice cream binge. I dashed toward the toilet and vomited everything I could.

Worthless bitch...

Jimmy appeared in my darkest moments (per usual), reprising his infamous role as the abusive tyrant that lived in my head—a.k.a. my mother's piece of shit boyfriend. I tried to ignore his voice and finished brushing my teeth, spitting out tooth paste and rinsing my mouth as fast as I could. Holding the sink, I forced myself to look in the mirror and face my reflection.

"You're okay," I whispered, tears stinging my eyes. "You're fine. It was just a relapse... you're gonna be okay."

Kill yourself, you dumb slut... it would save you a looooot of trouble, unlike your mama...

I ignored Jimmy's insults and got a grip on reality. The bastard deserved a slow and painful death for everything he put me through.

At what point had I started dreaming? I wondered, sorting through my confusion. It appeared that I'd gone to bed after pigging out on ice cream, which meant that Vincent had never come into the kitchen; our "conversation" was all a dream.

I washed my face again and dried off with a towel before I switched off the light and headed to bed. Tomorrow would be another day of torture, another day to love a man who was blinded by his hatred for me.

CHAPTER SIX

VINCENT

"Vincent, slow down!"

"Relax."

"You're driving like a maniac, and you're telling me to *relax*?"

I sped past a black sedan, hiding a smirk as Lana continued to rant. We were on our way back to the house from the supermarket. It was late in the evening and the sun was nearly setting. Dad wanted to make some grilled pineapple barbeque chicken for dinner tomorrow. I was more than happy to run errands by myself, but he insisted I take Lana with me, worried that I'd miss something on the grocery list. Although I had been reluctant at first (for obvious reasons), I wasn't in the mood to argue with my old man.

It was a twenty-minute drive to town from our property. I took Dad's red Corvette convertible since the weather was nice and had let the stereo play to avoid speaking to Lana. Our "shopping excursion" had gone smoothly. We had picked up everything we needed. But now that we were on our way back, I could sense an argument on the horizon.

"Who told you to switch the radio station?" I asked in annoyance, keeping my eyes on the road.

"You're always listening to rock music. Expand your horizons, Vincent."

She shuffled through several channels before she settled on a station that was playing an R&B track. I wasn't familiar with the artist, but he sounded decent.

Lana's long, golden locks whipped around in the wind, nearly grazing my face. I reached over and lowered the volume before I said, "You wanna take care of that?"

"Take care of what?"

"Your hair. It's out of control and obstructing my view."

"I don't have a tie on me."

I passed another vehicle at racing speed before I slowed down at a far enough distance. When I glanced at Lana, I noticed she was fashioning a side braid.

"Better?" she sounded irritated.

I said nothing and focused on driving, avoiding the urge to fixate on her bare thighs. She was wearing a short, spaghetti strap mini dress; olive green complimented her tanned skin, but of course I wouldn't tell her that. Lana received enough compliments from men drooling over her. The vanilla scent of her body lotion was pleasing to the senses, as much as I hated to admit it. How many men had breathed in that scent while fucking the life out of her? I wondered, afflicted by graphic flashbacks of that archived folder... the winding ropes around her perfect body, tightly wound over her limbs... blindfolded in complete submission. Something moved in my denim trousers as I gripped the wheel and tried to push out my darkest thoughts. BDSM had never piqued my interest, but ever since I opened that bloody email filled with Lana's *risqué* photos and videos, I seemed to have developed an obsessive curiosity about *Shibari.* The seductive song that was playing on the radio wasn't helping my current "condition," so I reached over and changed the station, only to have it switched back by the obnoxious woman sitting next to me.

Not bothering to argue, I changed it again, but this seemed to have started a stereo battle between us as Lana retaliated.

"Will you quit it?" I gruffly stated.

"I'm not in the mood for heavy metal, Vincent."

"How interesting, Lana"—I glanced at her—"it just so happens that I'm not in the mood for *bedroom* music."

"It's not a sex tune—get your head screwed on straight, please."

"She's singing about 'screaming through an orgasm'—and you say it's not sex music?" I arched a brow.

"The lyrics are open to interpretation. Your perverted mind just goes *there* of all places."

I sighed in annoyance as the artist continued to belt out falsettos before I reached over and switched off the music.

As expected, Lana leaned in to turn on the stereo, but I gripped her wrist and stopped her.

"If I can't listen to my music, then neither can you."

"I think I put up with enough of your shitty screamo rock songs while we drove into town—and I didn't even complain. It's only fair that I get to listen to whatever I want on our drive back."

"I'm surprised you're so combative this evening, Lana. Don't you like being bossed around and told what to do?"

"What the hell is that supposed to mean?"

I could hear the anger in her voice.

It means *you're a meek, little sex slave in the closet, Miss Lana McKenzie,* I wanted to say, biting my tongue.

"Interpret the meaning however you wish, love."

I could feel her eyes on me, knowing I had struck a nerve.

Good. Let her be upset. I didn't give a bleeding fuck.

"You don't have to be such a dick to me all the time, Vincent— it's getting old."

"You're too *tightly wound* up, Lana. I suggest you *unwind* and not take everything so personal."

My curious gaze wandered in her direction. I was dropping hints at the obvious, but she seemed confused.

"No snappy comeback?" I chuckled darkly. "It's your thoughts that keep you *tied in ropes of bondage...*"

More silence.

"You *blindfold* yourself to the truth..."

I was determined to provoke her.

"Must be so hard to admit defeat when the truth has you cornered... gagged... in absolute *submission*."

"Pull over, please."

"Why?"

"Just pull over, Vincent!"

She was getting hysterical. I slowed down to the side of the road and parked the car. The moment I did, Lana unfastened her seatbelt and swung open her passenger door before slamming it shut.

"Where the hell are you going?" I shouted after her, switching off the ignition and stepping out of the Corvette.

By the time I caught up to her quickened strides, I grabbed her wrist and yanked her back... only to find tears in her eyes.

"You saw it, didn't you?"

Diamonds dripped down her face, making my heart feel something I didn't quite like.

"What are you on about?"

"Don't play dumb, Vincent." She sniffled, angrily wiping her cheek, as if she resented her vulnerability.

"I'm genuinely confused..."

I knew I was being a prick. I had deliberately pressed her buttons, and now I regretted it. I had promised Dad to never mention the email to Lana.

What did you expect, you fucking bastard? My conscience scolded me.

"What did he send you? Photos?"

"Who?"

She searched my gaze.

"You're such an asshole."

Lana brushed past me and wandered into the woods. I had two choices: (1) confess about the email; or (2) continue to deny the obvious.

Sigh. For fuck's sake...

"Lana! Where are you going?"

I found her walking down a dirt path, hugging her arms to her chest.

"Hey!"

"Leave me alone, Vincent! I need to calm down."

I paused, angered by her stubbornness. I wasn't sure why I thought that provoking her would cause a boxing match of amusing banter, but I couldn't hold back. I hadn't expected a full-on breakdown.

"Why are you still following me?"

She was really pissing me off, so I deliberately chose my next words.

"I received an interesting email last year from a man I assume to be your ex."

Lana suddenly stopped in her tracks, slowly turning in my direction.

"He said you escorted all throughout your relationship with him—that you were unfaithful. He sent me a folder full of your nudes and videos as proof."

All the light seemed to fade from her eyes as I approached her.

"André emailed you?" Lana's voice quivered.

"He didn't give a name."

"He abused me, including my trust. I've never escorted."

"You sure about that?"

"What the hell is wrong with you, Vincent? You have absolutely no compassion for me. None."

"I mean... those videos were pretty incriminating, Lana—just saying..."

"Go fuck yourself, you bastard! I don't owe you any explanations."

"Because you can't admit the truth?"

"To a misogynistic prick like you?"

"Easy on the labels there, love. I know you're deflecting. It hurts to own up to your own BS, doesn't it?"

She was about to slap me across the face when I gripped her wrist and lowered it. Claire had done that enough to me out of anger.

"Let go!" Lana demanded.

"If you try that again, I won't be as 'nice' next time," I warned, releasing her. "But I guess you're used to that... being manhandled for money."

The earth seemed to vibrate beneath us as thunder clapped in the distance, shredding the sky with a violent storm. We were soaked in under a minute.

"You don't know me, Vincent. You have no idea what I've been through. All you have are baseless assumptions about my past."

"I've seen enough to make *accurate* conclusions."

I knew we had to get out of there, given the freak storm—and the fact that I'd left the top down on Dad's convertible.

"Have you been obsessing over my nudes? Is that why you're always pissed off at me and projecting?"

I laughed. "Don't flatter yourself. You *wish* I'd obsess over you, Lana."

"I bet you're so used to getting what you want... everything given to you on a silver platter. Everything and everyone but *me*."

"Who's projecting now? You may have my father wrapped around your little finger, but there is nothing about you I find attractive."

"No?" She suddenly peeled off her dress and stepped out of it, catching me off guard. "You sure about that, Vincent?"

"What the fuck are you doing? Put your clothes back on, you crazy bitch!"

"Is this what you want?"

Her bra was next to go.

"I'm a whore, right? You wanna fuck me like one, too?" She pushed me until I stumbled back and hit the ground, landing in a muddy puddle. The rain kept pelting down on us, as if I had angered the Olympian gods.

Surprised by Lana's strength, I was about to get up when she crawled on top of me and unfastened my belt like a nympho. I didn't even realize that I had a raging stiffy.

"Lana!"

Everything happened so fast; I could hardly process it.

"You've figured me out, Vincent. Well done... I know you wanna be inside me."

She gripped my cock, pulling it out of my trousers while I lay there, powerless beneath her. Lightning flashed in the sky before it poured down harder than ever, leaving us completely drenched.

"*Fuck!*" I cursed under my breath, unable to stop this sex crazed woman from taking what she wanted.

And then it happened.

Waves of pleasure.

Ecstasy.

A feral groan vibrated from my chest as soon as Lana dropped her weight on me, taking my length, inch by inch. I watched the way she parted her lips and moaned, rocking into me, submerging me deeper into her tightness.

How the fuck did I let this happen?

She took my hand and guided it toward her throat.

"All that frustration... [*pants*]... teach me a lesson, Vincent... pound my fucking—"

૭૪૦

BEEP! BEEP! BEEP!

My eyes snapped open to the blaring noise of an alarm clock assaulting my eardrums. It took me a moment to realize that I had been dreaming. Reaching for the nightstand, I switched off the alarm before I sat up, ignoring the embarrassing mess I'd made in my boxers. It was 8am on the dot. That nightmare felt so real... I had never dreamed so vividly before. It was a head fuck, but I was relieved to find myself firmly planted in reality.

Lana's voice echoed in my head as I stepped into the bathroom. I wasn't sure why I had dreamed of her. There was a part of me that felt guilty, even though it was nothing but the imaginings of my mind.

Subconscious desires?

No.

It was sexual frustration. Claire and I needed to work on our intimacy. I had no intention of sleeping with Lana. To be perfectly honest, I felt violated by her. How dare she infiltrate my dream state? This was entirely on her. Convinced she was a practicing witch, I concluded my nightmare was a result of her dark "spell work." If Lana had the power to penetrate my dreams, I could live with that torture. But one thing was clear to me: she could *never* penetrate my heart. Never.

CHAPTER SEVEN

LANA

Our vacation in Ocean City was going well until my husband had to fly out to Seattle on a business trip. He told me he'd be gone for a week, which shouldn't have been so bad, but I was a little upset because he had promised not to pick up any work-related calls. Max would always say he was happily retired, but he was clearly in denial about it; he was a *happy workaholic*, and that was the truth. It was that or he was having an affair. Maybe he had multiple girlfriends across the world that I did not know about. My husband had wealth, power, and status at fifty-seven years old, which explained why he could afford his luxury cars, expensive properties, and private jets. I often wondered why he had been in such a rush to marry me a year ago, but I wasn't complaining. He was a good man who took care of me.

Vincent and I had been keeping the peace with one another, but when Max had left, we reverted to old habits: constantly arguing—none of which I'd instigated. Thankfully, Claire was arriving tomorrow with some mutual friends. Denzel Forester had been one of Vincent's clients before they became close. He was married to his gorgeous wife Ciara, after they'd tied the knot two years back. I envied her cinnamon skin and hazel eyes. Although she was born in the states, she was biracial with Middle Eastern and Caribbean ancestry. Her mother was Lebanese, and her father was from Barbados. This woman was stunningly exotic. If I were to switch over to the other team, Cici was totally my type. She had an outgoing personality, a gorgeous smile, and intimidating intellect. It seemed fitting that she had chosen a career as a marriage counselor; Ciara always gave me expert advice. I never felt judged by her when I talked about my issues.

From the moment we had met, I discovered we had similar interests. Cici appreciated abstract art, theater, and indie music. We often went to plays and art exhibits together. I guess we had bonded so quickly because we were newlyweds, with no kids. Ciara and Denzel didn't have any children yet because she wasn't ready for motherhood. There was a three-year age difference between them, with Denzel being older (the same age as Vincent). He owned several restaurant chains in Atlanta and New Orleans. They lived very comfortably.

Spending a week at Ocean City had made me homesick. I needed to see a familiar face; one that didn't hate me. Ciara was the only close friend I had since marrying Max. She understood my introverted nature and was a genuine gal pal. Most of the women I met at my local country club were so stuck up and arrogant. I had no interest in establishing shallow friendships with bored, rich housewives that had no clue what to do with their free time and money. I guess that was the biggest thing I disliked about being Maxwell Luther's wife: his superficial friendships.

He often justified it by saying that he had a "reputation to maintain," but I disagreed. Rubbing shoulders with snobby elites wasn't exactly my idea of a good time. I had been to countless cocktail parties and charity balls. Most of the people I met at these places came from *old money*. They didn't know what it meant to truly struggle in life, it seemed. I was never the type of person to hate on someone for being rich, but to live a lavish lifestyle and resent the underprivileged by labeling them as the "scum of society"—this came straight from the mouth of a senator in Atlanta *in my presence* at a dinner. It was psychopathic and disgusting to me. We had enough reasons to be divided in this world; socioeconomic disparities only widened the gap.

Max had told me once that most of the plastic surgeons, lawyers, and politicians in our state were active participants in a secret society that hosted scandalous orgies in fancy mansions. When I told him I'd already seen *Eyes Wide Shut,* he'd laughed and admitted that he was "only joking"—though, I'm not too sure, to be honest. I didn't miss my old life, but I wasn't exactly happy associating with corrupted socialites who were more like frenemies to me and my husband.

I kept thinking about my day plans that morning while I hovered over the stove. Lilly and Milo had finished eating breakfast and were watching a Disney film in the living room... but I wasn't alone in the kitchen. Vincent was sitting on a stool near the island, waiting on his eggs and turkey bacon as he browsed through his iPad. It was fifteen minutes of unbearable silence, and he still hadn't bothered to start a conversation. I tried not to let it bother me and kept myself occupied. He looked so different with his black framed reading glasses.

Sophisticated... sexy.

No. I couldn't entertain such thoughts. He was a complete asshole and there was nothing sexy about that... but on surface level, he was hot as hell. He knew how to make clothing look good on his body, that's for sure. His style was attractive, whether he was in a business suit, semi-formal attire, or completely casual like he was that morning, clad in a black vest top and white shorts. I had a weakness for tall, muscular men, with a captivating smile and a head full of hair. Since I'd known him, Vincent often alternated various hairstyles that closely resembled Brad Pitt's short, to medium, to long length hair, except Vincent's "mane" was a little darker, like a soft, caramel brown. At present, he was fashioning a shorter hairstyle with a closely clipped fade at the sides. It made him look so dapper—especially with those glasses and his five o'clock shadow. I found it frustrating and difficult to admit that I was physically attracted to him.

In my younger years, I'd always been obsessed with men and women's fashion, collecting stacks of Vogue magazines, wishing I could wear the latest trends like all the models on those covers. As I grew older, my teenage dream was to become a journalist and travel the world, but that quickly changed when I discovered creative writing. It was a healthy escape from my nightmare of a life.

I grew up dirt poor in Michigan, raised by a junkie mother and her alcoholic partner in crime, Jimmy Harris. He was an abusive heroin addict who enabled my mother's addiction and damaged me in ways I still struggled to recover from. I didn't know who my biological father was.

The bastard left us and that's that. Accept it and move on.

I was just a child when Mom said this to me, and I never forgot.

I recalled finding a shoebox full of photos under her bed when I was nine. There was a picture of my mother in a gold sequin dress, sitting on a man's lap. He was dressed in a gray suit and looked West Asian or Middle Eastern, with hazel eyes, short, black hair, and a mustache. I had wondered if we were related, but it was hard to find my features in him. My mother never liked to talk about my dad and had told me early on to not bring up the subject again. I hadn't bothered to ask her about the photo because I was afraid she'd get angry and beat me for going through her things. She spanked me often whenever I misbehaved and it was always traumatizing, having my hair yanked or slapped across the face while she was screaming her lungs off and scolding me. Combine that with her weeklong silent treatments... no matter how much I cried and begged her to forgive me, it didn't matter. It was as if she got off on seeing me suffer. It was child abuse.

I'd like to unburden myself by expressing how much of a sadistic *cunt* my mother was (is), but my Higher Self knows better. She was just a damaged soul, miserably failing at child rearing. It's easy to "pop out a kid," but raising them right is a completely different story. There are too many damaged people populating the world and damaging their children, only for those young souls to grow up and continue the cycle of generational abuse by harming others. Did I regret being born? There were times I wished I wasn't, even though I had no intention of causing anyone harm.

As I aged, the pain I felt from having an absent father subsided into numbness, but it still hurt me deep down. I figured the man in that picture with my mom was either her "customer" or a former drug dealer. Whoever he was, she had held onto that photo for a reason.

I still struggled to release myself from my painful childhood. It was difficult to forgive my mother when a part of me yearned for retribution. I had cut her off and hadn't contacted her in years for my own mental health. She was dead to me. I wanted to give her a taste of her own medicine for the times she abused me. All I ever wanted was her love and approval, as if it would wash away her past mistakes and balance the scales.

Wrong.

"You got yourself a fancy degree and now you're too good for us? You just remember where you came from. I sacrificed everything for you, Lana! You would've been in foster care if it wasn't for Jimmy and me. Show some gratitude!"

Fuck you, Mom. Fuck. You.

That telephone conversation still haunted me.

I hated discussing my past; it was painful... but I had beat the odds. I could have wound up exactly like my mother: another sad statistic of the underprivileged. I didn't want that for myself. I didn't want to be like her.

Moving from Michigan to Miami to live with my aunt was the best decision I'd made, even though I was only sixteen. I just wished she had taken me under her guardianship much sooner. Throughout the years, I'd had many difficulties and struggled a lot, but it ultimately led me to pursuing higher education. It led me to

Maxwell Luther. He was old enough to be my father, being thirty years older, but I genuinely loved him. He cared about me in ways my family never did. I guess that's what I had been missing in life, an *actual* family of my own. It seemed like fate when our paths crossed a year ago in January. But to be completely honest, I never had a whirlwind romance with him. Our relationship never started out that way.

Max and I had developed a strong friendship from the moment we sat next to each other on a flight out to Florida from Chicago. We were like kindred spirits, the more we talked and got to know one another. He had never given me any creepy, pervy vibes—it was the opposite. He had been a perfect gentleman, and I found his British accent to be so charming. I had no idea how wealthy he was. He certainly could have afforded a first-class ticket. All I knew was that he was a retired investor who had lost his wife to cancer. I'd felt compelled to exchange phone numbers with him because he had mentioned having all the right connections in the publishing industry in New York and London. He was confident that he could open doors for me when I shared some of my unpublished work. Our mutual love for art, literature, music, and travel strengthened our bond.

The more I got to know him, the more I discovered how sincere he was in his efforts to help me achieve my "big break." I felt like I had met this guardian angel who wanted to take me under his wing. It seemed too good to be true. I never had that kind of support growing up. Yes, he was older, but his intentions toward me were truly selfless, at least in my eyes. Max used to fly me out on these extravagant trips around the world while I worked on my novel and editing business. All he wanted in return was for me to tag along as his "plus one" at certain events and business dinners.

The first time he had offered to pay me, I was so offended that I threatened to never speak to him again. I'd thought we were friends. I hadn't realized that by agreeing to be his "travel companion" I was consenting to a "business transaction." In sum, I had unknowingly entered the stereotypical dynamic of a "sugar baby"—something that I hadn't even sought. We never crossed any sexual boundaries, which explained why I believed our relationship was strictly platonic. Even though he had often introduced me as his girlfriend at social events, I always thought of it as me doing him a friendly favor. It didn't seem weird to me because he never made predatory moves to make me feel uncomfortable. His unwavering generosity and kindness had only made me love his soul. Max had nurtured me during a time when I really needed it. I was wounded and recovering from trauma.

When he had popped the question four months into our friendship, it had completely caught me off guard. We had been staying at a hotel in Vegas one night when he'd entered my suite and proposed out of the blue. Max and I had never kissed. We had never slept together. I was his girlfriend in the public arena of his professional life, and a best friend behind closed doors, not a lover. It seemed strange when he'd made his declaration of undying love, insisting that we were soulmates. It's not every day that a woman receives a marriage proposal from a wealthy man who offers her everything... including the freedom to sleep with other men. Max had told me I could see whomever I wanted. Marrying him wouldn't "cage me," he simply felt we were compatible and could help each other out in different areas of our lives.

I believed he was still grieving over Isobel and was afraid of being alone. I had told him I wasn't going anywhere and that he would never lose me as his friend, but he'd insisted on marrying me. Max had basically sold me this dream of never having to need for anything. He was retired, we could travel, and he'd focus on helping me reach the autonomy I always wanted. All he required of me was my lifelong companionship in return for his financial support of my career ambitions.

I hadn't been dating anyone, being fresh out of an abusive relationship. I was afraid of going back to that. Max made me feel safe and loved. He'd told me there was no rush for us to "level up" and have sex, and even admitted to suffering from erectile dysfunction. In hindsight, I think he was looking for a trophy wife to show off and parade around in his social circles. I guess I fit the profile of a "hot wife." Although I never felt an intense attraction toward him, I thought I could eventually grow to love him in that way. We made each other happy in the beginning. He had just lost his wife and needed companionship, and I was this pretty, young woman, disillusioned by romantic love, with broken wings that needed mending. It seemed as if the universe was pushing us together at the perfect time. I had given up on finding "the one"; I just wanted to be safe, taken care of, and loved. Max checked off all the boxes, which is why I'd agreed to marry him, as impulsive as it had been in that Vegas chapel.

The aftermath of that decision brought an onslaught of negative reactions in his family and some public scrutiny because of our age gap and the timing of our marriage. He truly did his best to shield me from hurtful gossip, but his son never hesitated to let me know how strongly he disapproved of our relationship, especially of *me* as his stepmom. I can't even express the shock, confusion, and horror I had felt when I met Vincent face to face after returning with Max to Atlanta as his new bride. That evening at the Sun Lounge... still hurt to remember. There was history between us. And while it had been short-lived and so *clearly* irrelevant to Vincent, it was still painful to me; so painful that even after ten years had passed, I couldn't even bring myself to write about it, let alone discuss it with my husband or Ciara. Aside from the agony of being around a ghost of my past, I was content in my marriage... but it didn't last very long. I had been contemplating an annulment for the past few months. It didn't feel like a marriage; we hadn't even consummated it.

My husband never seemed to desire physical intimacy with me. We even slept in separate bedrooms at home. He snored a lot and had said it was best to sleep separately. He always showed his affection in more of a fatherly way, showering me with gifts, trips, hugs, kisses on the head and cheek—never anything sexual. I hadn't forgotten his issues with erectile dysfunction. I wanted to be patient, but as the months kept passing in our marriage, it seemed like he had absolutely no interest in initiating sex with me. In fact, he had consistently encouraged me to "take on a lover."

Once again, I'd discovered that I had entered something that turned out to be so different from my expectations. I guess that's how life was. Strangely enough, I wasn't angry. As I noted earlier, we built our relationship on strong foundations of friendship and mutual respect; but if my husband was hiding something—whether a side chick or someone else—I felt I had the right to know. I knew I had a "pass" to date whomever I wanted (with discretion), but I wasn't searching for a "friends with benefits" kind of deal. I had devoted myself to my writing career from the moment I'd met Max, and that hadn't changed. But at present, I realized it was getting harder to ignore my desire for emotional and physical intimacy. My husband seemed to enjoy the way his friends undressed me with their eyes whenever we attended their fancy parties. He preferred I dress in traditional feminine attire, which included skirts, gowns, bikinis, and heels—no pants. I was fine with that because I already had a very feminine sense of style. My "tom boy" phase had ended when I turned twelve.

This morning I was wearing a nude chiffon skater dress that had a lace insert along the neckline, which flattered my slim body type. It was cinched at the waist with a gathering skirt that hung just above my knees. I had matched my outfit with a pair of open-toe, tie lace platform wedges. I confess, I had a bit of a shoe fetish (like most women)—Max had spoiled me. We often attended runway shows in New York, Paris, and Milan. I loved high fashion, and I was happy that my husband appreciated it, as well.

Never in my life had I possessed such an expensive collection of shoes, clothing, and accessories. Every time I stepped into my walk-in closet, I felt so out of place—like I was living someone else's life. I still struggled to adapt to my lifestyle as a rich and privileged woman, which honestly was a "first world problem" and nothing to complain about. I appreciated everything Max did for me, but if you knew what it meant to grow up in poverty, I think you'd also feel a sense of guilt for owning a hundred thousand-dollar Birkin bag and two million dollars' worth of jewelry. I had reconciled this guilt by starting my own nonprofit organizations for emergency relief in developing countries, including underprivileged children on home turf in the States.

My younger self never dreamed I would be where I am right now. There was a time when I used to walk out the door in tattered jeans, a messy bun, and old sweatshirts that I'd owned for years. I was rich enough now to wear designer brands, yet a part of me still felt like I didn't deserve it. Growing up poor had caused me to carry an inward shame throughout my adult life. My social status never mattered to Max, but Vincent never missed a chance to remind me of how inferior I was to him and the rest of the family—it was so dehumanizing. While my husband was patient and compassionate, Vincent was cruel and proud; he was a judgmental jerk with an over-inflated ego. How this happened, I did not know.

Careful not to burn the bacon, I switched off the gas stove and plated the dish with crispy strips and scrambled eggs before I served it to the Beast.

"There's no rat poison, is there?" said Vincent.

"Not funny."

"What?... just asking."

"Do you really think I'd confess if I were trying to poison you? That would defeat the purpose."

"Touché." He smirked, drinking his coffee.

Sigh.

He could get away with anything with that accent—rude insults and all.

I walked over to the fridge and grabbed a jug of orange juice, pouring it into a glass on the counter. Vincent was busy eating, seemingly disinterested in conversing with me. I couldn't help but notice how slowly he chewed his food. He kind of put me on edge. I was expecting a complaint.

"The bacon could be crispier."

There it was.

I must be psychic, I thought, rolling my eyes.

It was crispy enough, but there was no point in arguing, so I ignored his criticism and sat across from him.

He finished sipping his coffee and said, "You're not gonna puke your guts out afterwards, are you?"

I felt my face heat up: a silent mortification.

"What are you implying, Vincent?"

"I heard you vomiting the other night."

"I was nauseous and not feeling good."

"Well"—he pursed his lips—"can't be pregnancy, since we both know my old man can't knock you up." He took another bite of food. "So, tell me... whose is it?"

"You really need to watch how you talk to me. I'm sick of your insults."

"How else do you eat that much and not get pudgy? I'm genuinely curious, Lana."

You asshole.

It took every ounce of effort to hold my tongue and not stoop to his level. I knew exactly how Vincent operated. He just wanted to provoke me on purpose—probably because he was bored and found it amusing to humiliate me.

"I work out," I calmly replied. "Just like every other person."

"I see." He paused. "How are you feeling this morning? Any 'nausea'?"

"Honestly, I was fine until I looked at your face." I smiled sardonically.

"Is that right?"

"*Quite* nauseating."

He placed his knife and fork on his plate and slid it toward me. "Vomit on that—tastes like shit."

"You've tasted shit before?... *yikes!* I feel bad for Claire—she's gotta kiss that nasty mouth."

"You need to work on witty rebuttals, sweetheart."

Vincent stood up and walked toward the fridge. I caught a whiff of his cologne and felt my heart drop; it wasn't his usual scent. I remembered that smell, though. I could never forget.

"What do you have on?" I asked.

"Come again?" He shut the fridge and bit into a green apple.

"Are you wearing cologne?"

"Yes. Does that make you want to puke as well, Lana?"

"What is it?"

"Do you have a secret shrine I should know about?" He snickered.

"*Ugh*, you're impossible."

I had given up when he finally answered, "Pi by Givenchy. Not my usual scent—it was on the bathroom vanity of my guestroom." He finished chewing and added, "Is it too strong?"

"No."

There was a moment of silence before he turned and tossed his apple in the garbage.

"Vincent, that's wasteful! It wasn't even half eaten!"

"Too bloody sour."

"Then why'd you eat it?"

"Because you fucked up my eggs."

"There are people starving..."

"Cease your incessant virtue signaling, please. I've had enough."

"I'm not trying to—"

He turned on the radio and scrambled through some stations, as if to shut me up. When he finally returned, he reached for his plate that was still in front of me and took it back to the other side of the island.

"I thought you said it 'tasted like shit,'" I teased.

"I'm hungry. Beggars can't be choosers."

He sat on his stool again and started eating. Not wanting to argue, I reached for my phone to check my email when I suddenly froze.

Oh, my God.

This couldn't have been a coincidence. After all these years... was this truly synchronicity? Jon Secada's "Just Another Day" was playing in the background, and all I could feel was this rushing flood of emotions. This song was special; it brought back a memory I could never let go; a memory I had shared with him one night in Miami. Tearing up, I tried my best to erase all the flashbacks before I stole a glance at Vincent, looking for a sign... *anything.*

He was unphased, completely unaffected by the auditory trigger. Why couldn't he remember? And then I recalled perhaps he *did* but pretended like he didn't. What other explanation was there? That day was special to me, and I'd thought it was for him, too. But I was wrong. I guess it didn't matter. *I* never mattered. He had got what he wanted from me and never looked back.

Last year, when I had confronted Vincent about our history, he reacted as if I'd lost my mind and had mistaken him for someone else—mind you; I hadn't gone into detail about what had happened ten years ago. It was too painful to discuss, especially to a man who clearly didn't want to be around me, much less talk to me. He didn't even respect me, so how I could open up the sore subject? The man I knew seemed to have died, replaced by an evil twin. In retrospect, I realized that my friend Selena had been right; I was nothing more than a short-lived fling. It still didn't explain Vincent's selective "memory loss."

He hadn't shared his first or last name with me when we had collided all those years ago. I knew him as "Leo Cortez" *not* Vincent Luther, which explained why I never connected the dots whenever Max mentioned him before we got married. He hadn't shown me any photos of his son, and I was never curious enough to ask. They'd had a falling out last year when I met Max, so I'd made sure not to bring up the subject. It wasn't until I met Vincent in person that I realized we had already met before. I never discussed this with my husband because it was too embarrassing to tell him I had slept with his son.

I could never understand how some people claim to suffer amnesia after a drunken night out. I always remembered everything. Every. Cringeworthy. Detail. After my failed attempt to jog Vincent's memory last year, I had decided to never bring up Miami again, whether or not he remembered what happened, he clearly didn't care. But this song evoked so many feelings within me. It hurt that he wasn't affected the same way. Not even the slightest.

... Another day...

The lump in the back of my throat was painfully swollen, making it hard for me to swallow. I was having an emotional flashback that induced nothing but feelings of abandonment and trauma. He didn't care. He never did.

CHAPTER EIGHT

Atlanta, Georgia
April 10, 2016

It was jarring to see him again, Lana thought, hiding her anxiety as she stepped out on a wide veranda that overlooked a landscaped garden. Vincent had unexpectedly dropped by. As a new, young bride, she still struggled to adapt to her life as *Mrs. Luther*. Weeks had passed since she had moved in with her wealthy husband in his gorgeous Georgia mansion: a luxurious colonial property that was built on a gated five-acre estate. It had three-level private porches that overlooked a pond and dock. The property included a guesthouse, pool, an underground garage, and a tennis court. Max and Isobel had hosted many magnificent parties together while she was still alive. Lana felt as if the ghost of her husband's late wife was still present, walking the halls of her mansion. It had only been six months since she had passed in November of last year.

A staff of uniformed landscapers were quietly working in the garden when she approached the intimidating man who had fixed his gaze on a fountain in the distance. He was wearing a dark business suit, with his hands in his pockets, lost in thought.

"Are you looking for your father?" Lana spoke, heels clicking behind her.

Vincent turned and was immediately surprised by his "stepmother's" stunning visage. She was dressed in a long, silky champagne gown that had a plunging, deep V neckline that exposed the swelling curves of her breasts. He cleared his throat and stayed serious, keeping his hands in his pockets.

"Where is he?"

"On a business call upstairs. He should be down soon."

Vincent nodded and glanced at his watch; it was almost 6pm.

"Are you attending tonight's event as well?" Lana asked, tucking her hair behind her ear.

"No, I just came to see my old man."

"Oh, okay."

The awkward silence between them made her feel uncomfortable. Several weeks had passed since she had begun her new life in Atlanta. She knew she needed an opportunity to speak to Vincent in private. He didn't seem to remember their history, and it bothered her from the moment Max had introduced her as his wife. Lana had suffered many sleepless nights since that initial meeting at the restaurant. Her heart was in turmoil. There were so many unanswered questions. Why did he disappear? How come he never contacted her? Why did he behave as if he did not know who she was when they were reunited again? They had enough privacy to speak now; why wasn't he saying anything? She could not have hallucinated their entire encounter all those years back, Lana thought, ignoring the dread in the pit of her stomach.

Unsettled by Vincent's stoic stare, she turned to leave when he blurted out, "He shouldn't have married you."

Stung by his confession, she froze at the threshold and retraced her steps until she was standing inches away from him.

"Excuse me?"

"You're not fooling anyone, Lana."

"I don't know what you're talking about."

"I know you're after his money."

She frowned in dismay, confused by his hurtful accusation.

"You don't remember me... do you?"

"What are you on about?" Vincent scowled. "Why should I?"

"Miami? Spring break?" Lana's heart was racing. She hated confrontation. "Was everything just a game when you introduced yourself to me as *Leo Cortez*?"

"First off," he said, "Leo is my middle name—so I wasn't lying about my identity—and second, 'Cortez' is my mother's maiden name. I won't get into the details of why I hid my legal name from new acquaintances during my college years, but I suggest you listen carefully to *this*, sweetheart, because it's important: I was a notorious playboy back in those days, regularly abusing drugs and alcohol.

"I truly don't remember meeting you, but if we had a drunken romp in the sack once upon a time, there was probably a reason I didn't come running back for more. You must've been such a lousy shag that I can't even remember." He snickered. "The difference between me and my father is that I have enough sense to know that you can't turn a whore into a housewife."

Vincent's cruel gaze only amplified the harsh delivery of his baseless insults. Lana felt humiliated. She had suffered so much abuse in life, but no one made her feel as small and worthless as Vincent did at that moment. She couldn't tell if she was more in shock, angry, or completely shattered. But as she steeled herself, she found her voice.

"You never deserved me." Her voice quivered with pain.

"And *you* shouldn't have spread your legs—though I guess that's the *only* reason it's gotten you this far in life. I know your type. Women like you are all the same. Congratulations, Lana!" Vincent flashed a sardonic smile. "Welcome to the family! I'm sure my father flexed his wealth enough to keep you on his arm. Is that why you stuck around?"

"How dare you!"

"Enjoy it while you can. He'll move on to another once he's bored with you, though I suppose you're used to that—being discarded once you've served your purpose."

Lana could hardly process his words. She wanted to defend herself. She wanted to cut him down the same way he had attacked her dignity, driving a dagger through her wounded heart; but she was looping on a flashback that only resurfaced an unbearable sadness. She did not know about the defamatory email that Vincent had received from her ex, how it had tainted his impression of her. Her aqua eyes misted in tears as she fought them back with her stubborn pride.

"You're nothing like your father, Vincent. You're the most heartless man I've ever met."

"Only to those who deserve it, love," he condescendingly replied. "If you don't like it, you're welcome to leave. Frankly, he was better off keeping you a secret than to disrespect my mother's memory this way by parading you around as his new wife—and a cheap substitute at that. Both of you should be ashamed of yourselves!"

Vincent shook with anger as he balled his fist. He had lost control and crossed a line that never should have been trespassed in such an abusive manner. He had shouted so loudly that the gardeners had stopped working, looking up at the commotion that took place on the veranda.

A crystal tear rolled down Lana's cheek. Vincent's cruel tone and hurtful words were like pouring salt on her wounds. His assassination of her character was unbearably brutal.

"Cat got your tongue, Lana?"

"*Fuck you.*" She quickly wiped her tear away and turned on her heel, striding back inside, as if she couldn't get away from him fast enough.

Lana had not been prepared for a confrontation like this. She remembered what her best friend had told her about wealthy college boys on spring break... they only had two things in mind:

getting drunk and getting laid. That's all she had ever been to him: a sexual conquest, Lana thought. There was no point in discussing everything else she needed to say. Vincent didn't care. He had used her. He had worn the mask of "Prince Charming" to hide the ugly monster within. It had all been an act to achieve a selfish goal, Lana concluded, opening a door to the main level bathroom.

Fate had been undeniably cruel for reuniting her with Vincent this way. He was unaware of what he had put her through since he had disappeared for years without ever reaching out and explaining why. It was apparent to Lana that he had no remorse. Whoever he was back then, whether it was all an act or a misunderstanding, she had been so naïve to trust him and his intentions towards her. Vincent had never been serious about a committed relationship, she finally realized.

Her tears kept falling as Lana turned on the tap to drown out the heart wrenching sound of her heaving sobs. She was grieving all over again for a man she had loved and lost when she was only seventeen.

CHAPTER NINE

LANA

The memory of our terrible confrontation haunted me as I sat across from Vincent in the kitchen. He was still finishing his breakfast while I wandered down a ghostly hall in my mind. Ever since that fight on the veranda, I had kept my silence forever about those days we shared in Miami. He never gave me closure. It was something I had to find on my own—and I thought I *had*, but hearing this song again only ripped open old wounds that had hardly healed. There was no point in reminiscing. Whatever happened between us didn't matter to him. Life had taken us in different directions, and I was a married woman now.

"Could you pass me the salt?" said Vincent, avoiding my eyes.

I walked over to him and set the saltshaker next to his plate.

"Why'd you get up?"

"If you haven't noticed, there's distance between us."

On all levels.

"You could've just slid it over."

"It could've fallen."

He glanced at me with annoyance before he sprinkled some salt on his eggs. "You gonna hover over me now while I eat?"

Shit. I had zoned out.

"Sorry, do you need anything else?"

"No, thank you, *stepmother*," Vincent mockingly answered.

"I really wish you'd stop calling me that." I returned to my seat.

"Well, it's your legal title, is it not?"

"My 'legal title' is Mrs. Luther. Besides, we both know I can't mother you."

"Indeed, you can't, which is why your marriage to my father is bloody ridiculous."

"My marriage has nothing to do with you, Vincent. I've tried my best to improve our relationship, but it takes two to make a mutual effort."

"Is that what you think we have? A *relationship*?" He sneered.

"We're family now, whether you like it or not."

"You're not my family. You're an intruder, an imposter."

As much as his words cut me down, I refused to show a reaction.

"I'm not gonna argue with you so early in the morning," I expressed, playing with my food.

"Right," Vincent muttered.

We had no more exchanges as we finished our breakfast in peace. I sipped my tea and gazed at the open window to my left. It was such a beautiful, sunny day. The kitchen was bathed in natural light. During the renovation, I was worried Max would modernize the home too much, but he kept the classic checkerboard flooring and off-white color scheme in this communal space. I loved to cook and bake, so it was nice that he had updated the appliances.

Earlier that morning, I had cut some fresh white roses from the garden and had arranged them in a crystal vase; they stood in a majestic display on the kitchen table near the glass sliding doors. The flowers moved, caught in the breeze, spreading their fragrant perfume in the air. I loved the smell of roses; they reminded me of my grandmother's garden in Maine. She passed away when I was five.

Lilly's laughter echoed in the kitchen and pulled me out of nostalgia. I couldn't help but smile. She was singing along to Belle's opening ballad in *Beauty and the Beast*. I daydreamed about having children of my own one day. I even imagined Vincent as my husband. What kind of life would we have had? Probably fighting constantly. It was pointless to even conjure such absurd fantasies. The song on the radio had made me sentimental; that was the culprit.

I stole a few glances at Vincent when he wasn't looking. The nightmare I had of him was still so vivid in my mind. I was glad it wasn't real, though.

When he finished eating, he wiped his attractive mouth with a napkin and looked at me.

"So," he said. "What are your plans this afternoon?"

This man was so hot and cold. We had argued only two minutes ago, and he was acting like it had never happened.

"Um..." I cleared my throat. "I'm not sure. I think I might do some writing—you know... *finally* finish that manuscript. What about you?"

"I'm taking the kids sailing."

"Oh, that's nice. I'm sure Milo and Lilly will love that."

His blue-eyed princess suddenly sprinted into the kitchen, wearing a cute pair of denim shorts and a white T-shirt that had a sparkly pink butterfly in the middle. I had braided her hair earlier, and she looked so adorable. According to Lilly, Claire never had time to do her hair, so it was a special moment between us.

"Aunt Lana, may I have some apple juice, please?"

She was so polite, unlike her father.

"Of course, sweetheart." I got off the stool and grabbed her favorite blue cup from the cupboard.

"Daddy, when are we going on the boat?"

"In an hour, love."

"Can Lana come with us?"

"She'll be busy with work today, unfortunately."

Yeah. Right... unfortunate, indeed. Of course, he wouldn't want me to come.

"But... we're on vacation, Daddy!"

Lilly looked at me with those big blue eyes and pouted. "Why are you working when we're on vacation, Aunt Lana?"

"Oh, Lilly, I..."

Her little arms suddenly hugged my waist before I heard the desperate plea of a six-year-old.

"*Please, please*, come with us! *Pleeeeeeeease, Lana? Pleeeeeeeeease?*"

Lilly's persistence made me feel so loved. She was the sweetest angel, but I knew the man who was sitting across from me, and he did *not* want me tagging along.

"Your father's right, sweetie." I gently let her down. "I have some writing I need to finish up."

"When will you be done?"

"I'm not sure." I handed her a cup full of juice.

She took a sip, turned around, and looked at her dad.

"I wanna go when Lana can come!"

This child adored me. I absolutely loved her to bits.

Vincent let out something that sounded like a frustrated sigh before he regarded me.

"Lana, would you mind pushing that deadline to tomorrow and accompanying us on our sailing excursion today?"

Leave it to Lilly to get her way with that man. I found his sudden change of mind amusing.

"Hmm,"—I stroked my chin—"let me think about it."

Vincent shot me a look of annoyance while carrying his dish to the sink.

"*Please, please, please!*" Lilly bounced up and down.

"Okay!" I smiled at her. "I'll come."

"*Yaaaaaay!*" She hugged my waist again before she skipped out of the kitchen.

"Rambunctious little girl." I laughed, cleaning the countertop.

"Yes," said Vincent, "a little *too* much." He chuckled, rinsing his plate in the sink.

I stopped what I was doing and walked over to him. "You don't need to—I can do that."

I had grown up washing stacks of dirty dishes in a single sink. Mom had never been good at keeping up with house chores, and her asshole boyfriend, Jimmy always told me that a woman's place was in the kitchen, not a man's. We couldn't afford many things, especially a dishwasher, since they always spent half their wages on dope. Cleaning dishes the "old fashioned way" was something I was used to.

"You cooked," said Vincent. "I'll clean."

He held my gaze, and I instantly felt this invisible hand reach inside my chest, squeezing my heart till I couldn't breathe. His eyes were so penetrative and daunting at the same time. He made me nervous—which I hated because the feeling was comparable to a mild degree of social anxiety. I felt like the awkward, loner girl that finally got noticed by the popular jock in high school. But my reality was so far from a teenage rom-com.

"I got it," Vincent reiterated.

"Thank you." I smiled and placed my plate in the sink.

The least I could do was help with the drying, since he wouldn't let me wash up. I grabbed a kitchen towel and stood next to him, drying the plates and cups that he'd set on the dish rack. It was a quiet activity shared between us, almost like a picturesque moment of domestic bliss. I wasn't sure how to engage in a topic that would spark a conversation. Every time Vincent was near me, I was too distracted by an emotional flashback, or was looking for a way to escape all interactions with him to avoid an argument. He had so much power over my thoughts and feelings, and I hated it. He was attractive in a way that was movie star gorgeous. The modeling world would have been lucky to have him. Vincent was a worthy runway adversary—easily top three. I would never tell him this, of course; he was arrogant enough, but it explained why I'd felt like Cupid's bow had struck me all those years back.

I was jealous of his light olive skin. His mother had been darker in terms of skin complexion, compared to Maxwell's paleness, but together they had created a beautiful boy who grew up to become a walking sex symbol. Almost everyone darkened a bit in the summer (depending on the length of sun exposure), but I never seemed to get as bronze as Vincent. Admiring this man was dangerous. If a woman were wise, she'd avoid him at all costs. Direct eye contact was nearly lethal. Hearing his deep baritone voice and that sexy British accent was just as killer. I rarely heard him speak Spanish, but when he did... *my God...* it truly was a love language.

Those frosted eyes had the power to freeze you in place or burn you alive. The longer you stared, the more vulnerable you were to fall head over heels, which only left you open to complete infatuation. Being in proximity to Vincent usually filled me with nothing but excruciating turmoil. A sweet agony.

Emotional masochism? I wondered.

It had been such a long time since I'd seen him clean shaven. These days, Vincent kept a trim goatee. Whenever he walked into a room, the energy shifted with him—but that wasn't always a pleasant feeling for me. I had witnessed firsthand how he could make a person feel so special, and then crush them to nothing but worthlessness. Unfortunately, *I* was the one who was always in front of his war hammer. We'd had so many arguments during family functions. I can't even express the way this man had wounded me. My history with Vincent had scarred up my heart, and the damage was irreversible.

The song on the radio had stopped playing. I felt relieved. I should have just changed the station earlier, I thought, feeling awkward standing next to him. Vincent's energy was somber and ominous, which only heightened my anxiety. It was bad enough that I was trying to heal my damaged inner critic, but during moments like this, another voice took the podium in my head and did nothing but feed my fears with so much crap that I didn't want to hear.

He's judging you... you're nothing to him... he used you... he hates you... never meant nothing... stupid Lana.

"Thanks for helping." I smiled, masking my torment.

Vincent gave a brief nod, dried his hands off with a dishcloth, and left the kitchen without saying a word to me.

See? He can't stand you.

I had to distract myself. It was the only way to win the battle in my mind.

◌◈◌

After I finished making a chocolate pudding for the kids, I joined them in the living room and watched the rest of their Disney film. Lilly was singing along to "Be Our Guest," reminding me of my childhood years when my mother would plop me in front of the TV before disappearing with some strange guy into her bedroom. Apparently, that was her way of spending "quality time" with me. As a child, I loved watching *Beauty and the Beast, Sleeping Beauty*, and *Alice in Wonderland*. I used to dream of meeting my own "prince" one day... and I thought I had. But I learned a harsh lesson early on that the archetypal "white knight" and "Prince Charming" didn't exist; they were illusions. What's most problematic about these films is that they set up unrealistic expectations. Life didn't always imitate art. I wasn't too worried about Lilly, though. Despite the bad blood between Vincent and me, I knew he loved that little girl more than anything. He would protect her and be there for her to nurse her through her first heartbreak. The first time Jimmy found me crying over a boy, he ridiculed me and told me that if I "knew how to fuck" I wouldn't have been cheated on. I hated that man. I hated him so much.

I tried my best to ignore the painful memory as I sat on the end of a gray sectional with my sketchpad on my lap. Vincent was too distracted with the film to notice that I was drawing him and Milo; the cutie had fallen asleep in his arms. Honestly, that was the only thing I loved about Vincent: he was an amazing father. I could see how much he adored his children. Not everyone chose drugs and alcohol over their kids. Thank God for that. I could sum up my childhood in three words: abuse and neglect.

Stealthily, I stole a few glances at Vincent, drawing every detail as perfectly as I could with a charcoal pencil. I wanted to capture the flawless symmetry of his face. He was incredibly easy on the eyes, and I was sure he knew it. I never had art lessons, but apparently, I was a natural born artist, according to Max. Everything about the arts had offered me an escape from the horrors of my youth.

By the time the movie ended, I had finished my drawing. Vincent sat long enough for me to complete my sketch undetected. I was about to get up when Lilly ran over to the sofa and hopped next to me.

"*Wow*, Lana! You drawed Daddy and Milo!"

"*Drew*, Lilly," Vincent corrected her.

She reached for my sketch and held it up in her tiny hands. "Daddy, look!"

He placed Milo down in his playpen before he approached us and reached for my drawing. I was nervous. I didn't want him to know I had been sketching him throughout the film.

"Have you had lessons?"

Vincent's face was unreadable, which only increased my anxiety.

"No," I replied. "It's just a self-taught hobby."

"You drew my chin kind of strange." He narrowed his eyes. "And my nose is not that big. Also, your shading lacks proper skill and technique."

My face went bright red. He seemed to have missed the part where I had said that I'd never had a lesson in my life. Offended by his blunt criticism, I stood up, pulled my drawing out of his hands, and ripped it in half.

What a stupid idea.

Vincent didn't seem upset as he stared at me with a stony expression.

"That wasn't necessary." His tone was calm.

"Oh, I think it was."

"Can't take criticism?"

"I'm perfectly open to *constructive* criticism."

"Clearly you're not, otherwise you wouldn't have torn up the bloody drawing."

"It was hardly a masterpiece."

His glacial gaze pierced right through me as I stared back at him. It was a battle of wills. He was trying to break me. What he didn't know was that he had *already* broken me. Vincent always won these wars.

"You didn't have to do that."

"Too late." I flashed a condescending smile and cut our conversation short by leaving.

Like I always did.

ജ

I spent a huge chunk of my morning in my room, reading and writing. Once I got bored with that, I painted my toenails a fluorescent lime color to match my tequila green halter strap bikini that I wore beneath a white vest top and acid washed denim shorts. I sat by my vanity and curled my hair, tying it back in a high ponytail. I felt like Belle, locked away in her bedchamber... away from the vicious Beast. His tongue was too harsh for me. I wanted to take a raincheck on that outing, but when Lilly came in my room all excited, I couldn't say no. I didn't want to dampen her spirits. Kids were my weakness. So, instead of letting her down, I slipped on a pair of stylish gold flip-flops and grabbed my shoulder bag before I left the bedroom.

Vincent was waiting for me at the bottom of the stairs. His ocean eyes met mine as I came down, but we didn't exchange any words. Was he picking me apart in his head? Cussing me out? I questioned, hiding my nervousness. He seemed determined to make me feel like he didn't really want me there. I would have told him the same thing. I never felt like I fit into his family, much less this world. There was always a part of me that didn't want to be here. A death urge... the haunting whispers of the Great Void.

Jump...

I still remembered that day when I almost lost myself in a dark abyss before being rescued through Divine intervention. Was it really Divine timing, though... or "demon time"? I wondered, having flashbacks of the purgatory he left me in.

CHAPTER TEN

VINCENT

It felt good to be out in the open water. I loved the ocean, and I loved sailing more. Dad's luxury motor yacht was old but beautiful. He called it "Lady Isobel" after my mother. I was surprised he hadn't sold it yet, since he was determined to erase all reminders of her. This vessel had a cabin with amenities and built-in marine speakers that were great for outdoor entertainment. I had some music playing while we had set sail. The weather was amazing, perfect for spending the afternoon at the beach. Lilly loved boating. I had made sure she and Milo wore their life jackets, just in case. My daughter was already in swimming lessons and my son was due for his turn once he was old enough. He was safely sitting in Lana's lap, while Lilly sat beside her as we cruised at high speeds. I used to work as a lifeguard in my teens during the summers. I wasn't sure if the "stepmother" could swim, but I found the idea of making her "walk the plank" entertaining.

When I finally killed the engine, I put on my aviators and got myself a Red Bull before I took Milo off Lana's lap.

"I think he's sleepy," she said, sliding her sunglasses on her head.

"He's due for a nap soon."

"I can take him down to the cabin and stay with him," she offered.

"No, we won't be here too long. Thank you, though."

I watched her get up and make her way to the front of the boat. She removed her shirt and shorts before she maneuvered herself on the hard surface and stretched her body back. Her lime green two-piece was distracting; it especially stood out against her tanned complexion. Lana didn't appear to have any tattoos—I could have been wrong, though. She reserved the right to wear whatever she wanted, but I would have appreciated some modesty. Her bikini left very little for the imagination.

I turned around and focused on a boat in the distance. As a married man, I knew my boundaries, but I was still a man. Those who claimed to never notice attractive people while being in a relationship were flat out lying. Loyalty was a choice, of course. It just seemed absurd to deny the fact that anyone was virtually vulnerable to feeling physically attracted to another person, *outside* of the restricting confines of a monogamous relationship.

"Daddy?"

"Yes, sweetheart?" I looked at my daughter.

"Are there mermaids in the water?"

I let out a lighthearted chuckle. Do I tell her the truth and burst her innocent bubble of imagination? I pondered.

"Mermaids are part of fairytales—like Ariel."

"I wish I was a mermaid."

"Well, you *can* be... for Halloween this year. You can be Princess Ariel when she turned human."

This seemed to have excited Lilly as she chatted my ear off about last year's Halloween party at her school. At some point, I had zoned out. I hadn't slept too well the night before. I wasn't sure why the nightmares had started again. Maybe this place triggered something in my psyche. I wish I had never read my mother's journal. I knew she had bouts of depression here and there, but I had no idea how bad it was until I read her most private thoughts. She had *prayed* for death. Her cancer diagnosis had *actually* made her happy. I couldn't believe it. I specifically remember her writing, "I'm finally going home... Thank you, God."

In retrospect, she had been entirely at peace during that final year before her passing. I was still furious with her and Dad for keeping her diagnosis a secret for as long as they did. Mum had refused chemotherapy. I hadn't been prepared to let her go. I felt it was cruel to be kept in the dark all that time, not knowing the severity of her situation until it was too late to get her to do anything about it. She had been dying, and I'd felt like I had no choice but to compartmentalize my anger. Lock it away and throw away the key.

"Daddy?" Lilly tugged on my shorts. "May I have some water, please?"

"Of course, love, just open the cooler out front. I've got Milo in my arms."

I watched her as she followed my instructions and pulled out a bottle of Fiji water. She then skipped to Lana and asked her if she could twist off the cap.

"This weather's amazing!" Lana said, sitting on her knees. "The water shouldn't be too cold for a dip."

"You swim?"

She smiled at me as she got up and walked over to the edge of the yacht. I wasn't sure why I suddenly felt anxious as she shuffled across the edge, positioning herself before she did a backflip. Her feet pierced the water in perfect execution. I waited for her to surface, but all I could see were bubbles. Would it really have been the worst thing in the world if I had let her drown?

"Lana!" I called out, holding Milo closely. "Lilly, get back from the edge!"

Bloody hell. What was she trying to achieve?

I was about to consider diving in when Lana finally surfaced.

"The water's great!"

Damn you, woman.

I would have yelled at her, but my children were with me. I had to play nice, even though I could've sworn she was deliberately trying to fuck with my head. Lana tread through the water and swam toward the side of the yacht. She gripped the bars of the small stepladder and climbed back up.

I... was mesmerized. Her body was athletic. I could tell by the toned definition of her sculpted legs, midriff, and arms. Upon closer inspection, her breasts didn't seem to show any signs of surgical enhancement—not that there was anything wrong with that, but I preferred a woman's natural state. It's no wonder my old man married her, I thought, cringing at the idea of them going at it like wild rabbits. Clearly, he had been thinking with his head—just not the one that was resting on his shoulders.

Lana's half nude selfies appeared in my mind... see through lingerie... arching her back... bent over on a bed... the intricacy of the rope tightly wound around her arms and legs. *Shibari* is the Japanese ancient art of "bondage tying." My curiosity had got the best of me after I'd seen all those photos and videos of Lana tied up in submission. I had googled "BDSM rope bondage" before I had stumbled on an article that explained "Shibari: The Basics." There was a sensuality to it, I'll admit—at least from what I remembered in those X-rated snapshots.

Fuck's sake.

I had to stop this.

Lana finished wringing water out of her long, golden hair before she reached for a towel in her bag.

Something suddenly flashed in my mind; a split-second image of a long wooden bridge that stretched out for yards in the ocean; but the perspective was from a person standing *under* it. The vision had vanished as quickly as it had appeared, leaving me confused. I blinked, as if to conjure it again, but Lana thwarted my thoughts when she spoke.

"Do you mind rubbing some lotion on my back?"

Yes, I mind.

Even if I weren't busy with holding my son, I still wouldn't have touched her. I made my way over to her and grabbed the tube of sunscreen from her hand.

"Lilly, come here, love."

"Yes, Daddy?"

"Hold out your palms for me, sweetheart."

I squeezed a generous amount of sunblock into my daughter's hands while she giggled over the slimy texture.

"Rub it on Lana's back. Can you do that?"

Lilly wasted no time and spread her creamy palms on Lana's shoulder blades while the witch lay on her tummy on the seats.

I had made my point without being a prick about it. There was no way I was ever going to touch that woman. Lana didn't seem to care as she thanked Lilly and sat up.

"Make the boat go fast again, Daddy! Please?"

"So soon?"

"*Please?*"

It was pointless to deny her of anything. Lana took Milo from my arms and held him on her lap while I returned to the helm with Lilly. We were cruising again in no time. I tried to focus on the open water, but my eyes found their way to Lana. Her silky locks blew behind her while we raced ahead with the wind. She was a sight for sore eyes.

I hated it.

Thankfully, my wife would arrive soon. I had been hoping to mend our intimacy issues. Being sexually frustrated for so long only made me moodier. Last year had been very rough for me. I still didn't feel like I was over Mum's death—wasn't sure if I ever would be. It was a heavy burden to bear, going through the stages of grief with no siblings to share the pain with. I guess I had withdrawn a bit from Claire when Mum died. Everyone had their own way of dealing with grief. It didn't help that my wife had also become complacent with our suffering sex life.

The sky was a brilliant blue, without a single cloud in sight, a stark contrast to the dark and violent storm in my chest. Being on this yacht brought back too many memories. I missed her. Every day, I miss her. I had tried my hardest to be present for my children and resist the urge to drown in crippling depression, but I was still struggling with prolonged grief. I simply hid it well.

CHAPTER ELEVEN

LANA

Yesterday's outing had been fun. I had tagged along with Vincent and the kids to a festival along the boardwalk before we watched a movie on the beach in the evening. The activities had been more for Lilly and Milo than for us adults, but I loved spending time with his kids; they were much better tempered than their father. Lilly had had a blast going on all the kiddy rides. I'd won a prize for her when we played some carnival games. Vincent hadn't berated me like he usually did. I assumed he had kept the peace for his children's sake.

Mom and Jimmy always fought in front of me. I had lost count of all the times when things had escalated to violence. I used to sleep with a pillow over my head to drown out their abusive shouting matches, especially whenever Jimmy was ranting about me. It hurt to hear such nasty things as a child and feel so powerless to defend yourself. My self-esteem was not only decimated at school by mean girls, but in my home environment by my care givers. To this day, I still couldn't fall asleep unless I had a pillow over the side of my head. It was almost like an obsessive compulsion that made me feel safe enough to pass out. My childhood home was a war zone. The only sanctuary I had was the place that existed in my mind until I was old enough to move away and never look back.

Vincent's love and devotion to his children never triggered me. I knew I still had a lot of past traumas to sort through, but the abuse I'd endured had paradoxically increased my empathy. I guess I'd chosen long ago that I wanted to be a better person and not turn out like my mother and that asshole who lived with her. She never protected me from him. She didn't care.

Dinner conversation last night was sparse. Vincent had seemed to be in a world of his own, a place I couldn't reach—and even if I could, I was most likely banned from entry. I had wanted to ask him if he was all right, but I knew that he'd most likely snap at me, so I had avoided the effort altogether. He had put the kids to bed around nine and just disappeared into his room. I couldn't tell if he was avoiding me on purpose, but it was more than likely he was. Keeping myself preoccupied had been a peaceful solution, however. I had worked on my manuscript throughout the night. It was nearly complete, but it didn't *feel* that way to me. Around 5am, I had eventually passed out and slept in till noon. The good news was that I hadn't dreamed of Vincent.

Claire and our friends had already arrived by the time I showered and headed downstairs. Unlike her husband, she was always nice to me, though sometimes I wondered if she was forcing it. I couldn't recall a time where she and I had ever got into an argument. We were cordial with each other, but far from close. Denzel was a good-looking man. He had dark mocha skin, a tall, buff body, black shiny eyes, and a faded buzz cut. Charisma easily oozed off him. Ciara always told me he was a lady's man. I believed her.

Since Claire's parents lived in Ocean City, the plan was to drop off the kids with them for a couple days so that we could all relax with some drinks. She sent Lilly and Milo away so soon. I mean... she hadn't seen them for nearly two weeks. I would have thought she'd want to spend some time with her children before leaving them with her folks, but it wasn't my place to say anything about it. Claire was their mother, after all. Not me.

By two o'clock, Vincent and Denzel started barbequing in the yard while Ciara and I chatted in my bedroom. I was trying to decide on a bikini to wear, since I'd brought one too many with me. My guest room was spacious. Practically everything was white: the walls, duvet covers, curtains, dresser, vanity, including the table lamps. It was a stunning bedroom with a crystal chandelier that hung from the ceiling. The floor plan was dark (exquisite hickory hardwood). But my favorite feature was the large bay window that had a custom-built seat cushion. I liked to read there during the evenings. There was a gorgeous view of the ocean from my walkout balcony. Until my husband told me, I didn't know that this was Isobel's favorite room. I had wanted to switch, worried that Vincent would feel some type of way, but Max had insisted it wasn't necessary. Vincent and Claire were staying in the master bedroom right across the hall from me; the same one his parents used to sleep in before Max had sold all the furniture and replaced it with a new design.

"I love this house!" said Ciara, sitting on my bed with a margarita in hand. "The renovation turned out amazing! I've been thinking about buying some property up here, but Denzel wants to buy a villa in Florida."

I listened attentively while I rummaged through some collections of swimwear in my walk-in closet.

"I mean," she continued, "we could always purchase a place over here *and* Florida, then rent it out." She appeared at the threshold and smiled. Her leopard print sundress looked stunning in her figure. I especially loved her waist length box braids.

"Property is a substantial investment," I said.

"I agree." Ciara stepped inside and sat on a white ottoman. "We'll figure it out." She sighed. "Try that white one."

"This?" I held out the stringed bikini.

"Yes."

"Are you sure?"

"Girl, with *that* tan, that color will look *hot* on you."

I smiled and went behind the shoji screen, which was basically a room divider.

"How are you and Denzel doing?" I asked, wiggling out of my shorts.

"We're good... technically, swingers now."

"*What?*" I almost lost my balance. "When did this happen? And why?"

"Last month. I realized he has this tendency to gravitate towards provocative women. He told me he slept with someone at a club two months ago and that it meant nothing—just sex. I told him that if he wants to screw other chicks, he can... so long as I can have my fun too with men... *and* women." She giggled.

Her confession did not change my perception of her or our friendship.

"It's just easier this way, Lana, to be honest. We can sleep with whoever we want, as long as it's protected, and we don't get emotions involved."

The news had come as a bit of a shock to me, but if anyone knew the right way to go about navigating the "swingers" world, it was Ciara. She was a sex therapist and specialized in marriage counseling.

"You're quiet." She paused. "Which means I've freaked you out."

"No, I... I'm just speechless."

"Because I love to sleep with women, or because I agreed to give my husband a pass to screw whoever he wants?" She chuckled.

"I'm not judging you, Cici."

"I know it sounds like an enormous shock, but then again, most people have no idea how to separate sex from their emotions."

"Is that even possible for women?"

"You need to be in a *very* secure place in your relationship to embark on this lifestyle, hon. Trust and honesty are essential; they're the foundations of every partnership."

"Are you still in love with Denzel?"

"Of course! As much as I ever was when we started dating. Those feelings haven't changed."

"Then how come it doesn't bother you to know that he's sleeping with others? Sharing his body with another woman... giving *another woman* all the pleasure that should be only for you?"

"It's 2017, sweetheart. Times have changed."

I finally finished tying on my bikini and stepped out of the shoji screen.

Ciara's jaw dropped.

"How do I look?"

"*Um...*"—she sipped her drink—"the truth?"

"Obviously."

"You look like a hot-ass-bitch who belongs on Dan Bilzerian's yacht parties."

"Who's that?"

She quirked a dark eyebrow. "Seriously, Lana?"

I genuinely did not know.

"Look him up on Instagram and you'll find out."

I turned and examined my figure in the 360 mirrors while Ciara continued to drink.

"No wonder that man had to tie you down A-SAP."

"Oh, stop it." I laughed lightly. "You're avoiding my questions," I reiterated, putting some clothing away.

"Look, it doesn't bother me because I know I possess the most important part of my husband: his heart. It's all mine. Sex is just... sex." She shrugged. "It's totally possible to go to bed with somebody, wake up the next day, and not feel any kind of bond or obligation to establish something more. You can walk out and never miss them. Lust is different from love, Lana... it's transient, whereas love endures. If I walked out of Denzel's life, he would miss me. He would hurt."

I understood where she was coming from, but for me, sex and emotions went hand in hand. I didn't know how to separate the two.

"I don't know, babes," I finally responded. "I feel like the only way I'd be able to have that kind of relationship is if I weren't in love with my partner. Only *then* could I tolerate his womanizing ways while engaging in my own private affairs. Giving my body, heart, and soul... well, that's something I take seriously. And if I expect loyalty from myself, then I expect the same from my significant other."

"It's not for everyone." Ciara sighed. "Straight up, though... I could never be in a hybrid relationship."

"*Hybrid* relationship?"

"Yes. It's a type of relationship where one partner is non-monogamous, and the other is monogamous. So basically, one makes a full-fledged commitment, and the other doesn't."

Oh, my God. I suddenly realized that it almost mirrored my marriage.

"You're quiet again," she said. "Your thoughts?"

"I just can't see myself being happy in an open relationship."

"*Mm-mm*"—Cici shook her head—"That's a big no-no for me as well, honey."

"But I don't understand. Isn't that what you're already doing?"

"Swinging is so different from having an open relationship, Lana. The difference being, when you're a swinger, you're in a committed relationship, engaging in sexual activities with others—strictly on a recreational level. Having an *open relationship* is when you're in a committed partnership and you form this agreement that any romantic or intimate connection with another is permitted for however length of time.

"This can leave your relationship in a very vulnerable position because whenever feelings are involved with a third party, it becomes a potential threat to your marriage... unless you settle for a polyamorous relationship."

I felt so clueless about this stuff. It was enlightening to learn, though.

"... but with swinging," she added, "it's strictly about the sex. No strings attached, which means no commitment to your sexual partners. It's all super convenient, like the ultimate contract to fulfilling your baser, primal needs—and we *all* have them, trust me." Ciara paused and said, "I retract my statement. I meant *most* of us. Asexuality is real."

Ciara Forester was one of the best sex therapists for a reason.

"Are you ever worried that Denzel might fall in love with someone else?"

My friend seemed to contemplate before she answered, "I think we all have that fear deep down. But if you're able to be secure enough within yourself, to trust *yourself* enough to know that if the person you love betrays your trust, you *can* handle it, and you'll be okay. You need to have faith in yourself to move on if it gets to that point. You know that saying... 'we continue what we're willing to allow'?

"Life doesn't have to stop just because someone hurts you. I love Denzel, but if he ever betrayed my trust and wanted to end our marriage, of course I would grieve—but I also have total trust in myself to get over him. My happiness does not depend on him. Most relationships succeed the long haul when *both* people come together as happy individuals who have done all that necessary introspection and 'shadow work' in life. To put it bluntly: they've worked their shit out."

She wasn't wrong.

"What do you get when you put two broken people together?" Ciara continued, "more broken pieces. Everyone's always looking for love, validation, and fulfillment. You need to look *within* first. You need to genuinely love and accept yourself. Only then will the universe respond and manifest your soulmate. And once you're with them, you'll both be happier."

"Wow, Ciara, that's deep."

"I only speak the truth. I'm a love and sex guru, remember?" She boasted with a grin.

"How many marriages have you saved?" I asked, sitting on the ottoman with her.

"Girl, too many to count. I'm good at my job. If you and Max are ever having problems, my office is always open." She brushed a lock of hair out of my face.

Ever since I had met this intelligent woman, I somewhat suspected that she may have been bisexual. It wasn't like she ever confessed it directly—not till today, but I never asked her about it because it honestly never mattered to me. I wouldn't have loved her any less. She was my best friend. Everyone deserved to be loved and accepted, no matter their sexual orientation, race, gender, or faith. Her affection for me never made me feel uncomfortable. Ciara was like a sister I always wanted.

"Why do I feel as if you're hiding sadness behind those pretty eyes?" she said, squeezing my wrist.

"No sadness." I smiled wistfully. "I'm just so glad you're here."

"It's been that bad with Vincent, huh?"

"He's determined to hate me forever."

Ciara shook her head, laughing.

"What's so funny?"

"The dynamic of your relationship with this man."

"I don't get it."

"Let me tell you something, sweetie. I have years of expertise in human behavior, and it's become clear to me that your 'stepson' is suffering a very common case of 'I-wanna-fuck-your-brains-out-but-it's-wrong.'"

I blushed, which only made her howl in laughter.

"It's true, Lana!"

"Oh my God..."

"I wouldn't be surprised. Come on! You're hot! He's grumpy because he's sexually frustrated around you."

"He loves Claire. He would never—"

"*Unh-uh*"—she wagged her finger—"Let me stop you right there, boo. *Just because you're married doesn't make you blind to attractive people, Lana,*" she said in a sing-song voice. "Can you honestly tell me you never feel attracted to other men when you go out?"

She had a point.

"You say he 'hates you so passionately,' but... what if that hate has only eclipsed a passionate *lust* underneath? Dare I say... *love*?" Ciara smiled coyly.

"*Yeah...* I don't think he loves me, much less desires me."

The past doesn't count. Forget the past, I told myself.

"Has Vincent ever made any moves on you? I promise to keep it between us."

"Trust me when I say that he *really* can't stand being around me. Besides, I would cross no boundaries with him like that. He's Maxwell's son."

She seemed to study my face as she crossed her leg over her slender thigh.

"I've seen the way he looks at you, Lana. I'm a psychologist. It's my job to observe people. I'm an expert at reading body language and analyzing social interactions. I know what I'm talking about when I say that he has it *bad* for *step mummy* dearest."

"Cici!" I cringed. "Don't call me that!"

"Look, he's just in denial and projecting his frustration on you."

"I think it goes deeper than that. He resents me for marrying Max so soon, especially after—"

"Vincent needs counseling. He needs to make peace with Isobel's death. We've all gotta face the Reaper one day." Ciara paused and added, "But I'm serious about him being attracted to you. I'm surprised you haven't noticed this sooner. Surely, you must have suspected *something*. I mean, that last dinner party... I saw the way he looked at you... *secret glances* and all." She giggled. "I caught him a handful of times, I swear!"

I sighed and said, "He was probably throwing daggers with his eyes."

"More like *undressing you* with his eyes." She winked.

My face suddenly flushed with heat. Ciara was my best friend, and I trusted her, but I couldn't tell her about my brief history with Vincent. Nobody knew but him and I. He just couldn't remember (supposedly).

Ciara rested her palms behind her and leaned her weight back as she said, "I guarantee that if you two were stuck in a room together, your clothes would end up on the floor."

"Absolutely *not*," I adamantly stated.

"He would have his hands *all* over you... his tongue in your mouth... fucking you *hard* against the wall."

"*Ugh, Stop!* We're both married, remember?" I laughed off my embarrassment and tried to delete those images in my head. "Are you sure you're not projecting your own desires, Cici?" I joked.

"What if I am?" She bit her lip.

I wasn't sure how to respond, as Ciara leaned forward and added, "Don't worry, babe. I will not cross boundaries in this friendship... unless you..."

"Be serious, please."

"I am. I meant no disrespect to Claire or Max. I was just giving you my observation of our modern-day *Mr. Darcy*," she mocked in a British accent.

I couldn't help but laugh.

"Love Jane Austen," I said, "especially *Pride and Prejudice*, but Vincent is far from Fitzwilliam Darcy."

"He thinks he's better than you. Weren't you the one who told me about how he put you down because you weren't born into wealth? You said he has a hard time respecting you because he thinks you're after his daddy's money. I know you love literature, Lana, but I'd much prefer to sit you in front of the TV, pop in that famous film—the one with Keira Knightley—I love Colin Firth, but that series is *too long*—don't come for me, bitch!"

I laughed at her sassy witticism. Contrary to her, I adored that series.

"... my point is," she continued, "I could easily give you an oral presentation of the parallels between our *beloved Daaaarcy* and Vincent. You'll just have to put up with me fast forwarding and pausing the film throughout my analysis."

"Okay. I see your point."

Now I *really* needed a drink.

"There's so much tension between you two," Ciara expressed. "But it's the *good* kind."

"I think you're misinterpreting some things here, babes."

"I disagree, Lana."

My cheeks felt hot again as I stood up and rummaged through my closet. I needed a nice outfit to wear over my bikini.

"From an objective point of view," Ciara continued, "again, it's totally obvious that you and Vincent have chemistry."

"Yeah," I scoffed. "Like toxic chemical compounds." I pulled a red floral print dress off a hanger. "How's this?"

"Fab—love it."

"I just wish I could change his mind about me."

"So, you actually care about what he thinks of you?" Ciara smiled amusingly.

"No... well—yeah. I mean, he's Maxwell's son."

"How are you and Max doing, by the way? Has he fixed his little...?" She raised her index finger, as if to show a man's biological response to sexual stimuli.

"He still has erectile dysfunction," I said. "We... haven't consummated our marriage yet."

"Seriously?"

"Yeah... He encourages me to 'take on a lover,' but I don't like the idea of having random hookups with strange men."

"Has he tried the magic blue pill?"

"He said he had an adverse reaction to the medication in the past," I explained. "The weird thing is... I've seen him get... you know..."

"*Hard?*" Ciara laughed.

"Maybe he's still struggling with Isobel's death. Maybe Vincent's right."

"Or *maybe...* Maxwell Luther is gay."

"*What?*"

It hadn't even crossed my mind.

"He might be in the closet," said Ciara.

"No, that can't be."

"Have you seen yourself, Lana? You're gorgeous. I mean, if I were a rich old man, I'd want a hot young wife in the bedroom. I'm sure his friends think that's why he married you, to have his very own personal sex doll—no offense."

"None taken."

That was the popular belief among our social circles. Gossip always reached my ears.

"It wouldn't be too farfetched to consider my theory. Maybe talk to him? I could be wrong. People handle bereavement in different ways."

"I know I can never replace the love and history between Max and Isobel, nor do I want to—but sometimes I can't help but feel like... a daughter to him. Perhaps he'd just pitied me when we had met and turned me into a charity project. I fought with him last month over this."

"What did he say?"

"He told me I'm wrong and that he understands if I want to look elsewhere for sexual gratification. I got mad and told him I take my marriage vows seriously. His response kind of hurt."

"Well, I can offer you some free professional advice."

"That's a relief." I smiled.

"Marriage counseling. Consider presenting the idea to him in a non-combative way." Ciara paused. "But just between you and me... any man or woman would be lucky to sleep with you, Lana."

She made me blush.

"You know, now that I think about it," she added, "there have been plenty of men who have successfully sustained heterosexual marriages while hiding or repressing their sexual orientation. Max is old school. The British government used to put homosexuals in the slammer back in the day."

"Are you serious?"

"Just look up England's 'buggery laws.'"

It seemed as if the pages of world history were filled with more hate and violence than peace and love. No wonder I always hated history class.

"Has he *ever* started any kind of foreplay with you?"

"No."

"Kissing?"

"No."

The answer was as simple as that. I didn't need to think about it. But the more I reflected on Ciara's thoughts, the more it made sense.

My husband might be gay.

"I could be wrong," she said. "The best solution is to just talk it out with him. Worst-case scenario, you could always find yourself a sexy boy toy on the side!" Ciara giggled.

"You're such a bad influence."

"You have *no idea*." She flashed a naughty little smile. "So"—she got to her feet—"ready to head down?"

I grabbed my sunglasses and followed her out, contemplating the state of my marriage.

CHAPTER TWELVE

LANA

We spent much of the afternoon hanging out by the pool, drinking, and listening to music. Denzel's playlist had many exceptional hits that I was familiar with: Haddaway, Corona, La Bouche, PM Dawn, and Night Crawlers. I loved 90's dance music; that era was so upbeat and fun. While I had never been to a concert in my teens, I still remembered all the house parties I'd gone to in my senior year of high school. I rarely needed alcohol to have a good time. I *loved* music and loved dancing even more; it was the fastest way for me to dissociate from my thoughts. When you go through much of your life running away from trauma, you do whatever you can to cope. In my mother's case, she chose sex, drugs, and alcohol. And my dad?... who the fuck knows?

I had just surfaced for breath above the water when Denzel stepped out of the patio door with two beers. He handed one to Ciara as I swam toward the shallow end.

"Is that Milli Vanilli?" I shouted over the blaring music.

"Way back play-back!" Denzel hollered.

When I reached the steps on the side of the pool, I carefully made my way up and was suddenly mortified by my wardrobe malfunction: accidental *nip slip.* I quickly adjusted my bikini top, hoping that no one had noticed; but when I looked up, my face flushed in embarrassment. Vincent was lying down on a chaise lounge, right across from me.

Crap, I cursed in my head.

He was wearing dark sunglasses, which made it difficult to tell if he was looking in my direction.

Probably didn't notice, I consoled myself.

Like Denzel, he didn't have a shirt on, dressed in a pair of light blue swimming trunks. He looked comfortable, lying back with his hands folded behind his head, biceps bulging, per usual. He had put on a bit more muscle weight since a year ago, I discreetly noticed. His abs seemed chiseled onto him, sculpted to perfection. His flawless appearance only hid an ugly monster within, a demon he often unleashed in my presence. I had been hurt enough by good-looking men who used their charms to get what they wanted from me before moving on to "the new flavor of the month." Vincent was no different. I had forgiven him. But I would never forget.

I was relieved that I couldn't see his eyes, hidden behind his Aviators. If he was staring at me, it didn't matter. In fact, it was best to remain indifferent. I toweled off my body and kept my eyes straight ahead as I walked past him. No smiles. Nothing.

"Lana, you want a beer, babes?" asked Ciara.

"No, I'm good, thanks!"

I grabbed a bottle of water and gulped it down, nearly choking when I saw my best friend grinding on her hubby and slapping his butt; he was too busy flipping burgers to turn around. Denzel had a gym bod—it wasn't hard to miss. As a couple, they were both so attractive. I envied their closeness. They seemed so happy, given their constant PDA and the way they hyped each other up: a true power couple—at least that's how I thought.

The patio door suddenly slid open, catching my attention. Claire stepped out in a red bikini, waving a glass of white wine in the air while she danced and sang with the music. She seemed tipsy, considering that was her third glass. Her fiery hair was pulled up in a high ponytail, accentuating her prominent cheekbones and viper green eyes.

"I love this song!" she yelled out.

At least she was in a good mood. Claire was a chatty extrovert, unlike her husband, who always seemed to brood in a corner by himself and couldn't be bothered to engage with anyone beneath his level. That was Vincent's vibe: "can't be arsed" to do this, "can't be arsed" to do that. Gotta love British colloquialism.

"*Dance sandwich!*" Claire giggled, gyrating her hips on Ciara. "Vince, get over here!"

"I don't dance, you know that," he muttered within my earshot.

That was a lie, though. I didn't want to think about it. I didn't want to remember.

The memories no longer exist.

I was about to head inside when Ciara called my name.

"Girl, come sit with us!"

"I wanna make a salad," I answered.

"Bitch, it's a barbeque! Skip your bunny diet for a day!"

My stomach was growling. I had skipped breakfast and lunch—not intentionally. But I listened to Cici and walked over to where she sat with Claire on some patio furniture. Her husband was devotedly focused on his "world famous" burgers; they smelled delicious. I couldn't wait to eat. Denzel was a fantastic cook.

I chatted with the girls for a few about a fundraiser I was organizing for cancer research in honor of Isobel's memory. They were fully on board to help me with whatever I needed, which was a relief. I was about to ask Claire if she could help me arrange a guest list when she stood up and excused herself.

"Be right back, ladies." She grabbed her drink and sauntered toward Vincent.

"I think those two are heading for divorce."

"Ciara, don't say that, oh my God..."

That was random.

"It's just my opinion."

"Did she say something to you?"

"Nope. Call it intuition."

"Their kids are so young…"

"Honey, people have filed for separation, even with a baby on the way. You'd be surprised at how fast a marriage can crumble, depending on the situation."

She quickly changed the subject and started talking about her cousin's wedding, but I was too distracted to stay present in the conversation. Claire and Vincent were right in front of my view in the distance. She was sitting on the edge of his chaise lounge, rubbing his thigh. I couldn't hear their discussion, but I noticed Vincent seemed upset when he took off his sunglasses. His eyes were intense… angry.

"… there is *no fucking way* I'm wearing an ugly yellow gown as her maid of honor!"

Ciara's voice faded back into my consciousness.

"Like, *what*? I love my Cuz Rashonda, but she needs your help with fashion. I swear to God, Lana, if she picks a tacky wedding dress, I will call her out on it—I don't care if I get my head bitten off and removed from the guest list. The truth must come out!"

I tried to give her my undivided attention while she ranted about her cousin's wedding plans. Whether it was an outdoor or indoor venue, at least it wouldn't be at some crappy chapel in Vegas, like the one Max and I got married in. I wanted to tell her this, but Ciara was talking so fast, I could hardly get a word in.

Eventually, she finished her drink, and I was about to speak when I noticed Vincent get up. He seemed distraught, possibly yelling? I wondered, watching him. He looked at Claire and talked with his hands, upset over something I couldn't hear. Ciara twisted her head around just in time to see him storm off and head back inside the house.

I looked at Claire and noticed a hint of sadness in her eyes before she got up and fortified her social mask, heading toward us.

"I *told* you," Ciara muttered, half drunk.

Claire was all smiles when she returned to her seat.

"Everything all right, hon?" Cici asked for the both of us.

"Yeah!"

Claire sounded overly enthusiastic. I wasn't convinced, and neither was my bestie.

"Vince is just tired—should've brought our nanny along with us, to be honest. The kids can be a lot to handle." She reached for the bottle of wine that was resting on the table and topped off her glass.

"Now, *this* is *exactly* what I needed after a long work week," said Claire, gulping back her drink. "Cheers, ladies!"

Ω℥

After dinner, I went upstairs and showered again before I styled my hair, put on some light makeup, and changed into something cute: a white mini skirt and a black tube top. Dancehall music echoed from the den as I made my way downstairs. Whatever Denzel had on, the song was fire. I had to Shazam it on my phone: "Love Riddim" by Rotimi. I loved almost every music genre, especially Afrobeat. Music was a universal love language that brought people together. I recalled reading a journal article not too long ago about how the more open-minded a person was, the more likely they were to enjoy a wider range of musical genres, including world music... pretty sure I fit in that category. I found the girls hanging out on a sofa when I entered the space. Denzel and Vincent were busy shooting pool in a corner; he didn't look up when I came down, which didn't surprise me. Vincent always treated me as if I didn't exist. I was used to it.

The interior designer Max had hired had done an amazing job updating his "man-cave." All the carpeting had been replaced with hardwood floors and dimmable pot lights. We had a top-of-the-line home theater system with a giant TV, pinball machines, and a foosball table. The updated bar was impressive; it had a beautifully lit counter with modern light fixtures that hung from the ceiling. My husband's collection of expensive liquor bottles stood out on the glass shelves. I loved the stone fireplace that was built with New England fieldstone.

I was glad to see that everyone had changed out of their swimsuits. Vincent was wearing a pair of jeans and a black shirt with the sleeves rolled up. Denzel was clad in a baby pink T and white shorts, while Ciara had on a peach, strapless dress with a gold belt around the waist. I loved her hoop earrings and gold cuff bracelet. Claire looked amazing in anything that was green; the color really complimented her red hair and creamy complexion. She wore her hair down straight, framing her oval face.

"You girls are looking lovely," I complimented my friends and sat next to Ciara.

"Thank you!" Claire smiled. "If you ever need a personal stylist, let me know. Irina used to be my client, and she's amazing!"

"My cousin could use her," Ciara muttered, sipping her drink. "She's about to make a fashion *faux pas...* you should see what she's got in mind for her bridesmaid dresses."

"That bad?" Claire laughed.

"Here, look..." Ciara pulled out her phone and showed us some snapshots.

I'd thought she was exaggerating, but nope. The dress design was poor.

"By the way," she added, "is there any place we can get our nails done here? I accidentally broke a nail earlier and I'm in dire need of a nail technician to fix this monstrosity." She held out her hand.

Not that bad—just a little chip.

"I know a place," Claire replied, reaching for her glass of wine. "We can go tomorrow." She looked over her shoulder and told the guys to wrap up their game.

After a few more minutes, they finally joined our discussion. Claire started talking about planning a trip to Bali in late August. She knew someone who could book an all-inclusive package at a five-star resort for three couples—discounted rate. She invited us to come on vacation with her and Vincent.

"I'll talk to Max about it," I said.

"He's retired now. His schedule should be flexible."

"Yes, but he's always finding ways to keep himself busy with work."

Ciara chimed in and said, "How do you know he's not having an affair?"

"Babe, don't make her paranoid for no reason." Denzel frowned. "The man is Vincent's father."

"What? I'm just saying! How many times has he just up and left?"

"It's not like that," I tried to defend him, but Vincent interrupted me.

"*My* father," he spoke in a serious tone, "is far from virtuous, but he built his company from the ground up. Understandably, it's hard to let that go. He's guilty of having extra-marital affairs while my mother was alive. I wouldn't put it past him if he started now."

"Lana has nothing to worry about." Claire said. "She's beautiful! I mean, come on... he'd be an idiot."

"I know his habits. But you're right. He would be."

I was stunned. It was truly a rare moment, Vincent coming to my defense. It didn't take long before our group conversation gravitated to sex, which made me extremely uncomfortable for various reasons. Luckily, Ciara caught on and quickly changed the subject.

"Let's play a game then!" Claire suggested. "Move the coffee table over so we can sit on the floor."

Vincent and Denzel got up and rearranged the furniture while Claire threw some cushions on the gray area rug, forming a ring.

"Okay, everyone!" she said with a clap. "Have a seat wherever, and I'll explain the rules." Claire grabbed an empty bottle of wine and placed it in the middle of the circle.

Oh God. I knew where this was going. I didn't want to play.

"You can't be serious, Claire." Vincent sounded just as annoyed as he looked.

"Oh, come on, Vince!" she replied. "Don't be a party pooper! It's just some innocent fun, right, guys?" Her green eyes sparkled with mischief.

"Um," I hesitated. "Maybe I should sit this one out."

"Lana, *sit down*," Claire insisted. "It'll be fun! It's not like we're having an orgy."

Ciara patted her jeweled hand on a silver cushion and told me to sit next to her. Reluctantly, I caved and seated myself. Denzel joined us and sat by her left side, while Vincent was the last to sit between him and Claire. He leaned back against the edge of the sofa and stretched his legs at an angle, since the circle was wide enough. The next thing this man did was pull out his phone, which resulted in Claire snatching it away. He had already violated her first rule. Clearly, he was uninterested in playing this stupid game. I didn't blame him.

"We're gonna play a few rounds of Spin the Bottle," Claire stated, lowering the volume on the stereo. "I'm sure everyone's familiar with this game, but I'm gonna spice it up a tad and add a few *extra* rules."

"Let's hear them," Ciara eagerly replied.

I was already feeling a little buzzed. In fact, I think everyone was tipsy.

"We'll each take turns. You spin, and whoever the bottle lands on, you have to kiss that person."

"Oh, *hell no!*" Denzel laughed. "There will be no gay action between me and Vince. Sorry to disappoint you, ladies."

"Agreed." Vincent raised his drink and gulped it down.

Ciara scoffed. "You guys are such homophobes."

"Hey," said Denzel, "I got nothing against a gay brother, but it just ain't for me."

"That makes the two of us." Vincent gave him a fist bump.

Claire rolled her eyes and sighed. "Okay, *fine.* If the bottle lands on either of you guys while it's your turn, you can spin again until it lands on one of us *females.* Are we good with that?"

"Much better." Denzel chuckled, drinking his beer.

"And here's another important rule," she added. "You kiss your partner for sixty seconds. One whole minute. The kiss will be timed, so that means that you must make out in the hottest way possible. Items of clothing can be removed and groping is allowed." Claire smirked. "Skipping a turn is only permitted *once*, but your time will *double* on your next spin, so consider that consequence."

"Great." Vincent grinned wryly. "Full frontal snogging like fucking teenagers." He cursed under his breath.

"Stop being so grumpy! I'll sex you up later, don't worry." She winked.

"Christ, Claire..." He seemed embarrassed. "Care to say that a little louder, love?"

"Why don't you drink a little *faster*, darling? I think you need some more alcohol in your system." She poured him a shot glass full of tequila and passed it over.

"I have no choice but to get pissed out of my mind if I'm gonna play this bloody game." Vincent tossed the liquor back and squinted. "Keep the shots coming." He waved.

This felt like an episode of a shitty dating reality show; one that I probably would have watched if Joe Rogan were the host. The roasting would have been hilarious. But all jokes aside, I was a nervous wreck. The idea of kissing any of them made me anxious, but to think of that bottle landing on Vincent... there was no way I was going to kiss him. I couldn't. To me, kissing was an intimate act, an exchange of soul energy—far from casual.

"*So...*" Claire beamed, scanning our faces. "Is everyone ready?"

"Bring it!" Ciara cheered, downing a shot.

"Okay. I'll go first." Claire leaned over and reached for the dark bottle, twisting it as it spun around. The bottle rotated fast until it slowly came to a stop and landed on Denzel.

I felt so awkward, glancing at Ciara—but she seemed completely unbothered by the recent turn of events.

"You don't need my permission," she said to them. "Get to it!"

Claire set the timer on her phone and handed it over to Cici before she crawled over to my best friend's husband like a predatory lioness. It was shocking to see how easily they went at it—kissing with tongue and everything... and yes... there was moaning, as Claire seemed to take charge of the kiss. Things were quickly escalating between these two, and I had no choice but to bear witness. We were like modern day Romans, engaging in ritualistic debauchery in honor of Peitho, goddess of seduction.

I looked over at Vincent and searched for a trace of jealousy or anger, but he gave nothing away. Last month, Ciara had divulged something to me. She had a strong hunch that Claire had a crush on her husband. Evidently, her instincts were right. We watched in jaw dropping shock as Claire pulled off Denzel's shirt and swung it in the air like a lasso. She went in for another kiss when the alarm went off. They pulled back instantly, catching their breaths.

"You're welcome." Claire giggled, blowing Denzel a kiss before she returned to her cushion.

My eyes found Vincent's. It seemed as if he was indifferent about what had happened as he poured himself another drink. Were they swingers, too? I wondered, slightly horrified. Was this common among rich folk? Sleeping around and trading wives and husbands with each other? Where was the loyalty? Where was the Arthurian chivalric code? Even some of Shakespeare's tragedies pedestaled the beloved in such poetic ways as an honorable tribute to true love, or at least, the *idea* of it. But this... this was far from loving. It was a tame display of hedonism. Perhaps I was just a naïve, little fool for holding onto such an old-world view of love and romance.

"Not bad," Ciara finally spoke. "But I could do better. Three and a half stars from me." She finished her glass of wine and placed it on the table behind us.

"Denzel, you're next."

He reached for the bottle and spun it with his strength as it rotated until it slowed down and landed on Vincent.

We all laughed.

"Why am I not surprised?" He chuckled, leaning in for another turn.

This time, he was pleased with the outcome as the lip of the bottle pointed at Ciara.

She motioned him over with her index finger and said, "Gimme some sugar."

Lying back on her cushion, she parted her legs while inviting her husband between her thighs. We watched as Denzel pinned her hands above her head and kissed her passionately. They were obvious pros at this, having years of experience as lovers; countless hours of time invested in learning each other's body, synchronizing their frequencies to a higher vibration of being.

Of course, I was romanticizing it all in my head, like I usually did with almost everything in life. The *idea* of love seemed more appealing to me, especially when experienced through the eye of the mind, than reality itself. I guess that's why I chose writing as a career. My mundane existence was unfulfilling. I had spent much of my life pushing people away, only to *continue* that monotonous routine I often complained about; it all led to nothing but loneliness, apathy, and an underlying fear of dying alone. I had everything at my fingertips now: wealth, security, and yet... I was still unhappy.

"Grab her ass!" Claire cheered.

Her drunken giggles yanked me out of my thoughts. That was when I caught a rare moment: Vincent's laughter.

Glancing at Cici, I soon realized what they were laughing at: her thong. The black undergarment was hanging on her right ankle. I had missed it because I felt embarrassed watching them make out. I had been too focused on the wine bottle. Fortunately, the alarm soon went off, but they were so entangled in each other that Claire had to remind them to stop.

"I took her panties off!" Denzel proudly dangled it before us. "Y'all can't beat that! That's straight up Casanova shit right there." He chuckled.

Ciara laughed with him, sitting sideways, since her thong was in her husband's possession.

"Your turn now, Cici," Claire announced, wild-eyed with excitement.

My friend did not hesitate to lean in and spin the damned thing. We all watched as it rotated, slowly landing on Claire.

"Finally!" said Denzel. "Some girl on girl action!"

She crawled toward her and let their lips collide while I kept track of time. A dress was unzipped, and then a strapless bra came off like some Houdini magic trick (it was Claire's). That's when they *really* started going at it. I noticed Ciara was more sensual with the way she kissed a woman. She seemed to control the intensity and rhythm of their kiss as Claire moaned in pleasure.

As soon as their time was up, Ciara slowly pulled back and smirked at her husband.

"I hope you took notes." She gloated.

"Damn, babe... that was hot!"

It was my turn to spin. I felt sick to my stomach.

"I'm gonna skip my turn."

"Are you sure?" said Claire. "If the bottle lands on you, you'll have to complete *double* the time limit—that includes the next round when you spin."

I couldn't do it. I had to bide my time and come up with a good excuse to abandon this stupid game. Max wasn't here. *That* alone was a good enough reason to bail, but Ciara knew about our little arrangement—not that I'd agreed to Max's suggestion, but the option was out there. She was drunk, and I didn't want her accidentally opening her mouth.

"Again, are you positive you want to skip your turn?" Claire reiterated.

"Yes." I decided, trying not to look so tense.

"All right, your choice... can't say I didn't warn you, Lana." She turned her head toward Vincent and smiled. "Your turn, honey! If it lands on Denzel, I'm seriously gonna die." Claire giggled.

Vincent seemed just as hesitant as I quietly watched him. I was certain he was going to skip this round, but he subverted my expectations when he placed his hand on the bottle.

"Fuck it," he cursed, giving it a powerful spin before he leaned back against the brown sofa.

My anxiety was through the roof. I kept praying that it would point at anyone but me. Even if that bottle randomly shattered, I would have sworn it was Divine intervention, not a fluke coincidence. But the slower it turned, the faster my heart pounded, as it passed me over and over, until it landed on...

Our eyes locked.

Fire and ice.

I couldn't do this. I could *not* do this.

There was nothing but panic in my paranoid mind; a crippling fear that instantly pushed me into an unwanted flashback. This was not happening. They didn't know. No one knew our history.

"*See*, Lana." Claire smirked. "That's your punishment for skipping your turn." She set the stopwatch on her phone and looked at me. "Clock starts as soon as you make contact. Give us the best damn kiss we've ever seen!"

I wanted to get up and back out of the game to spare myself the unbearable humiliation if Vincent were to reject or insult me. But his next words were completely out of character for him.

"What are you waiting for, Lana?" He threw back a shot. "Let's be a good sport now, shall we? Our audience awaits." He patted his lap.

Alcohol. It was *definitely* the alcohol. Nothing like liquid bravery.

"Get on his lap!" said Ciara.

I could hardly move. No one had a clue that I was freaking out inside. I felt like a scared little kitten, approaching the king of the jungle, a ferocious beast who had wounded me many times when I had stupidly got too close.

"Come on!" Claire pushed me. "Don't be shy. Saddle up!"

Was I the only one in this room who struggled with sharing their partner? I couldn't believe she was perfectly fine with me kissing her husband.

No. Not a kiss, a *make-out* session; that's what they expected.

"Vincent, just pull her on your lap already! She's too nervous." Claire laughed, sipping her drink.

Peer pressure was real, I thought.

Ciara cranked up the music, which conveniently set the mood. I didn't recognize the artist, but the track was dark and seductive; it could have easily been added to an R&B "Bedroom" Spotify playlist.

"Drink up, Lana!" Cici handed a shot as a last-ditch effort to help me out.

Vincent's frosty eyes were on me; I could feel them as I finally gave in and tossed back the vodka.

"*Yeeees,* babe! Get it!" she hollered, clapping her hands.

I felt ridiculous, crawling toward an arrogant man who hated my guts. He was uninhibited only because of the alcohol in his bloodstream. He never would have agreed to kiss me if he were sober. Ciara continued hyping me up until I was finally in front of Vincent. His gaze was deep and intense, but I wasn't sure how to read him. Was he plotting an insidious way to embarrass me in front of our friends? I was afraid to even risk it, to give him the chance to prove me wrong. He had betrayed and wounded me in the worst way possible. But if my heart had recovered, then surely, so could my pride... couldn't it?

No.

That was a lie I fed myself. Whatever was left of that mangled thing that bled in my chest had never recovered, nowhere even close to healed, much less my pride.

You hurt me.

This wasn't an "innocent" party game anymore—never was.

"Kiss!"

Sitting astride in Vincent's lap, I gave myself the green light to step on the pedal, full speed... destination: self-sabotage. I could feel his energy infecting mine, now that we had touched, infusing my astral body with a sensation that was still so familiar to me. But I didn't want to feel it.

I can't do this, I repeated in my mind.

I didn't know whether to take charge or wait for him to initiate a kiss. He looked just as lost, staring at me. Our limbo state was short-lived when he finally reached out and made the first move.

Oh God...

My skin tingled, prickling with goosebumps when Vincent brushed his fingertips up the side of my arm... over my shoulder... wrapping around the nape of my neck. All he had to do now was lean in and kill me with a kiss or did he expect *me* to start that?

I was buzzing, which only heightened my emotional state as the music pulled me under its hypnotic spell. This entire situation was a recipe for disaster. Ciara always said to trust my intuition. I had to get up. I had to pack my things and *leave* Ocean City, leave Atlanta, and surrender my title as "Mrs. Maxwell Luther."

Run, a voice whispered in my head.

I didn't want this superficial life filled with superficial people. I had done my best to coexist with a man who didn't seem to have a clue about how he had nearly destroyed me.

"What are you guys waiting for?" Claire's voice echoed in the background. "Quit stalling!"

"Right," said Vincent, keeping his eyes on me. "Let's get this bloody well over with."

A rhythmic percussion of pounding 808s vibrated the floor and thudded through my chest, as if to fuel the fury in my heart: a powerful war drum that had suddenly turned into a bioweapon, or so it *wished.* My anger merely disguised my sadness. In my mind, I was sitting on a battlefield with Vincent, afraid and vulnerable, preparing myself for ultra-violence. I was too terrified to reach out and touch him, even though he had invited me to a "friendly" energetic exchange. My hands were trembling, but thankfully out of sight, resting on my thighs.

"Ready?" he almost whispered.

No. Far from it.

But I looked into his eyes and glanced at his kissable mouth before switching to his heated gaze. I held my breath when he leaned in and drew closer to my lips. Everyone's voice had suddenly tuned out.

This was it.

It was happening.

As soon as I shut my eyes, Vincent gently crushed his lips against mine, which thrust me into agonizing euphoria; an oxymoron, I know—but that's how I felt. My psyche seemed to transmute these feelings of pleasure into pain. It wasn't a gift. I didn't want to feel this heaviness.

Muffled voices echoed behind me, as if I were walking down a long, empty tunnel. I was losing grip of the present, falling into flashbacks that I didn't want to relive. Vincent's kiss was liminal: a transitory state that instantly blasted me into the past. I felt his strong hand wrap around my lower back, pulling me closer while he deepened the kiss.

My heart kept racing as a cosmic window opened in my mind; I didn't want to look through it. I wanted to break all contact, but something powerful had awakened in my soul, like a flaming phoenix, slowly rising from its ashes and spreading its wings in majestic glory; an exalted symbol of love resurrected.

My arms took on a life of their own as they coiled around Vincent's neck while we kissed each other with newfound intensity. I couldn't stay grounded. I was too lost in my head to focus entirely on the primal sensation. His warm tongue brushed against mine, conjuring feelings I had suppressed for so long... a sweet agony, a buried pain. I worried that when I'd open my eyes, my face would be wet with tears. There was no way I could handle his cruelty anymore, not after this.

I felt his heat, passion, and desire overwhelming me, wishing to myself that this wasn't all for show. Was I dreaming again? I questioned my reality. Had I fallen asleep upstairs after dinner? I decided that if this was, in fact, a dream... I would go all in and enjoy it as much as I could before waking up to disappointment.

Touch me. Breathe me.

Passion was all I could feel as I grew more confident and held Vincent's face, kissing him like it was the last time we would share this magical moment again. Possessed by desire, I drank his soul like a lust drunk succubus before I breathed his essence back into him as a final act of mercy. I was blind to the spectators around us. I wanted to devour this man and find salvation at the same time, as if the only way to look upon the eyes of God was through a mind-numbing climax achieved through Vincent's flawless vessel. Tantric sexual union. Was that enlightenment?

He squeezed my hips and yanked them forward, groaning softly in my mouth. Ecstasy surged through my bloodstream while our kiss gained momentum, transforming into something that seemed so unbreakable. It felt like a cosmic reunion... because it *was*. He just couldn't remember. I didn't want him to pull away, not when it felt this good. I never realized how much I had missed these things: affection, desire, liquid heat that filled up my emptiness. After years of aimless separation, somehow, we had collided again through cruel circumstances. Fate had been unkind to me. I had waited for this moment for so long, as I kissed Vincent with reckless abandon, losing all sense of time.

If this was nothing more than a charade, then it was truly worthy of an Oscar winning performance. But you can't fake chemistry. I was still in love with him. I was in love with a man who hated me with a burning passion, all because of his misguided assumptions and unwavering prejudice. And yet, the way he kissed me made me feel as if that hate were merely an illusion—that it never existed; it was only masking something else, something he couldn't seem to admit to himself. Perhaps I was entirely wrong, projecting my own thoughts and wishes.

Desperate to catch my breath, I broke our kiss, only to feel his hot mouth collide with mine once more, as if he couldn't bear the loss of contact. A soft, little cry escaped my throat when Vincent bit my bottom lip and tugged it back before he released it and kissed me wild and deeply. His inferno engulfed me. His fingers traced the curve of my spine, heightening my arousal as he pulled me flush against his body. I touched his chest, feeling his radiating warmth and the soft drumming rhythm of his beating heart. This wasn't a dream—it couldn't have been. These sensations were *real*, I told myself.

I wasn't sure what came over me, but somehow, I got brave enough to tear his shirt open, buttons flying with a satisfying *rrrrrip!*

Vincent didn't stop me.

He didn't pull back.

I touched his muscled chest, needing to feel his skin, as if he belonged entirely to me. At that moment, I had forgotten about his wife and my spouse. I had tasted Vincent's lust, and he had consumed mine; his intoxicating kiss certainly gave that impression. This wasn't a hedonistic pursuit—not for me. I craved his touch. I craved every part of him. I yearned for intimacy.

His hands glided over my glutes, igniting a flame in the pit of my stomach. I snaked my arms around his neck and drove my tongue deeper into his mouth.

He groaned.

I whimpered.

It was a battle for dominance, as we kissed our faces off. Nothing else mattered. All I wanted was to *take* as selfishly as I could.

A primal grunt vibrated from Vincent's chest while he traced my curves. Every part of me was sensitive to the touch. I could feel him stiffen below me, making my thighs quiver. His mouth was wet and slick, kissing me harder, dominating our rhythm. It was a dance of lips and tongues: a flawless choreography of unrelenting passion. I felt as if we were the only ones in our private universe, kissing on a beach beneath a blanket of stars.

"Aaaaand... time's up!"

Claire's voice suddenly jerked me back to reality as I snapped out of memory lane and quickly broke our contact. Vincent's labored breaths filled my ears while I stared at him, quietly panting. An entire year of pent-up passion had finally been unleashed between us... right in front of an audience, *his wife* and our closest friends. What was I thinking agreeing to this? What was *he* thinking?

"Ho-ly *crap!*" Ciara squealed. "That was hot as hell!"

"No shit!" Her husband agreed. "I didn't think we had any competition, but..."

Their voices were no longer muffled with echoes. I wanted to get up when Vincent gripped my hips, keeping me in place. Something had changed in his eyes. I couldn't find a trace of cold contempt, only brilliant warmth. Was it all in my head? Maybe it was nothing but his carnal desire, piercing through my soul and mirroring mine. Maybe that mind blowing kiss was nothing more than a drunken lapse in judgment. In that moment, though, everything about him had intoxicated me. I had tasted his passion, and it only left me feeling lightheaded and embarrassingly aroused. I could no longer think with logic, not while I was still in Vincent's lap. For the first time in forever, I finally felt safe with him; with *this* part of him; the part that reminded me of...

"You guys really went in hard!" Claire giggled. "I'll admit, I got a little jealous, Lana."

That was my cue to get up. I avoided Vincent's gaze and gracefully removed myself off his lap. As I adjusted my skirt, I returned to my spot and noticed Ciara biting her lip with a stupid grin on her face, wiggling her eyebrows. I could only imagine what she was thinking. I was sure I'd get an earful later.

"You okay, honey?" Claire laughed at Vincent. "You look a little winded." She turned her attention to our friends and asked, "What's the verdict? I rate it five stars!"

"Four and a half," Denzel replied. "I'd make it five, had he removed something from her body."

"Are you kidding me?" Ciara exclaimed. "You don't need to get naked to heat things up during a make-out session. Kissing is an art form—not everyone has mastered it. Lana could've kissed him in a nun's robe, and it still would've been hot!"

We all laughed, except for Vincent.

I watched as he picked up a few of his shirt buttons.

Can't believe I did that.

"We'll send you the bill for his shirt, Lana," Claire stated.

"I'm so sorry."

I felt so embarrassed.

"Relax, honey, I was teasing. Who's up for another party game? We can play 'Never have I ever...'"

"Count me out." Vincent stood up. "I'm gonna go change. Be back soon."

His eyes found mine before he turned and headed upstairs. Was that supposed to be a signal? It couldn't have been.

"No more drinking games for me." Denzel rose to his feet. He held out his hand and helped Ciara up.

"And *then* there were three..." Claire sighed. She swigged back a shot and encouraged Cici to join her.

"I think I'm gonna turn in early tonight," I said, hoping they wouldn't mind.

"Seriously?" Ciara frowned. "The night is still young!"

"I get up early to run—that's why I'm usually tired by midnight."

"Oh, *come on,* Lana," Claire persisted. "Drink some coffee and stay up with us." She poured another shot.

Her alcohol tolerance was next level. I would have been stumbling around and slurring my words if I'd downed all that liquor.

"Coffee won't do the trick, unfortunately," I replied. "I'll see you girls in the morning."

"*Afternoon,*" said Ciara. "I'm sleeping in."

"Lana, wait." Claire stopped me. "Before you go... tell me, what was it like kissing my husband?"

"Um…" My face went flush. "It was… nice."

"*Nice?*" She quirked an eyebrow.

"Quit grilling her and let her sleep, Claire."

"What? I was just curious."

"Girl, you're drunk as hell!" Ciara laughed. "Good night, Lana."

I was thankful for her intervention. I said goodnight to my friends and headed upstairs, praying I wouldn't run into an ill-tempered Vincent. I wasn't sure what to say to him since my mind was still in the past; a place he had deliberately erased me from. All I knew was how I *felt.* The pain in my chest was almost unbearable. That kiss… it would haunt me forever.

☙❧

My nighttime routine was usually simple: I'd wash my face, brush my teeth, change into something comfy, and hop into bed. I think it was Kat Von D who advocated "dressing sexy for yourself." Lingerie was supposed to boost a woman's self-esteem in the bedroom, so I put on a nude baby doll—strictly for myself; it was light and my skin could breathe while I slept. André used to control everything I wore—including my diet, my social circle, where I went… *everything.* But I was free from the abusive clutches of my ex. He was no longer part of my life, and I had to put him behind me.

I'm safe, I repeated in my head, struggling to erase the painful flashbacks.

André used to slice off my lingerie before forcing himself inside my body while holding a knife to my throat. He used to threaten to kill me while raping me—got off on it. It didn't matter if I wasn't in the mood. He had brainwashed me into submitting to his every need in our relationship. I felt ashamed for allowing him to brainwash me: a grown woman. I couldn't believe how much abuse I tolerated—complete lack of boundaries. All I wanted was his love. I went along with his sadistic role play fantasies because I wanted to make him happy, but somehow our roleplay blended in with real life. He went from wanting "a whore in bed" to accusing me of "whoring around," as if the roleplaying had manifested a hellish nightmare reality where I was constantly accused of cheating by the man I loved. He hurt me so badly.

Stop thinking about him, a voice of reason reminded me.

After I turned out the lights, I switched on a lamp on the nightstand and grabbed my glasses to peruse a self-help book I had purchased on my Kindle: *Complex PTSD: From Surviving to Thriving* by Pete Walker. I had been in therapy before when I lived in New York, but I wasn't ready to start again. At least I wasn't in denial about my cocktail of issues. Receiving some more counseling was inevitably the next step, I thought, propping a pillow behind me in bed. Just when I was about to read, there was a soft knock.

Probably Ciara.

I placed my tablet down and got out of bed. Twenty minutes had passed since I'd left my friends downstairs. I wondered if she had come up to talk about *that kiss.* Not bothering to wear a robe, I padded toward the door and opened it. Expecting to find my best friend's face, I felt like a deer in the headlights when I saw who was standing near the threshold.

Oh God.

I had stopped breathing.

It had been so long since I'd seen a glimmer of warmth in those frosted blue eyes; they betrayed nothing but vulnerability and a subtle gentleness that completely disarmed me.

"Vincent, what are you—"

His lips collided with mine, like a powerful wave crashing against the shore, sweeping me away into the deepest depths of its infinitude. I wasn't prepared. For the longest time, I believed that the only way I could feel anything deep was from a place of pain: *raw*, intensive agony. The existence of my anguish was a sobering reminder that I was still alive, still human, bleeding from my heart chamber, but breathing. Yet, in that moment of crushing vulnerability, between passion and panic, all I could feel was pure bliss. And it was paradoxically painful.

I retraced my steps to break contact, but Vincent wouldn't let me. He followed me into my bedroom, kissing me hard, making it seem as if *he* had been the one to move me in there. His lips felt so good, stimulating the pleasure center in my brain, which triggered a massive dopamine release. His kiss held an urgent intensity that hadn't been on display earlier. I could still smell a hint of alcohol on his breath, but the scent of Givenchy intoxicated me more.

The door slammed shut when he kicked it back, refusing to rip himself away. If I didn't make him stop, we'd end up with our clothes off. Everything was visceral, overtaking my senses... his touch, his kiss, his jagged breaths. I could hardly process the aftermath. I had to pull away. Since Vincent couldn't, I needed to find the strength. But each passing second made it that much harder to end our impulsive transgression.

Had he masked his desire for me all this time? I couldn't understand what was happening. He never gave me a chance to step back and try to make sense of this. His lips moved and glided against mine as he touched me in places my husband should have. He enveloped me in his masculinity, which only activated something inside... the energetic center that balanced sex, desires, and emotions: my sacral chakra. I could feel it pulsing powerfully within me, a luminescent orange. Vincent's kiss had revived a part of me that had died long ago. I wanted this. I *needed* this: his hands all over me, grabbing, tracing, possessing whatever he could claim as his own. It seemed impossible to break free from each other, but somehow, I tapped into my reservoir of strength and finally withdrew.

We panted breathlessly, staring at each other.

How... how?

I struggled to find my voice, overwhelmed beyond belief. It seemed as if we had shifted to a parallel timeline that starkly juxtaposed with yesterday's reality.

"I... I'm so sorry, Lana," Vincent murmured in a trembling voice. "Please forgive me."

"Vincent, I don't..."

I couldn't think as he stroked my face. His sullen eyes reflected a haunting sadness. It only confused me more.

"I remember." His tone was warm and gentle. "I remember everything."

How was that possible?

"The moment we kissed downstairs, it all came rushing back... I can't even express what I'm feeling right now." Vincent searched my misty gaze, reaching for my hand.

I recoiled from him. Who was this imposter?

"Please, just let me explain." He bridged the gap between us and opened his mouth to speak when he paused abruptly.

I heard it, too. Someone was coming up the stairs.

"You need to leave," I urged in panic.

"Lana, I—"

"*Please*, just go." I nearly snapped.

He stared at me for the longest five seconds before he turned and disappeared out the door, leaving only his passionate energy to linger in my bedroom.

Standing alone, I was paralyzed in place. The ghost of the man I had loved long ago had appeared in front of me. He had kissed me. He was real. Did he truly remember? What had happened? I had so many questions that kept me up all night, tossing and turning... yearning... for *him.*

CHAPTER THIRTEEN

10 YEARS AGO
Miami, March 12, 2007

"No falling in love, my dudes. We're here to party, get laid, and get drunk as fuck!"

"Exactly, bro!"

"Just don't let *this one* open his mouth around hot chicks."

"Yeah, man... he's got an advantage with that accent—should've left him back in New Haven."

Vincent chuckled at his friends as they carried surfboards out of a yellow Jeep. It was mid-afternoon when they had pulled up to Crandon Park Beach, a popular spot for tourists and locals. They were on spring break, vacationing in Miami together. Kevin and Trey were seniors at Yale, graduating with Vincent that same year in their Business Program. Dressed in dark wetsuits, they were the quintessential image of hard bodied, male athletes.

The coast was filled with people sunbathing and enjoying the Florida weather. When the boys found a clearing, they set down a Cooler and some towels before they headed toward the shore with their boards. Vincent loved to surf. The indescribable feeling of gliding across the aqua water made him feel so free. Racing through a tunnel of waves was the closest thing to a spiritual experience for him; an adrenaline rush that purified his mind.

Nearly half an hour had gone by when Vincent noticed a young woman with blonde hair drowning. Her mouth kept hitting water level as she tried to stay afloat, which instantly had him concerned. Contrary to common belief, most drowning cases were not always easily detected; Vincent knew this since he had lifeguard training.

"Hey!" he called out. "You all right?"

Her eyes found his as she gave him a glassy, vacant stare. A male lifeguard in the distance was already rushing in, but Vincent was closer. If he didn't act fast, her airways would close to prevent more water from getting in. Vincent knew he had a very short timeframe to rescue the helpless blonde.

Without wasting another second, he dove off his board and swam toward the drowning girl, slicing through the waves with his strength. By the time he reached her, she was already unconscious, which meant that she was likely to be in cardiac arrest. Fortunately, Kevin had been paddling toward them. As soon as he was close enough, Vincent lifted the blonde's slim body onto his friend's surfboard.

Once they reached the shore, a crowd of onlookers had huddled around them when suddenly, a panicked brunette sprinted forward in a black swimsuit.

"Oh my God, Lana!" she cried out frantically, clasping her mouth in horror. "Please save her!"

Vincent was already on it, performing mouth to mouth resuscitation.

Breathe, breathe, he repeated in his head like a scared mantra, as if to *will her* back to existence.

Staying focused, he heard his friends inform someone that he had Lifeguard Certification, to prevent them from intervening. An ambulance was called, but he was determined to save this young woman's life. Vincent gave her several chest compressions, hoping to restore some blood flow from her brain to her heart.

Come on!

He could not understand how God could let someone so beautiful die like this. But maybe God had nothing to do with it. Her life was in *his* hands now. He refused to let her leave this world in such a tragic way. It was not fair. The brunette, who was Lana's friend, started sobbing, as if she had given up hope. Seconds had turned into a minute and a half while Vincent continued CPR.

"Please don't let her die... *please!*"

A loud siren echoed in the distance, signaling its pending arrival. The crowd had grown bigger, and it seemed as if everyone feared the worst while they quietly prayed together.

Vincent gave Lana a few more breaths before she miraculously started coughing up water and opened her eyes.

A feeling of rushing relief had contagiously spread among the crowd as they cheered and applauded Vincent's heroic efforts. They had witnessed a poor girl's brush with death, which made her conscious state appear as a gift. An angel had kissed her.

"Oh, thank God!" Her friend raced to her side in tears.

"Medics are on the scene," said Trey, pointing in the distance.

Lana sat up, looking pale and disoriented. Her confusion was not out of the ordinary, since her brain had been deprived of oxygen.

"You gave me a heart attack!" her friend cried out, wrapping a towel over Lana. "What were you thinking, swimming out that far?"

"I... didn't mean..."

"It's a miracle you're alive, Lana!"

"I feel nauseous."

"Don't get up!"

Everything was spinning as Lana lost her balance, but Vincent caught her just in time.

"I got you..." He smiled, staring into her aqua eyes; they were deep and soulful, he thought, feeling a warm sensation fill his heart.

Before Lana could protest, he had already scooped her up in his arms, carrying her across the beach where the ambulance was waiting. Even though she was alert, Vincent knew it was crucial that she received a medical evaluation. He had saved her from the clutches of death, unaware that she had every intention of forfeiting her life: a silent shame that Lana kept to herself.

ಀ♌ಞ

"How is she?" Vincent asked the nurse, who had walked out of Lana's hospital room.

"Why don't you ask her yourself?" She beamed, letting him inside.

Uncertain why he felt so nervous, his anxiety instantly vanished when he saw those pretty eyes again. She was sitting up in a hospital gown. All the color had returned to her face, framed by her damp, blonde hair that was cut short with pink and blue streaks.

"Hope you don't mind a visitor?" Vincent smiled sheepishly.

"Hi!" Lana seemed to light up with life.

Her voice was like music to his ears.

"How are you feeling?"

"Alive." She nervously laughed.

"I see that."

"A doctor checked me out already. My vitals are fine. They drew some blood to screen my electrolytes. My lungs hurt a bit."

"Yeah, that can happen when you swallow large amounts of water. Hopefully, you won't have any respiratory complications." Vincent reached for a chair and pulled it near her bed before he sat down, smiling.

"Thank you," said Lana, "for saving my life."

"Don't mention it. I'm just glad you're breathing again."

So am I, she thought, grateful to be rescued.

Had she succeeded in her suicide attempt, she never would have met this gorgeous man.

God is real, Lana believed, shaking Vincent's hand when he formally introduced himself.

"I'm Leo, by the way."

"Nice to meet you, Leo. I'm Lana."

"A beautiful name for a beautiful girl."

She felt herself blushing, thanking him while averting her gaze. His eyes were intensely blue. She had met no one who was devastatingly handsome. It seemed as if her heart had already decided to love this man.

Vincent had not shared his first name with her. His closest friends called him by his middle name since it was his preference.

The brunette who had been panicking on the beach suddenly appeared. She made her way toward her friend and gave her the biggest hug.

"I'm so happy you're okay! You seriously scared the crap out of me!"

"Selena, this is Leo," Lana introduced them.

"I can't thank you enough..."

"I was there at the right time."

"You're literally a lifesaver," Selena replied.

"Well, that used to be my job some summers ago."

"In England?"

"Atlanta. I grew up in Leeds. Dad's British, Mum's from Spain. We moved to the states in my teens."

"*Ah,* I see. Hablas español?"

"Si, muy bueno."

Selena's jaw dropped. "I'm just gonna keep my mouth shut. You *don't* wanna know what I'm thinking."

"Por que?"

She flirted with Vincent in Spanish, secretly hoping he would take an interest in her.

There was a brief pause in the dialogue before Lana said, "I really hope they discharge me. I hate hospitals."

"So do I, chica"—Selena squeezed her hand—"but it's important they check your lungs and monitor your blood oxygen levels—doctor's orders!"

"I know," Lana sighed.

"How old are you girls?"

"Eighteen," she replied. "Actually… I'm seventeen. My birthday's in August, but it's close."

"Young," said Vincent, folding his arms in his chest.

"*Old enough.*" Lana smirked flirtatiously. She asked him his age and discovered that his twenty-third birthday was approaching in November of that year, which made him five years older.

"My mates and I are on spring break."

"Oh, that's awesome!" Selena cut in. "Which school?"

"Yale."

"Ivy league… damn!" She giggled, twirling her hair. "Sure beats community college."

Lana pursed her lips as she looked at Vincent. "Sorry for ruining your day."

"You didn't."

His smile was sincere.

"How long are you staying in Miami?"

"Two weeks," Vincent replied.

"We should all hang out soon!" Selena cut in.

"I'm game. The boys will be down for that." He pulled out his phone and got their numbers.

"I'm a local here," she added. "Born and raised, which means I know all the best bars and restaurants in the area, so if you need a tour guide, I'm your girl! My bestie moved from Michigan about two years ago, and we've been inseparable since." She glanced at Lana. "I don't know what I would've done if I'd lost you today."

"But you didn't." Lana weakly smiled.

A brown-haired nurse with a pixie cut returned to the room and informed her patient that she was due for a chest x-ray in five minutes.

"I should get going," said Vincent. "I'll be in touch, I promise." He took Lana's hand and kissed it like a gentleman.

Her eyes seemed to smile as she held out her arms, hugging him tightly when he leaned in to receive her affection.

"Thank you again, Leo."

"Of course, love," he whispered in her ear, rubbing her back. "I'm glad you're still here with us."

Lana could not wait to get out of that hospital bed. She was already excited to see him again, her guardian angel.

CHAPTER FOURTEEN

Miami, March 24, 2007

Two weeks had passed since Lana had been discharged from the hospital. She had made a speedy recovery without suffering lung complications. In that short time frame, she and "Leo" had grown closer, going on dates almost every day. Being young and naïve, Lana had convinced herself that she had fallen in love. In her eyes, Vincent was charming, intelligent, kind, and generous to a fault. He had refused to let anyone foot the bill during their group outings, which made Lana assume he came from wealth—though it was not a driving force in her attraction to him. His kindness and sweet nature only made her fall head over heels. As much as she enjoyed his company, sadness filled her heart that evening, knowing he was leaving tomorrow.

They were walking along the beach together, enjoying a Miami sunset. A gentle tide rolled in and kissed the shore, returning to the rhythmic ebb and flow of the sea. Lana noticed a flock of birds cascading across a champagne sky. Her golden tresses gently danced in the wind as she and Vincent strolled toward a bridge in the distance. She was wearing a white stringed bikini top and a sheer sarong, tied at her hips. Vincent had coincidentally matched her outfit, clad in a white dress shirt, rolled up at the sleeves, and a pair of knee-length khaki shorts. They looked like models walking barefoot in the sand.

Music echoed in the distance from a nearby bar, amplifying the romantic evening atmosphere. Lana had not felt this happy in ages. Vincent had restored her faith in men. His Spanish lineage made him more attractive to her; he had shown off his fluency frequently. She had discovered that not only was he physically desirable, but he had a wonderful personality that only heightened his masculine appeal. Vincent made her feel special and cared for; something Lana had rarely felt growing up. It was dangerous to place all her happiness in one person. But she was too young to understand the consequences of doing this. She had yet to meet a wise mentor in her life who would guide her the way she always needed.

While Selena had already hooked up with Vincent's friend, Lana had yet to experience a kiss from the man she wanted more than anyone in the world. Although their lips had already touched, she had been unconscious on her back when it happened, inching towards death. She secretly hoped he would make a move that evening and take their friendship to another level. It didn't matter that he was older; it didn't matter that they were states apart, her heart knew who it wanted.

The ocean seemed to sigh in peaceful breaths as Lana felt the water gently glide along the shore, soaking her feet and ankles. She was lost in her head that evening, dreading Vincent's inevitable departure. Her silent reverie was interrupted when he finally spoke.

"You're so quiet. What's on your mind, Lana?"

"I was just thinking about the ocean," she replied, gazing at the emerald water. "Are there beaches in the UK?"

"Of course." Vincent chuckled. "It's not all 'gloom and rain.' Pentle Bay in the Isles of Scilly is gorgeous—looks tropical with a white sandy beach and clear blue water. You'd love it. My Nan used to take me there on holiday when I was a boy. I had a seashell collection."

He didn't want to talk about the horrific deaths of his maternal grandparents. It was too soon to reveal personal traumas, Vincent thought.

"I'd love to travel someday."

"Where would you go?" he asked, leisurely walking beside Lana.

"Italy, France, Australia... *England, Spain.*" She giggled, hoping he would catch onto her suggestion.

"We should travel together! I need a proper holiday this summer."

Lana's heart swelled with joy. "I'm totally down—just need to get my passport sorted out."

"Don't delay, love. The beaches in Spain are stunning... Ibiza, Gran Canaria, Barcelona. You'd love the culture there. Ever been?"

"No, sadly. I've never traveled outside of America."

"I'd love to take you. There's so much of the world you need to see, and life's too short."

Vincent found it difficult to look straight ahead, as he glanced at Lana every chance he got. She was beyond beautiful, and the attraction he felt toward her was like nothing he had ever experienced. He had had many casual hookups at frat parties, but no one ever made him feel this way. Lana had an aura of purity; she embodied an innocence he had not found in another woman. In some ways, he felt unworthy of pursuing her.

"I love this beach," said Lana.

"Even after what happened weeks ago?" Vincent was still unaware of what she had planned to do that day... her tragic intentions.

"Can't hold a grudge against nature." Lana stopped moving and looked out at the water. "That was just stupidity on my part." She took a deep breath, unable to tell him the truth. "The sound of the waves... it's like the ocean is breathing. Do you hear it, Leo?"

Vincent cast his gaze at the vastness of the sea and said, "I do. It's beautiful, Lana." He paused. "But not as beautiful as your voice... all of you."

She turned, and their eyes locked.

This was it, Vincent thought: his window of opportunity had finally arrived. He wanted to pull her in and steal an insatiable kiss. But he hesitated. Instead, he played it safe and slipped Lana's hand into his as they continued their walk.

When they approached a long wooden bridge, they walked under it together. Vincent felt as if they had entered a private world; a portal that had taken them away from reality. The tide was low as it softly crashed along the shore, soaking their feet. Jon Secada's famous single, "Just Another Day" echoed all around them.

"I haven't heard this song in forever," said Vincent.

"I don't think I've heard it before."

"It's an early nineties track. I was eight when I'd heard it on the radio the first time."

"I love it." Lana smiled, brushing her fingers through her windblown hair.

He couldn't take his eyes off her. Everything about this young woman intrigued him. Vincent felt a connection that went beyond the physical. It was difficult for him to comprehend. Despite all the odds, he contemplated a long-distance relationship. Lana was not a girl to use and discard; he *knew* this. He had nothing but noble intentions, motivated by a genuine desire to build something real.

Vincent's train of thought immediately came to a halt when Lana playfully splashed him with water.

"Really, Lana?" He looked down at his wet shirt. "Are we twelve now?"

She splashed him again, beaming with mischief.

"Two can play at this game..." Vincent took several strides through the water and lifted her over his shoulder.

Her beautiful laughter filled his ears as he spun her around, till she begged to get off.

"You sure?" he teased. "I don't think you've had enough."

"Put me down!" Lana screamed, kicking her legs when he tickled her thigh. "Leo! Oh my God!"

A few more seconds of playful torture seemed fitting, Vincent thought, before he carefully slid her down his body. Lana was back on her feet, touching his chest. He had never believed in "love at first sight." In his mind, it was an illusion, packaged and sold to the masses by film directors who were more interested in filling their pockets than to give an honest portrayal of reality on the silver screen. But in that moment, right there, something glowed inside of Vincent's chest as he stared into Lana's eyes.

"Dance with me," he murmured, holding her waist.

Enraptured by the music, Lana wrapped her arms around Vincent's neck and slowly swayed with him while the tide swept their feet. She felt as if she was in a dream. He was too perfect to be real. All the time they had spent together had only intensified her attraction to him. She wanted more.

"Tell me something, Lana," Vincent murmured in her ear. "Do we have a summer of love on the horizon?"

"I hope not."

"Why do you say that?"

"It's too short." She looked at him and felt her stomach tighten.

"That's a fair point," he replied. "Have you ever been in love?"

"I wear my heart out on my sleeve, so... yes, I have."

"He broke your heart?"

She nodded.

"Bloody bastard. His loss, though... *my* gain."

Lana could not hide her smile. Everything felt so organic with him, she thought.

"I want to kiss you so badly," Vincent finally confessed. "Can't tell you how many times I thought about just 'going for it' these past few days."

"You seem brave enough." She giggled. "I mean, you saved me from drowning to death. I'm sure you can find the courage to take another risk."

"True... I'm a notorious risk taker, undoubtedly."

His penetrating gaze pierced right through her. She could not look away.

"Then why hesitate?"

"Because..." He leaned in her ear once more and whispered, "I'm afraid you'll steal my heart."

Lana laughed. "Do you say that to all the women you want to kiss?"

"No." Vincent chuckled. "I've been saving that line specifically for a mermaid."

"But I'm not a mermaid."

"For all I know, you could have magically lost your 'fish tale' when you were treading water that day... or was it intentional?"

"Now you're just being silly."

"You've put a spell on me."

Lana was speechless. He was too charismatic. She wondered if he was the devil in disguise. But would the devil have saved her from suicide?

Never, she told herself. This man did not have a mean bone in his body; Lana was convinced.

"I think I'm worth the risk, Leo."

"You *think?*" he raised an eyebrow, teasing her.

"I *know* I am."

"You're a heartbreaker, Lana; that's what I see when I look into those gorgeous eyes. You're gonna make me bleed one day if I let you in. I know it."

"I would never do that—not to you. Not to anybody. I'm harmless."

He found her earnest confession so endearing. She was nothing like the typical snobs in his social circle, self-entitled rich girls who were superficial and shallow. Lana was the opposite.

"You truly are as sweet as you look."

"I'm just me." She smiled. "What you see is what you get: a small-town girl with big dreams."

"And what are those dreams?" Vincent inquired.

"I want to be a writer... a famous novelist."

"I can appreciate the passion of artistic pursuits."

"I'm hardly an artist." Lana shied away.

"You weave stories in your pretty little head. Creative writing is an art form."

"I'm not very good, though."

"You have a dream, Lana. Do you believe in it?"

"With all my heart."

"Then you'll make it happen. I have faith in you."

Moved by his words, he had given her more encouragement than anyone in her life.

"Lana..."

"Leo..."

"I think I'm ready to take that risk now."

"You sure?" She smirked.

"You can't just dance in my arms, looking drop dead gorgeous, and expect me to resist the urge to kiss you, especially when you have such sultry lips."

"Maybe I've changed my mind."

"*Oh?*" He frowned. "Dare I ask why?"

"You mentioned you see a heartbreaker when you look in my eyes. I see the same thing when I look back at yours."

"What if I told you I fancy you?" Vincent stopped moving and gently stroked her cheek.

"What does that even mean?" Lana laughed nervously.

"It means, *this*..."

He slowly leaned in and pressed his lips against hers, tasting the peachy flavor of her lip balm. Lana slacked her jaw a bit and felt his tentative tongue slip inside, brushing over hers. Throwing her fears to the wind, she kissed him back with a sweeping passion while her heart soared with joy; a feeling she had not felt in a long time. Lazy ocean waves rippled along the shore, as if to celebrate the youthful love that was manifesting between the pair. It was twin flame union, a fateful collision of divine masculine and feminine, merging in full force. They did not know how fated and powerful this connection was.

When Vincent finally withdrew, he stared into Lana's eyes before he stole another kiss, over and over, until she giggled against his lips. He had never felt this happy, as he lifted her off her feet and spun her around in the safety of his arms. This moment was etched in his memory forever, Vincent thought. He looked forward to traveling with Lana and building more memories together. While their chemistry was undeniably palpable, a sexual connection was not the only thing he wanted; it was Lana's beautiful heart that he wished to possess forever.

"You're not gonna disappear on me, are you?" he teased.

"Not a chance." Lana locked her arms around his neck and kissed him long and deeply until they were breathless.

It was a beautiful beginning of young love, blossoming slowly. Vincent was lost in the heat of another passionate kiss when Lana pulled back and shivered against him.

"Are you cold?"

"A little," she replied, hugging her arms. "I should have brought my cardigan—left it in the car."

He unbuttoned his shirt and held it out for her to wear.

"You're such a gentleman." She smiled demurely.

"You can thank my mother for that."

CHAPTER FIFTEEN

A canvas of stars sparkled in the sky that night as Lana stood out on the balcony of Vincent's penthouse suite. She had never been to a five-star hotel, much less VIP accommodations, typically booked by the rich and famous. The terrace view was breathtaking, facing the Atlantic Ocean. Lana leaned against the railing and found herself mesmerized by the rolling tide caressing the shore. She felt so complete when Vincent wrapped his arms around her waist from behind and kissed her bare shoulder.

"I should get going," she quietly voiced.

"Stay the night with me, Lana. I promise we don't have to do anything. I just want to hold you."

She turned and faced him.

"Why are you so amazing?"

A subtle smile appeared on Vincent's lips when she touched his cheek. He never took his eyes off her as he kissed her palm and led her toward a cushioned chaise lounge. He sat down first and comfortably reclined, parting his legs so Lana could sit between and lie back. She curled up against him on her side, facing the glass enclosure of the terrace. Music softly echoed from inside the suite, adding to the magical ambiance of the starlit night.

Vincent gently brushed his fingers through Lana's hair, breathing in the sweet scent of her perfume. He rarely felt compelled to be overly romantic, but this beautiful young woman had truly brought out that side of him as he whispered, *"Eres tan bella... te quiero besàr."*

A lovely shade of pink spread across Lana's cheeks. "Translation?" She peered up at him. "Sorry, I'm not so good with Spanish."

"I can teach you." He lovingly caressed her face.

"What did you say?"

"I said... 'you're so beautiful' and..." Vincent leaned in and stole the softest kiss. *"That."* His gaze was deep and seductive.

Lana blushed with a smile.

"Te quiero besàr means, 'I want to kiss you.'"

"How do you say 'kiss me' in Spanish?"

"Bésame."

"Can you get any sexier?" She giggled.

"Am I stimulating you, Lana?"

"In more ways than one."

Vincent kissed her lips sensually before he withdrew and murmured, "I wish I could take you with me."

"Soon."

Lana had graduated high school early and was already completing her first year at Miami Dade College. She was looking forward to spending the summer with Vincent. They lay in each other's arms, enjoying the music and warm night air.

Vincent had not cuddled a woman like this in a while, he thought. Normally, he would have been hooking up with someone by this hour, but he had no intention of taking advantage of Lana. She had already hinted at a tough childhood earlier that evening over dinner conversation. They had bonded so much in a short amount of time. She truly was special, he thought. As much as he wanted to start a new relationship on the right foot, he was keeping something from her. Vincent was two months out of a four-year relationship. His ex-girlfriend Claire had cheated on him. While she had begged him for another chance, he had pulled the plug and had no intention of reconciling. Cheating had always been a deal-breaker for him. Ever since last year, Vincent had felt that their relationship had gone past its lifespan. Claire took the breakup much harder and had been texting him constantly before he changed his number to cut all ties. He did not want to look back. They were over.

A romantic song faded in, heightening the seductive atmosphere. Vincent filed his ex away in his mind and was pleasantly surprised when Lana shifted her weight and sat astride, facing him.

"Were you falling asleep?" He chuckled.

"I want to see your eyes."

"I'm not complaining." He took her hand and kissed it.

She gently brushed her fingers across his finely arched eyebrows, tracing his chiseled cheekbone before she held his chin and leaned forward.

"*Bésame*," Lana whispered, smiling when he gently pressed his lips against hers, boosting her heart with electrical pulses. She felt so alive.

"Why do I... [*kiss*]... want you so much?" Lana breathed between kisses.

"Let's see...[*kiss*]... the list is long... I'm irresistibly good looking... [*kiss*]... charming... [*kiss*]... amazing kisser..."

"Not to mention *cocky*." Lana giggled, kissing him deeply for as long as she could.

These feelings were new, and had caught them both off guard, but they seemed to be ready to take a leap of faith together. It seemed as if the universe had pushed these two in each other's direction. Now that Vincent had spent so much time with Lana, it physically hurt to think about leaving the following morning.

He stole a moment to gaze up at her. She looked so beautiful in the moonlight, he thought, admiring her feminine features. There was an innocence about her that seemed to touch the deepest part of his soul. Lana was a wounded warrior. Vincent had noticed the scars on her arms earlier but felt it would have been rude to ask her about them, especially since they were still getting to know each other. It would take a while before they would establish a stronger level of comfort to share their darkest secrets, but he was confident his patience would pay off.

She's worth it.

Vincent felt nothing but chills down his body when Lana unbuttoned his shirt and rubbed his chest in a languid motion.

"Enjoying yourself?" He flirted.

She bit her lip and smiled. "I know this sounds crazy, Leo—given that we've spent a handful of times together—but I kind of feel you're mine."

He folded his hands behind his head and grinned when she blushed.

"Do you want me to be yours, Lana?"

"Very much."

"Then you better work on charming me"—he reached for her hips—"I'm a hard man to impress, with a lineup of women just waiting to have a shot with me," he teased. "Just so you know, I don't mind chocolates, flowers, trips around the world..."

"Oh, really?" Lana burst out laughing. "I had you pegged for more of an Alpha type."

"I'm kidding, love." Vincent took her hand and kissed it again, completely enamored by her.

She adored his British terms of endearment, feeling her face heat again when he said, "I like the idea of courting you, however."

"*Courting?* That's such an outdated term."

"Come on, you're a romantic! Don't you want to be 'swept off your feet'?"

Lana slipped her hands under his open shirt and massaged his shoulders. "I don't think a love like that exists."

"What if it does, Lana? Would you be open to receiving it?"

Her heart already knew the answer. She stared into Vincent's glimmering eyes and drowned in his ocean.

"What's your zodiac sign?"

"You're avoiding my question," Vincent answered.

"I'm a Leo."

"Are you trying to find out if we're compatible?"

"Maybe." Lana softly kissed him.

"Well... I think *this* Leo"—he touched her tummy—"should let *this* Leo"—he pointed at himself—"prove it to her."

"Was that a pun?"

"I was referring to my name, love. I'm a Scorpio—on the cusp of Scorpio and Sagittarius, actually."

"Hmm... I don't know if we'll work out." Lana rubbed her chin. "Fire and water?"

"You forget I'm a hybrid sign."

"True." She leaned in and kissed his neck before she moved her lips to his ear and whispered, "The question is... which element dominates in the bedroom? The passionate flames of fire? Or the emotional state of water?"

"Speaking in metaphors, Lana?"

Their eyes lingered on each other.

"I'm sure you understand the implication, Leo."

Vincent smirked, enjoying her warm touch. He loved the way she called him by his middle name. His father had been the one to decide on naming him "Vincent" when he was born, while his mother had wanted to call him "Leo." They had eventually compromised in a way that made them both happy, but Vincent could not wait to change his name in all his legal documents to spite his father. It had hurt to discover his extramarital affairs before he left for university years ago. The only reason he had not started the legal process was because of his beloved mother. She had begged him not to hurt his father that way. Isobel had a loving and forgiving nature. They were working on their marriage, and she had told her son that she had no plans on filing for divorce. Vincent held a grudge, however; it lasted for years, driving a wedge between him and his father. He had reinvented himself while living in New Haven by rejecting his legal name and establishing his identity as "Leo Cortez," the proud son of Isobel Cortez. Lana did not know this, but he planned on telling her soon.

"Can't think of a witty response?" Lana teased.

"Well, to put it bluntly, would you like to find out?"

"Maybe."

"Careful what you wish for, sweetheart." Vincent flashed a sly little grin and pulled her hips down with his strength, as if to remind her of his primal instincts. He was a hot-blooded man, and Lana was more than seductive. Physical intimacy was just as important as emotional. He wanted to discover both worlds with the stunning blonde who had mounted him, sitting proudly like the reincarnated form of the Goddess Aphrodite.

He gazed at her with nothing but love and desire, hoping to worship at her altar one day when she was ready to invite him into her sacred temple. He wished to trace every curve on her beautiful body and kiss every part of her that yearned for affection, including those faded scars on her arms. If the power of touch had a healing effect, Vincent prayed more than anything to heal her with his warmth. He knew that they had come from different walks of life, but his kindness and empathy were two of his best virtues. His mother had raised him to be a responsible, caring person, a true gentleman.

In that magical moment, while he kissed Lana, Vincent realized that his heart had finally won the battle against his mind. He was falling in love with the broken woman he had saved from the sea. Their passion grew, burning stronger by the second, transforming into a beautiful dance of fiery flames that blazed across the ocean: a visual union of their elemental signs. He wanted her. He wanted to merge his soul with hers, the only way he knew how.

Lana seemed to read Vincent's mind as she reached for his belt and slowly unfastened it. Her lust for him had overpowered her logic. Although he was slightly inebriated, Lana was sober... but his kiss had intoxicated her. She felt ridiculously love drunk and uninhibited. She needed to feel him just as badly. At the cost of broken celibacy, she wanted to give him a memory he would never forget; a sacrifice she was willing to make, if only to deepen their connection. It was the soul that animated the flesh, Lana believed, not the other way around.

True intimacy demanded a mind/body connection where the ego would not be neglected (since sex was inherently primal)—essentially creating a balancing act between the higher and lower self. It was a transmutation of energy that allowed two souls to touch and unify. She wanted that. She needed that with him. The spiritual aspect of sex did not have to diminish in the least because of the intensity of the warring ego that only sought earthly pleasures. The rhythmic aggression of two bodies colliding could equally charge up every energetic center of the physical form, like a divine awakening.

"Lana..." Vincent broke their kiss. "What are you doing?"

"I want you." She pulled out his magnum shaft and stroked it, pleasantly surprised by his generous length and girth.

Vincent groaned, which only heightened her own arousal.

"*Fuck*," he cursed under his breath, clutching her waist. "I want you, too, but... there's no rush. I don't want you to feel pressured."

"I'm not, I promise." She kissed him tamely, pumping his shaft. "I want you, Leo."

He seemed to waver, as if to try to rationalize, but his desire for Lana was overpowering his logic.

"I hate to ruin the mood, love," he whispered, "but I need to get up and grab a condom if you're serious about doing this."

"I'm on the pill," Lana breathed with hooded eyes.

Vincent stared into her lustful gaze and trusted her completely. Deep down, he did not want any barriers between them, but he knew that safe sex was crucial, especially since they both had little knowledge of their sexual history. Talking it out at that moment would have been a buzz kill, he thought, contemplating the alternatives.

"Please, Leo," Lana whispered against his lips. "I promise I'm safe. I promise I'm ready."

Vincent's critical faculties had shut down as he wrapped his hand around the back of her head and kissed her to the point of breathlessness. He was powerless beneath her as Lana gripped his manhood, lifted her weight before she slipped her thong to the side and eased onto him.

He observed her face carefully, quietly panting through pleasure, in disbelief that he was entering the temple of a goddess.

Lana parted her mouth and slowly exhaled, never taking her eyes off him. Vincent stared back as if he were hypnotized, holding her hips while she took full control. His intrusion was achingly slow, moving inch by inch, spearing her tightness until he was fully submerged, buried to the hilt.

He throbbed.

She pulsed.

He inhaled.

She exhaled.

Their energies had fully merged at last. The indescribable feeling of completion and "oneness" suddenly overwhelmed them both. This was not a "one-night stand"; it was a divine union, as if the mysterious powers of the universe had orchestrated it. Everything in their lives had led to this critical point of realization: an agonizing urge to be together. Twin flame union was a curse and blessing. They were now bound forever by an energetic cord that could never be severed; a cord that had permanently connected their hearts as one through sacred sex.

They exchanged no words as Lana pressed her palms on Vincent's abs and slowly rocked against him, desperate to feel him deeper. Their passion for each other was so enraptured that the moon in the sky would have shied away from bearing witness as they made love on the balcony beneath the stars.

Vincent had lost himself inside of Lana. It was an altered state of consciousness that was new to him. He had never felt so emotionally vulnerable and connected to a woman during intimacy. He had saved Lana from drowning, like a selfless hero, but at that moment, Lana mirrored his heroism and revived his dying faith in something higher than himself. Their meeting was no coincidence; it had to be Divinely prophesied, Vincent believed, kissing her with everything he had.

A powerful climax was on the horizon as every cell in their bodies prepared for that glorious release. Lana felt Vincent's heart pounding through her hand. She breathed with him, keeping a steady pace while she worked toward a mutual goal. They had finally unleashed their sexual tension.

"You're so beautiful," Vincent whispered breathlessly, gliding his palm against her cheek.

He watched her slowly grind against him, admiring her in a way that went beyond the physical, as if he were truly seeing the magnificent soul that inhabited Lana's physical form. He could only imagine how mind blowing every sensation would feel if they were to get high on cannabis before getting high on each other. It was all Vincent could think about as he slowly thrust his hips into her, engulfed by her fleshy walls.

"I'm... close..." Lana's aqua eyes pierced through his, blazing with liquid heat.

"Come for me..." Vincent reached for her bikini top and parted the white fabric, cupping her breasts.

Beautiful, he thought. *Mine.*

He wanted to explore every part of her; to give her many "firsts" she had never experienced before. Their sexual union had sealed his fate. He knew it deep down: he was all in. They had found and saved each other in a unique way, unaware of the unspeakable tragedy that lay ahead waiting for Vincent. It would change the course of their lives forever. But the star-crossed lovers were too lost in euphoria to even think about any obstacles or catastrophe. New love was like a drug, a chemical reaction that induced an all-consuming madness.

Lana drew in a sharp breath and held it for as long as she could, as a powerful wave of pleasure crashed through her core and flooded her. She stared back at Vincent, watching the way his face twisted in agony before he growled low and gripped her hips, pounding into her while she climaxed uncontrollably.

It was sweet release, at last.

Lana leaned forward and kissed him, muting his pleasurable groans while grinding her hips. She desperately wanted to take him to the same place he had taken her seconds ago.

A string of expletives fled from Vincent's mouth as he dug half-moons into the outer part of Lana's thighs, achieving a violent release that overwhelmed his senses. The intensity of his rhythm pushed Lana over the edge again as she surrendered and felt her body quiver in pleasure.

He panted.

She matched his breaths.

He held her face.

She looked into his eyes.

Vincent's warm gaze seemed to express a gentle affection that could only be felt from the heart. He caressed Lana's cheek with his thumb before he kissed her slowly, taking his time until he lay back and let her collapse on his chest.

Their date had been perfect. Their evening had been so romantic. But that moment right there... it was pure magic, Lana thought, feeling blissfully at peace.

Vincent's body felt so warm as she molded herself against him. Having lost track of time, she knew it was late. Her aunt had probably left her many voicemails, wondering where she was, as Lana dreaded. But she focused on the present. All she wanted was to spend as much time with Vincent before he would leave Miami.

He didn't use any social media platforms, but he had promised Lana he would make a Facebook account when he returned home.

She had his cellphone number, which was the fastest way to reach him. As incredible as it was to experience deep intimacy, a creeping fear loomed over Lana like a dark cloud. She had childhood abandonment issues and worried that Vincent would somehow forget about her. Lana wanted to discuss this insecurity with him but feared that it would turn him off if she opened up. Everything was still so fresh. Her ex-boyfriend had told her she was too clingy and needy, which explained how he had justified cheating on her. She did not want history to repeat itself. She felt that Vincent had a right to know about her suicide attempt.

Am I over sharing? Lana questioned, trying to relax while he gently caressed her.

"Leo?"

"Lana?"

"I need to tell you something. It's... bad... just promise you won't be weirded out, please?"

He chuckled lightly and said, "*Confess, my child*, and absolution shall be given."

She appreciated his British humor, smiling to herself; it made her feel less on edge.

"That day you pulled me out of the water," Lana began, "I'd been in a bad headspace. Selena had insisted we go to the beach, even though I was depressed and hardly in a mood to go anywhere. She wanted to cheer me up. She was being a good friend. I feel horrible when I think about it now, but when she got up to use the restroom, something snapped in my mind.

"I just remember leaving our spot on the beach and walking into the water slowly until I was swimming out to the deep end. I was convinced that all my pain and suffering would go away if I just stopped breathing." Lana paused, offering Vincent a chance to respond. But he stayed quiet. He was no longer rubbing her back, which made her anxious.

"I would've most likely died if you weren't there, Leo," she bravely continued. "I owe you my life." There was a long pause. "Please say something."

Vincent felt lost, withdrawing into a silent panic that seemed to suffocate him. He had watched his mother battle with depression for much of her life, especially after suffering several miscarriages and losing her family members the way she did. It was rarely ever talked about, but *he* had been the one to discover her suicide note when he was sixteen. He had come home early from school and had found his mother passed out in bed, with a bottle of empty pills on the nightstand. She had overdosed on anxiety meds and antidepressants. While she had made it to the hospital in time to get her stomach pumped, Vincent had been permanently traumatized.

He often lived in fear that his mother would attempt to kill herself again, even though she had received proper psychiatric care for months afterwards. There was an underlying resentment that he could not admit to himself because he felt he had no right to resent her. It cut him deeply to think about his mother not loving him enough to want to stick around, at least for *his* sake. Hearing Lana's heartbreaking confession had triggered these difficult emotions to resurface from his past.

"Leo? Are you okay?" Lana was about to look up when he squeezed her tightly in his arms.

"Don't you *ever* do that again, you hear me?" Vincent's voice was stern and serious. "No matter what happens, you can't just throw in the towel and give up like that."

"I'm sorry."

"I mean it, Lana. When a person commits suicide, they devastate and destroy the ones left behind... all their family and friends. Those who decide to go through their own exit strategy don't know how badly they damage their loved ones in the aftermath. Permanently.

"It's like they're stuck in tunnel vision, completely blind to everyone else's feelings because they're too busy drowning in their own pain to pause and consider the *real* consequences of that irreversible decision. It's a different suffering that no one should go through... not the person who feels helpless, nor the families who try their best to help them."

"I know." Lana frowned, feeling a sagging sense of shame. "I wasn't thinking properly." She looked up and met his anguished gaze. "That's why I'm so grateful you saved me from myself. Please don't judge me."

"I'm not."

There was another brief pause before she asked, "Have you lost anyone this way?"

"No." Vincent tried not to sound so irritated. "And hopefully I won't ever have to."

Lana hugged him and found solace in his steady heartbeat. She prayed he did not think any less of her.

"It's getting chilly," said Vincent. "We should head inside."

Lana got up first and followed him in when he rose to his feet. Vincent checked his phone and noticed that it was almost 2am.

"You're welcome to stay the night with me, Lana. I'm just gonna quickly wash off... but you're *also* welcome to join." He flashed his sexy signature smile, which instantly made Lana feel better.

"It's a two-person stand-in shower... pretty fancy," Vincent persuasively added.

Lana did not know how amazing it felt to be held under steaming water until she finally got to experience it with Vincent. It took a level of courage and vulnerability to strip down before another soul, completely in the nude, scars and imperfections exposed. She had her insecurities, but Vincent made her feel so beautiful and perfect. His tall stature and muscled frame were flawless in her eyes. She wanted to hide herself inside of him, if only to be with Leo forever.

One body. One soul. Their kissing slowly led to another round of passionate lovemaking against the shower tiles before they washed up and stepped out with sore muscles.

As they got ready for bed, Lana collapsed on Vincent's chest and passed out naked in his arms. They looked like the perfect pair of Edenic lovers. Her time with this young man had been surreal, Lana thought, feeling like the luckiest woman in the world. She had finally met a guy who was not only handsome beyond description but was also an incredible lover and human being. She did not want to let go of him. Ever. The poor girl did not know that she would never see him again... not until *many* years later, when their paths would cross in the cruelest way.

⚜

When Vincent woke up the following morning, he was disappointed to find that Lana was gone. Confused about when she had left, he stepped into the bathroom and froze when he saw the mirror. A warm smile appeared on his face. Lana had written a poem for him in black eyeliner.

Found Heaven in your eyes
When you pulled me
From a sea of purgatory
Please don't forget me.
-Lana ∞

Vincent's gaze lingered on the infinity symbol. How could he possibly forget her? He questioned. Lana was unforgettable. She had knocked down his barriers and had infiltrated his heart in such a brief time span. It scared Vincent, but he was too in love to let that fear overpower his psyche. The magnetic pull between them was indescribable. He had never felt this way with anyone else. Even during the beginning stages of his relationship with Claire... their attraction was never like this, so intensely passionate. There was a soul-to-soul connection between him and Lana. A bond that only strengthened when they had made love. No one would understand it, Vincent thought.

They don't need to. She's mine.

CHAPTER SIXTEEN

LANA

Last night felt like a fever dream. I still couldn't wrap my head around what had happened between Vincent and me. I was conflicted and confused. He had wanted to explain himself, but I couldn't imagine hearing anything that would restore peace in my heart. Falling in love with him in Miami had been such a magical time in my youth; two weeks of absolute bliss that immediately thrust me in hell when he had broken his promise and never reached out after leaving. He had no social media. I didn't know his legal name to even look him up, and his phone had been out of service whenever I had tried to call him.

My best friend Selena hated seeing me in tears over a guy. She had convinced me that "Leo" most likely had a girlfriend back in New Haven and that I might have just been "a fling"; it was that or he had changed his mind about starting a long-distance relationship with me and didn't know how to tell me the truth, so he just disappeared. "Ghosting" still wasn't a recognized term back then, but essentially, that's what Vincent did: he ghosted me.

In the aftermath of his return to New Haven, I agonized for months, wondering what I'd said or did wrong to make him disappear, only to come up with my own conclusions that were equally devastating as the ones that Selena had provided me. I felt a toxic shame for sharing the truth of my suicide attempt when Vincent had saved me from drowning. I believed this was the reason he had changed his mind and never reached out, thinking I was unstable and clingy; or maybe he simply wanted to spare me from further heartbreak down the road, so he vanished. It still felt excruciatingly painful to be left in the dark like that. I didn't have the best self-esteem back then, so I had blamed myself, believing it was my own stupid fault for over sharing and pushing him away. Of course, I was worried that something bad had happened to him, but eventually finding him on Facebook under "Leo Cortez" was proof that he hadn't died... and he was happily dating someone. I was too devastated to reach out and confront him. I couldn't.

Discovering that I was pregnant a month after he'd left Miami had terrified me even more. While I had been on birth control (to regulate my periods), the pill had not been effective when we had slept together that one night. I'd had to struggle with the hard decision of keeping the baby or opting for abortion. It terrified me to imagine raising a child as a single mom. My mother had failed to nurture me properly. I was scared to death, dealing with mental health issues while working part-time and trying to graduate from college. I lacked the proper support I needed to decide the fate of our unborn child.

But God had decided for me when I had miscarried at eight weeks in my first trimester. I felt so guilty for feeling relieved. It was one less mouth to feed, one less problem to worry about, and a permanent end to my association with "Leo Cortez." I didn't have to worry about raising our son or daughter, triggered by the memory of the man who heartlessly abandoned me for someone else. It seemed as if the universe had offered me a chance to start fresh—a clean slate. All I had to do was heal and move on. If it was possible to delete "2007" from my mind, I would have—every memory... gone. Voluntary amnesia seemed to be the solution to mending my broken heart, but that was wishful thinking.

As the months passed that year, I tried my best to hate Vincent to cope with my loss and heartbreak. Narratives such as "he used you, he lied to you, he had a girlfriend" constantly looped around my head for the longest while until I believed all of them. How was it possible to form such a deep connection with someone, only to be discarded so quickly? I had no idea what Narcissistic Personality Disorder was back then, but in hindsight, Vincent's apparent "love bombing" and sudden disappearance mirrored the toxic traits of that disorder—specifically the stages of devaluation and narcissistic discard. I had learned about NPD in therapy after my breakup with André when I lived in New York. I'd always been a magnet for narcissistic people, being high on the spectrum of altruism and empathy. While those counseling sessions tremendously helped in unburdening me of blame, it didn't erase my memories, nor the scars Vincent had left in my heart.

I had suffered through a dark night of the soul and had done my best to heal from my childhood traumas, including the lack of closure I felt with Vincent, but I had completely resigned from my search for "the one" after I'd ended my three-year relationship with the toxic ex. Living with André had been the worst decision I had ever made in my life. It seemed as if trauma had become a recurring theme in my existence. Even meeting someone as amazing as Maxwell Luther had re-traumatized me when I stood face to face with his son. Had I known that they were related, I *never* would have married Max. I would have cut all ties and disappeared, if only I'd been aware that he was the father of a man who had caused me unimaginable pain. The universe had mocked me in the most disgusting way, or so it seemed to me, at least. I felt I was suffering from past life karma or had a new opportunity to understand Vincent's disappearance.

Prior to our initial confrontation, a part of me had still held onto hope, especially in the earlier years. I wanted to believe he had a legitimate reason for never calling or texting me. It hurt even more to realize that my therapist had been right about him; that he really was a covert narcissist who had tricked me with his charming persona and discarded me after he had gotten what he wanted from me. Perhaps the only reason he had even saved me was to boost his own ego.

The hurtful things Vincent had said on that veranda last year were burned in my mind forever. It hurt even more to realize how insignificant my drowning incident had been to him. The person I had fallen in love with at seventeen differed from the man who had stood before me on the terrace of my husband's mansion last April.

I had decided that it wasn't worth digging for the truth and humiliating myself further by being vulnerable with someone who had no respect for me, even on a basic human level. He saw me as a "whore" and a "gold digger" who was hellbent on taking advantage of his father. He had claimed no recollection of our time together, which only hurt and confused me more. I couldn't tell if Vincent was gaslighting me (a common method used by manipulative people, *especially* narcissists), or if he was truthful in his denial of remembering our time together.

At that point, it didn't really matter anymore. I was determined to stay in my lane as much as possible. We were both married, and the man I had fallen in love with never truly existed. Leo Cortez might as well have been a figment of my imagination; an idealized fictional character that was portrayed as a white knight in an unrealistic romance novel. Our time together in Miami that year was a pathetic attempt at "make believe" and a tragedy at worst—for me, at least. Regardless of how poorly Vincent treated me, I still felt grateful that he had saved me from suicide, whether it was selfishly motivated or not. Perhaps that was the *only* reason our worlds had collided in the first place: to stop me from making an irreparable mistake. My pregnancy and miscarriage may have been a karmic lesson I needed to value the precious gift of life. I found peace in that reasoning. It made it easier for me to try to get along with Vincent; to "live and let live."

Despite all the heaviness of last night's encounter, I knew I couldn't lock myself in my room and avoid everyone. My introverted nature required recharging in solitude. No one really understood that, apart from Max and Ciara. But that morning when I woke up, I knew I needed to go for a run and clear my head. Stagnant energy isn't good. Cardio always helped me feel better.

After I freshened up, I tied my hair in a ponytail and put on a pair of black shorts and a pink Nike shirt before I slipped on my running shoes and headed downstairs. The house was quiet, which meant that everyone was still asleep. I made a mental note of the chores I needed to do that day as I entered the kitchen... and froze.

He was sitting by the island, dressed in the same clothes as last night, with a cup of coffee in his hand.

Was he waiting *for me?* I questioned in confusion.

He knew I had a routine every morning since we'd been here. This wasn't a coincidence. I cautiously stepped into the large communal space, as if I were entering the wolf's den.

His ice-blue eyes found mine, nearly freezing me over.

This man is a narcissist... playing games with you, a voice warned in my head.

"Good morning, Vincent. You're up early," I calmly spoke, walking toward the fridge.

"I wanted to talk to you last night but was robbed of a chance," he replied.

An awkward silence floated in the kitchen as I avoided his gaze and quenched my thirst. I wasn't sure what to say or do. Vincent seemed to sense my discomfort as he got up and stepped in my direction. Instantly, my mind went into panic mode, which triggered a chain reaction in my chest.

"Lana." His tone was warm and gentle—something I wasn't used to.

When he reached for my hand, I immediately withdrew, as if physical contact was lethal between us. It seemed to hurt him when

I met his sullen gaze. Why? Why was he doing this now? Did he take pleasure in mind-fucking me?

"Let's go for a drive," said Vincent. "Everyone's still asleep upstairs, and I just want to have more privacy before I disclose some crucial details about what happened to us."

I don't want to be alone with you.

"I'm about to go for a run, actually."

"Please, it's necessary that I get this off my chest." He seemed troubled.

"I heard you arguing with Claire late last night."

"I'm quite certain you weren't the only one."

"Is everything okay?"

"Not really." He lowered his voice. "Can we just go for a walk, at the very least?"

Boundaries, I thought. I had to place firm boundaries.

I did *not* want to sit next to him in such a confined space. Driving around would have left me somewhat powerless with a difficult exit strategy (if I needed one). But a walk outside I could manage. I could always run away from him—literally.

"Please, Lana..."

Stop. Stop looking at me like that.

"Please?" Vincent begged.

Sigh.

"Just give me a chance to explain. I owe that to you."

He wasn't wrong.

"Okay." I met his pleading gaze. "Let's head out."

Several things were obvious to me at this moment: we would either end up arguing, or he would release me from a decade of pain. I prayed it was the latter.

♋

A sunrise in Ocean City was truly something else. The golden rays of that fiery disc seemed to birth new colors, painting the sky in crimson, coral, and magenta; a breathtaking vision of earthly splendor. I was mesmerized by the sun's powerful journey, as it lifted the veil of the night and slowly levitated on the horizon, bathing the earth with warmth. This was nature at its best, in an idyllic setting for the hopeless romantic. It was no wonder why I loved coming here.

Vincent was quiet as we walked on a gravel path near the waterfront. I wondered if he had slept at all, since he was still in the same attire from our last encounter, clad in a white Saint Laurent T-shirt, jeans, and white sneakers. Nothing ever looked baggy on his tall, muscular frame. I realized right then that it wasn't so much his fashion sense that I admired; it was his hard body.

Several minutes had gone by as we strolled down a path, pebbles crunching beneath our shoes. Birds were chirping all around us in a lovely cadence. We were far enough from the house to talk, but Vincent seemed to be lost in his thoughts, staring straight ahead with his hands in his front pockets. Was he expecting *me* to begin this conversation? I wondered, keeping a safe distance from him. But he seemed to read my mind as he finally broke the silence.

"I didn't sleep all night."

I stole a glance at him. I had hardly slept myself. Now that I thought about it, it seemed ridiculous to push through an intensive run on such low energy.

"I guess I should preface this conversation by saying that the kiss we shared in the den... it triggered memories I didn't even know I had locked away."

I frowned in confusion, folding my arms in my chest as we walked side by side.

"I'm confused, Vincent. What do you mean?"

He stopped when we reached a bench facing the ocean and asked if we could sit down. I seated myself first, noticing a deep trace of pain in his eyes when he sat next to me.

"I know I don't deserve this chance," Vincent began, "not after everything I've put you through, but you need to believe me when I say that I *genuinely* did not remember you when my father introduced us last March. If I had, things would have been different, I promise, Lana. But I'd already decided about you, convinced that you had malicious intentions when you married my old man." He paused and looked out at the water, as if to collect his thoughts before he met my gaze again.

"Please, just bear with me while I explain some things first. It'll all make sense soon, okay?"

I nodded, giving him my undivided attention.

"Lana, I haven't forgotten our big confrontation last April... when you mentioned Miami and spring break—I was a total utter bastard. I said things that were so disgustingly vile because I was blinded by my own judgments about you. There you were: this gorgeous, young woman who had entered a marriage with my father in such a short amount of time...

"It had only been four months since we'd buried Mum and I was so bloody furious with Dad. I was angrier at *you* because I felt you should have had enough sense to refuse his proposal, knowing he was not in his right mind."

I hadn't forgotten that fight. It still hurt to remember.

"People deal with grief differently," said Vincent. "In my father's case, I felt he had made an impulsive decision by marrying you so fast; one that he would eventually come to regret. It seemed as if he was running away from dealing with his loss, and you were a convenient escape for him.

"I truly felt as if he had disrespected and dishonored the memory of my mother by—and forgive me for saying this— marrying his *escort*. It didn't matter to me you were university educated. I had vilified you in my mind from the second I saw you last year. I thought he'd been paying you for sex before deciding to foolishly 'tie the knot.'"

We never had sex, much less shared a romantic kiss. But Vincent didn't know that.

"I found it hard to believe that such a beautiful—and again, I reiterate—*young* woman who had her entire life ahead of her would settle down with a wrinkly, old man, unless she was a gold-digging 'sugar baby.' I had never mentioned this to you, but my father had many affairs all throughout his marriage to my mum. Taking expensive trips with his high-end escorts had practically become a lifestyle for him.

"My mother always knew, yet she never divorced him because she loved him. I used to think that's why she was so depressed: his never-ending affairs with younger women. But anyway, discovering my father's infidelity had caused a huge rift between him and me for many years, since I was nineteen when I'd learned the truth. He had fallen from grace in my eyes. I practically wanted to disown him as my dad for his cheating ways.

"When I left home to start my first year at Yale, I'd assumed my own identity, introducing myself as 'Leo Cortez' to new friends and acquaintances. It wasn't a persona, but an alternative title—specifically, my middle name and Mum's maiden name. 'Vincent Luther' is directly affiliated with my father. I wanted to break free from any ties to him as his son—that's how angry I was.

"I'd gone as far as starting the process of a legal name change in my final year at uni, but Mum had begged me not to hurt her and Dad that way. Lana, I'm telling you this to give you some context *why* I had introduced myself to you as *Leo* and not *Vincent*." He stopped and took a breath.

"Fast forward to when Dad introduced you to me... I thought your intentions were to take advantage of him—his money. How can you love someone after only four months of dating? I was furious, but more so with *you*, as I mentioned earlier.

"My mother would have been ashamed of me had she heard me speak to you the way I did—and I know that wasn't the only time I'd crossed the line by humiliating you. I was dealing with unresolved grief. I was angry at my father, and it was easier to take it out on you than to put in the grueling work of sorting through my grief in therapy. I spent all night reflecting on this: my animosity toward you."

Vincent searched my eyes in anguish.

"Lana, have you ever suffered head trauma?"

"No." I frowned. "Why?"

He seemed to waver.

"I was in a horrible car accident ten years ago that put me in a coma for six months."

Oh. My. God.

"I don't talk about it because of the guilt I carry. I still blame myself, even though I was pissed out of my mind." Vincent paused and took a breath. "My best mates, Kevin and Trey... remember them?"

Of course I did, giving a nod.

"They died upon impact when we ran a red light and got T-boned by another vehicle... the *same evening* our plane touched down in New Haven from Miami in '07. We were all drunk. Kevin was behind the wheel—I was riding shotgun. I was the only one who survived, but my head trauma was so severe that my parents didn't think I'd wake up. Miraculously, when I finally opened my eyes, I didn't know where I was—couldn't remember a damn thing about myself, my past, and much less the weeping faces that had surrounded my hospital bed."

I had considered the possibility of a fatal accident, either by car or plane crash, which was why I had regularly checked the news and local paper that week for any updates. Unfortunately, I couldn't look up Vincent's friends on social media because I didn't know their last names or their contact info. It was the worst feeling in the world... being left in the dark, not knowing.

I think that's why I couldn't let go and had continued my search online until I finally found him under a "Leo Cortez" Facebook account in 2009. His timeline was filled with pictures of him partying with friends... and with Claire (I didn't know that was her at the time). I was so incredibly hurt. How could he just ghost me like that? I felt like a fool. Seeing him alive and well had only reinforced Selena's theory: I had been nothing but a fling, used and forgotten. I had cried so much that night. A part of me had wished I'd never found him. He was *alive* and had never explained to me why he had cut off contact. I couldn't bring myself to message him and risk getting hurt even more. Why reach out to someone who clearly didn't care, only to be accused of being an obsessive stalker? No, thank you. I couldn't park my pride and humiliate myself that way.

But that following year, I finally mustered up the courage to confront him and looked up his Facebook again, only to find his wedding photo on public display as his profile picture, with everything else set in private. "Leo" had moved on with his life and was happily married to someone else. I was crushed and angry, yet I couldn't retaliate. I didn't have the heart to, regardless of how he had shattered mine.

Accepting he had moved on, I avoided his Facebook profile like the plague until several years later, when I'd had a little too much wine one night and searched him up again. His "Leo Cortez" account had disappeared. Googling him had been a fruitless effort as well. Ultimately, I had taken it as a sign to let go and never look back.

"My entire identity had vanished," Vincent continued, ending our brief silence. "My parents worried that my amnesia would be permanent, but my doctor had told them not to give up hope and that it was possible for my memories to return. I didn't know it, but my mother had moved to New Haven to be there for me. She visited me every day for six months while I remained in a vegetative state.

"All I knew was that I came from a wealthy family with a patient, loving mother who was willing to help me through my struggles with rehab and memory loss. I'd also learned that I had a long-term girlfriend of four years who claimed to have miscarried our baby while I was in a coma."

My eyes filled with tears that I could no longer withhold.

"You may ask yourself, 'why didn't he contact me sooner?' Here's where it gets really fucked up. It's simple: *Claire.* She's the reason I went out drinking that night." He grimaced. "My phone had been out of charge all throughout my flight from Miami to New Haven. When I got to my house from the airport, I'd left my phone to charge on my nightstand while I showered. I was planning on calling you and letting you know that I'd made it home... that I missed you already."

Vincent paused. "Long story short, one of my roommates had let Claire inside while I was showering—she knew I'd be home. I had broken up with her two months prior because she had been cheating on me with a T.A. in one of her classes."

I could hardly process these details.

"I had changed my number and email address after the breakup, so she had no way of reaching me, but she still knew where I lived. Anyway, I digress... when I returned to my bedroom, my cellphone was missing. What I found instead was a nasty note from Claire... it flipped my world upside down."

Vincent released an exasperated sigh and lowered his voice. "I would have prioritized replacing my phone that same day or at least calling you on a landline, but I hadn't memorized your number, Lana, so it would have been pointless to rush out the door and get a new device. I knew you were on Facebook, and I was planning on making an account as soon as possible, but I was so angry at Claire that the first thing I did was get dressed and head over to her sorority house."

"Why?" I was almost afraid to ask.

"Her note. *Apparently*, she was twelve weeks pregnant... and *apparently*... I was the father."

I felt numb. And then I felt nauseous.

"When I confronted her that day, I noticed she was already showing. Mind you, I hadn't seen her in two months. She certainly *looked* pregnant, but I refused to believe that I was the father. I accused her of lying, and she insisted the dates matched up. She even promised to get a paternity test as soon as possible to dispel my doubts; she was *that* confident it was mine. I just... I felt like my life was over—everything I'd planned for myself, *our* plans, traveling that summer with you..."

He squeezed his eyes shut and sighed. "I didn't want to be with her, Lana. I wasn't in love with her anymore, but I also didn't know what to do. I was in rough shape mentally. Imagine, meeting someone so incredible while on vacation, only to discover that a ball and chain were waiting to be shackled around your ankle back home. I could hardly come to terms with the news Claire had given me."

Vincent paused again and exhaled. "I'm ashamed to admit this, but instead of contacting you to talk about the newest revelations in my life, I went on a drinking binge by hitting a bar with my best mates. I never should have let Kevin get behind the wheel. He said he was fine to drive. I was so drunk, he seemed sober in comparison."

"Were there any other casualties?" I asked.

A painful sorrow poured from Vincent's gaze. "The driver of the pickup truck was critically injured but eventually recovered from what I was told. Dad took care of the legal issues I was in. Kevin and Trey wound up six feet under, all their dreams stolen. I blame myself. They didn't even want to go out that night, but I didn't want to drink alone. I know I wasn't the one in the driver's seat, but it was *my* car... I pressured Kevin to drink with us. The accident was my fault, Lana."

My heart was bleeding pain while I resisted the urge to cry.

"My mum knew that I had ended things with Claire; they were close—used to be, at least. My guess is that Claire had contacted her about the pregnancy, which probably made my mother feel sorry for her. She always wanted grandchildren. I guess that's why she'd never told me about Claire's cheating and the breakup—infidelity had never been a deal-breaker for her and my dad.

"Basically, Claire had taken advantage of my vulnerable state and manipulated her way back into my life without me ever realizing her compulsive lying and cheating. She had tried so hard to get back together with me from the moment I'd dumped her two months before meeting you. My amnesia worked out so conveniently for her.

"I accused *you* of being a slut and a gold digger when *I've* been married to one all this time and had no idea... until last night. What sick irony, no?" Vincent snickered under his breath, shaking his head.

"In the aftermath of that accident, I'd successfully regained much of my memory through the years, but I had completely blocked out the last few months of my life before the crash happened. Claire had selfishly kept the truth of our breakup from me—that's why we were arguing last night, because I finally remembered and had confronted her. At first, she'd denied it and gaslit me to no end, hence all the shouting. She eventually confessed her crimes. She wasn't even pregnant, Lana. She had lied. I suppose I was lucky she was drunk enough to admit everything. I can't trust her now."

I couldn't believe how manipulative this woman was. I always thought she was nice. She sure had me fooled, not just him.

"Did you tell her about us?" I nervously asked. "Our history?"

"No. It's none of her goddamn business." Vincent scowled. "Kissing you last night was like... a powerful catalyst that changed my brain chemistry in seconds—that's the only way I can explain it... it unlocked a door I didn't even know existed."

He reached for my face and wiped a tear away, staring at me with what I could only describe as love and pain.

"After I got ninety percent of my memory back years later, I mourned my best mates' deaths properly and closed that chapter of my life for good. I'm a proud and private man, Lana. I didn't want anyone pitying me—I'd heard enough of it. My parents and Claire had agreed to no longer discuss that tragic event and my personal struggles with anyone. It was *my* trauma to share, *my* friends that I'd lost, not theirs." Vincent paused. "Did my father ever tell you about the accident?"

"No." My voice cracked.

"Denzel's my best mate, and even *he* doesn't know. I just wanted to put that tragedy behind me, believing I had grieved and recovered. I had no idea I was missing crucial puzzle pieces."

He shifted closer, placing a warm hand on my thigh.

I shivered.

"When you confronted me last April, I was so blinded by my hateful judgments that I hardly gave you a chance to speak your mind. What's worse is I lacked the ability to self-reflect and connect some dots. I remembered vacationing in Miami many times during my college years on spring break... partying from sundown to sunup, getting blackout drunk and high on coke. I'd slept with many women, but no one special enough to stay in contact with.

"So, when you mentioned Miami and spring break, I assumed you were just another slag I'd hooked up with while on vacation, even though I had no recollection of being with you. I dismissed the likelihood of us having any significant history that was worth remembering *because* of my prejudice.

"I couldn't remember that critical time frame... all the events that occurred in those two to three months before the car crash. I couldn't remember *you*, Lana"—he squeezed my hand—"... the beautiful woman I had saved from drowning... everything we shared."

Vincent stopped, seemingly conflicted, as he turned his head and stared at the sea. I fixated on his handsome profile, absorbing an unspoken sadness that radiated off him and pierced through my energy field, filling it with his pain. Without thinking, I reached for his face and coaxed it in my direction.

He looked at me.

For the first time since I'd known this man, the arctic frost in his eyes finally thawed, revealing an agony that had been frozen under a slab of ice. This wasn't an act. There was no way he could fake emotion like this. It was raw and real. It had to be. Fate had been so unkind to us. How could it rip us apart in such a cruel way, only to reunite us like this? Were there Greek gods up in the heavens somewhere manipulating our lives for entertainment? Our reunion last year had been painful for me, but now... now it all made sense, I thought.

"*Eres tan hermosa cuando lloras...*" Vincent spoke in a hushed murmur. "It's not fair." He held my face.

Oh my God... that accent. My heart bloomed in ecstasy.

It had been so long since I'd heard him speak Spanish.

"What's not fair?" I asked.

"You're so beautiful when you cry." He wiped my tears with his thumbs.

"Is that why you sadistically tortured me for a year and a half, Vincent?" I tried to lighten the mood, but he didn't laugh because it wasn't really a joke; it was the truth.

"You never deserved the awful things I said to you in the past. None of it. Forgive me."

I could see the remorse in his eyes as he held my hands.

"Please forgive me, love."

Love?

No. I was *not* his love. This wasn't him. Something shifted in my mind, as if that word alone were a trigger; one that immediately snapped me out of the mindset of seventeen-year-old me. The voice of my therapist faded into my consciousness and got louder; I was thankful for it.

What if there was never anything authentic about Vincent Leo Luther? What if the doting father I had seen and praised was nothing more than a mask he wore to impress those around him? Was he an absolute terror to live with behind closed doors? I couldn't tell if his apology was sincere, or nothing more than "narcissistic hoovering." Was this all a twisted act he'd scripted to deceive and seduce me? To prove to his father that I "really am a whore"? I questioned in my racing mind.

"Lana, I—"

"You remembered everyone and everything... but me." I observed his face. He *looked* distraught. He had *sounded* sad. But I was afraid to trust him.

"I can't even articulate the desperation I felt last night," Vincent admitted. "I can only describe it as a combination of horror, agony, anger, betrayal, *desire*... I feel like a madman, sitting across from you now. I know we've aged, but I'm just as youthful in my heart as I was when you stole it from me years ago."

"Vincent, don't—"

"I have to say it, Lana." He moved in closer and stretched his arm above the edge of the bench. "Being with you was the closest thing I'd ever felt to being in love. I often prided myself on being a realist— an unapologetic cynic." He lowered his head, hiding his smile before he gazed at me with those penetrative eyes.

"Here I was, judging you for marrying my father after four months of dating, when *I* had fallen so deeply in love with you in just two weeks." Vincent quietly chuckled. "No. That's a lie." He caressed my face. "It was love at first sight."

Who was this man? Where was his cynicism? I questioned, ignoring my injured heart as it cried and begged me to believe him, while my mind pointed a gun at it like a sadistic psychopath, threatening to pull the trigger if it didn't shut up. Ten years had passed... *ten years.* I was a different person now, a disillusioned romantic.

Vincent reached for my hand and raised it to his lips. "Please say something."

What was there left to say? If destiny was real, then it was unbelievably cruel, I thought, pulling my hand back.

"Lana, please don't cry."

"It's all just very sad. I feel..."

I shook my head, blinking through tears. As much as I cared about my husband, he never made me feel the way this man had all those years back. I contemplated telling him about the true nature of our marriage.

"May I ask you something?" said Vincent.

"Yes."

"Are you happy with my father?"

This was my chance to tell him the truth. But what would follow? Would he change his tone and accuse me again of marrying Max strictly for my benefit? The difference now was that I had an answer prepared: there wasn't a single person in the world who made a commitment unless there was *something* to gain, whether financial, emotional, or otherwise. Marriage is a transaction between two people who bring things to the table that are equally beneficial to the parties involved.

"Max and I never consummated our marriage," I blurted out, staring down at my hands.

"*What?*" Vincent sounded just as shocked as he looked, gawking at me in disbelief. "Why? How is that possible?"

"We never dated. We were best friends—still are. I was never after your father's money, Vincent," I confessed. "I'd signed a prenup and waved all my rights to alimony and spousal support—never wanted it."

"Why didn't you tell me sooner?"

"Would it have mattered?"

"Of course, it would've!"

"You wouldn't have believed me."

"I... I thought the most horrible things of you... it fills me with shame."

I had no idea why I had shared my sex life—or *lack* of it, but the look of shock and confusion on Vincent's face was enough to persuade me to explain further.

"No one knows this, but... your father and I never had a sexual relationship, much less a romantic one. I was more like his best friend, a companion. Ever since we met on that flight out to Florida, he often requested me as his plus one at business dinners and fundraisers, but other than that, we never even shared a kiss."

"But... why get married then?"

"Max wanted companionship, and so did I. I was in a place in my life where I had stopped searching for 'the one.' My expectations in a long-term relationship had changed. I wanted an understanding partner who treated me with respect. Max had offered to open doors for me in the publishing world. He wanted to take me under his wing and help me reach my dreams.

"The night he'd proposed, he told me he suffered from erectile dysfunction. Maybe I shouldn't tell you this, but... he insisted I could take on a lover, so long as I was discreet about it. Apparently, Isobel had that freedom, too—from what he'd told me. But I never took that option throughout our marriage."

"Bloody hell..."

"All he wanted from me was my affection, time, and friendship. Obviously, I didn't know you were his son. If I'd known, I would have stayed far away."

"Fuck..." Vincent rubbed his forehead. "My parents were swingers?"

"I think so." I pursed my lips and added, "Now that it's been a little over a year... I think... that *maybe*... Max is..."

"What?... *Gay?*" Vincent chuckled in disbelief.

I took a breath and slowly nodded.

"Honestly... I'm shocked," he said. "I mean, my father's never been the effeminate type, so... it's not like there were any blatant signs that made me question his sexual orientation—my mother certainly said nothing." He stopped a moment. "But the more I think about it, the more it makes sense why she stayed with him after I'd discovered he was cheating on her."

Vincent met my gaze and added, "Maybe she knew. Maybe all those 'affairs' were with boyfriends that she knew about. Dad's old-fashioned. Has he ever started any—how do I say this... foreplay?"

I shook my head. "We've slept in separate bedrooms since I moved in with him—he said his snoring would keep me up. At first, I was fine with it. I understood his 'condition,' plus he was grieving... but the fact that he took no sexual interest in me makes me feel as if my hunch is correct. Once we got back to Atlanta, I was planning on talking to him about it." I hesitated and said, "I've been considering getting our marriage annulled for quite some time now."

Vincent seemed surprised by this news.

"Are you unhappy?"

"I was lost and broken when Max and I crossed paths. He made me feel safe, loved, and supported. Many horrible things happened to me throughout my life, Vincent. I made one poor decision after another when you left Miami and never reached out—not to blame it all on you, but I was fresh out of an abusive relationship when I met your dad. I think that's why I rushed into marriage. More than anything, I just wanted to feel safe with a man. My ex had emotionally, sexually, and physically abused me."

Tears stung my eyes as I remembered those years. The nightmare chapters of my life. André was so charming and nice in the beginning... but it didn't last. For three years, I was constantly controlled and told that I was stupid and worthless by a man who claimed to "love me"; a man who blamed *me* for his jealousy issues; a man who punished *me* for all his own failures in life. I was degraded, beaten, humiliated, and raped too many times to count... all while believing that I loved this person, and he "loved me, too": a monster in disguise.

"I survived domestic violence and its vicious cycle of leaving and returning to my abuser," I admitted to Vincent. "In hindsight, I married your father to ultimately protect and *prevent* myself from ever going back to my abusive ex."

I hated André now that he was completely out of my system. Forgiveness was a step I was working on.

"My only regret is that I should have pressed charges instead of covering up his crimes against me."

Vincent looked visibly upset, reaching for my hand.

"Lana, I..."

"What is it?"

He wavered and said, "It's nothing. I'm so fucking sorry about what you went through with your ex."

"I don't want you to pity me."

"*Pity you?*" Vincent furrowed his brows. "I pity *myself.*" He sighed. "As much as I want to torture and kill the bloody bastard for hurting you, I suppose I'm no different from him in that regard. I'd never raise my hand on a woman, Lana, but I've said some ugly things to you. Apologizing isn't enough."

I tried not to remember our arguments by grounding myself in the present. Fidgeting with my thumb ring helped during moments like this.

"Please..." Vincent touched my face. "I can't live with myself knowing you hate me."

"I don't hate you, Vincent." I looked into his eyes, tearing up. "We're just ten years too late."

My chest felt so heavy. I didn't want to break down, not in front of him. Regulating my emotions was difficult to do, but I was much better at handling myself compared to my younger years.

"You were right," I said. "I can't fill Isobel's shoes—I never wanted to. I don't belong here. I don't belong in your family. Maybe I've known it for a while now."

"Lana—"

"Your father is amazing. He's showered me with gifts and more love than I ever received in my nightmare of a childhood, but I'll be turning twenty-seven in August. I'm at a point in life now where I'm ready to address my self-esteem and abandonment issues. I need to do this on my own without letting my fears control my life."

"But you're so confident," he stopped me. "At least that's how you've always appeared to me."

"I've been afraid of being alone, which left me little opportunity to truly find myself and figure out what will ultimately make me happy. Healing is a solo thing. No one can do it for you. I guess that was my first mistake: believing that the 'perfect relationship' with 'the perfect man' will heal me. We both know perfection isn't real. People are flawed." I paused and said, "Vincent, as a writer, I'm a pro with creating characters and plots in my mind, but I don't want to live a fictional life... it's not fulfilling to me. I got a taste of what it's like to be filthy rich, only to discover that it doesn't contribute to happiness—just comfort to an extent."

"You're serious about...?"

"Yes. This is gonna be my last vacation with the family."

He seemed to contemplate before he said, "I can't lie to you and say that I'm sad you want to leave my father. To be perfectly honest, I'm relieved you share no romantic history with each other... maybe because you were always meant to be mine."

Vincent caressed my cheek and slowly leaned in. But I stopped him.

"What are you doing?" I frowned, holding him back by the chest.

"I apologize, I... I'm overwhelmed with all these feelings for you... it's making me crazy."

"Vincent, you're *married*. As much as I appreciate the opportunity for closure, I refuse to be a home wrecker."

"That's so like you." He brushed my hair out of my face. "Always thinking of others."

"I'm serious."

"I want you."

"It was only yesterday that you thought I was a selfish, manipulative bitch."

"I wasn't in my right mind, Lana."

"And you still aren't."

"I need you. I *need* to be with you."

"Vincent, you're not thinking rationally."

"I don't need logic, Lana. I know how I feel. My marriage with Claire has been on the rocks for several years now."

"You have two young children! Don't put them through the devastating consequences of divorce. Lilly and Milo deserve the best shot at life."

"And they'll receive that, I promise. I'm miserable with Claire. I'm sure she is, too. We haven't had sex in ages—easily a predictor of divorce."

I couldn't believe this. While Ciara and I had sensed a rift between them, I never thought it was this bad.

"I can't allow myself to be the reason you end your marriage, Vincent."

"You and I... we're meant to be together; don't you see it?" He shifted closer, touching my thigh. "Everything has brought us here for a reason."

"No," I shook my head.

"Do you mean to tell me you don't feel the same?"

"It doesn't matter."

"It *does.*"

"This isn't just about you and me anymore, Vincent."

"For fuck's sake, just answer my question!" he demanded, losing his patience. "I'm sorry for raising my voice. I'm just... please try to understand... I feel like I've finally woken up from a nightmare."

"Don't say that. Lilly and Milo—"

"Will *always* be loved and looked after, but my marriage to Claire is over."

"I *can't* be the reason, Vincent," I reiterated, stress levels rising.

"Are you kidding me?" He glared. "Claire's the bloody reason I wound up in that accident in the first place. You have no idea how resentful I am."

"Please try to make it work—for the kids."

"She's been too focused on work to actually give a fuck about child-rearing. I'm pulling the plug. You're the woman I want to be with... the one I *always* wanted."

My head was reeling when I stood up.

"I can't do this," I said. "I can't do this with you."

"Where are you going?"

I walked around the bench and was about to retrace our steps down the gravel path when Vincent grabbed my wrist and pulled it back. I collided with him, feeling his lips crush my mouth.

"Vincent—don't—" I said between his needy kisses.

His hands claimed my body as if every part of me belonged to no one but him.

We were lip locked. He couldn't stop. Neither could I. There was nothing I could do to extinguish the inferno that was blazing around us. He kissed me fervently with untamed passion, piercing through my core with heat and desire. I could feel his desperation; the raging need to connect with me, as his hands moved along my curves... clutching, caressing, *possessing.*

It was easy to lose myself in him when he kissed me like this. It didn't matter that a decade had passed. I still yearned for this man and the intimacy we shared all those years ago. I knew we had to stop, but neither of us broke contact. My body was on fire, starved of lovemaking. I wasn't sure if Vincent's kiss had damned me to hell or had liberated me. Deep down, I needed him. I needed him in ways he could never comprehend. I had missed *this* so much: the part of him that made me feel as if I was the center of his universe. Touching him wasn't enough; kissing only worsened the chaos inside. I was so conflicted. But I finally found the strength to push him off.

His eyes were wild with lust when he stared back at me, breathless.

"I don't want this, Vincent!"

"I don't believe you."

"I don't care if you do or not!" I kept a safe distance, trying to calm down and rationalize. "I'm heading back to the house. *Please* don't follow me."

"Lana!"

Gravel crunched beneath my runners as I briskly marched ahead, hugging my arms to hold myself together. Our love story was a tragedy. The sooner I accepted that, the sooner I could finally break free and find myself. Starting a relationship with Vincent was just living in a fantasy; I had enough wisdom to realize this. As much as it hurt to surrender that dream, the same one I wanted a decade ago, I knew I had to make a head over heart decision. He never ran from me, and that gave me peace. But now... now *I* had to run... from him.

CHAPTER SEVENTEEN

LANA

"I *told you* he was bound to make a move! The sexual tension between you two has been obvious from the first time I studied his interactions with you."

"*Studied*?" I gave Ciara a queer look. "And technically, he didn't 'make any moves.' We were just playing a stupid game."

"Vincent enjoyed *every* second of that kiss. You can't convince me otherwise." She popped a cherry tomato in her mouth before she continued chopping vegetables on a cutting board while lecturing me in the kitchen.

Claire had gone out to do some shopping with her mom and the kids, so the task of making salad and dessert was left to Ciara and me.

"I have a degree in psychology, Lana, it's my job to analyze human behavior..."

I listened to her go on at length before I finally spoke.

"It was just a stupid kiss. It meant nothing."

I wasn't sure if I should open up to Cici. Vincent and I shared a past; a past he did not remember until last night. I had never told my best friend about my history with him. Ciara was trustworthy, but it just wasn't a good time to stroll down memory lane.

"Tell me, though," she said, "how did you feel last night when you two were kissing?"

Psychoanalyzing me again, I thought with a sigh.

"It was just a game, Cici."

"It's okay to admit that you're attracted to him, you know. It's perfectly normal. It just proves my point that people can never be monogamous—and I'm not judging you when I say this. I love Denzel, but I do lust after other men occasionally."

"I'd be lying if I said I didn't find Vincent attractive, but we kissed last night because we were playing a *game.*"

"Did it turn you on?" She giggled.

"No."

Ciara arched her eyebrow, as if to say she didn't believe me.

"Maybe."

"I knew it!"

"I'd rather just forget about it."

"Okay, Lana. But in case you've forgotten, there's doctor-patient confidentiality in effect between us. You know that, right?"

"I wasn't aware that I was your 'patient.'"

"I just meant that whatever you share with me will always stay between us."

"I appreciate that." I smiled. "Thank you for not judging me."

"*Judge you?* For what? Being turned on by a man who is hot as fuck?" She laughed. "Girl, please! I'm the last person to point the finger, although I blame that husband of yours. The man's got you sex deprived."

I moved away from the counter and was about to say something when I stopped in my tracks and turned to stone.

"My apologies." Vincent met my gaze as he stepped into the kitchen. "I'm just checking to see if those pepper skewers are ready."

"Not yet," Ciara answered. "Give me two minutes. I'm finishing up this salad."

"Yeah, no problem."

He loitered by the door, brazenly giving me eye contact. I couldn't look away.

Ciara seemed to sense our tension as she placed her knife down and said, "On second thought... be right back."

She opened the fridge, grabbed a bottle of Corona, and gave me a secret smile before walking out of the kitchen. She did that on purpose, I thought, wishing she hadn't left. I couldn't trust myself around Vincent now.

The energy in the space shifted as soon as he sauntered toward me, making me feel that magnetic attraction that always seemed to pull us together. I was tense, but I tried to distract myself by continuing where Ciara had left off with the cucumbers. It quickly occurred to me it was a useless undertaking; I only felt more anxious holding that sharp blade in my hand.

"Lana," Vincent murmured in a deep, seductive voice.

I felt his eyes on me as he hovered closer, heat radiating off his tall frame. The scent of his cologne grew stronger, intoxicating me, yet I was determined to keep my eyes on the cutting board.

"I can't stop thinking about you," he confessed, sending chills down my spine. "It's maddening." His hands landed on my hips and pulled me back against his hard body.

"Vincent, we can't—"

But before I could finish, his lips were on my neck, leaving a trail of soft, wet kisses. I felt his tongue caressing my skin, and it triggered nothing but instant arousal. The sex goddess that I thought had died was slowly coming to life, and I couldn't stop her resurrection. I didn't want to. A year and a half of celibacy had led to this: a desperate need for contact, to be filled and penetrated.

"When can we talk in private?" he spoke in my ear.

This was too much for me; all these feelings, seeing this new side of him. I should have been happy, but I wasn't.

"Stop." I placed the knife down and found the courage to face him. Those icy blue eyes were no longer staring back at me with hatred and resentment; they betrayed nothing but vulnerability... deep emotions that had been buried.

"I... I don't know how to deal with all this," I confessed. "I need some time to think. You put a lot on me earlier, Vincent."

"I apologize." He frowned. "I'm being a selfish bastard."

The disappointment on his face made my heart give a painful squeeze.

"I don't want to overwhelm you," he said. "I'll give you space. I'll leave."

Those last two words seemed to trigger my abandonment issues as the ghost of my seventeen-year-old self appeared and grabbed his arm.

"Don't leave," I said in panic. "I mean—you don't have to leave Ocean City because of me."

"That's not what I meant, Lana," Vincent gently explained. His gaze was calm as a tranquil lake.

My emotions had amplified in his presence. It frustrated me that we couldn't communicate the way we wanted, but I tried my best.

"Vincent, it's just... I'm not used to you acting this way with me."

He scowled in disdain. "You really believe I'm a sociopath? I'm not 'acting,' Lana."

"It's hard to forget everything we've been through this past year."

"You mean everything *I've* put you through?"

"No, Vincent. That's not what I meant."

All the light suddenly faded from his eyes.

"Lana, please, let's get away this evening. I need to be alone with you." He caressed my face. "It's killing me. I can't think about anything else. Do you understand that?" He spoke with such urgency that it made me forget about my pain. All I wanted was to reach out and comfort him.

"That's kind of hard to do. We're vacationing here with our spouses."

"And? My father isn't here. We've done errands together many times, you and I—it never raised suspicions."

He wasn't wrong about that, though the memories stung me.

"That was before," I explained. "Things are different now."

"What do you mean?"

"Do I really need to spell it out for you, Vincent?"

"Yes, perhaps you bloody well should!" He erupted.

I wasn't sure how to deescalate this situation.

"Forgive me if I'm slow to understand." Vincent sighed and calmed himself. "All I can think about is kissing you... holding you... *touching* you."

I felt his hand against my cheek and recoiled a bit.

"Lana."

A visible pain poured from his eyes, as if he were begging me not to send him away. I wanted to cry.

"Vincent, you've done a complete 180 overnight. I don't know how to handle this. For the past year, I've seen parts of your personality that I can honestly liken to Edward Hyde—"

"*Here we go again...*" He rolled his eyes, folding his arms in his chest.

"And now you're suddenly the friendly Dr. Jekyll."

"I know you're fond of gothic literature, but I'm a human being, Lana, not a fucking fictional character."

"I keep waiting for Hyde to show up."

"That's bloody brilliant." He scoffed. "You're comparing me to a psychopath from the nineteenth century."

"I'm not calling you a psycho. I just meant the shift in your personality is just..."

"I think you read a little *too* much," Vincent bitterly rebutted.

"I didn't mean to offend you."

"You didn't." He exhaled, pressing a hand to his forehead. "It's my own fucking fault. I shouldn't expect you to agree with me. If I could take back everything, all the nasty things I've said to you, I would. But I can't."

He was sincere. He had to be. I could see it in his eyes.

"I couldn't remember you, Lana. I know it doesn't excuse my behavior towards you, but—"

"You mean your complete and total apathy? Or the moments when you were so unjustly cruel? I'm not sure which is worse."

Vincent clenched his jaw, as all the hope seemed to vanish from his darkened gaze. "I feel like I've been cursed for the past ten years."

"Do you think you're the only one?"

"Lana, I'm begging you... just give me a proper moment alone with you tonight. We can't talk like this in the shadows. It's unnerving."

As if I didn't know that already; I was just afraid to be alone with him. Not because I feared he would hurt me, but because I was scared that we would do something I'd later regret. Being in such proximity was hazardous. My mind, body, and heart were battling each other. I wasn't sure who would win. All I knew was that all parties involved would end up injured.

"Hey, Vince!" Denzel appeared in the kitchen.

I panicked. It wasn't like we'd been caught kissing, but now I was paranoid, thinking everyone knew about us.

"What's up, mate?" Vincent coolly replied.

"Your old man wants to have a word with you."

"He's here?"

"Yeah, he just arrived."

"I'll be right out."

I avoided Vincent's daunting gaze and focused on chopping more tomatoes. My breath caught when I felt his lips brush against my earlobe.

"This conversation isn't over, Lana."

The way he murmured my name was so sexually charged, I had to stop what I was doing just to breathe.

"*We* are not over." He kissed my neck and whispered, "Never were."

I shut my eyes and listened to his footsteps fading in the distance. Vincent had shocked my system. How was I going to survive the rest of this vacation, especially now that Max was back? I wanted to write a letter to both men I loved before I'd pack up and leave forever. I didn't want to ruin Vincent's marriage. I couldn't live with that.

CHAPTER EIGHTEEN

VINCENT

I craved her. I craved her healing touch, her kissable lips, and beautiful voice. I needed to possess all of her. She was always mine. I craved intimacy with Lana on every level, as if our love transcended time and space. Had I enslaved myself to a feeling that was entirely idealized? Was love a deity? An illusion? Was I merely chasing after a dream that would never be realized? I wondered, sitting in a chair beneath an outdoor canopy that was covered in warm string lights. Lana sat across from me, chatting away with my wife and Ciara; she looked like an elegant goddess, radiating regal energy. I watched the way her sensuous mouth caressed the edge of her wineglass, leaving a glossy pink imprint when she placed it on the table.

Sexy.

Everything about her was dangerously seductive. She was wearing a white spaghetti strap sundress with her hair down over her left shoulder. I had tucked a white orchid by her ear earlier in the evening when no one was looking. It made me smile to know that she hadn't removed it, as if my romantic gesture was happily accepted, despite all the pushbacks whenever I tried to get close. Lana's soft, golden skin seemed to glow in the candlelight. I was mesmerized.

If I could have painted her right then, I would have. She still had her youthful beauty. The only difference between the girl I had rescued and the young woman who sat across from me was that her eyes held a penetrating sadness at present; it pierced through my chest as I studied her. Everything she had gone through, I felt responsible for. I didn't have the heart to tell her about that slandering email and the revenge porn. I felt ashamed for judging her the way I did for so long. I wanted to hunt down that son of a bitch who had abused her and torture him until he'd beg for death. That's what he deserved, not prison time.

The Lana that I had met ten years ago wore no makeup on her face. She didn't need it. It was obvious she was stunning. She didn't have French manicured nails and expensive jewels that hung on her neck and wrists back then. Lana was an untamed, free spirit, with pink and blue streaks in her short, blonde hair. But *this* Lana was different, at least on the outside. She was high maintenance and well put together, exuding an image of wealth and status. I couldn't tell if it was my father's influence, or if she always aspired to be a trophy wife. She seemed to have abandoned an extremely vital part of herself for a reason, and I needed to know why.

We were not alone, but in my mind, it was just the two of us. I wanted everyone to disappear so that I could pull her into my lap and make her feel safe with me. I wanted to stare into her eyes, tell her how gorgeous she was, how my feelings had never vanished—but had been buried somewhere deep inside of me. I guess that explained why I was so damn frustrated and hot-headed around her in the past.

The memory of our first encounter often flickered in my head throughout the years, but it was never long or vivid enough to restore those three months I had lost before the accident. I hated myself for hurting Lana. She was so young when we had met. Aside from her breathtaking beauty, there was something about her that had captivated me from the start. Our lives would have been so different had I never gotten in that car. I wanted to blame Claire for everything—that would have been the easy way, but I was ultimately responsible for my actions. I never should have hit a bar that night... should have called a cab. There was no point in dwelling on things I couldn't change.

Claire and I had kept a level of peace for the time being, but I was confident she knew where we were headed once we'd go home. I think we were both in denial of the failing state of our marriage. I wasn't happy, and from the looks of it, neither was she.

Throughout the evening, Lana had avoided me. It was driving me mad. I needed to touch her. I needed to be close to her. If my father had truly suppressed his sexual orientation, then I was relieved, as bad as it sounded. I didn't like the idea of him being intimate with Lana. It seemed as if he had stolen her from me. It wasn't fair. I felt like fate was mocking us, taking pleasure in my pain like a vicious cosmic master. Had I wronged someone in a previous incarnation? Were past lives even real? How could I possibly explain this unbearable tragedy? I couldn't. Maybe the only person to blame was me. I never should have gone on a self-destructive bender all those years ago. It was my own pathetic attempt at self-soothing, and I paid for it... so did Lana. Memories of that summer in Miami looped in my head as I stared at her.

Beautiful Lana.

Why in the bloody hell did it take me so long to remember? I asked myself. I would have chased her down to the ends of the earth if I had only recalled that she existed somewhere out there. Life had led me down in a different direction instead. I was a husband, a father, a man who had pledged his vows to his wife before God; in my heart I knew I had broken them, the second I remembered who Lana really was, and what she meant to me.

The sound of my wife's loud laughter pulled me out of daydreaming. Denzel had cracked a joke, but I could hardly pay attention. My eyes were glued to Lana, hoping to reach her telepathically. I had tried to steal a moment to be alone with her again, but that opportunity never came. She had deterred all my efforts.

Look at me, love, I repeated in my head.

Her alluring eyes never met my gaze. She was stunning... a rare masterpiece. How could I have been so blind? The saddest part was that she wasn't mine to possess. But I wanted a lifetime membership at that art gallery, just to see her every day, to admire her, even from afar. She had no idea what she did to me. Our undeniable attraction was instant from the moment we met. Desire is so complex; it can either be the root of all your suffering, or it can motivate you to attain what you seek. It's enough to make a person do crazy things. My desire for Lana had brought out the worst in me. I had been too proud to admit that I felt something for her. It wasn't lust—that's too shallow... it was *passion*, misguided energy that fueled my resentment. I wanted to hate her with a passion, unaware of the consequences that came with that transformative kiss. It was a painful awakening. Would I take it back?

Never.

There was a reason I was so drawn to Lana, and it all made sense now, as if my body knew all along who she was. My senses were familiar with her, but none of that registered in my brain, until I finally kissed her again. Either a curse had been lifted or I was eternally jinxed now that I knew who she was. Fate had taken us down two different paths, only to reunite us in the harshest way. Of all the women in the world, why did my father have to marry her? It couldn't have been a coincidence. All of this must have happened for a reason. If Claire hadn't made us play that stupid game, Lana and I never would have kissed. If my father hadn't married her, she wouldn't have been here at all. Would we still have crossed paths, regardless? I wondered. It didn't matter, though. These were the cards we had been dealt.

For the first time, I could finally see things with such clarity. It hurt to be in love with someone forbidden to you. Was I in love, though? I asked myself. I didn't feel like thirty-one-year-old Vincent anymore. I felt like I was twenty-two again, as if my heart had traveled back in time to recover all the feelings it had lost, while my physical body stayed present in the here and now. Fast forward ten years from 2007, and all I was left to face was an ugly truth: I had behaved like a heartless bastard toward Lana, accusing her of malicious things, like being a "promiscuous gold digger," all because she was young and beautiful. I believed every slandering accusation of her bitter ex-lover because it fueled my anger and resentment more. I didn't want to be attracted to her. I felt like my father had tried to replace my mum with another woman who was young enough to be his daughter. It enraged me. But I was wrong to project all of that onto Lana.

A dagger was plunged into her precious heart... so deep. It wasn't visible, but I could see it, because *I* was the one who had stabbed her with it. I had ruthlessly twisted that bloody thing every time I'd interacted with her, satisfied in knowing that I had wounded her beyond repair. How could I have been so sadistic, so fucking cruel?

Sitting there, wallowing in misery, I fixated on Lana's chest and imagined a splotch of red blooming onto the white fabric... a crimson rose. Was there beauty in this violence? Or had I simply lost my mind? I visualized her pain this way—what I'd done to her. I could finally see, no longer blinded by unjustified contempt. Despite her efforts to mask her agony from the world, she couldn't mask it from me. She could hide behind her contagious laughter and heart-melting smile, but she couldn't hide her pain from me. Her eyes betrayed her. Every. Single. Time.

My mother's garden was infused with the intoxicating scent of Hyacinth and Jasmine, but what dominated my senses was Lana's perfume; it had permeated the air, and it only made me want her more.

My father kept the conversation going at a fluid rate, as I occasionally glanced at him and nodded when he mentioned my name, but I just couldn't take my eyes off Lana. If I was under a spell,

I never wanted it to break. As agonizing as it was, at least I could feel something again. At least I *felt* alive.

Lana crossed her thigh over the other, making the hem of her dress hike up a bit.

Fuck me.

Her legs were toned. Everything about her was flawless and beautiful. I couldn't find a single imperfection. My eyes cascaded from her thighs down to her ankles, eliciting a fantasy in my mind: Lana in a bathtub filled with rose petals; a Greek goddess in mortal form. I saw myself sitting on the edge, reaching for her ankle, dragging my lips from her shin to her knee, kissing her inner thigh before I'd massage her pedicured toes... among other places.

Claire's howling laughter pulled me out of my steamy fantasy once more, like a bucket of ice water on the face.

"That's hilarious!" She slapped Denzel's arm. "Did you hear that, Vince?"

I didn't care about the bloody joke. I didn't care about small talk of any form. All I could focus on was Lana. I had one foot in the past and the other in the present. No one had a clue, except for Lana and me. She had to know how enamored I was with her. This wasn't shallow infatuation, nor obsession. It was a rebirth of what we had lost all those years back. She had revived something within me that had died long ago. I didn't regret that kiss.

Lana's face lit up as she smiled, while I watched in secret admiration. It did things to me... inside of me, which explained why I had avoided her so much; why I'd pressed her buttons and gave her every reason to cry or storm off, so that I wouldn't feel the way I did whenever those kissable lips smiled in my presence. I didn't want to feel like butter in her hand. I didn't want to accept my attraction to her.

How was it possible to feel so alone while surrounded by so many people? I had entered purgatory like Dante from the *Divine Comedy* and was suffering inside. No one could save me; no one, but Lana.

"Remember that guy from the gym?"

I looked at Denzel when he nudged me. "Sorry, mate, come again?"

"The one that shoots steroids, remember him?"

No.

"Uh, yeah... I think so. Why?"

He started talking about some random bloke I didn't give a rat's arse about, though Dad and Claire seemed to find the story amusing. Ciara and Lana weren't within earshot, as they continued a separate conversation—which was probably more interesting than what I was forced to listen to.

I observed Lana devotedly, admiring every detail that I had previously overlooked, locking it away in my memory so that I could never lose it again. There was no way amnesia could happen twice, I convinced myself.

I need to touch you.

Sending psychic signals, I couldn't take my eyes off her. I was determined to manifest what I needed. *Craved.* But she never glanced in my direction... not until the music changed to a track that was all too familiar to us.

Fuck. Not this song, I cursed in my head.

A low bass line played, followed by a soft, slow drumbeat and minor piano melodies. It was haunting and seductive. Abel Tesfaye's voice was magic, but this song was just painful. I wanted to get up and switch the playlist, yet somehow, I couldn't tear myself away from Lana. The memory seemed to materialize in her haunted gaze. I could see it; I didn't imagine this. The song, the lyrics, everything had suddenly triggered a flashback of events that happened on Halloween last year. One of many nights I wished I could take back.

CHAPTER NINETEEN

October 31, 2016

It was the first time Lana had dyed her hair in years, even though it contradicted her belief system regarding harmful chemicals dyes. For weeks, Ciara had insisted that she go for a full-blown makeover for the Halloween masquerade ball they were invited to at a ritzy hotel in Atlanta. Lana knew she could have settled for a wig, but a part of her desired a drastic change. She had felt this way for months. Her salon appointment had resulted in a transformation that she was not used to. Lana's silky hair had gone from blonde to black. Her eyebrows had been dyed as well to match her new hair color. According to her stylist, "dark hair accentuated aqua eyes."

Lana's makeup had been professionally done as well that evening: rose gold eyeshadow, winged eyeliner, and blinding highlights on her cheekbones that Javier (her stylist) described as "sickening": so stunning that it made any female "sick with jealousy." He had insisted that her ruby lipstick made her "irresistibly kissable." To complete the look, Javier had dusted glitter all around Lana's collarbones, shoulders, and arms. She looked like she had walked right out of a fantasy book, as a real-life queen of the faeries. Lana's dark hair was done up in a bun full of thick curls and waves, overlapping each other.

Her Halloween costume was an elegant gothic masterpiece. She wore a red corseted Victorian gown that was tailored and cut short above the knees, revealing her stunning legs. The only thing that bothered her was the tightness of the bodice; her breasts were pushed so high, she worried they would pop out. Ciara had convinced her it was worth the risky wardrobe malfunction. It was only one night, Lana thought; she would not wear it again. A black diamond choker sparkled on her neck, complimenting her pear-shaped ruby earrings. To match her costume, she wore a pair of black and gold peep-toe heels that had black feathers wrapped around her ankles.

Ciara's costume was a long-sleeved, gold Chiffon gown that had a hoop petticoat underneath and rhinestone accents around the bodice of the dress. She had dyed her hair a caramel color, styled in big, bouncy curls to match the Renaissance theme of her costume. She looked stunning, Lana thought, staring at her. The two of them were busy getting ready in Lana's boudoir when a phone rang. The limo driver had pulled up to the mansion and was waiting for them.

"It's too bad Maxwell won't be attending tonight's event," said Ciara. "What's the point in retiring if you're still a workaholic? He's always traveling and leaving you alone." She glanced at her friend, powdering her nose in the mirror.

"I know," Lana replied. "But he said it was urgent and insisted I go to this event without him. I already paid so much for this dress."

"Which looks *so* freaking hot on you, babes!"

"I don't know, Cici. You don't think it's too revealing?"

"Honey, if you've got it, flaunt it—and you *definitely* got it. Max is missing out tonight."

"That's okay, I have no problem going alone."

"No-no." Ciara shook her head. "You won't be flying solo on my watch. We're both sharing Denzel this evening."

"He's your date, though."

"And I have no problem sharing him with my best friend. Besides, it's not like I'm sharing his *you know what* with you." She laughed as Lana blushed. "There is no way I'm gonna let you walk into this event without a man next to you. You already rejected a list of eligible bachelors to stand in as your escort. The three of us will go to the ball and make a sexy ass statement while we're at it!" Ciara finished her champagne and stood up from her lounge chair.

"I feel nervous," Lana uttered. "I'm not sure why."

"Is it because of Vincent?"

"I think—"

"Hold it right there"—she held out her hand—"your face says it all. No point in denying it around me, Lana. You're completely transparent, despite *this* little prop." She waved Lana's mask in the air.

"I got into a nasty argument with him last week and we haven't exactly resolved it." Lana frowned, feeling nothing but dread.

"Girlfriend, he has issues that even *I* can't resolve for him, so stop torturing yourself. Vincent needs to grow the fuck up and accept the fact that you're not going anywhere. Harboring all this animosity toward you is not good for him—it'll ultimately damage him in the long run, more than it will affect you. Trust me."

"He still thinks I'm using Max. I've tried to reason with him, but he's convinced all I'm after is money. He really believes I've plotted to trick his father out of the family fortune."

Ciara folded her arms in her chest, shaking her head in disappointment. "Vincent's not dealing with his grief. He hasn't been the same since Isobel's death. He takes his anger out on you because you're the easiest target. 'Let's blame the stepmom.' It's juvenile." She scoffed. "He needs therapy."

"Don't tell him that. He'll bite your head off."

"I'm not afraid of him. I can be just as vicious, *believe that*, honey. You don't wanna piss off this boss bitch!"

Lana laughed, amused by her best friend's sassy attitude. Ciara always had an amazing ability to cheer her up. She was thankful to confide in her.

"You ready to leave?"

"Yes," Lana said, grabbing her clutch.

She prayed the night would be enjoyable. She prayed Vincent would come around.

⊗

A different world appeared before Lana as she stepped through a pair of dark double doors, arm in arm with Ciara and Denzel. Wide eyed in awe, she paused a moment and took in the magical atmosphere of the Venetian Masquerade Ball. Crystal chandeliers sparkled above a polished marble dance floor, with tall candelabras stationed near arch shaped windows. The banquet hall resembled a replica of the famous ballrooms in the French palace of Versailles. Everything was magnificently decorated to match the Renaissance theme. Round dining tables were placed around the perimeter of the hall, leaving plenty of room to gather on the dance floor. The guests appeared as if they had traveled back to the sixteenth century. Lana felt like she had stepped into a time machine. It was a mysterious wonderland of colors, music, fantasy, and art.

"This place looks incredible!" said Ciara, scanning her environment in awe. "Baroque meets *moderne*," she said in a French accent. "Love it!"

"I'm especially gonna enjoy that open bar," Denzel murmured in her ear.

"Did Vincent say what time he'll arrive? I tried texting Claire—she hasn't responded."

"I called him earlier, babe," he replied. "They're on their way." Denzel was about to escort the women down a wide staircase when he paused and noticed someone waving at him. "Never mind... they're already here."

Lana looked in Vincent's direction and immediately felt anxious. He was sitting next to Claire in the distance. His dark mask almost made him unrecognizable, she thought. When they finally reached their table, Claire was first to greet them.

"You guys look amazing!" She gushed, offering hugs.

Claire was wearing a silky green halter gown with her long, red hair flowing in waves over her shoulders; a fancy Renaissance version of Uma Thurman's famous role as "Poison Ivy." Vincent wore a tailored tux, as if to make a statement: he refused to dress up in costume. He put some effort, however, and wore a dark mask that covered half his face, though it did not take away from the intensity of his piercing blue eyes.

Lana was almost afraid to admit it to herself, but he looked so handsome, she thought, knowing he did not need her compliments. Claire's extroverted personality contrasted with Vincent's quiet, brooding nature. He was always indifferent and cold toward Lana. She was used to it.

"Love the new hair!" Claire said to her. "The dark color really makes your eyes pop! And your dress... *wow!*"

Compliments often made Lana uncomfortable, but she tried her best to accept them with grace, ignoring the discomfort of being in the spotlight.

"You look so beautiful this evening," she said to Claire. "I love your gown more!"

"Oh, this old thing?" Claire smiled. "It's been hanging in my closet for a while now. I didn't have the chance to wear it last year because I was still working off the baby weight." She glanced at her husband and said, "He's Bruce Wayne and I'm Poison Ivy, if you couldn't tell."

Vincent's arctic gaze was determinedly fixed on Lana. She could sense him picking her apart in his mind.

"How about some drinks before we mingle?" Claire suggested.

They sat down and waited on bottle service while Claire got everybody caught up on the latest events in her professional life.

She had been working on a big case and was expecting a huge pay out in court. Lana always felt like her profession as a full-time writer was so boring in comparison. She had ambitions of her own she strived to achieve one day. Sometimes, she couldn't help but wonder if it was her talent that had opened doors for her, or Maxwell's connections in the publishing industry.

"How's that novel coming along?" Ciara asked.

"Um… making progress." Lana sipped on a flute of champagne, avoiding Vincent's judgmental glare.

"What's it about?" he curiously asked.

She did not want to divulge any details. She knew he would criticize her ideas and make her feel more self-conscious than she already was.

"Well?" Vincent persisted.

"It's a love story."

"Is it the typical equation?"

Lana finally looked at him and calmly said, "What equation is that, Vincent?"

"*Alpha male meets damsel in distress…* she thinks she can save the narcissistic bastard and 'change him'—*that* kind of equation."

"No. My story's a tragedy."

She did not appreciate his condescending tone.

"Let me tell you something, Lana. In fact, you should all listen to this." Vincent paused and swigged his drink. "Romantic love is an artificial concept that is blown up in literature, media, and art to become exactly what it means today in mainstream culture: a *lie* that is fed to us from every 'blue-pilled' moron.

"Capitalist elites endorse this because the war on consciousness is real. Social engineering is real. People are brainwashed, and we, 'the consumers,'—in other words, *slaves*—eat it all up, day in and day out. Why? Because we'd like to believe in a 'soulmate.' We want our lives to imitate art. So, we buy into all that romantic bullshit, unaware that it's all engineered… smoke and mirrors.

"We go on our dates, follow social norms, we settle down, buy the house, buy the car, have 2.5 kids—because it's what every normal person wants—what we're *supposed* to want, right? Most of us don't even realize the ways we've been successfully primed and conditioned to chase after something that will never be enough.

"Don't get me started on monogamy because it's nothing but social construct. If we strip that all away, you're only left with human nature. Beyond our social grooming, we have animal instincts. The entire male population would prefer multiple sex partners instead of one for the rest of their lives. Just look at the statistics.

"People usually split up because of two reasons: infidelity and financial problems. So…"—he locked his gaze on Lana—"to write a book just to bank off a fairy tale romance that is so far from reality seems like the biggest scam from my point of view. Why lie to your audience?"

"I'm not lying to anyone." Lana frowned, feeling offended and attacked.

"You write fiction, sweetheart. What do you call that?" Vincent snickered under his breath.

Ciara seemed to notice Lana's embarrassment as she cut in and said, "All right, that's enough, Vince! No one asked for a fucking monologue in your philosophical beliefs about love."

"Far from philosophical theory, Ciara," he countered. "*Facts.*"

"Well, then you're a hypocrite, because you embraced the same 'illusion' that you criticize. Don't think I forgot about your extravagant wedding in Italy. You're married, successful, you're living the American Dream."

"Okay, you two," said Claire. "How did this turn into a debate?"

"Ask your husband that."

Claire was about to respond when her favorite song started playing.

"I love this tune!" She stood up. "I wanna dance!"

She practically begged her husband to get up and join her, dragging him on the dance floor. Lana was taken by surprise when Ciara took her hand and pulled her onto her feet, as well.

"Come on, girl," she said. "Screw whatever Vincent said. You have a gift. Your writing is magic!"

"You're amazing, Cici."

"With my dance moves!" She smirked, leading her toward the crowd.

The EDM got louder as it vibrated the floor. Lana expected to suffer a severe case of tinnitus by the end of the night, though that didn't seem to stop her as she found a clearing with her friend and moved to the house beats. A blanket of fog had crept in around them, glowing from red to blue. She loved to dance; it was the only time she felt carefree.

Vincent's harsh criticism had suddenly vanished from Lana's mind. She was present at the moment. She was unapologetically herself, dancing under flashing strobe lights like a magical being. As soon as Lana closed her eyes, she was flying through a portal to a different world; a place where she felt nothing but love vibrations. Music was powerful; it moved her. It helped her escape all the chaos in her mind, even though it was always short-lived.

⋈

An hour had passed into the evening, and Vincent still could not stop himself from searching for Lana in the crowd. It was frustrating him more than anything. His secret infatuation was psychological torment. He did *not* want to be attracted to her. In fact, he always denied it whenever Denzel brought it up. Despite the war in his mind, he watched Lana like a hawk, as if it were an obsessive compulsion. She was legally his stepmother, but that title alone sounded absurd to Vincent from the moment he met his father's young wife, unaware that they had already met before.

Mulling over his thoughts, Vincent hovered near a fancy bar and quietly sipped on a glass of scotch. Having lost track of time, he did not appear to be worried about Claire's whereabouts. He assumed she was on the dance floor or mingling about, being a social butterfly. Unlike his wife, Vincent hated dancing, though he had not always been that way. Ever since the accident, part of him had died along with his friends. Being married meant that his party days were over and done.

Watching Lana that night made him feel as if he were vicariously living through her. Her body shimmered like a gorgeous disco goddess, Vincent thought, gulping down liquor. She was certainly easy on the eyes—he was willing to give her that much. How many other married men were caught in her trap? He wondered, never taking his eyes off her.

She was seducing him, Vincent concluded, hypnotized by Lana's snakelike movements. Time seemed to slow down as he watched her dance beneath the strobe lights, surrendering to what appeared to be a trance-like state of bliss. Music can do that to a person, he thought, feeling slightly envious. Something stirred inside of him, triggering images that flashed within his mind: a white, sandy beach, footprints in the sand, a powerful sunset, ocean waves...

You're a mermaid, a voice echoed in his head.

Afraid he was hallucinating, Vincent contemplated if his subconscious mind had released some recollections before the car crash. His college years had been full of summer vacations on the west coast. He had casually dated many beautiful girls—no one that particularly stood out in his memory, however.

For a moment, he amusingly entertained the possibility of demonic possession. If the devil had a vendetta to collect his share of sinning souls, then clearly, he was doing it through the music industry, Vincent thought, entranced by the seductive minor notes that faded into the DJ's house mix. The darkest melodies always pulled his thoughts to a place that was forbidden; a place he was not supposed to visit. Ever.

But it was too late. He was already there. He could not erase those naked photos of Lana from his brain... wrapped in ropes on a bed. To make matters worse, his intoxicated mind was creating steamy images of infidelity with the woman he despised, like a dark magician, alchemizing transgression and desire. All he could think about was leaving with Lana, slamming her against a wall, and making her moan. Vincent could almost hear her cries of pleasure as his fantasy consumed him, the same way that scotch was consuming his sobriety. His father had been unfaithful plenty of times, Vincent recalled. He could have killed two birds with one stone by seducing Lana and exposing her. It was a wicked thought; one that would have stayed buried in his mind had he been sober. The music only seemed to fuel his dark imagination. After a quick minute, Vincent finished his drink and headed for a door that led to a large balcony. He needed air. He needed to get his mind off Lana.

◌৪৪৩

By 11pm, the banquet hall had reached full capacity. Vincent and Claire were back at their table chatting with their friends when the DJ caught everyone's attention with a birthday shout-out to a special guest. The crowd sang an off-key anthem, which only made Vincent cringe inside. He hated birthday celebrations. Claire always went over the top. In his mind, it was merely a consumerist trap. Spending an extravagant amount of money (in the hundreds of thousands—sometimes *millions*) on a "sweet sixteen" for example, was ridiculous to him. But this was the norm among wealthy families who had money to spend on the most frivolous things.

Lana seemed to be in a world of her own when he stealthily looked in her direction. Her glittery mask was on the table beside her. His friends were busy chatting away about things he didn't care for, while the bane of his existence sat across from him, teasing him with her untouchable beauty. Dark hair suited her, Vincent thought. Brunette or blonde, it didn't matter to him. It was Lana's *face* that had him mesmerized: free of plastic and Botox. He could always tell with other females, though he wondered if she would soon jump on that trend and start pumping her lips with fillers. She did *not* need it. The luxury of cosmetic surgery and noninvasive beauty procedures were more of a privilege reserved for the rich. Getting caught in the trap of unattainable beauty standards seemed to plague many women. Vincent knew this, though he was determined to shield his own daughter from that mind warping perception that typically spread on social media.

The false self, he thought, letting his eyes roam from Lana's face to her delicate neck.

A violent storm roared inside his chest as he sipped on his drink. He did not like this feeling. His train of thought was suddenly interrupted when the DJ faded a melancholy ballad into the mix: a slowed version of "Professional" by The Weeknd. It was dark, seductive, and hauntingly hypnotizing with its rhythmic percussion. Denzel asked Ciara to dance, but she quickly declined.

"I'm tired, babe, sorry." She turned her head at Lana and smiled. "Here, ask *this* one."

"Oh, no…" Lana refused. "It's okay—seriously. I don't mind sitting out on slow dances."

"You sure?" said Denzel. "The pleasure would be all mine."

Vincent nearly choked on his drink when Claire nudged him and said, "Honey, why don't you dance with Lana?"

"That's really unnecessary," she answered swiftly, looking just as uncomfortable as him.

He stared at his wife with a look that could only be interpreted as an obvious "*NO,*" but Claire dismissed his silent plea and asked Ciara if she could borrow her husband for a dance.

"It's hard to pass this one up when it's one of Abel's sexy songs, but these heels have murdered my feet! He's all yours."

As Claire got up, she leaned into Vincent's ear and murmured, "Be a gentleman and stop embarrassing yourself."

He begged to differ. Vincent was notoriously stubborn. He watched his wife disappear through the crowd with his best friend before he decided. Maybe the liquor had lowered his inhibitions, or perhaps he simply felt like torturing Lana; it didn't matter. He stood up and walked over to her seat, offering his hand.

"Well?" he impatiently grumbled, "are you gonna dance with me or not?"

Lana was stunned. She hesitated at first before she eventually slipped her hand into his and got to her feet. She did not desire this. Dancing with Vincent was the last thing she wanted. His presence was too triggering.

When they found an empty spot on the dance floor, Lana slid her arms over Vincent's shoulders and showed no reaction when he reached for her hips. There was an uncomfortable tension in the air as they slowly swayed side to side, but she could have sworn that was entirely Vincent's fault—the *vibe* he always put out around her: tense, serious, and unpredictably moody. Anyone would have felt uneasy had they been in her shoes. This was not a *Dancing with the Stars* kind of moment, Lana thought; it was torture. It was painful because she remembered everything that Vincent denied.

She shivered when he brushed his hand down the arch of her back. He *had* to remember the beach, Lana told herself, drowning in sadness.

Was I that insignificant? The questions were all-consuming as she pushed them back in her mind and tried to make small talk.

"Thank you for—"

"Don't."

Vincent rudely cut her off.

"I just—"

"Let's get this bloody dance over with, Lana." His tone was cold and devoid of emotion. His eyes were even more so, making her feel as if he were judging her.

This was not the man she had met all those years ago, Lana depressingly thought, absorbing his hostile energy. The Vincent she knew was kind, charismatic, and sweet. He had saved her from death, only to return as her executioner. Her face felt hot as her eyes filled with tears. She could not do this. Not there. Not in front of him. The traumatic events in her life had thickened her skin, but why was this happening now?

"You didn't have to dance with me if you didn't want to." Lana steeled herself. "Nobody forced you."

"My wife did."

"You have free will, Vincent. You didn't have to accept."

"And risk looking like an ass in front of my friends? I'd rather just be a bastard to your face in private."

His tongue was so venomous and cruel. Lana had reached her limit. From the outside looking in, they appeared to be the perfect couple, dancing intimately, as if they were absorbed in each other. Some might have even mistaken Vincent's serious intensity for passion, judging by the way he looked at the stunning goddess in his arms.

"I'd rather dance with the ugliest woman in the world than dance with you."

"Is that your twisted way of giving me a compliment?"

"You want a compliment?" He narrowed his eyes. "I'll give you one: love the new hair, at least now you don't look as dumb as you really are."

"Blonde jokes? *Really*?"

"Who said I was joking?"

"How mature of you, Vincent."

His constant criticism wounded Lana's ego, and he hadn't even opened fire. How much more could she take before she would storm off, bleeding in her chest? Lana asked herself.

"How can you be so disrespectful toward me? I've done nothing to invoke your wrath."

"Oh, but you *have*, sweetheart. You've done plenty of harm to my family."

"Your mother would be ashamed of you for the way you treat—"

"Don't you fucking *dare* talk about my mother." Vincent's eyes flashed with rage as he iced his tone. "You never met her. Don't disgrace her memory in front of me. You don't even deserve to say her name. In some ways, I'm glad she isn't alive to see the way this family has fallen apart. Knowing my father, he was bound to divorce her had she not gotten ill and died. He would've thrown away thirty years of marriage for a gold-digging whore like *you*."

Lana's heart was racing with adrenaline. It was fight or flight.

"I'm a married woman, not a whore. You're nothing but a misogynistic bastard." She desperately pushed back her tears, caught in a flashback of her abusive ex-boyfriend. Vincent's words cut her deep. He never spared her from his wickedness.

"You should've just kept your mouth shut, Lana."

"You are so unbelievably sadistic."

"Only to those who deserve it."

"And what have I done to deserve the way you treat me?" She stopped dancing and unraveled herself from him.

It was on the tip of his tongue. But he had promised his father to never breathe a word about the email.

"You're a class act." Vincent snickered. "I see right through you. I just want you to remember one thing"—he leaned into her ear—"You are *no one* without my father. You have nothing to credit for your reputation. You come from a bloodline of white trash—the kind of people that society doesn't give two shits about... and frankly, you are beneath me—always will be."

His cruel insults pierced through Lana's bleeding heart and butchered it like a merciless slaughter.

"You're a monster," Lana uttered, feeling a tear roll down her cheek.

"If I'm a monster, then you're a martyr. Are you a masochist deep down, Lana? Continuously sacrificing your character for assassination by *yours truly*... All because... what? You believe you can change my mind and help me see 'the real you'?" Vincent scoffed. "I already see who you are, and I'm not impressed, so be honest with yourself, please. You secretly get off on me making you feel like the worthless human being you are." He sneered.

Tell. Him. Off. NOW, LANA!

But the lump in her throat only grew bigger, swelling and constricting her ability to speak. She felt helpless all over again, trapped in the traumas that looped in her mind. It was a freeze response.

"My apologies," Vincent spoke in a patronizing way. "I'll correct myself: I can't make you *feel* anything. I'm only validating the truth. Lucky for you, I take pleasure in your pain." He paused, maintaining composure. "I won't thank you for the dance. It was torture from beginning to end... the stupid shit I do out of pity." His cruel eyes pierced through Lana's before he abandoned her on the floor.

The song had not finished. Standing in a sea of dancing bodies, Lana's face was wet with tears. She felt broken and dejected. Vincent had ruthlessly ripped her heart out, as if he had taken pleasure in squeezing it in his hand right in front of her before discarding it like it was nothing but a piece of junk. He made her feel like trash. She felt so humiliated. She wanted to leave the ball.

Marrying Max was a mistake, Lana scolded herself, disappearing through the crowd. Vincent had given her another psychic wound that was tragically associated with Abel Tesfaye's beautiful voice. She would never listen to this song again, no matter how deep the lyrics were. Never.

CHAPTER TWENTY

VINCENT

My heart was in turmoil as I flashed through memories from last Halloween. That song had triggered an onslaught of recollections that I'd much rather have forgotten. Lana seemed to have remembered, too, as I looked in her eyes and noticed a hidden agony. I was such a heartless bastard to her. I wanted to talk, but she abruptly got to her feet and headed back into the house. Everything I had said that night was disgraceful. I felt ashamed. She must have remembered that awful conversation. Why else did she have tears in her eyes? I fought with myself, uncertain if I should get up and follow her, or wait it out. My heart and mind were fiercely battling each other. It felt like an instinct to go after her. I had to let her know how sorry I was, how deplorable my behavior had been toward her—how uncharacteristic. There was so much I needed to apologize for. Somehow, I knew she was not okay—far from it. We needed to talk. The longer I sat there, the worse I felt. My guilt was unbearable.

"I'm gonna grab another beer," I said, pulling back my chair.

No one bothered to look at me, except for Ciara; she seemed worried as I walked past her and left the patio.

I entered the kitchen through the sliding doors and scanned the space, hoping to find Lana waiting for me, but that was wishful thinking. Without wasting time, I made my way upstairs and saw that her bedroom door had been left wide open. I never hated a central sound system more than I did at that moment. It probably would have been a good idea to have shut off the music before I came back inside, seeing as that blasted song was still playing. At the very least, I could have changed playlists... but I needed to be close to her. It was all I could think about, ignoring the flashbacks in my mind.

"Lana?"

I let myself into her space, only to discover that she wasn't there. And then, I heard something coming from the bathroom... quiet sobs.

Fuck.

Reaching for the doorknob, I tried to open it, but it was locked. Of course, it would be. Her walls were up.

"Lana, please let me in," I gently spoke.

There was a momentary pause before I heard a running faucet. It switched off shortly after.

"Why did you follow me, Vincent?"

"I just want to talk. I know you're not okay."

I pressed my hand against the door and desperately prayed that she'd believe my sincerity. I didn't care about us getting caught. I didn't care if I had raised suspicions about being up there with her. All I knew was that she was hurting, and it was my own bloody fault.

"I'm fine. You can leave."

How could I when there was so much pain in her voice? It was killing me. I wanted to comfort her. She needed to let me. I could make it right. I could make all of it right, I told myself.

"Lana, please... don't make me beg you so much. Open up and let me talk to you."

"I said I'm all right."

I clenched my fist, resisting the urge to punch it through the fucking door. It would have only terrified her, sabotaging my efforts to make her feel safe. I wanted to hold her, not give her more reasons to shut me out, even though she had every right to.

"I'm not the 'Big Bad Wolf' you believe I am." I sighed, feeling miserable, leaning against the door. "I wish I could take back that night... wish I could take back every awful thing I said to you. I'm disgusted with myself. Do you honestly believe last Halloween is the only time that weighs heavily on my conscience?"

I waited for a response... something, *anything*, but she was quiet. All I heard was silent weeping in the background.

"Lana, I swear to God I'm in hell right now. Please, let me in. Let me see your eyes."

Desperation was getting to me as I panicked out of frustration and fear. Through the years, I had mastered how to disguise my sadness as anger, but I couldn't let that ugly demon out in that moment. I knew I had to be vulnerable.

"Lana..."

Time moved slowly as I waited, cursing myself for hurting her so much. I cared. She had to know that I did. I was about to give up when the door finally unlocked. Immediately, I moved my hands off the barrier and watched it open a crack, noticing a sliver of light. She was letting me in. I felt relieved.

Treading with caution, I gently pushed through and shut the door behind me, as if it were the only way to shelter ourselves from the world. I found Lana sitting on the edge of a tub, mascara running down her cheeks. How many times had I made her cry like this in the past? I was gutted. I hated myself. Now that I could see her broken state, I struggled to find my voice.

"Lana... Please forgive me... I never meant the things I said that night."

"What are you talking about?" She stood up.

The orchid I had tucked in her hair fell to the floor, as if it also despised me for touching it earlier.

"I know why you're crying, all right? It's that bloody song... the masquerade ball... I may have forgotten what happened in Miami ten years ago, but I haven't forgotten all the shitty things I said to you last year. I didn't mean a word of it."

"You did."

"I swear I didn't. Just please let me—"

She stepped back when I approached her, hugging her arms to her chest as if to close off from me.

"Why would you want to be with somebody who is beneath you and will *always* be beneath you, remember, Vincent?"

I searched her tearful eyes and took a moment to gather my thoughts. How could so much ugliness exist inside of me? I didn't want to cry. Men don't cry, I repeated in my head.

"*I* am the one who is beneath you, Lana. I promise you that."

When I took another step, she raised her hand to stop me from getting closer, which made me feel like a cold-hearted tyrant. Maybe because I was. My immature insults had done a number on her.

"I don't deserve you," I said, fighting through the anguish in my voice. "I know I don't deserve your time. I don't even deserve your forgiveness, but I can't stand to see you suffer, Lana… it feels like my heart's bleeding."

She closed her eyes, black tears streaking down her face: a gut-wrenching torture to witness, but I continued to pour my heart out to her. I owed her that much.

"I know you've seen the worst of me, love, but I *beg you* to let me show you the best."

"How can you be so blind, Vincent?" she cried. "You're married! *I'm* married! I'm no longer that broken teenager you rescued from drowning, and *you* are not the same man you used to be. I don't even know if he's still alive in there."

"I admit I've been living somewhat blindly for the past decade, but I can see everything so clearly now for the first time." I paused, bridging the gap between us.

"I don't give a rat's arse that you're married—you're not even happy! My father doesn't deserve you—he's play acting, and it's obvious that my marriage is failing. Don't you understand? This is *destiny*, Lana. You and I... we deserve a second chance."

"It's too late for that." She wiped her eyes, shaking her head. "All this time, I'd hoped you would remember our history. I was convinced that you did but didn't care—that's the impression you gave me, at least. Now that you know who I really am, I almost wish you never did. Maybe it would've been better."

"How can you say that?" I glowered, controlling my anger. "You have no idea what it's like to wake up every bloody day, go to work, come home, be a good dad, be a good husband, all while feeling *dead* inside. That's been my reality for years now, Lana."

"I know what it means to suffer to the point of begging for death." She sniffled, wiping her tears as she stared through me. "You saved me from suicide, remember?"

It hurt to recall.

"You've had a privileged life from the moment you were born, Vincent—but *I'm* 'white trash' in comparison, right? A girl who was raised dirt poor by a junkie for a mother... my feelings, my experiences, and hardships don't matter because I wasn't born into status like *you*, and you've made that clear to me *many* times over. I'll never forget."

"I said those repulsive things because I *wanted* you to hate me. I felt attracted to you from the moment Dad introduced us, for fuck's sake... it made me lose my head constantly around you. It's no excuse, but it's the truth, I swear."

Her silence gave me hope. I debated telling her about that disparaging email. I wanted to come clean about it, despite my father's request. I needed to clear my conscience.

Fuck it.

"Look, it didn't help that one of your exes emailed me last year and accused you of cheating and escorting."

She froze, fresh tears filling her eyes.

"Oh, my god..."

I watched all the color drain from Lana's face. I didn't like this part, but she had to know.

"André emailed you, too?" she asked in horror.

"He didn't give a name, but he slandered you and said you were unfaithful throughout the relationship."

"That's not true!" She choked up.

"Lana, he had sent me a folder full of your nudes and videos, insisting that you were escorting behind his back."

This conversation felt like déjà vu, I thought, remembering my "nightmare" of Lana in the woods.

"I was never unfaithful to him, Vincent, and I never prostituted myself. Ever. But even if I did, what right do you have to judge me? How dare you!"

She was outraged, and I couldn't blame her.

"I've never worked in the sex industry. I don't look down on anyone in this profession because it's not my place to judge! Have you walked in their shoes? Do you know what it's like to struggle financially? Get off your fucking high horse, Vincent!"

I felt like shit. I couldn't argue with her.

"I apologize, Lana. You're right. I'm so sorry. Please, just—"

"Don't touch me!" She hid her face in her hands and quietly heaved. "I don't understand why that asshole won't leave me alone. I gave him my everything, and all he gave me was betrayal and pain."

I hated seeing her break down like this. It hurt my titanium heart.

"My father made me promise not to tell you about the email. I apologize for ripping old wounds, but I just need you to understand why I had such a terrible impression of you. I feel horrible."

"That explains a lot." Lana cried, avoiding my gaze. "Vincent, you need to know that my relationship with André was abusive." She finally looked at me with what seemed like newfound courage. "He broke my trust. *He* was the one who was cheating, not me. All I did was give him unconditional love—especially to the monster that

he hid from the world; I loved and nurtured that part of him, too...
which explains the photos and videos.

"I was uncomfortable with it at first, but I wanted to make him
happy. I wanted to be a good girlfriend, especially since I'd
consented to a more submissive role in our relationship. He often
recorded our intimacy and took nude photos of me, promising that
it was for *his eyes* only. I was so naïve, so stupid to trust him and
ignore all the red flags. I was clueless about what a healthy BDSM
lifestyle was all about." Lana collected herself as I handed her a
tissue.

"I don't even like saying his name—makes me sick to my
stomach." She wept. "He had so many side chicks that I was
suspicious about, but he always denied being unfaithful... until I
caught him in bed with three other women and broke up with him
shortly after. It devastated me. He thought I'd never leave, no
matter what. That's why he tried to destroy my relationship with
Max last year when he emailed him and slandered me with lies and
revenge porn. I had no idea that he'd emailed you as well." Lana
stifled her sobs, shaking her head. "I'm so embarrassed... oh my
God..."

I couldn't stand to see her suffering like this, knowing I had
caused her more trauma with my prejudice.

"I'll find him and kill him myself, Lana. Please don't cry. I'm
deeply remorseful for misjudging you. You have nothing to feel
ashamed about. I'm the one who's embarrassed."

She hugged her arms to her chest and cried, unable to face me.

"This is why I've been scared to kick off my writing career in the
'big leagues.' I'm afraid that André will leak all those scandalous
photos and videos he took of me to hurt my reputation. I don't think
I could handle suffering through a nightmare like that while in the
limelight—it would damage my professional career. Max assured me
that my fears will never manifest, but you don't know my ex... he's
a vindictive sociopath. I feel helpless and trapped."

"I'll hire a private investigator and have it taken care of, Lana."

"It's not your battle to fight, Vincent. I blame myself for getting involved with a man like that."

"He's not a man. He's a coward. I promise you I'll have this handled if my father hasn't already."

I wanted nothing more than to pull her into my arms and kiss the pain away. I had felt nothing like this in my life—to *this* depth.

"At the risk of sounding like a love-drunk, fool, I *need* to say this, Lana. I don't care anymore. I don't give a fuck if it sounds 'out of character' to me."

"Stop."

"You need to hear this." I reached for her face, searching her misty eyes. "Lana, you captured my heart from the moment I pulled you out of that ocean; you kept it with you all these years, only to return it to me when we kissed again in that basement last night." I paused, gauging her expression before I confessed something I probably should have kept to myself.

"I wasn't in love with Claire when I married her. I settled out of pressure from her and our parents."

"Vincent, that's enough." She raised her hand. "Do you even know what you're saying?"

"Don't you want to hear the damn truth? Let me give you full disclosure so you can understand my love/hate relationship with you this past year."

"I understand you hated me. You already explained your reasons."

Bloody hell.

How could I make her see my point of view?

"Lana, listen to me... I don't know how to handle all these emotions right now—too bloody intense. I've just been thinking nonstop about the possibility of us being—"

"Don't! Don't even go there."

She looked repulsed by my confession, but it didn't stop me from baring my soul.

"I want you."

"Stop it!"

"And I know you want me—"

"I won't listen to this!"

"You *will*, and you *are...*"

I reached for her waist, but she pushed me back, rejecting my touch.

"You're more messed up than I thought," she said with revulsion. "So, it's okay to insult me and belittle me to my face, but then turn around and fantasize about fucking me behind my back? What the hell is wrong with you?"

"Don't pretend like you haven't fantasized, Lana."

"I'm done."

This was not how I wanted this conversation to go.

"You should leave," she demanded. "I need to get cleaned up."

"*No.* I'm not gonna leave you like I stupidly did on that dance floor last year. I'm a stubborn prick. You won't get rid of me that easily." I stood my ground, searching her eyes for the longest while. "Tell me you have absolutely no feelings for me, and I will leave you alone. I will stay silent on this subject forever, I promise."

I made one last attempt to get closer.

"Say it, Lana"—I cupped her face—"tell me you don't feel a pull when I'm near you. Tell me your heart doesn't race when our eyes meet—that you don't fantasize about me touching you... kissing you." My words slipped out in a whisper as I looked for a sign in her gloomy gaze, praying I'd find something, anything to give me hope.

"Vincent, I can't do this with you right now. I—"

Fuck's sake.

"... you're not thinking clearly, and I've had a little too much to—"

I pulled her into me before she could finish and silenced her with a kiss that I'd been dying to give her all evening. I didn't care that it was wrong. I didn't care about my vows. I didn't give a bloody fuck anymore. All I knew was that she needed to know how badly I wanted her as I kissed her slow and passionately.

It was impulsive and desperate, but I had no regrets. How could I? It's what I'd always wanted—what I'd denied for far too long. Lana's lips seemed to hesitate at first, but the gentler I was, the more she loosened up and surrendered, letting me lure her into a thick, red fog. Her arms glided around my neck while I kissed her deeply, as if my life depended on it. Rationality had gone out the window when I gripped her thighs and lifted her on the bathroom vanity. This was wrong on all levels, but my moral compass wasn't strong enough to guide me away from the dangerous position I was in: between Lana's beautiful legs. I couldn't rip myself away from her. Every part of me wanted to selfishly take, until she was completely inside of me, a merged identity. Was that even possible? Was that even healthy? I asked myself, feeling my body come to life when she whimpered in my mouth. It was ten years' worth of repressed emotions, desires, and physical longing. I couldn't stop myself, even if I wanted to.

"Vincent," Lana breathed against my lips. "Please, stop—"

"I can't." I bit her bottom lip and sucked it back like a ravenous beast.

Her sultry moans triggered movement in my trousers. I wanted her. I wanted to take her right there and then. There was no way I could logically think this through. I felt like a man on fire, and the only way to put out the flames was through Lana... inside of her.

But everything came to a screeching halt when I heard Claire's voice in the distance. She called out our names and entered Lana's bedroom.

Fuck.

I had to think fast.

Lana was the first to break the kiss, panting breathlessly as we stared at one another. Fear and panic danced in her glistening eyes.

She seemed afraid that we had been caught. I brushed my thumb across her swollen lip and softly kissed her forehead while ignoring my arousal. I had selfishly acted on my own desires and had pulled her into something she did not want to be in. Reality was a hard pill to swallow. Lana was right: so much had changed. I couldn't turn back the clock. What was I thinking?

As I untangled myself from her, I glanced at the bathroom door, wishing I could enter a different dimension once I'd walk out—a parallel reality, an exclusive paradise where only Lana and I existed. My former self would remain here for Claire and the kids, but this parallel timeline... it was just for us.

Lana got off the vanity and grabbed a tissue to wipe her eyes. All that crying had left dark track marks down her face. I still felt bad.

"Lana?" Claire called out again, making us both panic; she was standing right behind the bathroom door. I knew how this was going to look.

Lana discarded her tissue in a bin and reached for the doorknob when I stopped her.

"Are you in here?"

I had to act fast as I unlocked the door and opened it.

"Hey... what are you guys—"

"Lana's unwell," I explained to my wife. "I came upstairs to grab my phone when I heard her vomiting."

"Oh, honey, you're not getting sick, are you?"

"I..." Lana glanced at me. "I think it's because I mixed my liquor tonight."

"Maybe take some Gravol?" Claire suggested. "We've got some in our medicine cabinet."

"The nausea's gone."

I could see the guilt on Lana's face. I felt horrible for putting her in this position.

"Do you want me to get Max up here?" Claire asked.

"I'm feeling much better, really. I kept telling Vincent to leave."
My wife didn't seem too convinced.

"I promise I'm fine. Just let me brush my teeth and I'll be down shortly." Lana looked at me and said, "Thank you for checking on me, Vincent."

I gave a nod and paused at the door after Claire walked out, but Lana wouldn't meet my gaze. We had almost been discovered. It was worth the risk. I didn't regret it. Not one bit. I wanted her. I wanted to fight for the possibility of us being together. She was worth it. *We* were worth a second chance, regardless of how much time had gone by. I wasn't ready to surrender hope.

CHAPTER TWENTY-ONE

LANA

"Aunt Lana?"

"Yes, Lilly?"

"Why is the sky blue?"

"Molecules in the air scatter blue light from the sun more than they scatter other colors."

"What are *molly-kewls*?"

"Um, well... it's a group of atoms held together by chemical bonds."

"*Adams?*" She giggled.

Gosh, I felt so out of my element. Breaking down simple science to a six-year-old was not my forte.

"What are *adams?*" Lilly asked, staring at the sky.

I tried to rack my brain for the easiest scientific explanation. "*Atoms* are something you will learn about once you start fifth grade, sweetie."

We were lying on a blanket beneath a weeping willow on the side property of the house. I had a pleasant view of a wooden dock that stretched out over the water in the distance.

"You're so smart, Lana."

"I wasn't as smart as you when I was your age."

"Really?"

"Really, really."

I met Lilly's vibrant blue eyes and tickled her tummy as her adorable laughter echoed around us. I spent a good portion of my afternoon catching sun rays and reading Elizabeth Gaskell's *North and South* on the dock. I loved 19th century British Literature. When Lilly had come by, I had moved the blanket under the tree to shield her from the sun and keep her away from the water. Surprisingly, she didn't get bored. She hung out with me and pointed out shapes in the clouds while we listened to music on my iPhone.

"Are you sure your mommy and daddy know that you're out here?"

"Mhm," she replied, curling up against me.

Lilly was such an affectionate child. She reminded me of myself when I was her age. I loved hugging everyone, but in my case, affection was rarely ever returned from my mother.

"Can we watch a movie later, Lana?"

"Of course, sweetheart,"

I felt so at peace out here. Having Lilly next to me was a comfort as well. Every time I looked at her, I saw her father in her eyes.

"So, *that's* where you've run off to..."

Vincent's deep voice caught my attention as I took off my sunglasses and saw him towering above us. He smiled, sliding his hands in the pockets of his shorts. I felt nervous. My efforts to avoid him were not so successful.

"I just wanted to hang out with Lana, Daddy."

"You should have told your mum and me before prancing out here on your own." Vincent crouched next to her and lay back on the blanket.

"I told Mommy," Lilly said, "I guess she wasn't listening."

"Maybe she just didn't hear you." He kissed her plump cheek and bent an elbow on his side, resting his head in his hand before he looked at me. "How are you doing today, Lana?"

"I'm doing well, Vincent, thank you." I tried to remain respectful. Things had gotten way too intense between us last night. We needed a cool off period.

"Daddy, we were looking for pictures in the clouds!"

"Is that so?" He charmingly smiled. "What did you find, princess?"

"A flower, a bird, and a bag of chips!"

"A bag of *crisps...* now, *that* I've never seen before." Vincent's laughter died down as he glanced at me again. "My daughter has quite the imagination."

"She definitely has an artistic perspective." I smiled and played with her silky brown locks.

This moment, this moment right here, was perfect. Lilly was so precious, so innocent, and pure. I didn't know I could love a child so much. It hurt to think of not seeing her one day. My own childhood innocence had been corrupted by traumas no one should experience, let alone a helpless little person. But I was determined to put those years behind me.

Was this how I imagined my life? Was *this* what I always wanted, to have the picture-perfect family of my own with this man? It was all I could think about, as I lay there, ruminating all the "what ifs."

For the first time, Vincent didn't snatch his daughter away from me. In the past he had accused me of "poisoning Lilly's mind," as if I were some evil Disney queen. Anytime she had been alone with me, it agitated him. But now, he seemed so relaxed. He looked content— almost like he was happy that Lilly was spending time with me.

Staring up at the swaying branches, I remembered the last time Vincent and I had stood under this tree. Our conversation had been heated. I had angered him—not on purpose, of course.

"Lilly, my love," said Vincent, "why don't you go inside and play with your brother?"

"No! I wanna stay here with you and Lana. Milo always knocks down my toys!"

"He's only two, sweetheart. You used to do the same at his age. How about you read him a book? I'm sure he will enjoy that."

I could tell that Vincent was conveniently trying to create some "alone time" with me. But I wasn't sure if he would succeed.

"I'll take you out for ice cream later…"

Lilly suddenly lit up with excitement. "O-kay!" She sat up.

"Good girl."

Bribing her seemed to have worked. She gave me one last hug and then kissed her father's cheek before skipping back to the house. Vincent watched her to make sure she got in before he turned his gaze on me.

I was about to get up when he pressed his palm on my stomach.

"Stay," he murmured.

"Vincent, we can't just—"

His lips crashed against mine before I could finish my sentence. As amazing as it felt to lose myself in the heat of his kiss, I hadn't forgotten what I'd read about boundaries in a self-help book. I didn't care how sexy this man was. I had boundaries that needed to be respected. I did *not* want to pull back, but I had to. Somehow, I regained control and pushed him off me.

"Have you completely lost it?" I nearly shouted. "What the hell is wrong with you?"

"Yes, I've gone bloody mad, I'll admit." He attempted to kiss me again, but I sat up and stopped him.

"Do you realize that our friends and spouses are inside and can walk out here?"

"I'm aware." Vincent smiled.

"This isn't a joke." I frowned. "You really need to exercise some self-control."

"I've been doing that for over a year." He looked up at the tree and then met my eyes again. "I'd say these branches have us safely hidden from any 'peeping Toms.'"

"You're kidding me, right?" I arched an eyebrow. "You can't just grab me and kiss me whenever you feel like it. Please take me seriously."

"I am, I just..." Vincent sighed. "I need to be close to you, Lana."

"We almost got caught last night."

"I don't care about getting caught."

"Are you trying to sabotage your marriage by using me as the scapegoat?"

He frowned, offended. "You really think I'm playing head games with you?"

"It's what you're best at."

"You sound resentful, Lana."

"Maybe I am. Can you blame me?"

Vincent Luther was all about mind games. It was all he did with me for the past year. There were so many arguments I could have used as ammunition against him, but I stayed quiet. Knowing him, I probably would have set him off on another raging tirade had I dissected his personality out loud.

"We can't do this," I firmly stated. "It's *wrong*. I know I told you I'm unhappy and planning on ending my marriage to Max, but you have children, Vincent. As much as I want to relive some memories with you, it's just not possible. Everything would lead to a dead end."

He looked at me with a painful longing in his eyes. It honestly hurt to reject him. All I wanted to do was hide myself in his arms and have a good cry.

"We can figure it out," he finally responded. "I don't want to give up a genuine shot at happiness with you. Don't you think we owe it to ourselves after everything?"

"Figure what out?" I hid my outrage. "That little girl of yours needs *both* her parents in her life—so does Milo. You can't be selfish here."

"Are you saying I'm thoughtlessly neglecting my children's happiness?"

"You're taking my words out of context."

"Really? Then explain what you meant, please—because it sounded like you were questioning my competency as a parent and labeling me as a selfish pig at the same time."

His stony gaze made me freeze up.

"Well?"

"I don't want to engage in an extramarital affair with you!" I blurted out.

Vincent slit his eyes and raised his voice. "I'm not some narcissistic, self-gratifying wanker!"

"Stop shouting at me!"

"I'm not!"

"Do I need to record our conversation and play it back for you, Vincent?"

"Don't be childish." He glowered. "Look, Lana, I'm just... I'm frustrated, okay? I can't function like this. There's history between us."

I got to my feet and looked down at him. "It's over and done. We can't turn back the clock." Tears clouded my vision as I weakly uttered, "I'm sorry."

With a heavy heart, I forced myself to walk away, but was quickly tugged back under the tree into Vincent's arms.

"I miss your fighting spirit," he whispered, gently ghosting the back of his hand across my cheek.

"I never had one."

"You fought to stay alive when I placed you down on that beach strip."

"That's where you're wrong." I shook my head. "*You* were the one who fought for my life. Not me."

My response brought a deafening silence between us as a gentle breeze whipped through my hair, caressing the leaves of the willow tree while they rustled in a low hush. I was battling with myself, unsure of what I wanted most. The air was humid, but being in Vincent's arms only spiked my body temperature to fever pitch.

His penetrative stare crumbled my walls and compelled me to not look away.

"I'm going to kiss you now," he confessed in a deep, seductive voice.

"Please don't."

"You'll have to slap me to stop me."

"Never."

I could never do that to him.

"Vincent," I pleaded, eyes filling with tears.

He gently rested his hand along the curve of my jaw and slowly closed the distance between our lips, until I felt myself soaring, weightless: that's what his kiss did to me. I was seventeen again, naively in love and completely blinded to the consequences of falling for him.

The longer we kissed, the more he lost control and abandoned his self-restraint. Vincent gripped my waist and pushed me against the tree. I had little time to register what was happening before I found myself lip-locked with such a racing force, unable to free myself.

"I can't function around you anymore"—he panted—"not after remembering everything."

He brushed his fingers up my outer thighs beneath my coral dress, causing goosebumps to form on my skin. We were two broken souls, facing one another, holding on to a thread of hope while believing that we could mend the damage of our past. All I could see was the demolition of our dreams and everything that could have been. But Vincent was blind to it. His perception of reality was filtered through a lens of optimism, passion, and the reminiscent feelings of young love. We were different people then; he had to accept this.

At present, I couldn't even recognize who he was. Was this the same man who had walked hand in hand with me on a beach ten years ago? The same man I had danced with by the shore under a bridge in Miami? His face had lost his boyish youth, but he was more attractive with age than when I'd first met him.

"Don't expect me to put on an act, Lana."

"Nothing has changed."

"*Everything* has changed!"

"We're both married."

"To the wrong people!"

I was at a loss for words before I finally said, "You don't mean that."

"I've said a lot of rubbish to you in the past—things I didn't mean. But I've never been more serious than I am at this very moment, right here, right now."

There was so much sexual tension between us; I could see it in his eyes, liquid intensity melting me to the core. I was familiar with that stare. He had looked at me like this during many heated arguments in the past. The only difference now was that he wasn't attacking me with insults. He was fighting for our love.

"Vincent, do you remember the last conversation we had under this tree?"

He stayed quiet and averted his gaze, as if I had injured him with a rude reminder.

"I'm sure you've long forgotten."

"I haven't," he bitterly replied.

"I remember it well." I blinked back tears. "I can't forget all the awful things you said to me this past year."

"Lana, *please*," he painfully voiced, "don't hold a grudge against me. I beg you."

I couldn't see the sun in his eyes anymore; it was hidden behind gloomy, dark clouds that were on the verge of pouring. My personal anguish seemed to disappear when I absorbed his emotions, as if they were my own to feel and process: the curse of an empath. It was torture. I couldn't bear to witness his turmoil like this.

"Let's get out from under this tree." Vincent took my hand.

"No." I withdrew. "It's not just about what happened last year." I took a deep breath and stared at him. "Just leave me in peace."

"Lana, you've been ignoring me all day. Don't do this to me. There's no use in retrieving painful memories that only hurt us."

"*Us*?" I scowled. "There is no us."

"There *is*. It's always been that way. You know it. *I* know it." He reached for my hip and caressed my face. "Tell me how to forget you, and I'll do it. How do I shred these memories of you in my mind? How do I stop myself from feeling the way I do every time you look at me with those soulful eyes? Tell me how to do it, Lana, and I will."

Where was the cynical man who had mocked love and romance? He seemed to have vanished as I stayed silent.

"You have no answer for me because you don't want me to erase you," said Vincent. "Isn't it bad enough that my memories of you had been repressed all this time? Why would you want to go back to that way of existing?"

"Vincent, I'm scared."

"Of what?"

"I'm scared you'll disappear on me like you did all those years ago."

"That bloody accident took me away from you, Lana. *Claire* took me away—her jealousy, her manipulation... I was planning to see you again sooner than you'd think. I wanted us traveling to Europe in the summer... going on adventures together. I wanted to love you slowly, despite how fast I felt things inside."

My head was in a state of chaos. I wasn't ready to have this conversation. It was pointless.

"I can't do this with you right now, Vincent. I'm sorry. Please, just go."

"Are you rejecting me?" He sounded hostile and threatening. "Yes or no? It's a simple question."

"Yes!"

I was expecting him to challenge me further, but he pulled away, fuming in silence.

"I'm not the monster you believe I am, Lana, but if I must act like one to get you to acknowledge my existence, then so be it."

High voltage currents crackled between us, making it almost unbearable to keep my distance. I wanted to say something, but my brain was paralyzed in panic. I never thought I would be in a situation like this.

Walking away, Vincent suddenly paused and turned around, striding toward me. My heart violently thudded in my chest as I tried to brace myself for whatever came. But before I could guess his next move, he took my face in his hands and kissed me long and hard. It was instant ecstasy, liquifying my soul. I couldn't rip myself away from him. I didn't want to. I selfishly surrendered and forgot all my boundaries.

When he finally broke contact, I was breathless and delirious with desire.

"I should've done that last summer," he confessed, "when we stood in this exact spot... God knows I wanted to. It was all I could think about when I saw you that night... ravishing you."

His gaze was intimidatingly intense, which made it that much harder to recover from his insatiable kiss.

"Don't worry," said Vincent. "That won't happen again, I promise. I just needed to taste you one last time."

Something about the way he said those words made my heart sink. He wasn't lying. I saw it in his eyes before he released me and left. Why did I feel like he was abandoning me all over again? I had told him to leave, but... this... *hurt*.

Standing beneath that willow tree, I was overwhelmed by a flood of memories that I wished I had never conjured.

CHAPTER TWENTY-TWO

VINCENT

June 21, 2016

Summer evenings in Ocean City, Maryland, were an artist's dream; the landscape was simply picturesque, extending from Sinepuxent Bay to the Delaware Line near the Atlantic. Sunsets by the boardwalk were even more breathtaking. Maxwell Luther's renovated beach house was one of many golden properties that was considered a hidden gem. Every summer solstice was a cause for celebration, as the Luthers hosted an annual event at their summer home. Paper lamps illuminated the long driveway that led to the family estate through a tunnel of trees. White cabana tents were set up in the yard, near the waterfront, as the guests chattered amongst themselves, enjoying the food, music, and the pleasant party atmosphere. The guest list consisted of a hundred people; family and friends that were close to the Luthers.

Celebrating the summer solstice was a tradition that Isobel Luther had started over a decade ago before her passing. Lana had followed Isobel's philanthropic footsteps by hosting a party every summer to fundraise for charity in her honor. While her initiative had delighted her husband, it did not sit well with his temperamental son, Vincent. He resented her for marrying his father, and his resentment only grew when she took over Isobel's charitable endeavors. He felt she had no right. But that did not discourage Lana from organizing the event to the best of her ability. For her, it was never about "dressing to impress," nor showing off her social status; she genuinely wanted to raise money for cancer research, the same illness that took Isobel Luther's life.

Everyone was dressed in formal attire that evening, mingling among the crowd, holding flutes of fizzy champagne. Some of the wealthiest guests were investment bankers, lawyers, and politicians who were more than willing to write a fat check for charity. It was narcissism disguised as philanthropy. Lana had always felt out of place with her husband's social circle. But if there was one thing she was good at, it was charming older men into spending money for a good cause.

She had hired performers from a reputable company to entertain her guests that night. A stage was set up on the lawn, where fire dancers performed, twirling their flaming staffs in beat with the lively music. Aerial dancers weightlessly floated on red silk that hung from an aerial apparatus, impressing the audience with their athletic flexibility. A trio of foot jugglers were up to perform later, including Hula Hoop gymnasts.

They had also hired a psychic medium by the name of *Madame Natalka*. She had set up her purple starry tent near a large gazebo in the garden, where curious guests could enter and receive a tarot reading. The festivities had a magical *Gatsby-esque* atmosphere that seemed to have impressed everyone who attended. Isobel Luther would have loved it, had she been alive to join the event. It was Lana's first year as hostess. She had truly outdone herself, though Vincent would have told her otherwise.

A soulful love ballad brought all the couples to the dance floor as they slowly swayed to a classical medley of Above and Beyond's "Satellite" and "Stealing Time." The male and female vocalist sang their beautiful duet on stage together, accompanied by a sinfonietta: a small orchestra that heightened the romantic atmosphere with the riveting sounds of cellos, violins, piano, and harp.

The pool area had been covered with tempered glass, transforming it into a dance floor; its beautiful design had required preparation weeks in advance. Lana had coordinated everything perfectly, from caterers to party planners to floral staff. There wasn't a single guest that was underwhelmed by Lana's extravagant efforts... except for Vincent.

He stood near an open bar, brooding, per usual, dressed in a tailored tux. Lana could have invited the Queen of England, and he still would not have cared. He watched his wife chatting away with their friends at a table while he waited on his drink, ignoring how much he did not want to be there. Beneath all his anger was prolonged grief. It hurt to return to their family's summer home, knowing that his mother's life had been cut short through such unfair circumstances. Vincent still could not come to terms with his loss. It had only been seven months since they had buried her in a cemetery. His father's impulsive decision to get married again had only worsened and delayed Vincent's grieving process. He was still stuck in the anger stage, resenting his father for moving on so quickly.

It was a quarter past ten when Vincent glanced at his silver Rolex. Maxwell and Lana were nowhere to be found.

Probably screwing her inside, he assumed in disgust, gulping back a glass of Bourbon.

He left the bartender a generous tip and turned around, letting his eyes roam through the crowd while he sipped on his drink. The twinkling fairy lights that hung beneath the dinner tents made Vincent feel as if he were at a wedding reception. The dress code on Lana's invitation card had clearly stated that it was a black-tie event. Beautiful women were dressed in colorful silk, chiffon, and lacey gowns—nothing that caught Vincent's attention... until he saw *her.*

She seemed to shimmer in the distance as she confidently made her way down the patio steps, wearing open-toe heels and a strapless, nude, sequin dress that tightly hugged her hourglass figure. Vincent could not take his eyes off her. He was spellbound, unable to tear himself away from the vision of beauty that had captivated him. Like a man possessed, his resentment suddenly vanished, replaced by a feeling that he could not admit to himself—not out loud.

Lana's tanned skin had a lovely glow that only made her stand out among a sea of faces. She wore her hair down in waves over her shoulder, with a white rose tucked behind her right ear. Her diamond necklace glistened and sparkled, accentuating her long, feminine neck. She looked as if she had walked off the set of a high fashion photoshoot. Her desirability was truly something to be coveted. But as stunning as she was, Lana's beautiful heart only magnified her natural allure. It was a shame that Vincent was blind to this.

Their eyes locked for a second before she looked away and stepped into the party atmosphere. Vincent continued to drink by the bar, observing the way she politely extended her hand and introduced herself to guests. He watched the way Lana's lips would curl into the softest smile whenever she was complimented; the way her cheeks would turn a rosy shade of pink, as she would laugh off her flattery. He studied her every move and interaction, unaware of the way she had bewitched him.

Time had seemed to stand still. Vincent could not understand his attraction to his father's wife. From the moment he had met her, he had labeled Lana McKenzie as an opportunist, and he still refused to change his mind. Yet, in that moment, right there, he could almost fool himself into believing that she was a good woman who truly cared about people. She had organized this fundraiser in memory of his mother, after all.

To feed her own ego, he concluded, forcing himself to snap out of the spell he was under.

A magical seduction was in the air that night, whispering through the wild orchids and rose bushes, spreading their fragrant scents into the vibrant ambiance, like invisible fairy dust, floating above the crowds. It seemed as if anyone could have fallen in love that evening.

Wherever Vincent went, Lana's perfume lingered. It frustrated him and increased his irritable mood, but he vowed to interact with her as little as possible. He had nothing of substance to say to her and was disinterested in making any effort at shallow conversation. She might have fooled everyone, but she could not fool him, he thought resolutely. He had decided about her, regardless of his sexual desires. Lana was not worthy of his respect, Vincent proudly believed. The sooner this evening ended, the happier he would be.

ڃڀ

Aside from the occasional secret glances, Vincent had avoided crossing paths with his father's wife for a couple hours. Maxwell had not appeared at the fundraiser, which only upset Vincent. He dealt with his disappointment by drinking more than he should have. Slightly tipsy, he took a stroll on the lawn with his wife when she begged him to come with her to meet *Madame Natalka*. Claire was curious and excited to receive a psychic reading. As a pragmatist, Vincent did not believe in horoscopes, mediums, or anything related to supernatural and paranormal forces. He was a practical man who believed in science and the empirical. But he humored Claire that night, sitting next to her in a dimly lit tent.

A woman in her late forties emerged through a silver curtain and sat across from the couple near a round table. She had a gaunt face with long auburn hair, dark makeup, and a case of heterochromia: one gray eye, one hazel. Decorated in jewelry, she wore bangles, rings, and several occult talismans that hung around her neck. At first glance, it was easy to assume that she was playing a stereotypical role of a "gypsy woman." When she introduced herself as "Madame Natalka," her thick Russian accent was noticeable, though Vincent was convinced it was all part of her act. He had to stifle his laughter whenever she spoke; it seemed so fake, he thought. Her collection of crystals, incense, candles, and tarot cards were all props from his point of view, not genuine divination tools that opened the mystical portal to the spirit world.

"Natalka tell your fortune!" The woman beamed, shuffling a 72 deck of cards full of major and minor arcana: visual archetypes of the human experience. Her English was not fluent, but she knew enough to get her point across.

"This is so exciting!" Claire clapped. "It's nice to meet you, Natalka! I'm Claire and this is my husband, Vincent."

They shook hands before the old woman continued shuffling her tarot deck while muttering an incomprehensible mantra to herself. She asked Claire some basic questions pertaining to her zodiac sign and date of birth.

"I'm a Libra. Vincent's on the cusp of Scorpio and Sagittarius."

"We focus on *you* for now," said Natalka. "Husband later." She took her time, placing ten cards down in a Celtic Cross spread.

Natalka flipped each card and explained their symbolism, speaking at length on the metaphorical meanings behind major arcana cards such as "Justice, The Moon, The Empress, and The Lovers." When she turned over the last card, she paused and pursed her lips.

"What does it mean?" Claire asked, slightly worried. "Is it bad?"

"Uh, no... not necessarily. Natalka sense you are feeling stuck in life." She picked up the card and reflected on it for a moment. "Something is troubling you and you need to get in touch with who you are because many, many time... you *feel*... life unsatisfying for you... you are hung upside down from sky, *lost*, just like this man here, see?" she explained in broken English, tapping her black polished nail on The Hanged Man.

"Hmm, I see," Claire nodded with genuine interest.

"You need emotional release from problem that makes you stuck. This card telling you must let go of something of less importance to gain something *greater*."

"You know what, that is so damn true!" Claire agreed.

"Overall, your reading is very, very good. Natalka impressed!"

"Thank you so much! You really put some things in perspective for me."

Vincent glared at his wife and muttered, "She really swindled us out of a hundred dollars, darling."

"Natalka's fortunes *real!*" The psychic woman frowned in contempt, offended by his bluntness.

"Yes, well, I'm sure if I wore a blue turban, grew a mustache, and called myself *The Great Vincenzo*, I'd be just as successful as you... can't forget the accent and referring to myself in third person—nice touch, *Natalka*."

Claire suddenly smacked Vincent's arm. "Stop offending her!" She looked at the old woman and apologized. "You'll have to forgive my husband. He's had too much to drink this evening, and he's not a very pleasant drunk. We'll be leaving now."

"*Finally.*" Vincent rolled his eyes.

He was about to get up when the Russian native grabbed his wrist and firmly said, "*Sit.*"

"Kindly remove your hand, please." Vincent glowered at her.

"Natalka prove herself. I tell your past, present, and future—no cards, just *these*..." She pointed at her eyes with two fingers and then aimed them at Vincent.

A lazy grin appeared on his face as he relaxed in his chair, amused by her proposal.

"All right," he said. "This should be interesting. Show me what *Natalka sees*," he mocked.

Claire quietly sat down next to her husband.

Natalka leaned forward across the table and peered into Vincent's cold, blue eyes, as if it were a staring contest. Twenty seconds went by before she spoke with intimidating authority.

"Past..."—she never blinked—"You experienced greatest love and lost it."

"*Please.*" Vincent scoffed. "That's so generic."

"Mermaid in ocean..." Natalka searched his gaze, as psychic visions appeared in her mind. "Beautiful, young woman under bridge... though, you don't remember this, it was where you shared love's first kiss."

Vincent's drunken laughter echoed around them.

"I've got to hand it to you, lady—wasn't expecting the rhyming scheme; it must be rehearsed. Please share a sample of whatever you're smoking. I'll even pay you for it."

Natalka ignored him and kept staring through his soul. "*Present...* mermaid walks on land. She's here. She remembers you. I feel her sadness very heavy. The cruelest destinies forced on you both... *tsk-tsk-tsk.*"

"Is there another woman I should know about, honey?" Claire teased.

"She love you still," Natalka continued. "She think of you always, even at this moment."

"Fantastic!" Vincent flashed a condescending smile. "I've got some fairy-tale mermaid in love with me, who also comes across as a stalker, to be perfectly blunt."

"*Future...*" The old woman ignored him. "You will kiss her again, and when you do, all will be restored to you. All that you lost, but it come with price..."

"Nothing's free in this world, lady," he chided.

Suddenly, Natalka gasped and went silent. Vincent waited for her to finish, but she said nothing.

"Well?" he asked. "What did you see? My inevitable pending doom? Premature death? Spit it out."

She looked at Claire with a sense of unease. "Natalka cannot say. Natalka cannot lie."

"Please tell us what you saw." Claire sounded worried. "How much are you charging for this session? I'll double your fee."

"No-no." The old woman waved her hands. "No money—free of charge."

"Then finish my bloody fortune!" Vincent angrily stated.

She glared at him and leaned in closer before icing her tone and saying, "*Future... you leave your wife.*"

There was nothing but dead silence. Vincent stood up, looking visibly upset.

"What a load of bollocks!" He glanced at Claire. "I've had enough. Come on." Impatiently, he took her hand and stormed out of the woman's tent.

"The mermaid is among you!" Natalka called after him. "Find her under the tree!"

Claire looked back at the purple tent and shuddered. "You were right," she sighed. "That old bat was totally conning us."

❧

The midnight hour was approaching 1am when Vincent noticed Lana was no longer sitting where he had last seen her. He quickly skimmed the premises but found no beautiful blonde in the lively crowd. He should have been relieved—ecstatic, in fact... but that was not the case. His suspicions about Lana made him quietly withdraw from the familiar crowd of socialites before he went inside the house to look for her. Vincent was hoping to catch her cheating... perhaps even *tied up*; he recalled those graphic images that were hid in a folder on his laptop. He had noticed the way a wealthy doctor had been flirting with her all evening. That same person appeared to have been missing from the party, as well. Vincent believed if he could prove Lana's "duplicitous nature," his father would divorce her in a heartbeat.

After entering each bedroom, he soon discovered that she was not in the summer home at all. Perplexed by her sudden disappearance, he stepped through a door that led to the side of the house and started walking down a lush green lawn that stretched out for acres. A full moon had cast its alluring reflection into the velvety waters of the tranquil sea. The humid temperature had cooled down, but Vincent still felt as if his skin couldn't breathe. He loosened the black bow around his collar and took off his blazer.

Expecting to discover his "stepmother" canoodling with another man, he was surprised to find her walking back from the dock, heels dangling in one hand, all by herself. She headed toward a weeping willow that majestically stood near the edge of the property.

Lana had not noticed Vincent approaching, as she dropped her shoes on the grass and leaned her weight against the tree. She stared up at the sky, losing herself in a sea of thoughts.

"I didn't think he'd find you boring this soon."

His deep voice gave her heart a sudden jolt as she turned and noticed him standing next to her. Lana's relaxed state of mind morphed into paranoia. She felt anxious around Vincent. His attractive physique only heightened her angst.

"Excuse me?"

"My father," he clarified. "Don't you find it odd that he pulls a disappearing act every time you host a party?"

"What are you implying?"

Vincent shoved his hands in his pockets and snickered under his breath. "I'm *implying* that he's out gallivanting, chasing skirts when he should be *here* chasing yours."

"Are you insinuating that my husband is cheating on me?"

"Clever woman," Vincent sarcastically replied.

"Max called and said he had an emergency business meeting. He's made some investments in solar energy. You know how busy your father gets—had to take a flight out to Monte Carlo."

"Right... 'busy.'"

Vincent hadn't forgotten about his father's extramarital affairs. Now that Max was married to a stunning young woman, he did not believe for a second that his father would stop his womanizing ways and remain loyal to Lana. Vincent pitied her.

"Maxwell loves me," Lana affirmed. "He wouldn't cheat on me."

"Sure, sweetheart, whatever helps you sleep at night."

His words upset her. All she wanted was to separate herself from those superficial people at the party, if only for a few minutes. She didn't need Vincent "whispering" poison in her ear like this. Despite her convincing smiles, Lana was miserable. She always felt out of place among Maxwell's social crowd. The fact that he had not shown up had disappointed her greatly.

"Why are you even here?" she asked with a hint of contempt. "Shouldn't you be with your wife?"

"Well, the party is quite dull, to be honest," Vincent replied. "So, I thought I'd come out here and berate you a bit. We both know that's my favorite form of entertainment."

He wasn't sure why he was being so mean to Lana again; she had not said or done anything to provoke him, yet he couldn't control his mouth whenever he was around her. It was almost as if she triggered the worst out of him.

"I practically hired our very own *Cirque du Soleil*, and you find it boring?" Lana questioned in disbelief.

"I hate the circus."

"They're professionals and incredibly talented! Those fire dancers were far from a hillbilly circus act."

"No," Vincent shrewdly replied. "That would require a band of redneck rodeo clowns that look like escaped convicts."

Lana laughed as Vincent tried his best to hide his own amusement. He felt an odd sense of déjà vu; it happened a lot around her. He couldn't make any sense of it.

"Well," she sighed, "at least you haven't complained about the food, so I guess it's not so bad."

"It could be better."

Lana rolled her eyes and shook her head at him.

"What? Just being honest," he said, unable to keep a straight face. Vincent watched her for a moment as the wind breezed through her golden locks.

Lana Del Rey's "Summertime Sadness" echoed behind them like a haunting melody that was written for a grieving lover.

"I love the ocean," Lana softy said, knowing it wasn't the first time she had told him.

"I don't."

"Why not?"

Vincent looked in her direction, feeling a poignant sorrow that he couldn't understand.

"I don't know. It's complicated."

For a moment Lana dared to hope that it had something to do with her.

"I feel sad whenever I'm near the sea," he added, "and I have no bloody clue why that is."

Vincent thought about discussing his car accident, but stopped himself. It was personal, and he still carried so much guilt. He did not want Lana to pity him.

"Repressed childhood trauma?" She risked a question.

"No." He frowned. "Like I said, I just… I feel a heavy weight on my chest when I'm near the ocean. I wasn't always like this, and it's not like I'm afraid of open water. I was captain of my swim team in college and a trained lifeguard."

"I know." She smiled.

He looked at her in confusion. "How do you know that? I never told you."

His hostile tone made Lana panic as she lied and said, "Max told me."

The song had reached its bridge as she listened to the beautiful lyrics, standing beside a man who had nothing but contempt for her. While they stared at the dark sea, Lana asked Vincent another question.

"If I were drowning in those waters right now, would you save me?"

"Well…" He let out a breathy laugh. "If I let you drown, technically, it wouldn't be murder," he teased.

"Have you ever saved a life before?"

"Yes, a few times—careless parents who let their kids play in the deep end, mostly."

Lana bit her lip and wondered if she should share what had happened to her. But before she could open up, Vincent changed the subject.

"I'm heading back inside. Don't wander into the sea. I won't be here to save you."

"Wait," she called out. "I didn't get a chance to thank you."

"*Thank me?*" He furrowed his brows. "For what?"

"For showing up tonight. I'm sure you didn't come on your own accord."

"You're right. Claire forced me to tag along."

Lana looked at him and blinked, injured by his brutal honesty. "Was that really necessary to say? I just wanted to be polite and thank you."

"Let's see... you hired some party planners to do all the work—all of which were funded by my father's wallet—hired a chef and caterers, also paid for with my father's money... oh, and you funded the monkey circus using what?" Vincent paused and flashed a patronizing grin. "*Sugar Daddy's* bank account."

"Why do you always look down on me?" Lana countered, visibly wounded.

"Because you're obviously a freeloader."

His laughter held nothing but cruel condescension. Everything he said had pounded her to the ground and crushed her dignity as she teared up.

"*Awww...* did I hurt your feelings?" Vincent jeered. "Trust me, sweetheart, I could do *much* worse."

Lana felt so torn. Every time Vincent was around her, all she could think about was that amazing summer that had faded away, as if it were nothing but a dream. She missed that man he used to be; she had fallen in love with that version of him. He had been so tender with her, so loving and sweet spoken. But the Vincent she knew at present was callous. He held no reservation with making her feel worthless. He had done it so much that she believed she deserved it.

"I just wanted to continue your mother's tradition," Lana uttered, her eyes filled with pain.

"This party is pathetic."

"I tried getting in touch with you so we could plan it together, Vincent. You avoided all my calls."

"Since when do I ever answer your phone calls?"

"You're the rudest man I know."

"Is that the best you can do?" He chuckled, folding his arms in his chest.

"That wasn't meant to be a 'comeback.' I was being honest."

"Ah. Well, in that case, you can keep your thoughts to yourself, because I personally don't give a flying fuck about what you think of me, Lana."

"No, of course you wouldn't."

His insensitivity stung her like a thousand bees.

But Vincent was lying. His cruelty was deliberate. Every time he was close to Lana, he felt a senseless need to pull her into his arms and kiss her. It drove him mad and the only way he coped with those unspoken desires was to push her away as best he could through unjustified spitefulness.

"That question you asked me earlier, Lana…" Vincent leaned into her ear and whispered, "I'd let you drown, and I wouldn't even feel like shit about it."

He glared at her in the most conceited way, putting her in what he believed to be her rightful place: *beneath* him.

"Now, if you excuse me, I need to join my wife and pretend to have a good time, for her sake, at least, since my father's too busy getting laid in Monte Carlo."

Lana held back tears, releasing them when Vincent finally walked off and abandoned her in the dark. He had shattered her once again. This time, she feared she was too weak to pick up the broken pieces of her dignity.

I made a mistake marrying Max; she told herself, desperate to break free; desperate to leave and never see Vincent's face again.

CHAPTER TWENTY-THREE

VINCENT

Vincent,

By the time you read this letter, I'll already be gone. Please don't be upset at me for leaving like this. I felt it was best for both of us. I understand your feelings are so fresh after everything that happened two nights ago, but I thought it would only be fair to remove myself from the equation, so you can think things through with a level head. I told Max everything this evening when you and Claire went out to spend time with your kids and in-laws. He now knows about our extraordinary history and has nothing but love and compassion for us. I think you should talk to him and hear his side of things for his past affairs. Your father's been hiding his sexuality from his family and the public for years. I was the first person he came out to, aside from Isobel. She knew. He told me it was okay to discuss it with you, since he doesn't know how to approach the subject one on one. Please, just talk to him.

There were tears, but I told him there's no shame in living your authentic truth. Love is love, regardless of gender. Please try to empathize. He loves you so much and didn't want to bring shame upon the family and ruin his reputation by coming out as a gay man. He's old-fashioned. I understand this more, having mingled in his social circles with all the powerful people in his life. We are getting an annulment. My needs have changed. I need to find myself, Vincent. I can't do that while relying on you, your dad, or anyone else.

I'm a romance writer, but even I know that I can't place all my happiness on a person. I think I'm strong enough now to be on my own and pursue my goals. Thank you for giving me the closure I needed. I was left in the dark for years, believing I had pushed you away or had done something to make you never want to speak to me again. Unlike Claire, who had lied to you, I was pregnant with your child. I had no way of reaching you and I was terrified of raising a baby on my own. I had considered an abortion but ended up miscarrying at eight weeks. I'm sorry I couldn't tell you this in person; it's still so painful. As much as I love children, I don't think I'm cut out for motherhood. I will miss Lilly and Milo so much—already do.

Vincent, it still hurts me to remember all our past arguments, but I don't want to hold a grudge. You misjudged me, and I understand why. I want to forgive and forget. I don't want to leave Ocean City convinced that you're a narcissistic villain who's out to get me. I've suffered a lot of narcissistic abuse in my life (still need therapy for it), but I'd like to part ways believing that you care for me. If you truly do, please let me go. Let me find myself. I've always known that love and relationships are nothing like what we see in films and stories... fairytale endings are rare. Like yourself, I don't believe they exist. Falling in love with you caused me more suffering than happiness. The only thing that gives me peace is knowing that you didn't use and discard me like I was led to believe for a decade. That was a critical pain point for me, one that I'm ready to release.

I don't want you to agonize over all the "what ifs." Maybe you had to have children with Claire, whether or not you're in love with her. Lilly and Milo deserve to have the best of you... they're a part of you, Vincent. I know you love them more than anything and anyone in the world. Please don't go off the deep end by going on another alcoholic bender. Things are different now; we're older, wiser. I want you to be happy and find peace. I want you to look back and remember me with fondness, not hatred and resentment. We shared some magical nights in Miami. You saved my life and I'm forever grateful. I'll always think of you if I hear Jon Secada's "Just Another Day." That evening under the bridge was... incredible.

When you have a chance, listen to "Sun & Moon" by Above and Beyond—I love the chill-out remix of the track. The chorus is magic. I know I'm a writer. I should be able to express myself just fine with words, but I'd rather let music communicate my feelings for you. Consider this my last romantic gesture, whether or not it's "overly sentimental." There's still so much of the world I need to see. When I'm in England, I'll remember you. When I'm in Spain, I'll remember you. I'll think of you if I ever smell Pi by Givenchy on a man. You were always <u>unforgettable</u>.

I know you're not a very spiritual nor religious person, Vincent, but I pray for your healing as you work through your grief. My mother's still alive, but I lost her a long time ago when she decided drugs were more important than raising me. I suppose much of our suffering in life originates from unaddressed childhood wounds. I hope I can heal from mine. Maybe we'll see each other again, ten years from now, and laugh about all the ways the universe fucked with us... maybe not. But right now, I think the best thing for both of us is distance. Please don't be destructive. Please don't come looking for me. This isn't some backwards way of me telling you to chase me. No games. No manipulation. Just pure honesty.

I'll always care about you. I'll always want the best for you, which includes your happiness, even if it's not with me. To truly love someone is to love them selflessly, Vincent, even if it hurts so fucking bad. I know this because I've had to suffer through it for a decade. All my life, I believed I needed a man to complete me... but I was wrong. My soul was <u>always</u> complete. We all yearn to be loved, to share a slice of happiness with someone. I can't achieve that while still being so miserable inside. I don't want to embrace an epic love with an empty cup, expecting my partner to fill it. I'm no longer looking for a "white knight" to come and save me from myself. I learned so much while being married to your father, even though it was hardly a proper marriage; it opened my eyes to a lot of things. Introspection through shadow work is terrifying and excruciatingly painful, but that's when <u>true alchemy</u> can happen, which leads to the transmutation of darkness to light. I had a lot of darkness inside, Vincent—

still do. The difference now is that I know how to help myself. I know I can transform.

I'm ready to chase my dreams with confidence. I'll always be indebted to your father. He helped me mend my broken wings at a terrible time in my life when I was susceptible to returning to a toxic relationship that could have killed me. He loved me like a father; one that I always needed and felt safe with. Please be kind to him. Forgive him, Vincent. You, Milo, and Lilly are everything to him. We never know when death will come knocking. You've experienced this firsthand with the loss of your beloved mother and your best friends. Try to forgive and love with an open heart. Life is too short to live it being angry inside. Please find it in your heart to forgive me, too... for leaving.

I wrote a poem inspired by you many years ago. It's in the prologue of my romance novel I've been working on—no title yet, unfortunately. I think it's only fair to share it with you in case I scrap this project and never publish it. Please take care of yourself, Vincent. I don't want you to stay sad. It's okay to cry, it doesn't make you any less of a man. I used to believe I was an overly sensitive person, because that's what my ex used to say to me to justify his abuse. But he was wrong. Emotional intelligence is a <u>gift</u>. There's beauty in pain when you work through it and come out on the other side stronger and more compassionate with gratitude. Never forget that. You'll always have a piece of my heart.

Love you forever,

-Lana

I sat on the edge of a dock, facing the water near the bank of our summer estate, holding Lana's letter in my trembling hands. Tears stung my eyes as soon as I flipped to another page and started reading her poem in the darkness, guided by a dimly lit lamp post.

My flame,
How I've suffered many nights without you
In silence,
In darkness,

Lana's beautiful words pierced through my soul and moved me as I wept in silence, allowing my heart to grieve after many years. I didn't deserve her love; this much was clear to me. I couldn't even be angry at her for packing up and leaving while I was gone. I wouldn't have let her, had I been in the house. I would have stupidly made a scene. I did not deserve this beautiful woman, and it absolutely gutted me to realize this. She wanted me to let her go, but how could I? How was I supposed to live my life and pretend as if I had never met her? Lana had been *pregnant* with my child... whatever doubts I had about her character... I felt so bloody ashamed of myself. I needlessly wounded this loving soul that was already in so much pain. I had senselessly contributed to her suffering because of my own fucking issues. I hated myself so much as I sat there feeling as if my heart had been broken for the first time; it *was.* I was shattered.

Why did this happen? What was the bloody point in remembering everything, only for the woman of my dreams to slip through my fingers and fly away? Was I paying a karmic price? Was our reunion destined to increase my suffering in life? Lana had mentioned getting closure... but I felt the opposite. How was I supposed to reconcile these feelings now?

"Bloody hell," I cursed under my breath, fighting tears.

Anger filled within me as I warred against it. Without thinking, I pulled out my phone and called her, which immediately went to voicemail. I cleared my throat and tried not to sound like a wreck as I left her a message.

"Lana, it's me... please give me a ring. Let's talk this out. I read your letter and your beautiful poem... you don't need to disappear... *please* don't disappear from my life—I can't... [*exhales*] ... I don't want you gone forever. It's fucking painful, Lana. I've been through enough. Please don't do this. Don't shut me out... Just text me, at the very least, I beg you. Let me know you're all right..."

I paused for the longest while, debating my next words.

"You can't just pour your heart out and deny me the chance to respond... you owe me at least that. I promise I won't try to kiss you—as much as I'll want to—just please contact me. I... I hope you're okay."

Lingering in silence, I eventually hung up and resisted the urge to hurl my phone into the water. It wasn't easy being vulnerable. I felt stupid.

She wants to go? Fine. Leave me, Lana. Fucking leave and never look back.

I was livid as I rose to my feet, folding her letter before I shoved it in my back pocket. If this was how she wanted to say goodbye, I had no choice but to accept it, even though I felt like dying inside. It was tempting to hop in my car and race after her, but I knew I had lost her forever. There would be no reunion again. Her farewell was permanent. My emptiness and despair were all-consuming. Love was evil. Love did nothing but gut you into pieces and toss you on the side of a road to get run over. I wanted to hate her for punishing me and leaving me this way, but I could only hate myself. Lana deserved someone better than me. She deserved everything that I had wanted to give her ten years ago when we had met in Miami.

I wish I never remembered you. I wish I didn't have to feel this pain, to suffer through another loss.

My thoughts buried me in depression as I walked back to the house in the darkness: a prelude to the beginning of the darkest night of my soul.

CHAPTER TWENTY-FOUR

LANA

Two years later...
New York City, March 3, 2019

I was nothing but nerves as I was ushered into Brooklyn's Tavern by my publicist, my agent, a security guard, and my personal assistant, Valerie; she was biracial, fluent in Japanese and French, with a quirky personality and incredible organization skills. I had an entire publishing team now that I was a best-selling author. After two years of grinding hard, knocking on the doors of one literary agency to another, my determination had finally paid off and resulted in one of the most climactic moments of my professional career. I couldn't even describe the feeling of walking into a bookstore and seeing copies of my novels front row and center: *His Heart, Frozen; His Heart, Open; His Heart, Mine* by Lana McKenzie. I was beyond ecstatic, dressed in a black blazer and leggings, with a white shirt underneath, and red stilettos. I had professionally styled my hair and makeup that afternoon before we carpooled to the big event. I had pink and light blue streaks in my long blonde locks. I wasn't sure what had compelled me to rock a "retro look" that closely resembled my teenage self; the only difference was that my hair was much longer, reaching my waist.

Valerie had really come through for me on organizing my book launch. My publicist, Matt, had gone above and beyond with my marketing team to promote my novels. Our venue was filled with people, smiling faces of friends and supporters of my creative works. I felt so blessed and grateful. All my hard work and sleepless nights had led to this moment. They expected me to speak that evening and read a few excerpts from my first novel. Public speaking was always a daunting experience for me. I hated it while in college and it still terrified me. Even though I had nothing but supporters who were there to praise my writing and congratulate my success, it was still so scary to stand before an audience with all the spotlight on me. I preferred my art to speak for itself while I took the backseat. The pitfalls of fame were truly nothing to envy. Celebrity status was not something I had ever sought. I only wanted to share my gift with an audience of people who would be moved by the power of my words. Years ago, I had decided I had a story to tell that was worth sharing, and I had committed to the grueling process... and it paid off.

"You ready, Lana?" Matt appeared in front of me, gripping my shoulders.

"I think so," I nervously sighed.

He was a tall man in his late thirties, with short blonde hair and hazel eyes that were hidden behind his dark-framed glasses. Valerie always teased me by saying he had a crush on me, but I figured she was reading one too many romance novels.

I took the podium to speak into a microphone and address a crowd of people who were sitting with copies of my novels in their hands. I couldn't afford to have stage fright now. I had to push through the fear. A team of people were relying on me to make this event a success; the same team that believed in me and helped me achieve my dream. I could not let them down.

Matt had coached me on how to answer some hard questions, especially when doing press interviews. As I spoke into the mic, I slowly gained more confidence when I introduced myself and discussed my novel.

After I read a few significant passages, my reading audience was given the opportunity to approach the mic on the floor level to ask me questions. While I was still nervous, I was pleasantly surprised when my first few fans did nothing but shower me with accolades before they got to their questions.

I discussed my inspiration behind my decision to build the story in the Victorian era, which set the tone as I delved into an in-depth discourse on the character analysis of my main protagonists, including the villains. It was such a rush to have a bunch of strangers connect with my imagination. It made me feel as if everything I had suffered through had to happen to bring me to this moment in life. All my anxiety slowly vanished as I stood before my crowd of supporters, discussing my passion project, a labor of love that had taken me years to complete.

Everything was going smoothly when the next person approached the mic and adjusted the stand, raising it higher to reach his tall height.

My heart dropped.

I stopped breathing.

He cleared his throat and smiled. "Good evening, Ms. McKenzie."

Everyone's focus shifted to the attractive man who spoke with a charming British accent. His deep voice echoed all around me while I stood there, panicking inside.

"First off, I would just like to congratulate you on your well-deserved success. Your novels blew me away. I couldn't put them down."

Oh, God... those eyes.

"Your ability to move your audience with your words is truly a gift. I felt everything... the love, the pain, the constant push and pull between Theo and Ava, the angst... it was quite the roller coaster. It seemed as if the direction you were taking these characters was headed for a heart crushing tragedy, but I was relieved to find that you gave them a happy ending. I'm sure I speak for everyone else who agrees, no?"

My audience clapped and whistled before their applause died down.

"My question then, Ms. McKenzie, is this: what, or *who* inspired you to write this beautiful love story? Because I can't help but find reflections of myself in Theo's characterization."

Breathe, just breathe, I told myself.

"Um..." I paused and took a sip from my glass of water. "That's a great question."

My heart was racing so fast I could hardly think. Vincent's piercing blue eyes remained determinedly fixed on me while I struggled to plan an answer. He looked just as handsome as the last time I'd seen him in Ocean City, if not more, dressed in black, clean shaven, his beautifully, thick, brown hair cut short and styled like it always was. I had never expected him to show up at this event. We hadn't spoken in years. Had he really read my novels? Did he fly all the way to New York just to get a signed copy from me?

"Sorry"—I cleared my throat—"I don't own a time machine, so it's not like I can stand here and say that Ava's experiences in that time period directly reflect my own, *but...* I tend to place pieces of myself in some of my characters when I write, including Theo."

Vincent looked at me and said, "I strongly identify with him."

"And how does that make you feel?"

"Proud." He smiled. "Your characterization of him is spot on, even when he was acting like a total bastard toward Ava."

The audience laughed.

"I couldn't help but feel as if he didn't deserve her, even though he loved her so passionately and did everything he could to redeem himself... that shows your strength as a writer. You made me empathize and identify with your characters, regardless of the temporal setting of your novels."

I smiled and said, "I knew a 'Theo' once upon a time."

"Past tense? May I ask what happened?"

"We drifted apart."

"How unfortunate," Vincent replied. "But what if he came back?" He paused. "What if he's standing in front of you right now, ready to offer his heart to you?"

Before I could respond, Matt intervened and pulled me back, calling on security to seize Vincent and toss him out.

"What are you doing?" I shouted. "Stop! I know him! I *know him*, Matt!"

Everything happened so quickly as I was rushed backstage, fighting with my team to let me speak to Vincent.

"He's not a stalker, for fuck's sake! I know him! How many times do I have to stay it?"

"You *know* the guy?" Matt looked confused.

"Yes! Now let me go!"

I finally broke free and rushed out of the venue onto the street, where my security guard had restrained Vincent.

"Lana!" he called after me, holding out an envelope. "Please, just read this!"

I walked over and took what appeared to be a standard envelope from his hand. My security guard, Jax, had eased off and released Vincent when I told him we were familiar with each other.

"I didn't come here to disrupt your event, I swear," Vincent said, slightly winded. "I just wanted to give you that letter. Please read it when you can. I know you're a busy woman."

A flurry of emotions hit me at once as I stared into Vincent's eyes. I wanted to ask him something when Matt's domineering voice echoed behind me.

"We need you back inside, Lana," he said, touching my shoulder. "You're on a tight schedule."

I looked at Vincent, apologizing. "I'm sorry we can't talk, I—"

"It's okay." He tried to smile. "This is your big night. You've worked hard for this. Like I said, I just wanted to give you that letter. Now that you have it, I can leave in peace."

"*Lana*," Matt nagged me again.

Uncertain of what to say or do, I thanked Vincent for coming and offered to sign his copy of my first book, but I didn't have a pen on me—go figure.

"Don't worry," he said. "I already have something with your signature on it, and I think you know what it is."

Something that couldn't be seen with the naked eye. I think I knew what he meant. We had a moment right there, as we stared at each other before Matt got in my face and nearly yelled at me.

"There are people inside waiting for you! Wrap this up, please!"

I was about to ask Vincent if he had time to stay till after the event, but he was already getting into a cab down the street. The only thing I had of his now was an envelope with my name on the back in his handwriting.

As frustrated as I was with Matt, I knew I had to remain professional. Being a successful author meant I had to honor my deadlines, meet-ups, and press interviews. My personal life had taken a backseat so that my professional life could thrive. I was happy with that choice, but seeing Vincent again only reminded me of why I had gone no contact in the first place.

There were questions about what had happened when I headed back inside to continue the Q&A; but I assured everyone it wasn't a dangerous incident, just a personal matter with an "old friend." I hadn't been prepared for the tidal wave of feelings that washed over me when I saw Vincent again. All I wanted was a moment alone to read his letter. My book launch went from me being super excited to discuss my novels to me counting the minutes until the event would end so that I could finally satisfy my curiosity.

⋐⋑

By the time I got to my hotel room, I was dead tired. My wrist was sore from signing so many books. I wanted to shower and pass out. I had an early flight in the morning to Chicago, booked for a TV interview with a popular talk show host. I was nervous and honestly hated this part of my rising success, but I understood the business aspects of the publishing world. Thinking like a businesswoman was not something I particularly liked, but I knew it was important for book promotion and sales.

Now that I was finally alone, the first thing I did was open Vincent's letter and collapse onto my queen-size mattress. He had written several pages, front to back, in a black fountain pen that showed off his beautiful handwriting.

Feb 27, 2019

Beautiful Lana,

I can't express how ecstatic I was to walk into a Barnes & Noble's last month and see your books on display with your name on the cover. I knew you'd make it. You deserve this success, love. You always did. From the first time you shared your ambitions with me all those years ago, I believed in you. All you needed was to believe in yourself. Congratulations are certainly in order! While I wish more than anything to wine and dine you to celebrate your success, I understand why you needed distance from me, though that wasn't always the case in the beginning. I tried to look for you after you left Ocean City two years ago, despite your wishes and my father's advice. I'd been guilty of stalking your socials now and then, but I had enough sense not to reach out because I wanted to respect your wishes, as hard as it was.

Lana, please forgive me for making you feel you had to run. I was selfishly acting out on my own feelings that were extremely impulsive and careless, to be certain, but I promise you they were entirely motivated by the heart. As I'd mentioned to you that summer, Claire and I were not in a good place in our marriage. In the aftermath of your absence from my life, I did try to receive some counseling with her, but even that was pointless. She had confessed to having an office affair in the last six months before we vacationed in Ocean City. I filed for separation and went through a complicated divorce procedure because of her, but I've been a free man for a while now. We both have shared custody of the kids. I know you had said that you did not want to be the reason I leave Claire, but our marriage had already been falling apart. We tried to save it. We're both happier this way. Divorce is not always bad, Lana. In some cases (like mine), it's the best option.

I can't tell you how many times I've thought of you... how many times I broke my promise and tried to reach out. I guess you receive so much fan mail now... I'm sure my messages are lost in your inbox somewhere if they haven't been deleted. The purpose of this letter is not to make you feel bad or burden you with sadness. That's not my intention at all, love. I did struggle to release you throughout the years. I won't lie. But I understood why you needed space from me.

You'll be happy to know that I didn't self-sabotage. I got my shit together and finally received the grief counseling I desperately needed. Everything you had said in your letter to me was rational; so rational that it made me angry to admit that our roles had reversed. I'd gone from being a cynical misanthrope to a lovesick fool, possessed by emotions I could not control. Lana, I resented you for leaving me at first, but I couldn't stay angry at you. I was angry at myself.

I still have your beautiful poem. I've read it so much, I've memorized it. I'm honored to have inspired you, and even more so to have been your secret muse in your trilogy series—incredible writing, by the way—I read them all in a week and a half... I especially enjoyed the love scenes. But you never needed me to tell you you're talented.

Lilly still asks about you. She misses you. I always tell her that "Aunt Lana" has traveled for work and will come back soon. Milo is finally walking and talking, which has put Dad at ease. He's happily dating an Italian fashion designer named Massimo—ten years younger, but hey... who am I to judge, right? I learned a harsh lesson with you, but I'm grateful for it. I took your advice, Lana. I worked things out with my father and forgave him. You were right: my mother always knew about Dad's sexuality. She wasn't exactly happy about it, but she had told my father that she would keep his secret, so long as he was discreet about his affairs. Their marriage had been more of a business partnership, but they cared for each other, and that gives me peace.

I'm not sure where you're living at present, but I moved to California last summer when Claire did, so I could still be close to the kids. The weather's amazing and I still surf. Would be great if you could visit me one day. I'd love to take you out and show you around. I found out about your book launch/meet and greet through your website last week, which led me to book a flight, hoping I could have time to see you face to face and give you this letter since it's virtually impossible to reach you these days.

Lana, I hope you're not upset with me for showing up unannounced. I promise it was by no means an attempt to sabotage your big event; I simply needed an opportunity to give you this letter. Consider it my way of finding closure with you.

The anniversary of your second chance at life is coming up: March 12th. I have a proposition for you, Lana. All I ask is that you think it through. It's been two years since we last had a proper moment to talk, and so much has changed in my life, as well as yours. I don't want to wait another ten years. The older you get, the more you realize how precious time is.

I'm going to be in Miami next week, closing a deal on a condo property I'm purchasing along the strip of Sunny Isles beach. There's this beautiful bridge/pedestrian overpass that stretches out on the water—Newport Fishing Pier... I'd love for you to meet me there after sunset, anywhere from 8:30-9pm—it'll be less crowded. I'll wait for you. If you show up, I'll take it as a sign that you'll say yes when I ask you out for a drink. If you don't come, I promise there will be no hard feelings. I want your happiness. Should you feel the need to contact me sooner, please call or text: 209-727-6367. My email is: vluther@flymail.net

You can reach me by phone any time. Your beautiful voice really did things to my heart. I miss it. I really hope you take me up on my offer, Lana. I miss you so fucking much. If you are married, engaged, or dating someone else, please consider leaving the prick and flying out to see me. I'll make it worth your while... kidding (but not really). I'm sure that made you laugh, though...

It did, as I laughed through tears and wiped them away.

As long as you're happy, I'm happy—well, no... again, not really, but I shall try. It isn't easy being the bigger person. I bloody hate it. But... as I mentioned earlier, <u>the ball is entirely in your court</u>, no pressure, love. In closing, I've never really been a poet, but I will leave you with this, though you should know that my poetry can't hold a candle to yours.

My heart is an ocean, roaring with waves,
Violently crashing on the shore of your soul,
Pulling you into the depth of my love.
You drown and sink into me,
Resurfacing, resurrected.

All my love,
-Vincent
P.S. You <u>are</u> my sun and moon... and I <u>never</u> got over you.
P.P.S. Listen to "Wasted Times" by The Weeknd.

My face was wet with tears as I went back and read Vincent's beautiful poetry. It warmed my heart to know that he even made an attempt. I loved his use of water imagery and metaphors. Seeing him earlier that evening had woken up feelings inside of me that had been dormant since our separation. I knew I had a big decision ahead, one that would either make or break us.

CHAPTER TWENTY-FIVE

VINCENT

The week had passed slowly at a snail's pace, as I stood by a wide railing at Newport Fishing Pier in Sunny Isles Beach, Miami. I was surprised to find that there weren't many people on the pedestrian overpass that evening, but I suppose it worked to my advantage. Privacy was something I preferred. I was worried if I had picked a more secluded place, Lana would not have shown up. A public setting was more appropriate, especially after two years of no contact. All week I kept hoping she would call or text, but I'd received nothing. It was a bit nerve-wracking, to be honest... walking down that pier not knowing if she would show up or not. By June, it would have been two years of not seeing each other.

I was genuinely happy that she had reached the level of success she always dreamed of having. She truly deserved it. I would have liked to have been by her side throughout the process, but you can't force someone to be with you. Besides, my marriage had been falling apart. Lana didn't deserve to be mixed up in that mess. I eventually told Claire about my history with Lana. She hadn't taken it too well, of course, especially since I had blamed her for my accident and how she had deliberately kept the truth from me during my amnesia recovery.

As I stood on the end of the pier, I glanced back and noticed that the lampposts had turned on while the sky had darkened, which only made the setting more romantic.

Please don't let all this pain be for nothing. I prayed to every higher power and held faith that Lana would show up.

The emerald sea was calm, but I could still hear the peaceful sound of ocean waves rolling along the shore behind me. My stomach was in knots when I leaned over the railing and took a deep breath. I don't think I had ever been more nervous than I was at that moment. Preparing for this highly expected reunion had been equally stressful for me. I had gotten a fresh haircut and shave at a barbershop earlier in the afternoon and had spent a decent hour trying to figure out the perfect outfit at my hotel. I had Massimo to thank for helping me decide—the man had a great sense of fashion. I was wearing a white shirt with a few buttons undone at the chest, tailored gray trousers, and black leather loafers—*business chic,* according to Massimo. He was confident Lana wouldn't be able to resist me. I prayed to God he was right.

I had every intention of convincing her we belonged together. All I needed was a chance. I wouldn't mess it up this time. I wouldn't let anyone, nor the universe, fuck with me and Lana like it had twelve years ago. But perhaps the universe was always on our side— be it "angels" or "cosmic forces." Maybe they were always working hard to bring us back together. I wanted to believe it. I wanted to believe that our story wasn't finished—that it had *never* finished.

Lively music echoed behind me, which only made me more nervous as I glanced at my watch and waited. I had arrived on time, just in case she was already waiting for me, but half an hour had already passed. It was almost 9—8:58pm, to be exact. Was I nothing but a bloody fool for coming here and believing that she would show up? She hadn't called. She hadn't texted. She hadn't given me any sort of sign that she would meet me. I was standing on that pier, holding onto nothing but blind faith that the woman of my dreams would not let me down.

I tried my best to dissociate, as I shut my eyes and listened to the musical melodies. But the lyrics only made me think of Lana even more. This had to be a sign, I told myself.

She'll show up. She'll show...

I gazed at the dark water in the distance and reflected on my feelings. This woman had lured me into her ocean and made me feel things I never thought I could access inside myself. I wanted every part of her. I had tried to date here and there a few months ago, but no one made me feel the way Lana did, which explained my single status. It wasn't too late to begin a new chapter together; she *had* to see that. My desire for her had not diminished in the least; it had increased. She had looked so stunning and confident when I saw her take the podium to speak at her book launch event. I was so proud of her.

The possibility of only having a few chapters in Lana's book of life depressed me to no end, but I knew if she didn't show, I'd have to respect her choice and silently back away. It was a tough pill to swallow, accepting that she may be happy and fulfilled without me, but at least I had peace in knowing that my letter had reached her. I could try to move on, knowing I had done my best to give us one last shot.

It still hurt to remember how she had tried to kill herself on this same day, twelve years ago. Had she succeeded... had I never been there... she wouldn't have reached her dreams. Perhaps that was the only important part I played in her life: rescuing her from an irreversible decision. If God was real, then I had nothing but gratitude. Society was populated enough with shitty people. Lana made this world a better place. She had to know that. Loving her made me a better man.

My broken mind had forgotten her existence for years, but my heart always knew. It had echoed signals to me from the moment Dad had introduced us; I had simply ignored it, transmuting those feelings of passion to hatred and anger to disguise my pain. Grief work wasn't easy, but I was much more at peace inside, having accepted my mother's passing. She would always be with me, even though her physical presence was gone from this earth.

Maybe humans had it all wrong. Maybe the sole reason we were here was to learn how to heal ourselves, let go, love one another, and return home... our *true* home. If reincarnation was real, was *that* why we constantly returned to this plane of existence? I could appreciate theosophical perspectives, especially Buddhist thought, though I suppose we'd never really know the true nature of reality until we release our final breath... even then, no one lived to come back and offer objective truths. NDEs were subjective. I often wondered if Lana had seen anything on "the other side" when she had nearly died in my arms all those years ago. Whether or not she had, I was grateful she was alive.

Glancing at my watch, I realized that I'd been standing there for almost forty-five minutes. It was a quarter past nine and she was running late. I wanted to cling onto hope so badly, but I knew if I did, I'd only prolong my suffering. My romantic endeavor had been rejected. While I would have appreciated a text at the very least, I realized I had told Lana I'd have no hard feelings if she didn't show up. I had given her the impression that I had no expectations, when in reality... I did. It stung inside to accept this as I cursed myself in my head. I had taken a risk, only to end up standing alone with my heart in my hand. I could only imagine her pain when she had believed I had deliberately cut her off from my life. My pain was nothing in comparison; I knew this as I exhaled deeply and tried not to pity myself.

Five more minutes, ten more minutes... it wouldn't have made a difference. She had decided loud and clear. I cast my fretful gaze on the ocean one last time and tried to make peace with her choice.

I'll let you go, love. I understand. I wish you all the best.

My heart felt so heavy. I had underestimated the agony of rejection. A part of me had desperately hoped that once she'd see me at her event, her feelings would come rushing back. I was wrong. I was naïve. Was it hubris or merely blind optimism?

Turning to leave, I halted in my tracks.

Bloody hell... fuck... me.

There she was, approaching in the distance. Her beautiful face and hair were unmistakable, as I stood, statuesque, feeling as if I'd been revived. The closer she got, all the heaviness in my chest suddenly lifted. I could feel my heart powerfully pounding away in my ribcage, vibrating my body. No one had ever made me feel this way; no one but Lana.

She was wearing a short, white, strapless dress that clung to her feminine figure and showed off her toned, long legs. I noticed her platform wedges when she got closer, until she bridged the distance between us and stood before me, face to face, with a beautiful, timid smile. I melted, at a loss for words.

"Please tell me you're real," I finally spoke.

"I'm sorry for running late—there was traffic."

Every cell in my body yearned for contact. I wanted to pull her into me and kiss the fuck out of her, but it wouldn't have been very gentlemanlike. I wouldn't force another kiss on her like I'd done last time, maddened out of my mind. Lana had returned to me as the delicate rose that she always was. I had to temper my passions, regardless of how intense these feelings were.

"You came."

"I had to," she replied.

No idle chit chat. Get to the bloody point, Vince.

As the seconds kept passing, I knew I had to find my bravery. I had asked her for this chance. I did not want to fuck it up and make her turn around.

"Lana... I spent two years hating myself for letting you slip through my fingers," I confessed. "It should have been you."

"Don't say that."

"It needs to be said. Please forgive me. I know I don't deserve it. I've been a wreck... I can't explain how fucking sorry I am... for everything... all the years I wasted. It should have been you... it was *always* you."

"Vincent, what happened to us wasn't your fault. I told you in my letter that I don't hold a grudge."

Her smile seemed sad as she stepped closer and touched the side of my face. My skin instantly tingled. I had longed for her touch so badly. Lana's perfume intoxicated my senses. I was wearing her favorite cologne, hoping to induce a familiar sense of nostalgia for happier times that were shared between us.

"Please don't cry," she whispered, caressing my cheek.

I laughed off my embarrassment by averting my gaze. It was never easy for me to shed tears in private, let alone in front of others. I hadn't even cried when Claire had walked down the aisle on our wedding day. When my children were born, I got emotional. I recalled eventually breaking down at Mum's grave when I was finally alone, but other than that, crying was not something I did regularly. In that moment, however, I could no longer control the intensity of my emotions... everything Lana made me *feel*, being in her presence, feeling her touch, *breathing* her. I was so overwhelmed that the only way I could achieve catharsis was to surrender to my human nature.

"Seeing you again is so bittersweet," I finally admitted, meeting her warm, aqua eyes.

"Why?"

"All the years we had lost together, Lana... remember what you used to say about my 'titanium heart'?"

She smiled, nodding.

"You were right... except you were in there all along. I had only shielded myself from the truth."

"What truth?"

I searched her gaze and gently slid my palm beneath the curve of her feminine jaw. It was now or never. I had to tell her.

"I'm so desperately in love with you. I always was. From the moment I brought you back to life on that beach, I was so completely yours, even when my mind couldn't remember through the years, my titanium heart always did; it kept my feelings and memories of you a secret until you finally unlocked it with a kiss."

How's that for a declaration of love?

"Did you rehearse that, Vincent?" She giggled, touching my chest before she slid her arms over my shoulders.

"I had several versions, I'll admit." I chuckled. "You gave me ample time to think about it." I rubbed her lower back and murmured, "Are you disappointed?"

"No." Lana smiled, staring at me with what I could only interpret as admiration and desire.

I pulled her in close, feeling her soft breasts push against my shirt.

Contact.

This is what I needed. I needed so much more than this. I wanted this gorgeous woman lying naked under me, while I took her to the deepest depths of pleasure, for hours until sunup. It was hard to ignore my arousal in her presence. She was stunning beyond description. She always was. Any hot-blooded man would want to ravish her—women included. I was a proud ally of the LGBTQ community, especially since my father had finally found the courage to come out publicly with his truth.

The pink and blue streaks in Lana's blonde locks reminded me of the first time we had met.

"Mermaid hair," I said, brushing my fingers through her silky tresses.

"Do you like it?"

"I love it. I love everything about you."

I wanted to kiss her so badly. I wanted to taste her lips and lose myself in her.

But she seemed to read my mind as she leaned in and whispered, *"Te quiero besàr."*

I couldn't help but smile.

"If I kiss you, Lana, will you let me take you out for a drink?"

"Risk it and find out." She smirked.

Without wasting another second, I held her face and looked into her soulful eyes before I softly brushed my lips against hers and poured passion into our kiss. A supernova blasted in my chest, sending chills down my body. This woman belonged in my arms. She belonged in my life. I wanted to share my happiness with hers, with both our cups full, not empty. Everything that had happened had brought us to this moment. My cynicism had died, replaced by a hopeless romantic that dared to believe in second chances.

I felt her healing energy flow through me, reviving my faith as I kissed her on that pier, molding her body with mine. We were together at last. I was happy. I was hopelessly in love. I had loved this woman in silence long enough. Now it was time to show her the lengths I would go for a future with her, to be worthy of her devotion. Twin flames were real. I had found mine, only to be separated *twice* and reunited in the most epic way possible. Lana was proof of this metaphysical union—our experiences were proof of that runner/chaser dynamic and the reversal of roles. We had both endured a dark night of the soul, only to come out stronger. Not only did she level up in those two years apart in her own personal journey, but so had I.

I was ready to love her with an open heart. I was ready to go all in. It was all I could think about as I kissed her fervently, tasting her vanilla lip balm.

"*Wow,*" she breathed, pulling back.

I kept her locked in my arms, leaning against the railing. Her beautiful neck was exposed, enticing me to kiss it, so I did just that, leaving a trail down to her naked shoulder.

"I missed your kisses." Lana shivered against me.

"I'm more than happy to be generous with that," I said, placing another kiss on her neck.

My God, she smelled divine.

"Does that include tonight when we go to your place after drinks?"

"As much as you want, love."

I smiled from ear to ear as I slid my hands over her curvy peach and gave it a firm squeeze.

"I look forward to it." She simpered, kissing me long and deeply.

Everything we had gone through had happened for a reason—the separation, the pain... now that I had her in my arms, I knew I'd never let her go. Never again. We had completed the tiresome journey of soul searching and finding ourselves embarking on our own individual paths, only to return to each other, as if we were Divinely destined to get to this point all along. This meeting wasn't the ending I feared; it was a beautiful beginning. So many people fall in love, very few *rise* in love. Every day I would rise in love with Lana. This was my vow. I was hers forever. I always was.

ACKNOWLEDGEMENTS

First and foremost, I'd like to thank the Divine, my guardian angels, and the Universe for always having my back.

A huge heartfelt thank you to my dearest friend Charles—you'll always be my Billy. Thank you for being the father I needed in life and for always believing in me. You helped me mend my broken wings. Your love is like the sun. I love you forever.

Carolyn, thank you for believing in my gift and for all the wonderful feedback you gave on my writing.

Next, I'd like to thank my amazing, loyal fanbase who have watched me grow as a writer, especially my beta readers who volunteered their time on this project. I appreciate all your love and support throughout the years.

This novel would not have reached completion if it weren't for the unwavering support of my amazing mentor, my best friend and confidant: Jay, I love you beyond love. Thank you for helping me heal. Thank you for crying with me and being my rock throughout this publishing process. You are the Neo to my Trinity.

To my soul tribe: thank you for supporting me with unconditional love, especially during rough times when I felt like self-sabotaging. Much love to Shebz and Keela, my cosmic siblings.

Mom, thank you for *innerstanding* my creative needs and always encouraging me to keep going with Vincent and Lana's love story. All your sacrifices were worth it. I love you so much.

And last, but not least, thank you to Black Rose Writing for recognizing my talent and handling all the publishing requirements. I am forever grateful.

MUSIC PLAYLIST

Novel Soundtrack

- Azee - Summer Highs (slowed + reverb)
- Two Hearted - Better With Time (slowed + reverb)
- Darci - These Nights
- Kid Riz – Nightmares (slowed + reverb)
- Palastic - Through The Fire (ft. Sam Welch)
- Ja¥en x District - unknown
- JAHKOY - Firefighter
- Thilo - Flight Risk (slowed + reverb)
- Black Atlass – Something Real
- Dxvn. - Subtle Things
- Daniel Di Angelo x Dxvn. - Love Is Evil
- EMIKA - Flashbacks (Gnothi Seauton remix)
- SWIM - Eyes On You
- Fred again.. - Angie (I've Been Lost)
- Xavier Omär - If This Is Love (slowed + reverb)
- Kwota B. - Get You Off My Mind
- Abra Taylor - Feels Like This
- Daughter - Numbers
- KAVI - Worst
- Darci – Tell Me When (slowed + reverb)
- The Weeknd - Wasted Times (slowed + reverb)
- Jake Hope - Where Do I Belong?
- SEV - To Be Loved
- BLVCK VIØLET - Make You Mine
- Alina Libkind - Songs About Love
- Eloy - On Your Mind
- PNK FME - You Never Said

- Lounatic - Hold Me On
- Kadebostany - Save Me (Hijazi Remix)
- The Weeknd - Professional (slowed + reverb)
- Sobhhï - finders keepers
- Lana Del Rey - Summertime Sadness
- CamelPhat x Eli & Fur - Waiting
- Lindsxy Mesenburg - Divine (slowed + reverb)
- Darci – High Speeds (slowed + reverb)
- Moonkay - Make Me (slowed + reverb)
- JOY – Compromise
- Aaryan Shah - Dissociation (slowed + reverb)
- Alyxx Dione - Don't Stop (slowed + reverb)
- Thrizzy - Tell Me You Love Me (slowed + reverb)
- Dimi (ft. Anders) – When You're Lonely (slowed + reverb)
- Fred again.. - Faisal (Envelops Me)
- Ross Quinn – Away With Me (Fideles Remix)
- Otnicka – Sorry
- BONNIE X CLYDE - ANOTHER YOU
- Brady Goodyear - Dreaming (slowed + reverb + lyrics)
- Jay Aliyev – All Night

ABOUT THE AUTHOR

Mina Alexia was born in Tehran, Iran. She moved to Canada with her family at the age of three and was raised in a small town in Ontario. She graduated from Wilfrid Laurier University with a Bachelor's Degree of Arts, Honors English.

Having faced many adversities in life, she decided to use her artistic gifts to heal through the medium of creative writing. Mina uses her social media presence to spread awareness on trauma recovery and mental health. Her novels include trauma-informed themes that are rich with emotion. She believes "we need to feel to heal."

NOTE FROM THE AUTHOR

Word-of-mouth is crucial for any author to succeed. If you enjoyed *Pain Loves Passion*, please leave a review online—anywhere you are able. Even if it's just a sentence or two. It would make all the difference and would be very much appreciated.

Thanks!
Mina Alexia

We hope you enjoyed reading this title from:

www.blackrosewriting.com

Subscribe to our mailing list – *The Rosevine* – and receive **FREE** books, daily deals, and stay current with news about upcoming releases and our hottest authors.
Scan the QR code below to sign up.

Already a subscriber? Please accept a sincere thank you for being a fan of Black Rose Writing authors.

View other Black Rose Writing titles at www.blackrosewriting.com/books and use promo code **PRINT** to receive a **20% discount** when purchasing.